Nix Romipen

by Lyz Russo

P'kaboo Publishers;
Amazon Paperback version.
2020

www.pkaboo.net
ISBN: 978-1-68454-606-0

*

Disclaimer:

This book, as with the rest of the two series ('The Solar Wind' and 'Shooting Star') is a work of fiction. Any potential similarity between names, people, relationships, places or any other aspect of this story to anything in the real world is purely coincidental.

*

Acknowledgements

Thanks for this sequel goes to my editorial and beta-reading team consisting of my beloved husband Iain Moncrieff Rossouw (deceased in 2017) and our three awesome young people Robin, Ray and Meggi (you were so small when the Solar Wind series started!); my dear friend and editor Les Noble (also now deceased, in 2020); my team of graphic designers who did the beautiful cover, and (always) my family who supports me in all these ventures.

*

For my Iain.

You who are now an angel. You who were the original Federi, in inventiveness, humour, and being more colourful than life itself. You who in an unbelievable act of courage, to protect your wife and children, tackled four armed robbers bare-handedly and in doing so, drove them off... and laid down your life, a bullet in your lungs.

Nothing can quite describe the darkness. They were not even human; pure distilled evil. Why? Why would they disrupt a perfectly normal, happy family? Why did they shoot? Couldn't they just have run, as they did anyway?
Questions I will never have answers to.

It is 2020. We have found a home among Ireland's beautiful and gentle people. But I have not been able to write since that night. I miss your feedback, your pithy comments and jokes, your chronic music quotes and your very sane context edits. I miss you being alive, I miss your loud hearty laughter. The Solar Wind and Shooting Star series were some of the best fun we had together.

I know you'll be waiting for me on the other side of the Gate, when my time here is up. In the interim I feel your love, you are around us often, a beautiful golden angel with huge wings and blazing red hair, wielding your electric guitar. When you are not at the Great Ceilidh in the Sky and jamming with Freddy Mercury.

I love you, my Iain.

Forever.

Dedication

To my wonderful children,
Robin Shea,
Ray Leander
and Meggi Stella.

And to my Iain.
Forever.

1 – The Solar Wind

Niciuna. A small town in the Transylvanian Alps, surrounded by wintry forest. November winds cutting through the trees. Dry leaves crunching under feet that moved lightly, cautiously. A *kumpania* of ghosts, phantoms… a tribe of Free Tzigany moving through the woods, their worldly belongings in bundles on their shoulders.

This is Romania. Free Gypsies here don't have the luxury of caravans, horses, beaten-up hybrid cars driven with home-brewed tequila. Here, life is harsh. You own what you can carry, and the only attachments you form are to your loved ones. Because there is always the risk of losing it all in a few minutes…

Almeira moved ahead of her *familia*, silent as the night, her gypsy senses on hair-trigger. It should be here… Lanina had said they would be here, waiting to meet up…

The smell hit her first. A cold, dreaded scent carried on the icy wind. Minutes later she had traced it and was staring at what was left of her cousins, the bottom dropping from her world…

*

The Solar Wind's large white sails billowed against the night sky, illuminated scantily by deck and mast lights. The ship cut through black water, churned up into white luminescent foam at her prow. Reflections glinted off the two sleek discoid shapes of the jets, the Comet and the Probe, that followed the Solar Wind silently, tagged onto her with a magnetic positioning function. The outer deck was deserted; Captain's sharp eyes peered into the dark from the bridge.

Not much remained hidden from those piercing, steely-blue eyes; but the Free Gypsy in the jib deck at the prow did. Federi gazed out of the darkness between the boxes, catching a last "thinking break" in his favourite meditation spot of many years. He'd been the last to check on the winches, lines and rigging. Tonight's Ceilidh had been long and arduous, but it had eventually died of natural causes, with the crew drifting off to go to sleep, or to play cards in Wolf's cabin.

So, technically, now was the moment to escape. Federi was taking a risk sitting here motionlessly, mulling over things. He and Paean had already been retained far too long; first losing two whole days in a coma, then being kept back by Captain's endless orders, work and more menial work, because dear Captain could not let go. Three further days had slipped away like that, with some or other "emergency" arising spontaneously every time Federi was on the point of calling Paean to get into the Comet, and leaving.

He had promised her a honeymoon. Young bride of his, barely an adult, still full of childlike fun and mischief, but owner of one of the sharpest and most competent minds on the Solar Wind or for that matter, Earth. Gutsy and temperamental. All that, packaged in a body that was small and light, bird-like – as though she had decided to put a halt on growing at age fourteen. It was genetics, she had told him: Her mother had been small and dainty like herself. It suited him. "Short guy gets the girl."

The honeymoon however was a lie; a cover-up. The Mission loomed in his mind like a freak wave, refusing to go away any longer. He had been hiding from it for twenty years, the last twelve in the safety aboard the Solar Wind. But it was who he was, and it had found him. He couldn't ignore it any longer. It burnt inside him

8

like a plutonium fragment picked up at that evil place, the Hub.

The diminutive redhead was suddenly there next to him, the light of her ice-blue eyes cutting a ragged trail through his soul.

"Federi?"

He swallowed back the bitterness. And here it was. He was her slave… but she didn't feel that way about him anymore. That light was deceptive.

"Mind if we take Shawney with us?"

"Sure, little luv. No problem." Her younger brother? It could have been her honeymoon. It probably didn't matter.

"Only… he wants Mindy to come along too."

"Mindy …?" – Wait!

Mindy with the broken back? Little smuggler's daughter Mindy, whom they had salvaged from the Golden Walrus?

"Wolf has created a bridge for her spine," explained Paean. "It spans the dead spot in her spinal column. And Doc put pins in so that her bones don't get dislocated again. She can walk, but carefully."

Federi rolled his dramatic eyes. It sounded like an amazing risk to take, to allow Mindy off the ship. But if Captain… and Doc…

"Whatever, little luv. Whatever makes you happy."

"Thanks!" She jumped up, moving off towards the hatch like a quark in a nuclear stew. Federi shook his head at himself.

Sure, little luv. Shawn, Mindy. And while you're at it, bring Captain too, so he can boss Tzigan around. He saw himself going off alone, disappearing off the radar. But heck – that was impossible these days, with the teleporters finding everyone by their own genetic signature! He'd have to switch his bioelectric field off for that, die and become a ghost… he needed a new planet…

The Morrigan had corrupted Paean's thinking, and thereby broken Federi's marriage. His soulmate didn't want him any longer.

She'd had a vision of princes, castles, a life of luxury in a place of peace. All illusions; for which that vile alien had been assassinated, but the damage was done. So all Federi was doing taking her along off the ship, was keeping an outdated promise. She had made it clear that she'd leave with or without him.

He scowled.

Mindy? Well, that put a time-frame on his mission!

His most recent wrist-com sounded. Like a little birdie on steroids. He started plotting where he could leave it.

*

"So," Radomir Lascek greeted him as he arrived on the bridge. "You really want to go?"

Leave the Solar Wind? Federi stared at his Captain of many years, and shook his head.

"I've got to, Captain! Got a mission!"

"I'm going to miss you, my friend," said Lascek gravely.

Federi ground his teeth. Captain wasn't making this easy!

What did Captain need him for? The cook was Lyr. The chars were the croaches. There were plenty of sharp assassins aboard. Ailyss, Jon... Able sailors? When last had they actually flown a storm? Quartermaster...

" 's just a holiday, Captain," he said sanguinely. "Showing Paean a few places."

"You're going for the jugular this time," predicted Lascek glumly. "You're targeting the Unicate."

Federi nodded. There was no point in denying it.

"Didn't work that other time," he said. "You noticed, Captain."

"Yes." Lascek clasped Federi's arm. "Be safe, my friend. And look after my foster-child."

10

Child! Paean was no child. The comment riled.

"Keeping her safe," promised Federi a little sourly. Ha! While she is under my control, he added in his mind. Those days were numbered!

"Federi," said Lascek with a heavy sigh, reaching for two tumblers from the drinks cupboard, changing his mind and putting them back, "have a seat!"

Federi pulled the second console chair closer on its track and waited for Captain to sit down on the main one before making himself comfortable, cross-legged. And he folded his hands, giving Captain all ears.

"My friend," said Lascek gravely, "while you were comatose, your friends disclosed all."

Federi blinked. "What!"

"When you returned from the mission, all four of you were leaving holes in your reports. You didn't collude on that, did you?"

"Captain, I did suspect that Ailyss and Jon had seen more than they were letting on…"

"…and so had you and Paean," completed Lascek. "So! Both parties decided independently on mushroom therapy for their Captain! I understand."

"Captain, that information would have been…"

"Destructive, I know," completed Lascek. "And in fooling me, the four of you did achieve that world peace was negotiated. But Federi, understand a number of things. Firstly, don't breathe a word to aliens!"

The Romany cocked his head to one side, studying Radomir Lascek in puzzlement.

"Dana," said Lascek. "Perdita. Even Rashni, though I can't see why you'd want to disclose to her. Don't talk to them about this. I identified an inner circle of conspirators that is safe to confide in, and

11

who have all come forward to back you up when you need it."

Federi nodded sagely. "Who?"

"Ailyss, Jon and Johnny Anyhow," said the Captain. "Sherman will help with information, as much as he can. And of course, Federi, you can call on your old Captain if you need help. Is that understood?"

Federi smiled, feeling light-headed. An awe-inspiring team! He couldn't have wished for better superheroes. But...

"Johnny Anyhow, Captain?"

"He was in the Secret Service," said Lascek. "You'd like to talk to him and Ailyss some time to find out what they know about the Unicate. It's bound to be useful."

"Thank you, Captain!"

Radomir Lascek stood up. Federi followed suit, nearly losing his balance when the Captain heartily slapped his shoulder.

"Go well! And don't be too long, Federi!"

"We'll be back sooner than you think," said Federi brightly. "Not getting rid of us that easily!"

What was he doing? The plan was *not* to return! But it was maybe not a too wild idea to keep that door open...

Ha! If he survived the first sortie into Unicate headquarters! If he went about it carefully, he might have moments to check up on the ship. By March perhaps. He might stash Paean back here much sooner though. If she didn't leave him first. And if she did...

Good thing that nobody could escape their own genetic signature, he thought, his hand sinking into his pocket to touch the new teleporter Wolf had given him. An improved model; Wolf was trying to get the process kinder to the human bioelectric field. He'd still be checking on her to make sure she was safe.

"Good." The Captain grinned. "I'm counting on you both being fully back aboard by Christmas!"

~

Federi was still nodding to himself and shaking his head when Paean and Shawn helped Mindy onto the Comet, and as he climbed into the jet after them. Behind them the Probe slid into motion and curved away over the sea and up into space, lighting up like a meteorite.

Christmas! Well, that gave them precious well less than a month, anna bottle! How was he going to unravel Falco's curse in a single month? And try to undo the Morrigan's damage to his marriage? Was there even a glimmer of a hope for that? Should he waste time trying? Could he even stop himself from trying?

The Comet's hatch closed and she detached from the Solar Wind. Federi activated his wrist-com.

"*La revedere*, old ship."

There was no reply. The Solar Wind hadn't spoken to him since he returned from annihilating the Morrigan. In fact she spoke to nobody. Ailyss was spending whole days trying to coax the Solar Wind back into communicating. She was learning that an artificial intelligence could out-stubborn humans any day.

Ailyss was the only one apart from him who insisted that the personal awakening of the Solar Wind's AI had been hundred percent real and could not possibly have been a Morrigan illusion. She should know! She was the specialist.

Well, tough, thought Federi. The Solar Wind would get over it. Hopefully she'd miss him soon enough, what with Lyr in the galley and the croaches cleaning her decks…

Luigi the Croach peered out of his sleeve. Federi nodded, content. He keyed something into the console, and the Comet followed the Probe at a fast pace. There was something he wanted to check on.

13

2 – Dublin

The Earth fell away beneath them. Soon the Solar Wind disappeared from view, then the blue planet got smaller and smaller as they headed into the void, focused on that single bright speck before them.

"Why are we following the Probe?" asked Shawn.

"They're out treasure-hunting again," said Federi. He laughed dryly. "Silly really. The planet is the treasure. Those gold-hungry Atlanteans haven't twigged that yet."

"I know why they are going there," said Shawn with a smile. "But why are we?"

He got a feral smile with a silver tooth in it as a response.

"See, Mindy," said Shawn sagely, "that's what you get when you hang with pirates."

"Yeah, treasure," Paean chipped in. Mindy laughed.

"I know," she said. "You guys are preaching to the initiated!"

Right, thought Federi. She must have seen some things by now. Daughter of a smuggler. He thought back to the slaughter on the Golden Walrus. It had been pure luck and intuition that he'd found her alive aboard that ship, along with Derrick and Peter. He wasn't so sure about Peter's 'alive' though. He turned.

"Mindy," he asked, "what happened to your mom?"

"Mom left us when I was very small," said Mindy. "Dad says she wanted to be political, and it was safer for me to stay with him."

"How small?" asked Federi.

"I was one, I think," replied Mindy. "That's what Dad said. I can't really remember her."

"What was her name?"

"Angelina Carter," said Mindy. "They never married, see."

Federi scowled. Blast. He'd been right!

"You know her?" asked the perceptive girl.

He shrugged and returned his attention to the pathway of the Comet through space. Angelina was dead – brutally murdered by Semanchio Sancho. She had been avenged, equally brutally, by Radomir Lascek; but it didn't fix things.

Bubbly, sanguine Angelina had been a close friend of the Solar Wind. She had been too independent for Captain to draw her into his projects. If he had, she might have been alive today. Then again, maybe not, thought Federi, remembering the Unicate's destruction of the Ice Base. They were all in permanent danger.

And unease hit him.

It came from space. He peered into the void, wondering. They didn't have megalithic sharks out here, did they?

~

A small dot spun into view, a brighter star… no, a planet. Mindy watched in fascination as the blue sphere came closer.

"But – we just left Earth!" she objected.

"This is not Earth," smiled Federi. "Observe!"

He activated the Comet's com system. "Perdita, come in."

"Tail-gating us, Federi?"

He laughed softly. "Perdita, does our planet have a name yet?"

"No," said Perdita. "Captain keeps wanting to call it Earth Two, but he can't. Earth Two did exist."

"So, you girls are on another treasure hunt?"

"Actually I'm just taking Michelle around the place," said Perdita. "Want to see how far this planet is from defrosting."

15

Federi nodded to himself.

"Calypso," he said then, turning back to the teens in the Comet. "Her name is Calypso. Earth's twin. We name planets after Greek and Roman deities."

"Calypso wasn't a deity," laughed Paean.

"She wasn't?" he asked, confused.

"She was a seductive nymph," retorted the know-it-all young lady.

Federi laughed too. "Fine. And Pluto was a dog."

~

The Comet skimmed low over the surface. The ice on the seas of Calypso was beginning to crack and form shoals. Planting the planet in an orbit closer to the sun to break her ice age had been a good plan. And Perdita's engineering on her jets was brilliant. They withstood a good bit of celestial heat.

"Looks like the ice age on this planet is pretty much over," commented the Romany. "Got to move her into Earth's orbit before all her oceans evaporate."

"We're going to plant her?" asked Paean with keen interest.

"Michelle is going to, little luv," said Federi. "Us – we just keep tabs, see. Personally Federi would rather sort out Earth."

They orbited the beautiful planet once more. Paean gazed down at it.

"I'd like to be in on the terraforming," she said wistfully. "I could help."

Federi studied her. Of course she could! New species to cover a planet! A GM designer's heaven.

Well, if that was what she wanted – maybe their honeymoon should be spent on Calypso. And hang the mission! He knew he'd

16

go anywhere she wanted to, right now, even if it had to be into the Devil's aunt's tea party to steal her a hellish cupcake.

Actually that particular thought struck him as quite tempting. Hang the mission? Ha! He grinned.

"We'll organize it," he promised. And he punched a sequence into the Comet's console and she sped away from Planet Calypso and completed her arc around the sun. A while later Earth grew back into view.

"Where now?" asked Paean.

"Dublin," said Federi.

She scowled. "I thought, Romania! Why Dublin?"

"Loose ends," he snarled softly. "Anna bottle, yodiho, and so on."

He saw how she set her jaw. It wasn't the destination of her choice – but she was going to tackle it, with all the gutsy toughness in her. She was reasserting her right to her city of birth.

And that was good. Any healing was good. Even if it took her away from him, eventually.

"Federi?"

He glanced at her again. All his bitter sadness had to be reflecting in his eyes, because she looked at him with pity – always pity! – and reached out, and nearly touched his arm... only almost.

Damn it!

~

The Comet touched down on the docks in Dublin. Rain was seeping down in veils, greying out everything – the docks, the ships, the sea, the quayside pubs and other establishments. Shawn released a heart-rending sigh.

"You've been missing the old place too," commented Paean with sympathy.

"Never going to be the same again," replied Shawn. Federi

glanced at him sideways. And then at the younger girl.

"Mindy!" pounced the gypsy. "You're not dressed warm enough!" He opened the hatch. "Come, little luv. Leave the two young ones in here. We're getting some clothing for them."

Paean put on her rainskin over her T-shirt and followed Federi out of the hatch, which was closed quickly by Shawn to block out the falling rain.

There was always some life on the docks, even at this late hour. A number of louts came over to goggle at the space jet that was hovering half a metre above the ground, parked securely on Earth's magnetic field. But Federi didn't worry, because the hatch was secure. It needed his or Paean's fingerprint to open, or – hah! – Perdita's security override hack that he hadn't authorized!

"Why Dublin?" enquired Paean, gifting him a scowl.

"Loose ends," repeated Federi, taking her by the hand and leading her out of the rain and into a roofed-over mall. "Didn't I say so?"

"What loose ends?" She wasn't pulling her hand away. Well, at least that was something.

"Want to find out a few things!"

"What kind of things?"

"Stuff that's been bothering me."

Paean shrugged and lapsed into silence. He peered sidelong at her. Good that she was accepting it. He wasn't yet ready to tell her. Annie Donegal's assassination site was as good a beginning point for the Unicate riddle as any.

In the middle of the quiet mall Federi stopped Paean. They were quite alone.

"What now?" she asked with her red eyebrows sky-high.

He'd had enough. If he was going to give her back to the mainland, at least he was going to do it with flair. He could out-flair

18

any bleeding alien! He was not Tzigan for nothing!

"Owe you something," he replied and pulled her into his arms, and kissed her thoroughly. Blast that Morrigan with his false promises and illusions!

It took a few surprised moments before the magic set in. But it did set in. By the time he released her, she had all the appropriate stars back in her eyes and was staring at him in bewilderment, her lips slightly parted. Asking for more? He smiled.

"Owe you a few hundred more of those," he pointed out, "but we can cash in as we go, what do you say?"

She gazed at him out of hazy blue eyes. Federi nodded, feeling infinitely better. Yes. This was the way to do it. If she was going to leave him anyway, he wanted to make doubly sure that she could at least never forget him.

"Was a good start, I think," he muttered to himself and overrode the lock on a clothing store, looted some warm stuff out of the winter section for Shawn and Mindy, broke into the cash tills, left a generous amount in there for the clothes – he wasn't hung up about that bit of change – locked the cash tills again and re-locked the shop's doors on their way out. The whole operation had been stealthy and fast, with Paean shadowing in what they called at home gape-mouthed wonder.

Well, it wasn't dishonest because he'd paid correctly, right? And it wasn't his fault that the Dublin clothing shops were closed at such inconvenient hours! It was only midnight.

He grinned and decided to repeat the stunt. This time, it was a small boutique that received an unexpected night-time visit. He deactivated the alarms and also the movement detector, and pulled Paean into the little shop.

The boutique was better defended. Just in case this went wrong and they had to vanish fast, he first stuck a nice sum of cash down on

19

the counter. Ha! Prince Vlad? The fiend didn't even have any own money! This was thirteen years of a quartermaster's wages and a pirate's loot that Federi had at his fingertips here; not even counting the rest of his ill-gotten professional fees, which were in Southern Free in an account, in Marge's able hands. And Paean thought that only Unicate officials were really rich...

He rifled through the ladies' clothes and pulled out a beautiful two-piece in soft pearly sea-green, with a short knitted skirt and a dreamy lace-and-knit top, and told Paean to put it on. Elegant; but warm, too.

She was still in the habit of complying unquestioningly. Federi inwardly thanked Captain for placing her under his command. As she emerged from the change-rooms, his breath went missing. She was gorgeous!

"Does it work?" she asked, worried. "I rather like it."

"Better keep it on," he told her. "We'll need to look smart in the near future." For the Devil's tea party, he added in his mind.

She gave him a puzzled look.

"Shoes," he said. "Pick a pair!" The deck sneakers didn't really work with this kind of outfit.

She picked some innocuous-looking white sandals. Federi shook his head.

"Going to freeze to death in those," he advised. And he directed her to a pair of fake-fur-trimmed ladies' boots. He could see that it was on the tip of her tongue to say they were too old for her – and then she changed her mind. Great. Thanks, Vlad! Federi smiled to himself.

"But... does it work? I like it, but... is it still me?"

"You look sweet," he told her and pulled her close and treated her to some more Tzigan-style 'flair'. And he stood back and looked into her glazed eyes, and grinned. Much better! "I lied. You look absolutely breathtaking."

~

They returned through the rain to the Comet with arms full of warm clothes for Shawn and for Mindy. Shawn gawped at his sister.

"Wow, Pae!"

She grinned and did a self-conscious little turn on the slightly pointy heels of her white boots to display the outfit. "Nice, you say?"

"Stunning," said her little brother. "Keep it on! At last you're making use of your position, married to a pirate!"

She laughed.

~

Paean made both Shawn and Federi wait in the tiny ablutions cubicle while she helped Mindy get into the jersey and long pants, as the girl was scared of dislocating the artificial bridge on her spine.

"And now where?" challenged Paean.

Federi turned to Shawn. "You got an aunt here?"

"Oh no," said Shawn with a frown. "Not Auntie Katie! She's a regular horror! We're not paying her a visit!"

"We are," said Paean with a vicious little smile.

3 – Katie McLochlainn

Katie McLochlainn, in her winter dressing gown and slippers, her blonde-dyed hair in curlers, opened her front door.

There was a moment of frozen silence as she stared at the four figures in orange rainskins, on her doorstep, in the rain. Two of the four were unknowns, but the other two were nightmares from the past, whom she had hoped never to see again. Her hand on the door handle started trembling and she played with the thought of slamming the front door in their faces.

Her nephew's bright smile and his fast boot in the door forestalled that.

"Aren't you going to invite us in, Auntie Katie?"

She shook her head, still unable to speak. These children were hunted by the Unicate! Now the Unicate would come sniffing around her place, maybe imprison her, possibly kill her the way her sister-in-law had been killed…

She gaped at Paean. The girl had grown up! In only eight months? She was dressed like a VIP from the embassy. What on Earth? Somehow she must have come into money.

But for heavens' sakes, the company they were in! The dirty Egyptian stepped forward and extended a hand. She nearly shook it but withdrew hers at the last moment. Common sense prevailed: Who knew what diseases he carried? The gypsy laughed softly.

"Who is there, Katie?" a bass voice boomed across from somewhere inside the house.

Kate still didn't manage any answer. Séamus McLochlainn, the size of a bear, moved up behind her.

"I canna believe it," he exclaimed, highly delighted. "Shawn! Paean, *mo chrói!* And you're looking so well! Is it Christmas already? I've been praying for you to come to no harm, me wee bairns! Come in, my children! Where's Ronan?" He got very serious of a sudden. "He's alive, isn't he? Paean, tell me that nothing bad has happened to him?"

"He's alive and happy," said Paean with a smile. "Don't worry, Uncle Séamus."

"Séamus," Katie started protesting. "The Unicate…"

"Rubbish, Noodlekins," said Séamus with a laugh. "What are you kids still doing standing in the rain? Get yer bums inside! Katie, put the kettle on. I see you two brought friends? And am I not delighted to meet you, lassie!" He paused just long enough to hear Shawn's mutterings. "Mindy, you say? Welcome, my heart! Welcome! And you, er – mister?"

Federi smiled tightly and nodded, ignoring Séamus's extended hand. Paean glanced at the Free Gypsy, baffled. He seemed all formal suddenly, stuck for words! Intimidated?

Uncle Séamus clapped first her, then Shawn into a bear hug. Mindy got one too, for good measure – but Shawn protested that her back was injured, and Uncle Séamus let go of her very cautiously. She assured him that everything was still fine. Paean worried about this too. That bridge was a fragile piece of equipment.

All four followed Séamus in through the hallway, to a cosy living room that spoke of wealthier days. Auntie Katie disappeared into the kitchen, taking her unbelievable stress levels with her, to Paean's relief.

"Federi!" hissed the little redhead. "Introduce yourself!"

She collected a dark glance as a response. She blinked. What was with Federi? Did he feel unqualified in any way?

Prince Vlad and his impeccable manners flashed past her mind.

He wouldn't have had a problem... Prince Vlad was a bleeding illusion! An alien shape-shifter! And it didn't take the brain-power of a nuclear physicist to put on a black cape and perform a sweeping bow. She remembered Federi's exaggerated bows to the Goddess Bridget, and suppressed a smile.

He'd dressed *her* up to a T for this encounter. He'd equipped her beautifully so that she didn't need to feel like a poor relation. So that she could walk in like the queen of an empire. Or a syndicate. But he'd forgotten to equip himself! Or maybe he hadn't planned to? He didn't need any of that! He was Federi!

"Must I introduce you?" she offered in a whisper. And wobbled a bit on those heels of those boots. They might be ultimately sweet, but she'd have to get used to them before she could move in them like Perdita.

Uncle Séamus sensed Federi's reserve.

"I'm Séamus McLochlainn," the huge man with the greying mane of once-red hair introduced himself once more, this time simply grabbing the gypsy's hand and shaking it heartily. "Séamus to you. And you are?"

"The bodyguard," said Federi. "Call me Shadow."

Paean gasped.

"That's na true!" she exploded. "He's my husband! Uncle Séamus, and he's the sweetest guy under Earth's sun! And various other suns too, hah!"

Silence descended. Séamus stared at Paean, shocked; Federi gazed at her with a quirky smile. Auntie Katie came out of the galley – the kitchen, Paean corrected herself – just at the wrong moment, overheard Paean's heated little speech, and nearly fainted in the doorway.

"Oh Mary, mother of Jesus!" she exclaimed theatrically, her arms thrown aloft. "There, you see, Séamus? Didn't I tell you? Just like

Annie?"

"Katie, hold yer tongue!" commanded Uncle Séamus. "I'll not have you say bad things about my poor sister, may she rest in peace!"

Paean reached for Federi's hand and interlaced her fingers with his. Nobody was blasted well going to rubbish her husband like that! She glanced at his face. He was peering at her, seeming dazed. Why did her uncle manage to intimidate him? Not even the Admiral's opinion had unsettled him as badly as this!

"Your precious sister was all banged-up at sixteen too, Séamus," ranted Katie. "By that drunkard lout Donegal. Or she wouldna've got herself into such a fine quandary as she was in, living in the slums, working her fine hands to the bone in the factory, dancing in taverns at night…"

"She never danced in taverns!" snapped Shawn, madly angry. "She was a waitress! Pae, let's go! We're not welcome here, and we've never been, now have we?"

Paean was staring at her aunt in disgust, lost for words. There was a deep ache in her heart where her mother had been. How that stupid Kate could even utter such things…

"Katie!" thundered Séamus. "You hold yer poisonous tongue and get back in the kitchen!"

"Don't tell them my name," Federi mouthed at Paean under his breath. "'s critically important!" She blinked at him in surprise, but then she passed the message to Shawn and Mindy. He must know what he was doing.

"I'm so sorry," Uncle Séamus addressed Federi, taking his left arm and ushering him to one of the couches. Paean followed closely. "Please don't mind her foul manners," added Séamus with a significant glance in the direction of the kitchen. "She's a regular banshee, that one. And wouldn't she talk the ears off a deaf mule?"

Paean sat down next to Federi, nice and ladylike as the high-heeled boots demanded, but she shifted right up close to him and took his hand again. He was the one who had taught her to smile again, after she had escaped Dublin. She was sort-of counting on him to buffer her against her aunt's attacks.

"There's a story to be told here, that I can see," said Séamus with a placating smile. "Paean, Annie didn't raise you to rashness and foolishness, this I know. Surely you've good reason to be married to this man at your young age? Do tell me the story, won't you?"

"I'll spin you a yarn," muttered Paean darkly. "A right Ceilidh yarn!" It was none of it Uncle Séamus' business!

"He's a prince," piped Shawn. "From the north of Egypt."

Once again Auntie Katie appeared in the door, just in time to hear the wrong end of the 'yarn'. Her mouth dropped open.

"Oh, Jesus son of the Holy Mary!" she exclaimed and nearly dropped the tray with tea cups. "A prince! Under my humble roof!"

"Calm down, Katie!" commanded Séamus, running out of patience fast. He returned his attention to Federi. "Shadow? Do the travellers not give their children any names?"

"We do," said Paean. "But you wouldna understand a word of it, Uncle. It's a *lot* of names, three pages long, and all in Aramaic."

"So of which country are you a prince, Shadow?" asked Uncle Séamus with a smile.

"None," replied Federi. "As I said, I'm the bodyguard."

"He's the prince of Romania," piped Shawn, just as Paean jumped in with "Prince of the Romanian Kalderash." Take that, Mr Morrigan!

Séamus laughed.

"Shawn, Paean – let the man speak!"

"I do have a question, Mr McLochlainn," said Federi. Paean knew instantly from his tone of voice that the question meant

27

trouble. "On the twenty-fifth of March this year, three minors came to you for protection and shelter from the corrupt authorities." His voice dropped to subzero levels. "They were hunted for their lives. They were your blood family. They had just lost their mother. And you turned them away. Could you explain?"

An icy silence fell for the second time.

"That day I came home," said Uncle Séamus darkly, "and got the news that my sister had passed on. I asked after the children, but nobody knew what had become of them. I feared the worst. I contacted the police to find them; they told me that the three children were on the Unicate records as missing, but that they would let me know if they found them. Only much later did Mrs Flanagan tell me that they had been here, and Kate had turned them away." He shook his head and glared at his wife, who had lost all colour from her face.

Federi watched carefully as the uncle talked, listening for more than just the words. His inner lie detector did not get triggered. The man was genuine. As for Kate…

"The Unicate," she started, got lost, repeated "the Unicate," and stopped talking.

She wasn't telling everything. Not anything, to be exact.

"If I had known," said Uncle Séamus with regret. "If I had only been home!"

"That's alright," said Shawn brightly. He couldn't stand the tension. "That way we managed to board the best ship in the world. And Paean got to marry a prince."

"At fifteen!" yapped Katie.

"Sixteen," corrected Shawn patiently. "Small legal difference, see?"

"And Ronan?" pressed Séamus, ignoring his wife completely. "Where is he?"

"He's currently setting up house in Miami," said Shawn. "Going to have twins, in March."

"What!" gasped Auntie Kate. "See, Séamus -"

"So he is married too?" asked the uncle.

"You see," Auntie Katie started again, "didn't I -"

"To the daughter of the Planetary Ruler, Radomir Lascek," completed Shawn triumphantly.

~

It was unreal. From the moment Shawn dropped that particular bomb, Auntie Katie fell over herself to make them all comfortable. She turned from a haughty, unpleasant dame into the perfect hostess, to the point of embarrassment. Obviously she didn't quite buy into the 'prince' yarn; but the daughter of the planetary leader! She cooed and twittered around Paean, Shawn and Mindy and only stopped flapping when Uncle Séamus sent her out of the room to fetch some shortcakes.

"Tha's another Ceilidh yarn!" he said with a sceptical smile. "Shawn, what happened to your truthfulness? I honestly want to know where Ronan is!"

"'s the plain truth," said Shawn, incensed. "Tell him, Federi?"

Paean iced, her eyes darting to her uncle. Hopefully the name would not be noted?

"Actually, no," Federi replied, shaking his head, ignoring Shawn's slip-up. "Mr McLochlainn, Shawn is an honest boy. Only these last few months have been rather traumatic for all three. Understandably, would you agree?"

Uncle Séamus nodded, a bit guiltily.

~

Paean watched her uncle as the conversation rolled over her with its hypnotic music. She could almost believe the tale Federi spun about the Solar Wind being paramilitary under cover, rounding up

29

survivors out of bad situations in various ports, Mindy being a classic example. Mindy's and Shawn's mouths hung open at the lies the Tzigan so lightly and convincingly invented. Radomir Lascek was a man of a high military position who had been elected for a term of taking the highly responsible position of leadership of the global panel of political heads, for organizing peace between the various groups.

There were no space trips, alien invasions, Atlantean horrors or anything of the sort in his tale. Just plain, common-sense heroism on a small personal level, and political progress. A tale a sensible citizen like Uncle Séamus could believe more easily than Shawn's wild confabulations, a.k.a the truth.

Paean snuggled up to Federi as the music of his voice spun her along with the others into a mild trance. His arm went around her without him pausing in his saga. She had very nearly discarded him, hours back. Forgetting that underneath the unassuming exterior lurked a hero, and a storyteller, and an entertainer, and a man with more facets than she'd ever be able to figure out. A man who had managed to get rid of – she had to face it – an alien pest who had been making everyone's lives miserable.

She had thought that she wanted to leave him, after all the nasty stuff on the ship – chains, and Jodi, and all that; but she wasn't so sure now. Actually, what she wanted to do was take him with her and protect him from the chronic work and nonsense that was just his daily life. Except that the man was chained to the Solar Wind. Rats. She sighed glumly.

Uncle Séamus scowled at her overt closeness to Federi. And she noticed, and moved even closer. She didn't care. Maybe she could come to an agreement with Federi about her independence; but right now his warmth and closeness was what the doctor ordered, for her sore heart. And his arm tightly around her told her that he hadn't written *her* off.

"She's only fifteen, you know, Mister Shadow," Uncle Séamus pointed out.

"Sixteen," Shawn corrected, irritated. "In any case, Uncle, if you weren't there to provide a landing place for her when Mom died, who are you to judge those who did? She's married to him."

This brought some more hysterical reaction from Auntie Katie, but Uncle Séamus cut her short.

"The boy is right," he stated. "This is your doing, Kate!"

Paean closed her eyes with a sigh. Issues she didn't want.

"In any case," Shawn piped up again, "as you are aware Shadow's a diplomat. You got something better to offer to a poor orphan girl?"

Federi didn't argue again that he was merely the bodyguard. He also didn't pull Shawn up on his blatant disrespect of his elders, noted Paean. He must be in agreement that in this case it was warranted.

"So you're here to bring us Shawn?" asked Auntie Katie, that panic still edging her voice. "I've never raised boys, and they say teenage boys are difficult..."

"And Mindy," said Shawn with a grin. "She has special needs. She has a broken back and needs specialized medical care so she can keep on moving normally. Can't keep her on the ship."

Paean, with her eyes closed, chuckled. Auntie Katie went into another fit of hysterics just as Uncle Séamus said, "Of course, Mr Shadow! Shawn is always welcome here, and we'll most certainly have space for another young lady. We're not exactly impoverished, so the medical needs shouldn't be too much of a burden..."

"Séamus, you're off of your mind!" exclaimed Auntie Katie. "Wi' the food prices up like that and the medical licenses..."

Paean felt more than heard the silent laughter from Federi. And

31

his fingers moved into her hair and combed out a few tangles.

"If that were the case, the state would be covering her expenses," he pointed out. "Besides, medical licenses are removed from the New Constitution. But we're not leaving anyone here. Don't stress yourselves." His voice dropped. Paean opened an eye and saw him peering calculatingly at Auntie Katie.

"Séamus," he said quietly, "Annie Donegal was a good woman. I see this by the beautiful values she taught her children. Sounds to me as though she was a very hard-working woman, too. A good citizen. I really have to wonder why the Unicate executed her."

Aunt Katie turned pale, got up, excused herself and escaped into the depths of the house.

*

Federi had prised Paean away from the posh company of her aunt and uncle. It hadn't taken much. In fact he'd nearly had to prise her eyes open, she was that tired; but now she was awake, out in the very fresh air of late November.

It had stopped drizzling and the Rose Garden, a park two blocks away from Auntie Katie's place, was glistening in the dark, its rose bushes scraggly and bare, not yet trimmed for the winter.

"I'm still scared of Dublin," commented Paean quietly. "If you weren't here with me, I wouldn't be here."

Federi nodded and broke a late straggler of a white rose off from its bush and tucked it behind her ear, into her wild hair. She smiled at him.

"Auntie Katie's a horror, an' that's a fact," he said, and pulled her into his arms to pay her one of those owed items on his list. When he released her, tears were glistening in her eyes, in the reflected glow of the street lights.

32

"And this?" he asked, catching one of them with a finger.

"I'm sorry," she sniffed. "You're the best there is, Federi. I so badly want to be free… but I can't leave you! You're gold."

He laughed softly. "'m nothing of the sort, little luv. Federi's just an old vagabond."

She shook her head. "I don't get it."

Federi wrapped his arms back around her and held her tightly, his mind spinning around what she had just told him. She still loved him? It was precarious, fleeting, possibly just momentary – but it was a chance, and he grabbed at it.

"Let's be free together?" he suggested.

"If I could only believe in that!"

The wispy flame of hope went out. Rats! He clung to her, despondency moving in again, blocking out the light.

Time. He needed more time.

"Do me a favour," he improvised desperately. "Don't talk about it until you really want to walk away. Okay? Because you're just breaking your heart on it. 's pointless."

She nodded.

"Okay," muttered Federi, resting his cheek against her lush shock of hair, thinking frantically. She wanted freedom. She didn't believe he could be free. She was right: He wasn't. There was the mission.

Stashing her back on the Solar Wind had been a hundred percent part of his plan. He didn't want to expose her – the light of his life – to the dangers of the Unicate! But she wouldn't stay on the Solar Wind. She had quit the ship and was not going back.

Would it make sense to abandon the mission and put her freedom first? He wanted to – hells, anything she asked, he'd try to give her right now – but how? There was no freedom as long as the Unicate survived.

Her hand had wandered into his hair, playing with some strands.

"Little luv," he started, and that feeling of doom hit him, making him inhale sharply. That shark from space swam closer to the surface again. Federi peered at the cloud cover, trying to see beyond it with his second sight. Something was definitely out there trawling for him!

And not only from space! He eyed the empty Dublin roads with suspicion. It had been a long while since the Unicate hounds had last chased him around the mainland. But Paean's escape was a lot fresher. Could they sense her presence?

"We'll have to move," he said intently, releasing her.

"What are you getting?" she asked with a scowl.

"It's a trap."

She nodded. "But…"

"We wait it out," said Federi. "But I'll get you your gun from the Comet."

"Got it here," said Paean and reached underneath the cardigan part of her lacy top, and produced the small machinegun that looked almost like a toy.

"Proud of you," muttered Federi with a grin.

She shrugged. "'bout Uncle Séamus and Aunt Kate," she said. "As their niece I'd forgive and forget them."

Federi nodded. That sounded about right.

"But as an assassin," she added, "I feel there's something awry. Something nasty."

He took her hand. "C'mon. Let's get back there. Shawn and Mindy aren't exactly safe."

~

They returned to a much quieter house. Shawn and Mindy had been given rooms to sleep in: Shawn, the room of the younger cousin, and Mindy that of the eldest. The two cousins had long since grown up and left the house.

34

Uncle Séamus showed Paean to the original guest room. It had twin beds in it; for her and Federi to share a room, but not a bunk. The chances were that Aunt Kate would have quartered her together with Mindy instead, if she'd dared be openly rude to the diplomat she believed Shadow to be. Paean had to smile.

Federi checked on Mindy and on Shawn. Both were asleep in their respective rooms. When he returned to the guest room, his young wife was sitting on one of the two twin beds battling a comb through her wild curls, having changed back into a clean pair of daily jeans. Not her ducky pyjamas? It occurred to him that he might have to buy her some nightwear... but maybe not yet. Not where they were going, in the near future.

"C'mere," he said and took the comb out of her hands and attacked that unruly shock of red hair with significantly more gentleness than she had.

"So what's the plan?" she asked.

"You pretend to go to sleep," he said. "I interview your auntie a bit. But little luv, please don't really fall asleep! Anything might happen!"

She rummaged in her pack that was next to her on the bed, and found Leila.

"Girl, wake me up if I fall asleep!"

"Yes, mistress!"

Federi gave her comb back and got up with a sigh. "See you later." And he slunk out of the door.

~

It was about an hour later when Federi opened the door to the guest room again. He moved into the dark room without activating any lights; instead pulling the curtain back a bit and letting in the patchy moonlight, thankful that the extra satellite had been moved out of Earth's way again. By his improved night vision, now that the

35

clouds had parted, things were as bright as in the dusk. He slipped into the single bed in which Paean had curled herself into a tight little ball. She relaxed and turned in his arms. And two blue eyes snapped open and studied him.

"You're cold," he whispered. "I thought for a moment you were sleeping."

"As though I could sleep," she countered. "There's too much stuff here."

He nodded. The feeling of being in a trap hadn't let go of him either.

"What did you find out?" asked Paean in whispers.

He shook his head. "Nothing much. She's too scared of the Unicate."

Paean closed her eyes. "Glad you're here. Missed you!"

"You too," replied Federi, his cheek against her hair. "You too, little luv!"

He closed his eyes. He could sense how she slipped into dreams at last; having stayed awake so long. It was very late. Three or four perhaps. Much was not left of the night.

And that sense of foreboding slammed into his guts. It was happening now! He got up again, with Paean being awake in a frightened instant, and stuck her machinegun into her hand.

"Hold the fort, sweetness! I'll be back in a second." He moved out of the door, and down the passage, and into the place where Shawn was sleeping. The boy was in fact not sleeping!

"Come, Shawn," he whispered and included the youngest Donegal into his teleporter field, taking him to the Comet.

"But – Paean," protested Shawn. "And Mindy!"

"Getting them. Wait for me here!" Federi teleported back into the house of the McLochlainns, and slipped from Shawn's room to Mindy's. The young girl was fast asleep. Federi lifted her precariously and teleported a second time. Shawn was waiting for him; the astute boy had flattened one of the Comet's seats so that Federi could put Mindy down. She muttered something but didn't wake up.

"And now, Paean," insisted Shawn.

"Got that right," replied the Free Gypsy and teleported back to the mansion.

Shawn shook his head to himself. "'e shouldn't be teleporting!" He was going to ask Wolf for a teleporter when he returned to the Solar Wind.

~

Federi checked on Paean. She was still fine; but he couldn't get her convinced that she needed to return to the Comet.

"Your backup!" she insisted. "Already pulled you out more than once! Remember the mutant!"

"Then back me up!" he demanded.

Paean scrambled to get her clothes bundled up and her backpack shouldered. Not a fly was she leaving that beautiful two-piece and those cute boots here if things blew up – which they would. And she followed Federi out into the passage, her machinegun lowered but ready.

~

Federi stealthily led the way to where he'd heard a murmur come from. Aunt Katie, talking to someone at this time of night? Either Uncle Séamus was a night owl who never got tired, or she wasn't talking to him. Federi set his jaw, considering what he'd found out about that woman.

Auntie Katie knew about the assassination of Annie Donegal. She had been Annie's superior in the structure of the clothing factory. She had in fact been the director of that whole division. And she had dined with the owners every so often. This she had proudly related

37

herself; seeing that Shadow Kalderash was in with the Unicate Top Leadership, it ought to impress him. At which point he had asked who owned the factory. Unicate, of course.

The going got a little bit tougher from there. Aunt Katie had retired with a headache; Uncle Séamus had completed the story. Katie had discovered that Annie had hacked into the factory's console. The electronic seal on some of the files was broken. This was following the disappearance of a co-worker, about which event Annie had voiced a suspicion. She and four others were investigating, not trusting the police report. So Kate conscientiously reported what she had discovered. And the owners had got a strange smile that had frightened her, and commended her for her loyalty…

Days later those five women were called aside for a medical check-up. Blood samples were taken, and the next day the follow-up came in the shape of "vaccinations". But strangely enough, while the others were a bit off-colour for a few days, Annie was the only one who died of a disease.

Federi was by now sure that Annie had seen something she shouldn't have. How he wished he could ask her what that was!

Yes, little luv, we do remember the bleeding mutant! That creature that had tried to invade and take him over, was impossible to forget, seeing that it had left him with its memories, a fair amount of its reflexes, and its improved senses – so improved that it would drive him insane if he didn't watch out. In fact, if he didn't constantly filter out the over-active hearing… he was an idiot. He stood completely still and listened.

It wasn't as bad as it had been at first. His hearing was returning to almost normal. But still, he managed to pick up a phrase, in a half-whisper.

"Yes, I think it's him!"

He led Paean all the way down the passage, to the other end of the house, and moved closer to the door behind which this conversation was happening.

"Yes," Aunt Katie was whispering to an invisible conversational partner. "From the Solar Wind. Federi. Demonos?" There was a second's puzzled silence. "What? I don't understand what you're saying, ma'am." Another silence, and a strange little strangled sound, and then, "Alright, we'll get out of the way. I knew there was something strange about him!"

Federi burst into the room and wrenched the com shell out of her hand, twisting her arm on her back and holding her wrist in a vice grip. He listened into the com, but it was silent. Katie squealed.

"Séamus! Séamus, help!" She wriggled in Federi's grasp. "Federi Demonos, you brute, let me go!"

"So you can get out?" asked the Assassin coldly. "Sorry, lady. You've spoken the name. You get to witness what happens next!"

Séamus appeared in the doorway. Federi registered how Paean stealthily cut off the way to the passage, guarding at the door.

"Excuse me, Mr Kalderash!" the uncle stated indignantly. "Get your hands off my wife!"

"Tell him what you've done," Federi challenged Kate. "Your poor husband has no idea, does he! McLochlainn, here's the low-down. Your wife is a Unicate informant."

"But…"

"Make him let me go!" screamed Katie. "They'll be here any minute! They warned us to get out!"

"Now she's finally telling the truth," said Federi. "And why, Katie?"

"Because – it might get vicious…"

The window shattered. Federi heard several other windows shatter through the house at the same time. He released Katie and confronted what came catapulting through the broken glass. Paean slipped into the room behind them. Thank the Stars!

"McLochlainn, lock the door!" he shouted.

"The children!" bellowed Uncle Séamus.

"They're safe," snapped Federi, grabbing the apparition by its neck fur, sticking its own gun into its mouth and blasting its head off. He dropped the dead Unicate hound to the floor. "McLochlainn, I took the children to a safe place. There's Unicate," he said and flashed Katie a silvery smile, "and then there is this!"

"Federi Demonos," coughed Katie. "Descendant of Falco Demonos."

"Traitor to humankind," completed Federi. "That's me. Excuse me." He left them staring at the unearthly Unicate corpse that graced their studio's floor and moved off into the house. Paean was once again right there, shadowing him. Good girl.

"Did you see him move?" choked Katie. "That was uncanny!"

"What the hell have you invited into our house there, Kate?" asked Séamus, pointing at the Unicate thing's remains, white with shock. "Look at it! That's never human!" He locked the door behind Federi.

~

Paean's machinegun was rattling non-stop. Those monster dogs came bursting in through every door in the passage. She had followed Federi back out and was now shooting a circle around the two of them.

"Should have blasted well – allowed me – to teleport you out!" scolded the gypsy between bursts of gunfire. "Crickets, how many of these monsters are there?"

"They come through portals," said Paean.

"Looks like it!"

There was no Prince Vlad to growl them down. But in any case these dogs were different, thought Paean. They looked like Vlad's shifter beast hounds, but they acted like something else. Like trained soldiers. Vlad's hounds would have taken off with their tails tucked in, long ago.

There were several dead Unicate hounds lying around them now; and silence as the last one hit the ground.

"Come!" said Federi and grabbed her hand once more.

Something in him had changed, she thought as she followed him. She'd come across the Assassin before; but this was Federi, fed up. She remembered the concealed terror in his voice back when he had first told her about the Unicate slaughtering his family. There was none of that terror now; only a grim determination to leave none of them alive. The hounds should be terrified.

They moved systematically from one room to the next, looking for more hounds. Eventually they returned to the study, and found the door locked. Federi cursed, shot out the lock and kicked the door open. No time for Tzigan tricks now.

Uncle Séamus was still standing next to the fallen hound, holding a quivering Katie tight with her head turned away so she didn't have to look at the monstrosity on the floor. She was stammering. Federi thought he picked up an incoherent stream of saints and archangels. Séamus glared briefly at him as he broke in through the door; but then the man returned his attention to the dead hound as though he expected the thing to come alive again.

Hell, he had no idea!

"Kate," said Federi, "and Séamus. Come. This place is not safe any longer."

Katie looked up in fear.

"But -" she objected, "Maire is coming home for the weekend, tomorrow!"

"Call her," commanded the Assassin coldly. "Call your older daughter too. Tell them, under no circumstances must they come to

41

the house. They must stay where they are! This place is not safe!"

"Mr Demonos," countered Séamus angrily, "the police will sort this out in the morning!"

Federi held up his hand.

"*That* is the police," he pointed at the hounds. "And if you want a repeat of this whole thing, just say my name again! Didn't you hear when I asked you to call me Shadow?" He snorted. Bodyguard indeed! Heck.

Katie stared at him in numb horror. Federi saw that she was registering only now that the hound was wearing a Unicate police uniform.

"Now call your daughters, blast you!" he snapped impatiently, glancing about. More hounds might come pouring out of everywhere in another moment. But it was alright; he had more than enough rounds for them, and he had noticed Paean reloading, a moment back.

They died from normal old bullets. This came as a surprise to him. He'd begun to think that it needed something supernatural – perhaps his mutant-Assassin-blend rage, and ripping out their jugular with his teeth, like back in Miami.

While Katie shakily made those two calls, he puzzled about something else. The monster dogs were equipped with standard Unicate-issue guns; not only stun guns, but also the firing kind. Yet not one of them had used any. They morphed into hounds, bared their terrible maws and attacked like wolves, or lions, going for the jugular. And never reaching it, because their prey was armed with a gun. How logical was that?

They probably relied on their victims to be frozen with fear, he thought. It would make sense. Most would be. Except those who had previous experience. What was he thinking? People never survived to *get* previous experience!

Katie finished her two calls; and Federi escorted her and Uncle Séamus out of the house, with Paean shadowing and covering their backs, and frog-marched them to where the Comet was parked, hovering above the ground in the Rose Garden. There were sirens in the distance; but no further dogs came pouring out of any portals, doorways or windows. But the Unicate had clearly noted the shoot-out and was on its way to investigate.

That, too, puzzled him. Was the ordinary police force not connected to these hounds? Was it bad administration – good old red tape? Left-handed confusionary state incompetence? He had to think of Buddy Ruggiero. No, indeed. The ordinary police knew nothing of the Romanian Hounds. Those were very special forces. What hotline did Aunt Katie have there?

He shooed Uncle Séamus and Aunt Katie into the Comet, followed them, waited for Paean to board and close the hatch, and then took the jet into the stratosphere. The little craft was cramped with those two and their loaded auras; both Shawn and Paean had to sit on the floor. Well, he knew exactly where to park the traitorous McLochlainns.

He included both Séamus and the bleached Katie into his teleporter field.

*

"Federi!"

The Romany grinned at the space goddess who was once again perched on top of his antique Ironwood Table with a mug of something in her hand. Not coffee. It smelt of something else. And she had messed on her priestess robe from the fright. Johnny Anyhow glanced up from filleting a fish. He nodded a greeting at the gypsy. Federi laughed softly.

"Dana, if someone ought to be used to teleportation, that should be you!"

"Not every Talita, Diana and Aine on New Dome has a teleporter," she snapped at him. "It's a Special Forces item."

"Figures," grinned Federi. "Look, my friend. Do me a favour. Take this confused couple here and get them to New Dome?"

"What?" Dana stared. "Friend? New Dome? You've never even seen the planet! How would you know if it's suitable?"

"Well," said Federi, "do you have Unicate there?"

"Unicate?" She laughed out loud. "No, you birdbrain! Of course not! No Unicate or other aberration sets foot in Dana's Empire! Unless I've designed the aberration!"

"So there," said Federi with a theatrical gesture, *"isda!* The place is suitable. Would you?"

Dana studied the couple thoughtfully.

"And you would give me…"

"I'll entertain your young one when the time comes," said Federi. And chuckled. It sounded a bit evil. "Actually, Dana, I've already notched up a life-time's worth of entertaining Rushka for you. Shall I send you the bill?"

She grimaced. "All right then, let's station them on my planet! At least this time it's not my treasure you're after!" She led the way out of the galley towards Perdita's space jet, beckoning Séamus and Katie to follow.

"I'm going along," said Johnny Anyhow, abandoning the fish. "She mustn't fly alone! She's with child!"

Federi smiled and said nothing. The young marine had to be badly smitten to be that protective of the tough, immortal space raider! He glanced at the eye in the corner of the ultra-glare oven.

"Hey, old ship."

Once again the Solar Wind cold-shouldered him. He shrugged

and teleported back to the Comet.

Paean had finally fallen asleep. But Shawn was waiting for him, wound up. "Federi, what happened?"

"Taking you and Mindy home," snarled the Romany. "This mission is getting too dangerous for you kids!"

"Then it's too dangerous for Paean too," stated Shawn.

"Wrong, Donegal. I can protect her. But I can't protect all three of you. This, just now, was nothing but luck."

"But," said Shawn.

"Basta," retorted Federi.

"… you shouldn't teleport so much, Federi," Shawn reminded him. "Doctor's orders, 'kay?"

Federi laughed. "Fine. There goes our stealth."

4 – Mrs Flanagan

Paean woke up to the ship rocking, and the hundreds of wind chimes tinkling softly. She stretched contentedly, and realized she was in the bunk rather than the hammock.

Back on the forsaken ship?

Federi was sitting cross-legged on the bunk next to her, something small in his hands.

"What's that?"

"New mind-twister from Wolf," said the Romany, studying her with soft eyes. "Slept well, Twinkletoes?"

"Fine," said Paean and frowned. "Only... Not complaining, Federi, but what are we doing back on the ship?"

"Not complaining, huh," he smiled.

"Any place away from Auntie Katie is a good place," said Paean with a shudder.

"Right," agreed Federi. "So I sent her to New Dome. With Dana."

It took Paean a good few moments to digest this.

"Yay! Genius! Why? With Dana? Federi – I mean, she's a horror, but – sure she deserved that?" She thought for a second. "Dana, I mean. Sure she deserves Auntie Katie? The woman is capable of ruining New Dome for her!"

Federi laughed. "They deserve each other, believe me."

"And Uncle Séamus?"

"He's gone with her," replied the Tzigan. "Dana is setting them up. In exchange for favours."

"What favours?"

"Babysitting," grinned Federi.

"Hay!" exclaimed Paean.

He had to laugh. "Not you, my sweetheart! Me! Federi has a track record, remember? Dana already owes me a lifetime of favours for that, she'll get the idea sooner or later. Or possibly the bill."

Paean sighed and studied the many jewels hanging from the ceiling, swaying hypnotically with the ship. Babysitting! Incredible, that she'd have that in common with her gypsy!

And she glanced at Federi, and got a mischievous glint in her eye.

"Ten," she said. "Nine, eight…"

"Stop that!" exclaimed Federi, shooting to his feet. "Alright, enough loafing around on the Solar Wind! Let's -"

Paean's wrist-com made an alarming noise.

"Alright, you vixen, *you* go see Captain!" snapped Federi.

~

After all, Captain didn't hold them back long. He only wanted to ascertain that they had enough ammunition, enough explosive, the guns were in working order, the teleporters and the wrist-coms…

"Wha's that team Captain spoke about?" asked Paean, munching on a piece of salmon. She'd never tasted the stuff before; it was lovely. Federi had taken her to a hovering restaurant that hung above the shoreline of some or other place – possibly Portugal. Suspended on an enormous beam from the mainland. Waiting for a freak wave.

Federi shrugged. "Not important. But now you'll tell me," he added softly. "I've left little brother and girlfriend on the Solar Wind and sorted your pet horror relatives. 's just you and me now, little luv. Now you'll show me Molly Street?"

She stared at him in dismay. "But Federi, we were filthy poor. You're na' going to like it!"

He stared at her quizzically. "What's it matter if I like it?" And he shook his head. "Would have followed you home there anyway," he commented. "Would have tracked you there. Good at tracking. Never expected musicians to be rich! Not while they play in such a bad pub as you kids were!"

She pulled a face. "The place was paying us cash!"

"Not enough," said Federi with a smile. "Anyway, whom are you calling poor? I'll bet you half of my fortune you weren't as poor as the Romanian Tzigany!"

"You're on," she challenged. "And this time you're not wriggling out of showing me Romania!"

Federi laughed.

*

Some time later they were trailing through the forlorn streets, rain whispering on their wind jackets, erratic gusts blowing pieces of rubbish about. Paean had sunk into a blue funk, kicking at empty cans and other pieces of litter. She had refused to take the Comet; she wasn't going to afford Federi a look from the air. And so, he thought with an ironic smile, he got a much more close-up look at the increasing poverty and squalor.

It was a wise decision, he thought. They could move more stealthily like this. After last night's fracas at the McLochlainns, the chances were that the Unicate was out looking for them. And he really wanted to see Molly Street – without drawing attention to it by navigating a highly visible flying saucer there in broad daylight.

The place was filthy. He had to admit that in this respect, Dublin was more depressing than the Transylvanian Alps. At least the Free Tzigany didn't have to live in rubbish.

A purple-haired youth walking by hissed "filthy Tinkers!" and spat at Federi, who side-stepped the missile automatically. Paean's

49

fists came up and high colour rose in her face. Federi placed his hand over her fists and gazed at her until she calmed down.

"'s not worth it, little luv," he said. "Don't get angry – 's his problem, not ours."

By now the road was not much more than a muddy track, with potholes full of water. Yes, they were definitely in the impoverished parts of Dublin now. Houses were in bad repair; broken windows were patched with paper bags; broken and rusted washing machines graced over-long lawns, unkempt gardens were strewn with junk.

"Got to make an initiative!" growled Paean. "It never looked like this when we were still living here!"

"Because the Donegals cleaned up for everyone?"

"I organized the children," said Paean, ignoring the jibe. "Gave them a sense of pride, like Mother gave us. Ronan fixed things for people, in exchange for food and sometimes for free. I babysat. Shawney…" She laughed. "He went around stirring trouble. Hence the name. Shawney actually cut lawns and planted gardens for a bit of quid, or treats, or games."

"All subversive activity," Federi pointed out with a smile. "Children under sixteen aren't allowed to work in exchange for anything, not even in kind."

"Stupid law that," retorted Paean. "There's nothing wrong with a kid earning a few bob polishing some rich person's car! Teaches work ethic. I hope Captain took that law out."

"Law's there for a reason," said Federi. "Your old Tzigan saw to it that it stayed in! Don't want our children being exploited in compounding factories."

Her eyes flicked to him at that 'our children'. And her steps slowed down, and her face dropped, and she ended in front of a small house, thunderstruck, rooted to the street.

"That was it, right," said Federi, peering into the garden through the drizzle.

Paean only stared at the little off-white house with the green window frames and the grey compounding roof with home-made patches in places. The Tzigan could see the beginnings – or rather what was left of a herb patch; the chamomile had overgrown everything. Some flower bushes hadn't died, but the lawn was knee-high, and graced with paper packages, beer bottles and not-quite-clean clothes that had blown off a line in the rain. Toddlers' toys were strewn all over, languishing in the wet grass. From inside came baby squeals and adult shouts. A broken window was banging against its frame in the wind.

The house and garden didn't look particularly worse than any of the other houses in the street. But Paean turned away, heartbreak in her whole posture. Federi placed an uninvited arm around her shoulders.

"It didn't look like this," he guessed.

"Mother would *never* have allowed it to run down like that!" said Paean emphatically. "And neither would I!"

"Or any of you," agreed Federi. "Let it go, little luv! Close your eyes and remember it the way it was."

"Don't want to," she said, suddenly tearful. "The way it was we had to leave Mother behind in it."

Molly Street! He had expected an emotional reaction. This was the first time she saw her old home again after that dreadful night. He knew from Shawn that Paean had wanted to stay back with Mother's deceased body and let the Unicate kill her too. The two brothers had jointly blackmailed her into fleeing with them. He locked her into his arms as he gave her time to cry about it.

This was it, he realized with a pang. The last time he could hold her like this. The last time she needed him to help her over her past. He had done a good job; she was strong now, ready for freedom.

51

Federi's function in Paean Donegal's life was finished.

She looked up at him and wiped those tears away and freed herself.

"I'm now officially homeless," she stated with a lopsided grin.

Federi shook his head. "Your home is on the Solar Wind," he tried half-heartedly. The devil made him say it.

"Exactly not!" she snapped. "The Solar Wind is a job, not a home. And I quit, remember?"

"Fine," countered Federi, "but you're independent! You could set up house anywhere you like."

She laughed. "With what, my dear Arthur?"

"With the money you wring out of your husband when you divorce him," growled Federi. "Remember, half of all my assets are yours. 's the deal when you get married. 's a legal thing. Even in a gypsy marriage."

She laughed brightly. "But Federi, you don't have anything!"

"Nu?" He studied her critically. "You really think I don't?"

"But…"

"Besides," he said, "it's not what you have; it's whom you know. I'm quite sure Perdita would be happy to cut a deal with you. And your cloning."

She became thoughtful.

"Tell you what," said Federi. "I'll set you up with… say… a trillion Unicate dollars. You can buy a comfortable two-bedroom home for that and still have half left. You can get the rest when you really want to finalize things."

She studied him in silence.

"Anywhere in the world," he said. "Southern Free is nice. Besides you've got the jet. Can always go on holiday if you want. Visit old friends."

"Federi, where on Earth are you going to get a trillion… ?"

He smiled.

"You source it," she deduced. "You have nothing, but you need nothing because you can lay your hands on anything you like, whenever you want."

Federi shook his head. "Close."

"You raid Captain's state coffers?"

He laughed brightly, shaking his mane back. Wrong again! And a movement caught his eye, from across the road. An elderly woman from one of the neighbouring houses was watching them intently from her window, through a half-closed curtain. And then she disappeared from the window and her front door opened. She peered furtively up and down the road and beckoned to him.

He steered Paean in that general direction. "Look!"

The little redhead's eyes lit up. The elderly woman hurried them inside and quickly closed the door.

"Paean! It's you! It's really you?"

Paean grinned and gave the woman a stormy hug.

"Federi, this is Mrs Flanagan!"

Ah! Federi smiled. Right on track!

"Federi?" asked the woman and studied him thoughtfully. He scowled at her. He had known that she was sharp – but how sharp precisely?

"Not Federi Dem-"

Paean shrieked as Federi's hand closed over Mrs Flanagan's mouth with mutant-speed. "Don't hurt her!"

"Not trying to," said Federi apologetically, slowly releasing the old lady. "Mrs Flanagan, that name is bad luck. Promise you. The Unicate comes with their beasts from the Sixties and everyone gets ripped to pieces. Please don't say it! Or I'll have to station you on a distant planet."

"Trouble is, he means it," Paean put in desperately. "He's a good guy, Mrs Flanagan, just please, don't cross him!"

Mrs Flanagan nodded, recovering her breath, her hand over her heart. She glared at the Tzigan. "You're the one. Thought so! And your grandfather was Falco."

Federi nodded gravely. "The Traitor. Yes."

"Paean," said Mrs Flanagan, "let me show you something." She led the way through a door… Federi blinked. As she and Paean crossed the threshold, they both disappeared! He fairly jumped through the doorway after them, finding his stiletto reflexively in his hand. And his other hand on his gun.

He found both of them on the other side, in that little study with the messy desk and a console that looked as though it came from the dinosaurs. And Paean – the mischief – was laughing at him.

"Welcome to my study," said Mrs Flanagan as she switched that prehistoric machine on. It whined as it spun into life.

"This is where Mrs Flanagan hid us when the Unicate came digging," mentioned Paean. "You can only see through the door one way."

He shook his head in confusion.

"We think it's a time pocket," said Paean. "A forgotten little piece of last century, or something."

"You mean, the house is that old?"

"We think this is in another house, back then," said Paean. "It's a bit spooky, don't you think?" She grinned.

"Does it go anywhere?" asked Federi.

She shook her head. "Was a mission getting out of here when we were escaping. Unicate everywhere! We had to wait hours!"

"Here it is," Mrs Flanagan beckoned them closer to that ancient console. "Look!"

Federi moved closer. It was a newsletter with a large, full-colour image of him as a boy. 'Wanted. Reward.' Paean looked horrified.

The Tzigan studied the old photo. Funny how time went by when one wasn't looking. A rare shot, taken by a Unicate surveillance camera, of him at one of the Romany community soup-pots waiting for his share.

"You look hungry," said Paean softly as she studied the pic.

"That was you, right," Mrs Flanagan stated. "Young man, you've no idea how we all prayed that you'd get away!"

"Why?" he asked, incredulous. The grandson of the Traitor? "And when you say, 'we'…"

"My friends," she replied vaguely. "Paean, where on Earth did you find him? What's your connection?"

The little redhead's eyes darted to him. "'e's my husband," she said.

Mrs Flanagan stared at her in horror. "But, wee lass… och no! How did that happen? You're set up for such a lot of pain! Didn't you know?" She shook her head in dismay. "But Federi, how could you do this? The poor wee lass! Have you no heart?"

"'parrently not," said Federi. "No soul either. 'm the Devil. Lugh, or Loki, y'know?" He peered at that ancient console in fascination.

"Have a look," invited Mrs Flanagan. "Feel free, there's a lot in here that you won't find anywhere today." She indicated for him to sit down and investigate into the files. "And you, Paean," she added, "come, help me get the tea set up."

"Mrs Flanagan," Paean asked, "please – the day we left. Did you see… what happened…"

"To your mother?

Paean nodded.

"They took her away to the mortuary," said Mrs Flanagan. "Cremated her. Because of the virus, Paean."

"They know it wasn't real," growled the little redhead. "That

55

virus was designed to break on contact with air. Nobody could die from it except Annie Donegal!"

"You're informed," commented Mrs Flanagan with a lift of her eyebrows.

"You apparently know about it too!" replied Paean.

"Wasn't entirely unexpected," agreed Mrs Flanagan. She sighed. "Poor wee lass! Your mom was politically active."

Federi lifted his eyes from the computer and fixed the old teacher with a sinister, unreadable stare.

"You had better tell us," he said quietly.

5 – Unicate

Paean gazed at the grey building. It could have been of compounding; except that this structure was older than that. It hailed from the last part of the Industrial Era when factories like these had been erected by the dozen, from cement blocks that were cheaper than brick. Anyway compounding was never that rough – or that cold. The place seemed to drain the life energy out of one's very spirit.

"Sad place," commented Federi next to her.

"She never allowed us to see her workplace," said Paean. "Said she didn't want us to get the idea that it was any kind of job option for us! Wanted us to reach higher."

He nodded sombrely and touched her hand. "Come?"

They went up the steps on the side of the squat block, and in through the unassuming door. That was supposedly the main entrance? Paean cast one last glance at the drizzly grey sky before turning and facing the sickly indoors lighting and the dismal inside of the factory.

Three dozen sewing machines hummed. An electronic cutter whinged softly as its unoiled blades carried on with their patterning overwork. Women in moss-green overalls busily fed material into hungry machines and into the cutter, and out came the kind of poor rags Molly Street had bought second-hand when the richer poor had finished wearing holes into them. Paean knew them too well.

"Mind-killing work," said Federi softly by her ear. She nodded. "They had it all automated, by the Forties," he added. "There were no more seamstresses involved. The Unicate brought all that back.

Job creation."

Paean shook her head. "'s not a job!"

"Dead right, little luv. They brought it back because they studied their history and found it a good way to prevent people from getting creative and enterprising. Plain ol' oppression. So where was your mother's station?"

She shrugged. She had no clue.

A stern-looking, tall woman in a tidy beige suit walked up. "Can I help you?"

Federi clasped Paean's hand firmly. There was a command in that.

"Looking for Annie Donegal," he said and registered the shock that went through his young wife. She didn't say anything. He hadn't expected that she would.

"Annie Donegal?" asked the woman, a panicky edge in her voice. "She is not here! She left months back. Who are you?"

"Family," replied Federi with an evil lift of his left eyebrow. "How did she leave?"

A small sound came from Paean. He placed his arm around her shoulders and pulled her close. If they were to get to the bottom of this, she had to be brave now, *basta!*

"She resigned," said the woman impatiently. "Now I'll not waste your time any further, shall I, Mr...?"

"Demonos," supplied Federi with an utterly evil smile.

The woman went grey with dread. "Fed-" she managed before the dart found her. Paean's dart. The little redhead glared at him.

"What in hell do you think you're doing?"

"She's one of *those*," Federi pointed out. "Just don't say my name now!"

"But Fed – you blasted pirate!" She shook her head.

"They're covering," said Federi. He raised his voice over the din of the machines. "Where can I find the boss of this fine establishment?"

"You've just shot her," said one of the women dryly. "What did you want with Annie?"

Federi placed his arm around Paean's shoulders again. "This is her daughter," he said. "Paean Donegal."

A hush fell over the whole place. Sewing machines stopped humming. The cutter whinged away petulantly. Federi had the surreal impression that the name had echoed all across the universe.

Paean stared back at the room full of stares.

"Half o' them are *Others!*" she observed in a whisper.

The woman who had asked the question, got up and took a closer look.

"Poor child," she whispered. "Did you then lose yer mind when yer mother passed away? May her blessed soul rest in peace!"

Paean looked straight through the woman's head.

"You're Lennie," she muttered. And the next moment they were in the Comet, including Lennie. The woman screamed.

"Lennie," said Federi, putting his teleporter away. "You're one of the five. What did Annie Donegal see?"

Lennie stopped screaming and stared at him.

"You're Unicate," she emitted in a half-hysterical whisper. "What have you done wi' the real Paean? Oh sweet Jesus, I failed – I promised Annie to look after her children, but then, when she died I couldn't find them – I was too late – you guys already had them, didn't you? Oh sweet Mother Mary…"

"We're not Unicate," said Paean. "I *am* Paean Donegal. What do you mean? What have you seen? What did me mother see?"

"I canna tell ya, now can I?" snapped Lennie. "I don't know! Don't you remember? And didn't you question me before? Gave me that shot, an' made me all drowsy and grilled the living Bejeesus out

60

o' me concerning what I knew – I knew nothing! Nothing! And didn't ya kill all the others – Annie, and poor Bonnie, an' she in the family way an' all… seven months along she was, poor Bonnie, and what they found o' her… it wouldna' filled a teacup."

Federi glanced at Paean. She looked grey; her freckles stood out sharply against the pallor, and her arms were covered in goosebumps.

"And Nita," Lennie continued her hysterical tirade, "she disappeared, now didn't she? I went around her house, I did, to check that she's alright – and there was the open door, blowing in the wind, and no Nita anywhere to be seen… I knew you'd come for me, sooner or later, didn't I? But what's the point?" She suddenly collapsed into tears. "Why did you spare Kate?" she sobbed. "Why? Because she's your informant? She's human too, you know! And she's really evil – she knows everything! She was there, you know! Ask *her* what Annie saw that night! *We* don't know!"

"Paean," said Federi quietly, "hang tight!" He included Lennie in his teleporter field. Thirty seconds later he was back.

"Where did you put her?" asked Paean, still rattled from Lennie's disclosure.

"Stationed her with Itzak for now," he said. "She's got to be rehabilitated before we can question her." He peered doubtfully at her. "Ready to go back?"

"What for?" she asked shakily.

"Finish what we started," he said. He navigated the Comet back down to the factory. And his back straightened, and he listened, his hand still hovering over the console.

"What's wrong?" asked Paean.

"Got this feeling as though there's a fly buzzing around my head," said the Free Gypsy. "'xept it's not a fly. It's a… spook or something. From space." He checked on his teleporter whether any

61

traces of sticky carbon were present. Of course they were not. The Morrigan was dead. "What the hell is it?"

She listened too. "An' ya shouldn't've bandied my name around like that, Federi," she scolded. "The Unicate's hunting for me too, don't you remember?"

"Hang that," he exclaimed, locked down the Comet outside the factory door, jumped out and stormed back into the building, his gun raised.

Paean locked the hatch of the Comet and followed the Tzigan, her gun ready too. As she ascended the steps she heard Federi's machinegun rattling in staccato bursts of five bullets at a time. She emerged in the doorway. Unicate hounds were laying waste to the place, attacking the women, upturning machines, ripping cloth. And going down in sprays of blood where Federi's fire hit them.

The Unicate leader of the place was not on the floor any longer. In fact Paean couldn't see her anywhere.

Federi was in the grip of a very strange mood.

"Federi Demonos is here," he kept on shouting. "Come on out, you stupid hounds! C'mon, doggies! Yum-yum time! Come and get Federi Demonos!" Paean realized that he was laughing.

The hounds that still had their wits about them, turned and moved towards him, presenting such easy frontal targets for his marksmanship that it almost seemed unfair. He mowed them down five at a time, with every burst of rounds from his Federi Special. Paean could hear that he'd tuned the gun down to a slightly lower speed, so that he could control the accuracy of his aim better. She stood frozen to her spot, noting in amazement how fast those dogs went down; almost in synchrony with the rattle of his gun. One could nearly imagine that not a single one of his bullets went astray.

More hounds poured in through windows and doors – anything that looked like an entrance, was used as one. Good gracious, how many were there? What on Earth was he doing? Was he trying to clean up the whole population of hounds in one go? She realized that that was exactly what he was attempting. His mission. Eliminating as many as he could before he'd go down with them. As though nothing else mattered, anymore.

She couldn't take her eyes off him. Completely reckless, half-insane, enjoying himself. And that accuracy! He was the master of his dark trade, there was no question. He was a one-man army.

But he'd run out of rounds sooner or later; the hounds had to know that too. And they just kept on coming, an endless lot pouring in through all those entrances. From where? Definitely not from the street; that had been empty. She fiddled with her teleporter, ready to get her Tzigan out of there when that moment arrived.

And then, as if there had been some inaudible signal, all the surviving hounds swerved and escaped into the office.

Federi cursed heartily and charged after them. Paean lost a few moments assessing the damage on the floor – Unicate *Others* and ordinary human women had been mauled without differentiation. A number looked dead; but more lay writhing in pain.

She couldn't leave them like this. They would die! She activated her com.

"Ailyss? Please get the Ginavian rescue village to come and help here! I'm leaving my com, just follow it." She stripped off her wrist-com, unsure whether Ailyss had actually heard her message; but there was no time. She stormed after Federi into the office.

"Federi?"

He was not in that room. He had only just run into it, and now he was gone! The office was empty; no sign of any hounds either. On the desk sat a presence, staring mutely at her. She moved up to it and ran her finger lightly over its screen. On the console stood in bold letters, in the search field, "Federi Demonos".

For a creepy moment she had the impression that the monitor had swallowed Federi. She shook herself out of that thought and stared at the walls, and the open cupboard, looking for a trap door. Or a trap. Something like that Morrigan had set for her, back in Romania.

Well, if he was on the planet… She cast a fearful glance at the door behind which the Unicate Dogs had left such a battlefield. She tried to block the ghastly images from her mind as she reached for her teleporter. Just before she activated it, she heard Ailyss' answer come through on her wrist-com, which was lying on the floor in the other room.

"Paean! Paean, come in! Are you guys alright?"

There was no time. Paean teleported.

6 – Vlaşta

"This goes to prove," said Radomir Lascek, his boots carefully stepping between the injured and the dead, "that he's in it much deeper than he let on, this morning. Honeymoon, my foot!"

Ailyss scanned the room, moving between the victims too with her gun ready. She had contacted the forces at Las Village; they were on their way with Perdita jets and first-aid kits.

"These," said Lascek, prodding a dead Unicate dog with his boot, "are bad news. By the stars, look at the sheer numbers he has mowed down here! Where the hell do they come from?"

"I think that is what he's investigating," said Ailyss.

"Those weren't the ones you came across on your mission?" prodded Lascek, glancing over to where his First Mate was kneeling down at a hound. The crew from Las Village was arriving; they came in through the small door, and stopped, and gasped, and got to work.

"No," said Ailyss. "Wasn't them."

"Keep an eye on Federi for me," said Lascek. "And especially on Paean. We must not be fooled. He pretends to want privacy, but it's a foil so that we don't interfere with his harebrained heroism. I've invested too much training into that man to lose him now." He moved into the office, Ailyss two steps behind.

On the desk sat the machine with 'Federi Demonos' in the search field. Lascek hit the activate button. The machine spun through various options. There were sirens outside, and the police came in.

Radomir Lascek met them with a salute. The officer leading the small squad saluted back and enquired politely what was going on.

"We're investigating a crime scene," said Lascek.

"Sir, unfortunately civilians aren't allowed at such a scene," said the young officer, and swallowed. Even strangers found it difficult to stand up to Radomir Lascek.

The Captain smiled.

"Young man, you're not facing a civilian, however," he said and produced his official ID from the Peace Talks. Instantly, the Unicate officer backed away under humble apologies.

Lascek noted with satisfaction how efficiently his Ginavian team was taking care of the injuries and clearing away the fallen hounds.

He turned to Ailyss.

"Then show me what you and Jon meant," he instructed under his breath.

"Captain, I would suggest that we take all the real people up to Space Base," she replied equally quietly. "These girls have seen too much. They weren't meant to survive; Unicate will see to it that they don't. And then, Captain, you can have a good look at the remaining girls. Maybe you'll see what I mean."

"We give assistance to them all," said Lascek with a scowl.

"Of course, Captain! But we don't invite all of them onto your secret base." She moved ahead and started indicating to the marines who should be taken to the Space Base, and who not. The Captain stalked two steps behind, taking a good look at the Unicate girls.

He couldn't tell the difference. He had no idea how she decided that.

Ailyss turned back to him with a smile.

"Captain, please don't feel singled out," she told him under her voice. "It takes years of training to spot them – or a very special gift."

"Paean's voodoo radar," he growled. He had pocketed the girl's wrist-com from where he'd found it lying on the floor. So now she was out there without a com. And Federi – he'd tried calling the man on his com earlier and had instead connected to a very nice elderly lady. Whom he'd handed over to Sherman to deal with. He had no time for old 'dears'.

*

Stars. Myriads.

It peered up overhead, wondering what had been the cause of it shuddering awake out of its comatose sleep.

The stars weren't stars, it realized. It was deep inside the cool bowels of the mountain, and the only light there was, was generated by tiny spiders, who built their starry webs to lure their prey. For many aeons it had felt soul-kinship with these minute creatures. Luring and spinning webs was its speciality. Lulling hapless prey into a state of mindless contentedness before eating. But today it couldn't get that connection anymore. Things had gone wrong.

It sent out tentative psychic feelers, out of the mountainside and into the planetary grid. And it realized the reason for the disturbance. Doors had opened and closed, unsolicited. And a presence had passed through… a presence that evoked a deep sense of dread. And with it, memories.

An urgent voice inside its head.

Shrn!

It groaned a psychic groan.

Shrn! Wake up!

It – he – came out of dream-state. There was a Blue Furry hovering right above. It thought he couldn't see it; it probably also thought it was funny, waking him up out of his near-death state, just so that it could see him die some more.

"What do you want?" he groaned in the intergalactic language of telepathy.

"You've got to help! The Demon is back!"

The name vibrated across the Morrigan's being, rattling the sticky carbon. The pain hit, as sharp as any broken shard. It twisted back on itself and sent out a piercing psychic shriek, cutting across the layers of reality.

The Blue Furry blinked out of the third dimension in fright.

*

Paean found herself in a very cold mountain village, surrounded by scraggy wintry pine trees and grey flat blocks.

She looked around in amazement. A wonderland! The most noticeable feature was the complete silence. There was no wind; no rain; no constant drizzle like in Dublin. The place was cold, but dry. No snow. No traffic, no human buzz. Nothing. The little village might be a ghost town.

The valley lay below, vast and desolate in its threadbare autumn garb. Scraggly, forlorn; yet a hush was over it as if it were waiting for something. Or someone.

Had she crossed over into the world of the Dead?

And Federi was next to her, glaring at her.

"Hand over!"

She meekly handed him her teleporter. "Where are we?" She shivered.

He shook his head, and shook it again.

"This is such a sick joke, whoever thought of this…"

He knew this place! He'd been here before!

"Where are we, Federi?"

"Trrransylvania," growled the gypsy softly. And he lifted his head and listened. "Quiet! There's something…"

Paean listened too. A ripple of unease went through the Earth. The wind picked up; a shower of icy droplets blew down from the grey overhead. Paean stared at her gypsy, whose face was dark and unreadable. She herself was sensing something akin to a cry of despair, from a dying animal – except that the animal somehow wasn't there.

"What do you think it is?" she asked in a hushed voice.

"Something in those mountains over there, something unnatural…" He stared at her.

"The Morrigan," she mouthed at the same moment as he spoke it.

"Damn," added Federi. "Didn't kill him quite dead enough, did I!"

"Poor thing," said Paean.

"Right," agreed Federi. "Shouldn't leave an animal wounded. 'nother mission for your old Tzigan." He got up from the Unicate hound tracks and their abrupt end, across a time line, just like those in Miami. And he stretched. And peered critically at Paean.

"Federi," she said, reaching for his hand, "there's something I should have told you."

He scowled at her, his heart plummeting. What had the Morrigan done to his bride?

"Prince Vlad saved me from the Unicate hounds," she said. "They came for me."

Federi gasped. "They hunted you? Little luv?"

"I fell through a portal into his world," she said. "His planet is called Shrn. The Unicate hounds found me practically immediately. They're shape-shifters, Federi – but you know that. They come from the Shifter Universe."

"Damn!" He grabbed her shoulders, staring intently at her. "Are you alright?"

She laughed softly. "That was then, Federi!"

"How did you get away?" he asked tonelessly. "Did they hurt you?"

She shook her head.

"Prince Vlad – or rather, the Morrigan – took on the shape of a huge hound, much larger than the rest, and he chased them off, and then he turned into Prince Vlad and led me to his castle."

He nodded, releasing her. "So the forsaken Morrigan... I owe him your life? Again?" And he scowled more. "Could it have been an illusion?"

"Was there blood over my t-shirt when we got back?" asked Paean. Federi nodded. "Wasn't an illusion then," she said. "I shot a few of them."

"My brave Paean!" He shook his head. "Was wondering why you were in such a mess."

"But there were too many. They'd have had lunch... Federi, I could nearly understand their language."

"And he chased them off? What is the connection between the Morrigan and the Unicate?" growled Federi, staring at those tracks again. "You're saying, they come through portals from a parallel universe?"

"Perpendicular," said Paean.

"So there is a portal here?" He stepped across the invisible line where the tracks ended. Nothing happened. "Was," he corrected himself. "If the bleeding Unicate hounds are shifters, they're not Unicate hounds! What the hell is the connection here? Got to interrogate that blasted Morrigan!" He peered back at the village, and into the mountains ahead. "How to get there, anna Dana."

"She's na going to help you find the Morrigan," said Paean with conviction. She watched in surprise as his eyes lit up and he gazed at the little village with calculation. "Federi?"

"Got a friend here," he said and reached for her hand. "Coming, little luv?"

~

Vlaşta. Part of the reason Federi was so angry, was because they were in Vlaşta – the closest town to where he was born. 'Town' was probably exaggerated. Paean peered doubtfully at the small settlement of compounding homes in the grey drizzle. Stack-houses, they'd called them at home. Their compounding was only beginning to get wet; and the dry dust that was the ground was only beginning to be transformed into a sticky layer by the droplets, not yet wet enough to be mud.

Block-buildings of ten to twenty apartments each; with two rows of people living on top of each other. It was economic on compounding; one saved outer walls. But one couldn't build them higher than two storeys without running into strength trouble with this 'econo'-version of compounding.

There was no need to save space; Vlaşta was surrounded by sprawling meadows and forests, breathtaking mountain spires and plummeting valleys. This was just simply cheap.

She shivered lightly in the fine rain. Federi glanced at her and fetched the Comet – by remote control, via the mechanism Wolf had programmed into Paean's teleporter. And he ordered her to put on her weather jacket; and absently put on his, and sent the Comet back into the stratosphere. These rainskins weren't enough though. They would need polar gear; it was cold.

A tiny village forgotten by time.

"What keeps it together?" asked Paean.

"Compounding factory in Tirgu Mures," said Federi. "There are four such towns. Vlaşta is the smallest. There's Sat Gri; Verda and Niciuna."

"Cute name, Niciuna," said Paean with a smile.

"It means 'nobody'," replied Federi. He peered at the little village of Vlaşta. Sabie in Southern Free was a metropolis by comparison.

The stack houses came to an abrupt end at the edge of a steep drop. Paean blinked in shock at what she saw on that slope.

There had been a family of Free Gypsies camping on the banks of the River Liffey one time, when she was twelve. They had put up a house using old grey blankets, tying them together into a gazebo-like structure, using old cardboard and bits of metal and compounding salvaged from the scrap yard to add into the structure of their "house".

As compared to what she saw here, those had lived in luxury!

Deep trenches had been dug into the mud, to keep it away from precarious front doors. The trenches were at this point turning into quagmires in the rain that was fast thickening to a downpour. They were dotted with stepping stones which had probably been found in the meadow.

The homes themselves were embedded to three quarters in the muddy slope. They weren't much more than dug caves. Pieces of compounding had been weighed down with rocks and pegged down with pieces of wood to prevent them from flying away in a storm; these were the roofs. Paean's heart stuck in her throat.

"Come, little luv," said Federi, extending a hand. He was in an oddly light mood. "Welcome to Utopia!"

She nearly threw up. "Federi! How can you?"

"They called it that themselves, little songbird! The Romanians call it the Țigania, but the Rroma got tired of that, that's like calling it 'the ghetto', so we gave our place a name."

She clasped his hand, battling down tears as he helped her down the steep muddy slope into the first trench. Alright, Federi won the bet. Hands-down, poorer than Molly Street. Her old home was a downright mansion compared to this.

73

The place was a slippery, slithery labyrinth. She tried staying on the stepping-stones of the gulleys, but before long her deck sneakers were soaked through with muddy, icy water. As were her socks. Miserable and cold.

"See, when it snows the ground shelters them from the worst cold," said Federi. Paean glanced at the embroidered blankets that paraded as walls and front doors.

"'s an illusion," Federi assured her. "It's compounding. They paint it and decorate it."

"And when it rains really hard?"

"Then this place turns into a river," he said. "But it's on a slope, so it all runs off. No flooding of any homes."

"Don't people drown in that?"

"They stay indoors, little luv. And the adults know how to negotiate the place."

"And in spring, when the snow melts?"

"Same effect," he smiled. "Should see it in winter, little luv. Snowed under, sometimes right to the roofs."

"Don't they collapse?"

"Sometimes," said Federi, losing his smile. "They are reinforced, inside. But not enough."

"What happens then?" she asked anxiously.

"Funerals, sometimes," said Federi quietly. "Depends how the roof comes down. Injuries, mostly. Can't prevent that."

"But can't one build them proper houses?"

Federi smiled and spread his hands, palms-up, and shrugged. "'s the definition of poverty, little luv. That 'can't'."

She set her jaw. "Well, with all Captain's resources…"

"Any idea how many really dirt-poor people there are in the world?" asked Federi. "If you think for these, you must think for them all. And, no, you Donegals weren't really poor. Not really."

She nodded. Federi was right.

"But I don't understand," she said. "How do people *get* this poor? I mean, they have hands, they can work…"

"… in the Unicate compounding factory," he completed for her. "That's exactly it. They all do. Where a Unicate *Other* decides how much you can feed your children today."

"And they none of them think of taking other jobs?"

"If they do," said Federi quietly, all humour gone, "the bleeding Unicate comes after them. Hunts them down, takes them away for 'truancy'. Those never come back."

She was shocked into silence for a moment. And she squeezed Federi's hand to console him. Oh hell, there was no way she was leaving him! He'd had enough hardship.

"So you were born in here?" she asked, in horrified fascination.

"No, anna bottle," he replied, baffled. "By my boots! What gives you that idea? Federi was born in the forest! Like a true free Tzigan! Warm and safe. In a proper gypsy tent if my parents had any sense."

"In a *tent?*" She tried to envision a tent in true Romanian winter weather.

"Warmer than this here," said Federi.

She peered at him, trying to find the string to pull, that would make the tall story unravel.

"Plain truth," he insisted. "You'll see." And then he scowled at her. "Stop that," he commanded.

"Stop what?" she asked, injured.

"You're feeling sorry for me," he growled. "Can forget that. Federi's a big old ugly man. Can look after myself, can sort my own karma. Either you stick with me or you leave me, but if you feel sorry for me, I'm putting you back on the Solar Wind." And he turned away abruptly, shaking his head.

A few children appeared on the path ahead of them, skipping out of a side alley. Paean could hardly call these canyons of mud 'alleys'; she thought of them more as tunnels. The children, with skin still tanned from the long hot summer and wild black hair, and the brightest smiles she'd seen in a long time, came closer and encircled them curiously. They were wearing colourless rags though. She had to think of Miami and the colourful kids of the Gitanos. A little girl picked up a tendril of Paean's hair that was spilling out from the raincoat's hood. Her bony little fingers were icy where they touched her cheek.

"Federi," said Paean accusingly, "aren't there more warm clothes on the Comet?"

"If I'd known we'd end up here I'd have stolen some," said her Tzigan.

"Well... can't we quickly teleport..."

"Paean, get it out of your head to teleport!" said Federi sternly. "We don't need to. We've got the Comet. But they need more than warm gear. They need homes where the cold can't come in."

Paean took off her raincoat and draped it around the little girl, who instantly called an even smaller girl closer and shared it with her. And Paean started shivering in the rain.

"You've made your point, yodiho," growled Federi. He remote-controlled the Comet closer and looted all the space blankets out, and handed them to the kids. And gave Paean one of Perdita's weather suits to put on over her clothes. The children streamed onto the Comet, peering into every corner, chattering loudly in a language Paean could very nearly understand.

"So," ordered Federi, "now wait for me!" And he boarded the Comet again, chased all the kids off and whizzed off into the greying dusk.

76

~

Paean tried her Latin Romani on the children and asked whether they had had lunch. They took her by the hand and led her to a metal cart a few gulleys further down. It looked nearly exactly like the one from the photo on Mrs Flanagan's computer, that 'wanted' poster of twelve-year-old Federi. A youngish teenage girl was manning the cart, tendrils of her black locks plastered against her pale cheeks. The rest of her long hair hung in a limp, wet plait over her left shoulder, all the way down to her waist. There was a small fire going in the bottom of the cart – peat fire, Paean realized; it kept a huge pot boiling that sat atop the cart. The girl asked something in a Romani that Paean nearly understood, and then took a compounding bowl out of the side of the cart and dished some hot soup from the pot. There was a lot of soup in the pot; potatoes mostly, with green vegetables, but too thin to be called stew. Paean, who hadn't eaten anything since the morning, ate hungrily and then dug in her pockets to pay.

The girl gestured wildly that she shouldn't. Paean couldn't understand this; she tried her Romani from Cassandra's gypsies once more and asked why she must not pay for the food.

"You're poor," came the answer from various of the kids, in that other, heavily Romanian Rom. "You wear rubbish bags for clothes. Don't pay."

~

By the time Federi parked the Comet next to the soup kitchen, he found his young bride in a huddle of kids, all of them with tears of laughter in their eyes.

He opened the hatch and brought out what he had fetched. Waterproof rain jerseys with hoods, in all colours of the rainbow, all sizes, lined with some warm material. Rain pants. Gum boots. And he stuck a pre-ultraglared chicken into the soup pot. They wouldn't

77

have to wait for that.

And then he chased Paean back into the Comet to change into some dry clothes and a polar parka he had secured from Itzak.

"That stew is a community effort," he explained to her. "Everyone adds something into it; everyone may eat from it. When there are Tzigany close by, their children join the effort and put interesting stuff in. Poached rabbit. Wild bird's eggs. Mushrooms. Makes the stew colourful."

She grinned and bit back a comment about the mushrooms.

"But there aren't any around, at this point," he said, peering critically at the small crowd.

"How do you know? Aren't the Tzigany and the Rroma genetically one people?"

"They are. But Tzigany children are – different. You'd spot them. Move differently; dress differently. You'd know." He grabbed her hand and led her onwards, scrambling down more gulleys, step-skipping along the large rocks in the rivulets. The gaggle of kids followed them for a while, then got distracted. All the while the grey drizzle seeped and seeped down, somehow wetter than in Dublin, and somehow colder.

And then Federi turned at one of the mud-cave-houses and rapped on the compounding flap that acted as a door.

Compounding didn't make any significant noise when you knocked on it; it was slightly elastic, especially the cheap type. That was part of the reason for the hazard of collapsing roofs. Still, someone inside had heard him, because the door opened – shifted aside, and a small girl stuck her head out of the door.

"Hello," said Federi in Romani-jib. "Is this the mansion of Mihai Barbulescu?"

The little girl stared at him with large eyes. And then she stared at Paean, and said something in that heavily accented Romanian

78

Romani. Federi replied with a smile. Paean caught only part of it. Some little joke. The girl giggled. From the inside of the dark behind her came sounds almost like a guitar.

"So you are...?" prompted Federi.

"Esma," said the child. She glanced uncertainly at Paean once more. "My father is not home," she said. "But you can wait inside. She" and she indicated Paean with her head, "won't steal anything, will she?"

Paean giggled so brightly that Federi turned in surprise. "You were not supposed to understand that!"

She laughed at him and turned to the little girl.

"Mi sim a Paean," she said. *"Ande Irlandia."*

Esma relaxed and smiled at her.

"And I don't steal," added Paean in her Latin Rom. "But he does!" Federi nearly choked. "But only from the *gadje*," she specified, giving his hand another consoling squeeze. "Don't worry."

The cave-house was dark. Paean's eyes took a few moments to get used to the gloom as she entered. There were no windows. Further to the back of the room a boy sat on something like an Ottoman, plucking on a guitar. He looked much younger than Shawn. Ten, perhaps.

Her eyes adjusted slowly and she gazed in wonder at the countless jewels and flashies that glimmered secretively, adorning pillows and walls, some even suspended from the ceiling in mobiles. It looked like a magical forest of gems. Amazing! She suddenly understood the Cabin of Dreams.

The boy stared at her and Federi with wary eyes.

"Friends of Dado," said Esma shortly before indicating to Federi and Paean to sit down on cushions on the ground. "Remi! Where are your manners? Stand up and offer the man your seat!"

79

Her voice was like a whip. Remi shot to his feet, chastised by his younger sister. Paean smiled secretly. How exactly had the girl now sounded like her mother?

Federi smiled and waved the offer of the seat away, and sat down cross-legged on one of the large cushions on the ground, comfortably leaning back against a wall-hanging. "Don't worry, Esma!"

Paean eyed the fireplace that had been dug into one of the walls, with a tin pipe leading the smoke away and through the roof. That stack of peat sat there, ready to be lit. But the children made no move to do so. An oil lamp stood on the table, unlit as well.

They're conserving fuel.

She glanced at Federi. It took her by surprise; she had forgotten about the telepathic link. It zinged through her like a small electric shock; confused her and made her heart beat faster. And why was he contacting her telepathically?

Ah. He didn't want her asking questions that would put the children in a corner. As though she would!

"You've been playing long?" she asked the boy Remi.

"A year," he said, glancing at his guitar.

"Will you play something for me?"

~

It was nice sitting here, out of the rain. The house was cold; but not as cold as outside, and it was dry. Paean and Remi started exchanging riffs, getting so involved in the music that they didn't notice how time passed. Esme had returned to what she was doing before, which Paean suspected was her homework – in the dark like this! Paean dug one of her green luminescent tubes out of her moonbag, shook it into action and gave it to Esma to help her with a bit of light.

Federi sat so still that at some point Paean wondered if he'd fallen asleep. But when she glanced at him, she did get that

80

answering sparkle from his black eyes.

And then the compounding flap opened, and a woman came in. She paused in surprise.

Federi came to his feet, and Paean arose, too, from where she and Remi were exchanging guitar tricks.

Right behind the woman, a man came into the room. He, too, paused and stared at his two unexpected guests; and stared some more, squinting in the dark.

"Mihai," said Federi. "Don't you recognize me?"

The woman moved over to where the oil lamp sat on the table, and lit it. Paean blinked. The lamp turned out to be a modified tin-can. The "jewels" hanging from strings turned out to be colourful glass shards. The "table" was a cheap compounding packing crate, barely concealed with the scrap of table cloth. The "Ottoman" Remi had sat on, revealed itself as another box, with a cushion on top. The large cushions of patchwork material that they had been sitting on, were stuffed with who-knew-what, and lovingly embroidered with pictures from fairytales. Pieces of glittering wrapping paper had been worked into the embroidery like gemstones.

It was a shock how the whole artful illusion suddenly became what it actually was; and it was amazing to realize that even so, by the very care with which it had been woven, the fairytale failed to come apart.

"Mihai," repeated Federi. "You don't remember me?"

Mihai only stared.

"Pardon our manners," exclaimed the woman. "Welcome in our home! I'm Mirela."

"Mi sim a Paean," said Paean politely, with a little smile, *"ande Irlandia."* Just like Cassandra had taught her to say. "Sorry that we're invading your house like this," she added in her Latin Rom.

Mihai was shaking his head, and then he laughed out loud and clapped Federi in an embrace.

"Federi! You're alive! All these years! Mirela," he turned to his wife, "look! It's Federi!"

Now it was Mirela's turn to stare, rather more critically, at the Free Tzigan.

"Impossible," she said. "Mihai, Federi was killed, twenty years back. The Unicate ate him. Impossible."

"It's me," confirmed Federi with a grin. He studied Mihai appraisingly. His old childhood friend had acquired a receding hairline. His hair was cut short in required Unicate fashion. He was dressed in a blue overall, as was his wife. Factory work.

Mihai was still struggling to believe his eyes.

"Old friend, you're alive! You made it through! How did you get away?"

"That's such a long story," smiled Federi.

"And her?" Mihai gestured to Paean, who was watching with wide eyes. "Where does she fit into the picture?"

"Mi sim a Paean," repeated the little Irish redhead with a smile in the corner of her mouth. *"Ande Irlandia. San Romanian Tzigane."*

Federi stared at her, speechless. Mihai exploded into laughter.

"Sunt la soție de Federi," added Paean with a smirk, in Romanian.

Mihai's laughter got even louder.

"Is true," said Federi, struggling for a straight face. "She *is* my wife!"

"So she's a Romanian gypsy from Ireland," concluded Mihai, still breathless with mirth. "And she's your wife? She looks so young!"

"Nimic! She's… old enough!" An assault from within his own ranks?

82

"Federi, you brute," replied Mihai, still grinning.

Federi shrugged. Old enough to leave him, he added in his own mind. Old enough not to need his protection any longer – she thought. He'd stalk her to see that she wouldn't come to harm... Donegal bait... to lure out the Unicate... dammit...

~

Mirela scuttled around, getting food ready, fussing over her guests and over her children. Paean offered to help, but was instructed to sit. She watched how the Rroma woman efficiently lit the peat fire and put a pot of something on it, adding bits and pieces from crates into it.

No electricity; no fridge. This place had to be difficult to live in, even during summer. Worse in winter, but at least one could light a fire. Paean studied the little house in fascination once the fire was going and there was enough light. She should give them...

"Don't insult their hospitality!" said a very low voice by her ear. She turned.

"Okay, Federi."

The walls were covered in beautiful patchwork tapestries, sewn together from rags, with glittering bits of junk added into their story lines. Behind these, Paean spotted crates. A wall of crates, right up to the roof. Raw branches, straight and strong, were arching from one wall to the other, across the strange, glittery ceiling. She realized that the ceiling was patched together with corrugated iron pieces, and pieces of compounding, and in places, cloth that was plastered over with something. A cloth curtain separated the room from a second one. She followed Mirela into that second room after the supper of vegetarian stew, and watched as the lady helped her children get ready for bed; and then Paean sat down and spun them an Irish fairytale about a Pookah in an old mill, in her Latin Romani. Esma and Remi seemed to appreciate the story, and so did Mirela.

This second room didn't have as many wall hangings, and the crates were more clearly visible. Old tomato crates, making a wall. Paean went up close and touched the compounding of one. Through the slats she spotted that the whole box was filled rim-full with rocks.

A sturdy wall indeed. But enough to keep the roof up when it rained really hard? This whole place must melt every time there was a deluge, she thought dismally. Mud slides. Images of terror filled her mind. She had to get these people out of here, and into proper accommodation!

The children's room also had a small fireplace, which Mirela lit. Paean saw to her relief that it too had a functional chimney; but she was worried about the carbon monoxide, as this room had no windows either.

"There is no window," said Mirela when she asked her, "but there's a lot of air coming in through the wall."

That was when Paean realized that one of the walls was an outer wall. Yes, she'd thought it was rather cold in here. In winter, the snow drifts themselves would insulate the place a bit. But it hadn't snowed yet. The children huddled closer to the fire before falling asleep. Paean returned to the front room with Mirela, feeling depressed.

*

"So how old are you actually?" asked the voice.

"Ah," smiled Sherman Dougherty, "that would be telling!" He paused. "The Forties now – that was a nice era," he said pensively. "Would like to take you dancing in the Forties, tonight. They had style. Fine wine, the old Ritz hotel…"

The mellow feminine voice on the other side chuckled. "I was a tiny wee bairn in the Forties! You wouldna've got much dancing out of me."

"So then the Sixties would've been ideal?" probed Sherman. "You wouldn't've liked me much in the Sixties. I was an old man then, trying to age gracefully, now wasn't I just?" And he laughed.

"It doesna sound as though you ever got that right, did yer?" came the reply. "Do you still climb trees, then?"

"When the opportunity arises," Sherman fibbed shamelessly. "Ah, here's Captain now for his shift – was a pleasure talking to you again, my dear!"

"And the pleasure was all mine, Sherman," came the sweet response. "Keep well now!" And then the com went dead.

Sherman Dougherty switched his side back to the default setting and pocketed that feeling of quiet glee. Bless Paean's soul for telling him about Mrs Flanagan and then forgetting her com there! It made his watch – exciting.

*

Paean woke up shivering. The room was dark. Federi was next to her, in another sleeping bag on the floor. She couldn't remember how she'd got into her sleeping bag. Probably hadn't, she thought. She looked at him and saw him watching her, his eyes like two reflective sparks in the dark.

"Federi?" she whispered.

His hand crept out of his sleeping bag and into her hair.

"I'm cold!" And that even though she still wore the polar Parka. The cold went right through her bones.

He sat up and got out of his sleeping bag, and helped her out of hers.

"Federi?"

85

He put his finger across his lips and led her out through the compounding door flap, into the icy Romanian night.

The drizzle had stopped. Everything was glistening, washed clean. There was momentarily no wind, only the wispy clouds overhead chasing each other past a partial moon.

"High winds," whispered Federi. "Come!"

She followed him, shivering, her hand linked with his. The night wasn't all that icy, surprisingly. The creeping, malicious cold that had crawled its way into her every bone through the floor and the sleeping bag and her parka, was gone. It had been floor-cold.

He led her out of the Țigania and into the open meadow, the mountain slope. They clambered on and on, by the light of the moon and the chasing clouds. Slowly Paean defrosted and stopped shivering.

"Why didn't you want to say anything back there?" she asked.

"Mirela and Mihai," said Federi. "Didn't want to wake them up. House only has two rooms. 's no good, little luv! If you can't sleep because it's cold, we'd better sleep in the Comet, *nu?"*

"Nu!" replied Paean. "'s okay. I'm getting used to your Romania."

"My Romania." He smiled. "So you like it here?"

"Love it," said Paean.

"Should see it in summer," said Federi. "Yoy, I wanted to bring you here, show you this, back in Miami…"

"Love it here in winter," said Paean. "We should stay until summer! And then into autumn, and winter again."

He eyed her warily. "So you don't want to leave me… right away anymore?"

Her heart constricted. Leave him? It was as she'd said. She couldn't! But he didn't understand. It was not enough.

She stopped him, and waited for his undivided attention. It was amazing out here, a partial moon, high winds up in the sky, a nippy breeze that had started up around them; a wild meadow in the moonlight. It reminded her of another meadow under a different moon; balmy in summer. She had been confused and overwhelmed by emotion, back then. But this fitted too; the crisp, cold, unpolluted air, the wind of decisions. There was a sharp edge, a stress, a sadness; the fear that this was the end, that between them both they would conclude that their love, as crazy as it had been, was not viable in a world of realities. Full circle. She heard another voice on the wind; it was called Freedom. And she didn't know which she would choose.

"Federi," she said, unsure where to begin, "remember!"

He scowled and said nothing. Waiting. He knew.

"I jumped out of a Stealth for you," she said. "And I'll do it again, every day of my life, if it takes that until you can believe me. Federi, I don't care about poverty and riches, and dashing princes and diplomats. All that is pretence. I married you, Federi."

He gazed intently at her. The "but" hung between them.

"Now pay attention!" she carried on, an edge to her voice. "You're making it damned difficult for me to be your wife. You're married to the Solar Wind. You're married to Captain! When we're on the ship, you're just not there. I can have five seconds of you at a time." She took a shaky breath. "Do you think I can go through life like that?"

"'s just my job," said Federi quietly.

"It's not! It's slavery! And you choose it, Federi! What are you running away from?"

He stared at her in surprise.

"You think I'm sorry for you," she continued heatedly. "Well, yes, I am! But I'm also pretty fed up. You can be so much more! I didn't fall in love with your broken bits. You don't have to stay

87

broken to keep my love!"

Federi gasped for air. She cut pretty close to the core tonight! He needed to listen carefully now.

"It's a trap, you see," she said. "You're always running. Away from yourself, and from me. Committophobe!"

Federi laughed and pulled her into his arms. "So what are you saying?" he asked. "You want more of me?"

"You don't understand," she said and stepped away from his embrace. "I'm not going back."

"You'll miss your brothers," he predicted.

"Och, another excuse! Can you hear yourself? I've got the Comet, don't I? Can visit! That's not the point!" She stood with her wild mane whipped about by the wind; her parka's hood flung back. The wind was cold, but it energized her. "I spent so long being a prisoner, hiding in a hole, not daring to move... I need to breathe, Federi! I'm finally free."

This was it, she realized: The wind of change was calling her; she had grown up, and she couldn't be a jealously protected treasure anymore. She'd had to make a choice, and in the end it was no choice at all. She couldn't pick even Federi above her own truth any longer.

He stood studying her in silence, an odd look in his eyes. They seemed to glint in the overly bright moonlight; there was a smile on his face, she battled to read it – was it pride?

"My Paean," he said quietly. "Yes, you're everything a Free Gypsy should be. And then some!"

She watched him with bated breath. He took her teleporter out of his pocket and handed it back to her.

"Don't use this," he said. "Only if something attacks you."

She took it with a scowl.

"You left your wrist-com behind," he said wistfully. "Would

88

have been nice to keep in touch. Then again I don't exactly have mine, either." He chuckled wryly. Paean noticed the catch in it.

"But…" she said, not understanding.

"You're right, Paean," said Federi sadly. "I'm *not* free. Federi never was free. Falco loaded a mission on me before I was even born, and until it is completed, Tzigan can never walk in freedom. I can't take it away from you any longer. *Kathal*, little luv." And he started walking away, further up the mountainside.

She watched him for a moment.

"Federi!" she called after him.

He paused and turned, waiting.

She hurried to catch up with him.

"The mission?" she asked.

"That's the name of the game," he confirmed.

"This was never meant to be a honeymoon," she said accusingly.

"No," he confirmed. "Never. It's our prison break. Not going back either." And he turned away and retook the climb up the mountainside. Paean stared at his retreating form, as it made its way higher and higher up. And then suddenly he was gone, absorbed by the half-shadows of rocks and trees in the uncertain moonlight.

~

It had to happen. Federi dashed away the leaks in the corners of his eyes and smiled grimly. Too late. He should have done more of that flair stuff, should have made her not want to leave him. But he'd known this was how it was going to go. Romania did this to a free spirit.

And it was in any case more sensible. No way was he taking her along where he was aiming to go next. He made his way up the steep slope, retracing the steps of two decades past. It had been summer when he'd last walked here; the hot breeze had brushed against his face as he had stood gazing over a panoramic sunset. Just

Federi and his violin. He needed to find Falco's instrument again. Right now there was a massive gash in his soul, and the only thing that had a chance of filling it – or drowning it out – was that instrument's music.

*

Paean stood on the icy mountainside, staring at the place where her gypsy had disappeared. And at the teleporter in her hand; the choice he had given her. To be wherever she wanted to be.

The silence was amazing; it did remind her of the parachute jump. She thought of the cosy camped-in atmosphere of Nuku Hiva; of what Federi had said. "It takes some of us like that. It's too safe." There was nothing of that here. The land was vast, the possibilities endless. Danger was also very present, always at the edge of one's awareness. A person could definitely die here, and never be found. It added a sharp zing to the freedom. She felt that she had found the country of her soul.

He had set her free. For several minutes she stood in disbelief, merely savouring the feeling, the icy wind numbing her cheeks. She stood so still that a fox came up to her to investigate; a quiet little shadow. Federi's spirit animal. Her hand dipped into her pocket and closed around that strand of soft black hair. He had made amazing sacrifices for her, these past nine months, ever since she boarded. And this was the greatest yet.

And now, where to?

The wind had died down. All was silent, waiting for her. She gazed at the imperfect moon, trying to read its expression.

*

Federi had found the place again. High up in the mountainside, the little cave entrance was waiting for him as it always had been. The Cuckoo Caves. He shone a torch beam into its depths, his mutant eyesight making it easier to establish that nothing had set up its home in the cave mouth. The place was empty; he listened with all his senses to determine whether anything moved deeper in the cave system where it tunnelled away into the mountain. No: All was as it should be.

A fire? No, he decided. Not tonight. He'd sleep here, as invisible as Tzigan, and continue tomorrow. It was warmer in here. There was a sound of water trickling; he knew from his childhood that there must be an underground hot spring. He'd never thought about it before, but that might mean some volcanic streams running closer to the surface here. The Transylvanian Alps were not volcanic in origin; but Nemesis II had caused world-wide seismic ripples, and it might have opened a small fissure where before there had been a weak point.

The bare rock floor didn't look very inviting. Twelve years of comparative luxury on the Solar Wind had softened him up, he acknowledged wryly. He teleported to Mihai's home, collecting his sleeping bag. And Paean's, and checking briefly whether there were any more of their belongings. There weren't. But the stark poverty in which his friend lived, ate at his heart. He dug a generous pack of notes out of his pocket system – pirate loot and quartermaster's wages – and tied it into a square cloth, one of those he used for polishing his woodcarving knife, found a piece of paper from Esma's school books and wrote a quick note.

"Thank you for your friendship, please accept this for Esma and Remi." It was okay to bestow money on a friend's children. He glared at the message. He was not good with words. They might be offended anyway.

91

He teleported into the Comet, depositing Paean's belongings in there – he should get a message to her, he thought, but then again she'd return to the Comet first thing. So it didn't matter. And he reversed his leap with only his own backpack, sleeping bag and ground mat, back to the Cuckoo Caves. He hoped he had all his necessary equipment; because he was not going to return to the jet. It was now a part of his past.

It didn't take long to spread the ground mat and roll out the sleeping bag on it. But he couldn't sleep. This was Romania. Where werehounds tore gypsy families to bits. Paean's independence worried him. Sure, it also cut him up; but he'd told his heart to shut up. His mind however wouldn't.

He moved back to the ledge, staring out over the wide-open land. Tomorrow he'd begin his search. By daylight. How often had he sat up here, feet dangling over the abyss, chirping birdcalls on his violin to the wind? The temptation to steal Paean's violin, just for a little while, was overwhelming.

A movement in the corner of his eye caused him to swivel around in a flash, his jack-knife open in his hand. And he gasped.

There she stood in the moonlight, with a huge question in her eyes.

Federi put the knife away and held out his hand.

"Hand it over!"

Her eyebrows sky-high, she obediently gave the teleporter back to him. "But…"

"Doc Judith said, a week," he pointed out. "Didn't give it to you so you could hop around. Just so nothing would eat you, okay?"

"Okay," she said meekly.

"Okay," agreed Federi, studying her. And now what? "Want me to pull your Comet closer for you?" he offered. "Forgot how to do that?"

She shook her head.

"Wanted to tell you," she said.

He waited. Tell him what?

"Thank you for setting me free," she said, searching for the right words. "It feels fantastic."

He nodded. It didn't feel fantastic to him.

"But it's not enough," she said. "Federi... I can only really be free if you're free along with me."

He shrugged wistfully. She knew the parameters.

"So I've made up my mind," she said. "I'm with you on the mission, Federi. All the way."

What ...? No! It was wrong! He took a breath to object, but she held up a hand. "No. I'm an adult. I make my own decisions. If we both die, it's still a risk worth the prize. I'm with you. That is..." she was suddenly unsure.

"What?" asked Federi, transfixed.

"If you still want me?"

He took her in his arms. There were a few hundred 'owed' items queuing up. Payback time.

7 – Romipen

"Shrn!"

The Morrigan groaned dismally as he surfaced.

What do you want, you little pest?

"Anthrim sends me," said the Blue Furry. "He demands your help in destroying the Demon."

The Morrigan wailed. Not enough that the sticky carbon was still vibrating from the double teleporter field, frying him further. It was a terrible, slow, drawn-out death. He was nearer to it than the last time this Blue Furry menace had disrupted his sleep.

At least when he was sleeping, he could partially forget the pain. He could dream of a white ship as he slowly slipped away. But this…

Anthrim was bad news. He'd always been bad news. Couldn't they even let him *die* in peace?

"Anthrim does not want to make this a council matter," warned the small creature.

The Morrigan doubled over and let out another drawn-out psychic shriek, broadcasting his agony. And he didn't stop until the Blue Furry had escaped in terror.

*

A cold, wintry mid-morning sun peered down from a hazy-blue sky painted with long trails of feathery cirrus. The frost crystals that had been everywhere earlier on had mostly melted by now and only remained in the deeper, shadier places under trees, in the middle of groves and in the shadow of rock overhangs.

Paean trailed after Federi through the fairyland that was this morning. They had been going for hours again, clambering along the steep slope, over roots and around rocks, descending deeper and deeper down into the valley. She was getting the full Free Gypsy experience.

She had never yet felt so moved by a place. Not even Southern Free and the beautiful beach at Sedgefield or Marge's Eastern. Here, it was as though the ground itself spoke to her, whispered at her. Even the muted colours of early winter seemed luminous. There was a music in the ground, and in the wild nature; a quiet, faraway ancient music of a different world. And her Federi like a visitor from the wild Alb World, his wiry shape finding the trail ahead of her, lifting twigs out of her way, taking her hand when the path got very steep or slippery…

"Where are we actually going?" she asked as they picked their way down the steep slope, closer to the ravine.

"Wait and see," was his cryptic response.

Federi had left his spare wrist-com that Wolf had given him for emergencies, at Mihai. Paean grinned. There were no coms left now. One for Mrs Flanagan, one for Mihai… her own left behind at the factory…

It didn't even matter. Captain calling them would have been ignored. They were not Solar Wind slaves any longer. That was in the past. Finally, her husband really belonged to her.

Federi stopped her and pulled her closer. He pointed down into the ravine. Paean gazed down. She leaned her head against his shoulder. And turned to him and cashed in on one of those addictive kisses. He owed her a few thousand? She was going to make sure that by the time those were used up, he owed her more.

"Pay attention now!" he whispered when he had his wits back.

This dual reality was going to split his mind. He'd have to drop the mission for a while and focus on the honeymoon.

"Down there! What do you see?"

"I don't know," said Paean. "Trees? Rocks? A bird?"

"Tents," he helped her.

She peered down, but still she couldn't see anything.

Federi laughed softly.

"I didn't see the Island base either, at first," she said defensively.

"Right! And who, do you think, designed Captain's Island base?"

She smiled at him. Her happy was drowning out all his thoughts.

"Quit that!" warned Federi and took her hand again. She was dangerous! "Come!"

She followed him down a horrendously steep path of rocks and tree roots, into the ravine.

Federi approached the grey tents with caution, indicating to Paean to hang back a little. The whole way here her sweet presence had been like a drug on his mind. All he could think of was her; nothing else seemed even remotely real. It didn't help that he knew that her state of mind was the same. Between the two of them they could easily wander into the Alb world today and never find their way back.

Which might be a very short 'never' if he allowed that. This was Romania. Dublin had been tricky; this place was potentially a minefield. The bleeding Alb world was real. More real than Paean could guess, despite all her Irish fairy tales. Things went missing in these forests.

So, while she would have preferred solitude for them, he was going to put safety first. The Comet wasn't exactly a very romantic place to spend a honeymoon. But it wouldn't hurt them to be amongst people – people who respected them; who were as invisible as Federi and who knew how to negotiate the dangers of this forest.

He crept closer to the tents, aware of her eyes on him. Something was too quiet here.

This wasn't right! The fire was dead. In this cold? There was absolute silence; not even the chirping of a bird or the movement of a small mammal in the carpet of frozen autumn leaves. He moved in between the tents. And the sense of absence hit.

He lifted the flap to a tent. Empty. A few belongings lay scattered; further nothing. He opened another tent; the same scene. One after the other he investigated the dwellings. In the last one he found evidence.

They weren't out gathering nuts or ground roots or bunnies or something. The insides of this tent were splashed in dark blood, frozen on the ground and against the canvas. But nobody. Nothing left. Federi emerged from the tent, feeling shaky. His Paean was waiting for him. He went to her and accepted her arms around his neck, and held her, saying nothing.

"They're dead," she whispered, shivering.

*

Some time later they sat by the small fire Federi had lit, some distance away from the dead camp. Within view, but not right in there. Paean had brought the Comet closer with a setting on her teleporter, which had miraculously found its way back into her possession. She had made them both coffee. He nursed his in silence. He had scoured the entire circumference for tracks. Any tracks. Bear prints, three-toed fire lizards… trails that stopped abruptly across a time line, a portal – there were none.

Either whatever had done this had access to teleporters too, or the tracks had been eliminated by a tracker more experienced than

Federi. And there was only one such kind of tracker…

"Bin amongst the *gadje* too long," muttered Federi and sipped his coffee, his right arm around Paean, who was leaning against him. "Federi's losing his edge!"

"What do you think happened to them?" she asked.

He shrugged. The same, he presumed, as was happening to gypsies in Romania all the time. Stupid of him to forget this for a second; to believe he could bring her back into the fantasy realm of his childhood, when the world had been whole. He wondered how many Free Gypsies were left, at all.

And then he paused, and listened again. His gypsy radar was trying to say something.

"They're close," he said. "Come!" He got up and kicked ground over the tiny fire. It sputtered and died. With Paean's help he piled more ground on it, then scattered leaves over until the remnants of his little fireplace weren't visible anymore.

"Why do that?" asked Paean.

"This is the wild. Free Tzigany always delete their tracks. Technically we don't exist." There it was again. Those dog-men of the Unicate hadn't deleted their tracks; the tracks had merely stopped in mid-nowhere. At the portal through which they crossed over to their own planet. And the fire lizard – she had slunk along, leaving tracks the way an animal would. He frowned and listened once again to the signal. And then he went off through the forest, bearing away from the running stream. Paean scrambled after him.

A mound, all covered with leaves. Federi stared at it, absently drawing Paean into his arms as she moved up next to him.

"That's it," he said. "This is where they are. Someone has buried them." He closed his hand over his eyes for a moment, giving a mental last salute to his fellow Tzigany. One more whole tribe, deleted. Who? When did this happen? Recently, his radar told him.

Just at the onset of the cold weather: Week or two back.

His wife held tightly onto him, mourning with him for the people she had never met. He wondered which of his friends and cousins were buried in this mound.

His senses warned him and he raised his head and listened intently. There was complete silence; but they were not alone in the forest. He threw his head back, cupped his hands to his mouth and made a careful noise like a bird call. Of a rock pigeon.

The breathless silence stretched. Federi began to wonder if he were wrong. But then another rock pigeon answered, not too far away. Aha. He led Paean in the direction of the call. They walked through the trees, the ground nearly level now.

'Close by' was once again an understatement, thought Paean as she trailed after him through the forest. The doomed camp was a good half-hour back by now. Federi was grim and determined, putting a lid on all her attempts to console him. Every now and then he stopped and uttered another rock pigeon call, listening for the answer.

He led the way through the forest, unable to stop the feelings of guilt. He had left the Tzigany to this. It was his fault. He ought to have returned years back, jumped ship the moment his skills were sharp enough, maybe made it a mission to take someone along, Jon or somebody, to help him clear up here. But he'd hidden himself away like a coward, leaving the Unicate monster dogs to decimate his people. They ought to cast him out for this!

He was going to find those Unicate dogs and put an end to them. But if he just called them to him – he couldn't do that. There might be hundreds. He had tried it, in the controlled environs of the Dublin factory, and they hadn't stopped pouring in from everywhere. He'd run out of rounds if he tried it here; and he couldn't shoot to all sides at the same time. Paean would get killed even before they tore him

100

to shreds, and there was no guarantee that their bloody rampage would stop with his death either.

And then what he had hoped to see, materialized before his eyes. Another bit of grey neo-nanomer tenting was barely visible through the trees. And a woman in flowing grey rags came walking towards them, suspicion radiating from her black eyes.

"Who the hell are you?"

Federi stopped.

Right. He hadn't considered this. They might not recognize him; they might not accept Paean.

He took off the warm parka and revealed his purple flared shirt underneath, with the orange waistcoat. He handed the parka to Paean and turned his hands palms-up to show they were empty. Entertainer; harmless. And he peered at the woman. Cor, had she grown up...

"Almeira," he said. "Guess you won't recognize me."

"So you know my name," said the woman. "It's not going to help you any. You look like one of us but you dress like nobody. You move like a psychopath. Your aura says you've killed. Your hands look full of blood. You bring with you," and she glared scathingly at Paean, "a *gadchey*. You are none of us. Now leave before I put a curse on you!"

Federi sighed and held out his hand to Paean, who gave back his parka, biting her lip. He put it back on. He had sensed how the *"gadchey"* had rippled through her, leaving a mark. His hand found hers to interlace, to take the sting out of the comment for her.

"I'm Federi," he said. "And this is Paean. She's no *gadchey*. She is my wife. I was born in these woods, Almeira. Last saw you when I was a boy. You were younger than me, so I don't think you'll remember. Who was killed back there?" And he pointed back into the forest, in the direction of the mound.

101

She stared angrily at him. "You're a liar, whoever you are! Federi is dead."

Federi stared darkly back at her. The silence stretched.

"I can't expect you to welcome me," he said eventually, with a sigh. "I left my people to die, here in the mountains, and I ran. But I'm here to tell you that I'm back, and this curse following the Romanian Tzigany is going to stop. They call me the Demon."

Almeira's eyes widened and she started backing away.

"Yes," he drove the point home. "The legends are true. And Federi did get away. And Falco's curse sticks to me, can't get away from it, so I've come to put an end to it. I only hope that someone made a grave for my family too."

The Tzigany moved out between the trees like shadows, surrounding him and Paean. He glanced at his wife. She mustn't be scared now.

She stared at them, scruffily clad figures with light eyes and black hair, each armed with a branch, a knife, a rock, a slingshot... no guns, but Paean didn't doubt for a second that one well-aimed rock could kill her before she could even lift her gun.

In a way they were a lot more frightening than the Unicate hounds. These were humans. And they were wild, and angry, and borderline insane; and they were in a corner.

"Almeira," said Federi, lifting his hands once more in a gesture of peace, and Paean's hand with his. "You don't remember me. I remember you though. You were a little girl of five. Your mother was the Manya in those days. I made you a toy. A dolly. From wood. It fell into the river one day and you were scared to get it because the river was so wild. So Federi ran downriver, climbed into a tree over the river, and picked your dolly right out of the current. I was eight. You were five. Remember?"

Almeira's eyes stretched in surprise.

"It's a trick," she muttered.

"And you," Federi pointed to one of the men. "Jehan. You were my age. Don't you remember me?"

Jehan shook his head, worried.

"We figured out together how to build a kite," said Federi with a smile. "From a piece of your parents' tent. And then we tried to fly it and the wind took it away. Your mother was furious."

Jehan nodded. The message was sinking in.

One by one, Federi pointed at the gathered Tzigany and called them by name. There were a few who'd come over from other *vetsas*, whom he identified too. His own family had not stuck to one place, ever; the legacy of Falco the Demon had forever weighed on his mother, so they had moved from tribe to tribe, spending some time in each. They had been known as the wanderers amongst the wanderers. The result was that the only gypsies he could not identify now, were those who had been born after he'd left Romania at age twelve.

They listened in suspicious fascination. But – the Unicate had many tricks. Tzigany didn't survive by being fast to believe a stranger.

"And you, Aneşca," continued Federi, pointing to yet another woman who had a baby on her skinny hip and a rock in her free hand. "We always teased you, me and Jehan. Because you were so pretty. Remember? Until one day you threw mud balls at us. Caught me -" he indicated his nose, grinning, "right there. Your aim was fantastic. I hope you're not going to release that rock on us!"

Aneşca started laughing. "It is him," she told the others. "Federi, welcome back! Where were you all these years?"

One by one the sticks and rocks were dropped to the ground; the slingshots and knives disappeared in pockets. The Free Gypsies gathered around him, shaking hands, clapping his shoulders and

103

hugging him. Federi accepted the wave of greetings with a smile. Paean stood back, smiling too. She was getting used to this emotional home-coming type reaction Federi got from everyone. And he needed it so badly right now…

Almeira remained coolly outside the circle, watching all this with deep scepticism. Paean felt the iciness of the Manya's stare whenever she was at the receiving end of it. When Almeira did open her mouth to comment, it was nothing good.

"You may then be Federi," she acceded. "But are you still a gypsy? Your hands are full of blood; I can see it in your aura. You do not hesitate to kill."

The knot of Tzigany around Federi backed away, staring uncertainly at him and at the Manya.

"You are right, Manya," he said acridly. "You are perfectly right. I have killed. More than you could possibly imagine. I have killed terrorists and hijackers and Unicate *Others* and Romanian hounds, and merrows… I have killed a ship processor, and an immortal alien slime… every time something tried to kill me or mine, I killed it first. This is my style. I choose to live. So cast me out for surviving."

"It is against the Romipen," she insisted.

"Yes. Apparently survival is against the Romipen," agreed Federi angrily. "The Romipen comes from a time of peace and plenty. In case none of you have noticed, those times are past. We are dealing with an invasion like humankind has never seen before. Yes, my family; the Unicate is murdering everybody. They don't distinguish between gypsy and *gadjo*, European or Chinese, rich or poor. I thought they were only after us. I thought they were *gadje*. Boy, have I learnt a lot of truths!"

They stared at him, spellbound.

"You surrounded us with weapons and rocks," he pointed out.

"What was this about the Romipen? In the old days all of you would have been *marimé* for not greeting another gypsy properly and welcoming him to your fire. And that is the *old* Romipen," he added scathingly.

Shocked gazes all round.

"I shall not welcome a murderer!" snapped Almeira. "You have killed for money. A gypsy no longer!"

The silence that settled, was icy. Federi stared at her, dumbstruck. She had cut away the very basis he'd hoped to establish here.

His shoulders dropped; his face fell. He seemed to shrink into himself, become less than he had been in his darkest moments. Paean watched this in horror. Oh, Federi! Almeira was destroying him!

"That's right," he said quietly. "You're right. I was – I *am* an assassin." And he turned away.

Paean bristled. And her Latin Romani clicked into place, nice and fluent.

"You fools!" she spat. "Do you think you're alone in the world? So proud to be so free! So much better than the lousy *gadje*. And when the Unicate comes and eats you, just like they eat everyone else, where is your Romipen then?" She pointed an accusing finger at Almeira. "Manya! It is your responsibility to keep your people safe! When the hounds came and tore up my Federi's parents, and his brothers and his sister – where were you? Where are the Tzigany when Tzigany need them? When a little twelve-year-old boy was running for his life, who protected him? Who took him in and gave him food and clothing? Who got the men together and organized guns to shoot at the dogs when they hunted him?"

She grabbed Federi's hand as he had quietly started retreating, and pulled him forward. "Not a damn! You gypsies abandoned one of your children to his death! You guys are cowards! It would *never* have happened in Dublin!"

She glanced at Federi and saw his eyebrows shoot sky-high at this last statement.

"Okay," she amended, "it did happen in Dublin too, we got cowards there too. But where were you? When he had to learn to steal just so he could eat? When the bullies and rowdies of the street taught him to fight dirty, and someone taught him how to be really dangerous, and turn it into something he could use? Where were the sacred Tzigany with their sacred Romipen? Gah!" She turned away from them abruptly, lapsing into English. "Federi, let's go. I don't want to associate with these. They're exactly like Aunt Katie. Bloody hypocrites!" She got an evil grin. "Shall we station them all on New Dome?"

Federi drew her into his arms with a hopeless smile.

"I love you," he whispered. "Don't need anyone except you. Don't throw them away quite yet, that's not actually why I looked them up." His magic Paean had just refuelled his power.

He eyed the stupefied Tzigany.

"I'll take my wife and leave," he promised. "But first, Almeira, I'll sit by your fire and share some rum from *my* flask with your family whether you like it or not, and tell you all my story. So that you know. I don't care if you curse me or cast me out, Manya. Your power ends here." He smiled, exposing his silver eye tooth.

"I'll supply your family with guns," he added. "*Gadjo* guns, of the finest quality. And you will learn to use them, and you will let me train you all. You, Almeira, will not make any rule to forbid them. You can't keep risking the children like that. It's harebrained folly."

Almeira snapped her mouth shut. He knew he'd snubbed her amazingly, calling her, the Manya, irresponsible. But she was, anna

106

bottle! She turned and stalked off between the trees, head held high.

Jehan put a hand on Federi's shoulder.

"Come sit by our fire and share some *rakija*," he invited. "And your wife is welcome too, even though she is a *gadchey*."

"She's a gypsy," said Federi, drawing Paean closer as he allowed Jehan to lead him towards the camp. "In Ireland, gypsies have red hair."

Paean smiled. Two unrelated facts. The fox!

~

She nearly fell asleep leaning against him at the fire, a little while later. He was talking to Almeira's people in his native Romani, the music of the language gentle like himself; she understood more of it by the moment. It wasn't at all as different from the Latin Rom as she had first thought.

Telling them all his story. He wasn't cropping the tale half as much as for her Uncle Séamus. And there was a reason. The gypsies needed to know. He was arming them with information – as much of it as he had himself.

And then his tale was done and so was his *rakija*. And he stood up and stretched, all his joints crackling loudly into place. The response from the gypsies was rather funny, thought Paean; they glanced around furtively, worried that this noisy *gadjo* habit would betray their presence.

Paean was surprised at the fact that he'd accepted their strongly alcoholic drink. But it would probably have been a snub at Jehan if he'd refused. All it meant was that she'd have to be on a sharper lookout herself.

"I'm going to get you guns now," announced Federi. "And I'll show you how to shoot straight. 's easy enough. This is nothing to do with the Romipen, my family. You won't be shooting any humans. And then," he added, "we're going to keep close, we'll be in the area. Got to get to the bottom of this mess!"

"Stay with us, Federi," said Jehan. "Don't put your wife in danger out there."

Federi eyed the lot of them speculatively. Paean could see that he wanted to stay, to reconnect. It was what he needed.

"What about Almeira?" she asked the question he was avoiding, her eyebrows drawn up in worry.

"She'll come round," said Jehan.

"She," said Almeira, approaching from the other side of the camp, "has already come round. Federi, forgive me. Your return took me by surprise and I'm mourning my cousins. So it was a quick thing to blame you for the way the Unicate is hounding us."

Federi went quiet. It was his fault. If he hadn't run, if he had stayed and allowed those dogs to kill him too…

"Your wife is right too, though," said Almeira. "The Tzigany failed you. You were only a child. It is our responsibility that you became… what you are."

"An assassin," repeated Federi acidly. "Nobody's choice but my own."

Paean's fingers intertwined with his. He shut his mouth. Her magic calming him down.

"I'll call a *kris*," said Almeira.

Paean iced. A *kris* – a gypsy trial. The Manya was planning to alienate him from all surviving tribes!

"Keep your *kris*," snapped Federi. "Call me an outcast right away, save yourself the bleeding trouble. Come, little luv!" He grasped Paean's hand firmly, his other hand reaching for his teleporter in his pocket.

"We need to change the Romipen," said Almeira. "I need to call a *kris* for that."

"Leave me out of it," snarled Federi.

"But there should be exceptions to the rules," said Almeira. "We need to allow for guns, and self-defence."

"Allow bloodshed and murder," agreed Federi. "Yes, Almeira. What you do with your outmoded little system, has nothing to do with this filthy murderer. My only drive here is to make sure the family survives; and when we're all alive at the end of it, we can all get holy again and call those who did the dirty work, outcasts. Don't change your silly little rules just because of survival!"

The Manya studied him for a dignified moment. Of course she understood why she had been so hostile towards him. The safety of her clan was in her hands; yet Lanina had failed to keep her own clan safe, and Almeira had no idea how long before it was her turn. As a leader, her position was balanced precariously; only on the fact that she was the wise-woman, the seer of the tribe. But leadership amongst Tzigany was a matter of practicality and respect. And here Federi had come waltzing in, and had taken the leadership right out of her hands.

It was maddening. But she *was* in fact a wise woman, and it was patently logical that the man, assassin or not, made sense. The tribe needed him. They needed the protection of someone like the Demon, to stand between them and the Unicate. For that, she needed to yield the leadership to him; and make sure that every other surviving Manya did the same, because he came with the first solution that made sense since Falco Demonos.

It would not do to point out that now he'd insulted the Romipen, the whole traditional basis of gypsy life, the set of rules that defined a gypsy. He was hurt; worse than she could imagine. She had rubbed salt in that by her first, territorial response. She'd wanted to cut him down with any fact she could use, and she had. But the tribe needed him, she couldn't afford to alienate him further. And what was more, she had begun to remember, a light-hearted, caring boy who had enough heart to carve a dolly for his little cousin and rescue it out of a raging river. If any part of that boy's character had survived, she'd like to welcome him, indeed.

"Federi, peace," she said. "You killed mainly to defend yourself and to save the lives of innocents. If ever you killed one who was not scum, it must have been an accident. The *gadje* have a word for someone like you."

"Filthy assassin," growled Federi.

"Freedom Fighter!" Paean put in.

Almeira glanced about, then bared her dazzling white teeth in an unexpected grin.

"Poliţia!" she said.

8 – Tzigany

The days that followed, turned into something dream-like for Paean. She relaxed into the mellow rhythm of the days. Nights she fetched her violin out of the Comet, and played for the Tzigany just as she'd done for Cassandra's clan. Sometimes Federi let himself be talked into playing some tunes for her while she took burning sticks out of the fire and did her fire-dance.

The fires were kept small though; the roaring bonfire of the Miami gypsies would have been a dead giveaway. Paean missed it, but it was alright. Federi's presence more than compensated. The constant heartache that had accompanied her music and her dancing in Miami was gone. He was here; and he was hers. The single gypsy girls were all very interested in him – as in any male from outside the *vesta*, he explained to her – but he made sure that he kept her close, usually with his arms around her or playing with her hair while he spun his stories to his circle of rapt listeners. Stories from the Solar Wind, which had Paean as mesmerized as the others.

When the fires died down, she'd crawl into the tent the Manya had given them; usually long before Federi turned in. He sat and chatted with the clan deep into every night. But that was fine, because the rest of the night he belonged to her.

Surprisingly, he had been right. The cold did not penetrate these tents. It was the material they were made of, he said. Wolf would be able to explain the molecular principle to her.

During the day, the two of them went on long walks through the forest, sometimes with company but mostly on their own. Federi was showing her all the magic of his Romania. He was also teaching her how to track. Paros from Cassandra's Gitanos had already taught her a bit of that; so Federi had quite a lot of cause to be proud of her. They practised spotting the forest's animals and birds, and once she managed to creep up on a fox – from downwind, of course – so close that she could touch its tail.

It was a magical time and she found herself deeply in love with everything: The forest, its wildlife, the mellow rhythm of the days, the gentle gypsies and their quirky sense of humour and personal warmth, and most of all, with Federi. If he decided that he wanted to spend the next five years like this, she'd be alright with it.

They did other things too though, on a more practical level. Federi armed the gypsies to the teeth, teaching them in fine detail how to handle their guns. Hair-trigger traps were set up around the camp, of spider silk-thin threads of – well, spider silk, which were connected to motion sensors that would set off alarms if anything tripped them. Perdita checked in a few times, brought by Federi. She was behind the supplies of guns, and she donated them gladly. Paean buttonholed her when she was there, and used the time to catch up with her.

Federi, too, had relaxed. The constant haunted look had left him, replaced by something sharper, more primal – but infinitely more powerful. He was as alert as any wild creature, and then some; but it was a focused, positive alertness rather than a paranoid edge. A man at the top of his game. The gypsies had not cast him out; they had made them both welcome and were showing Federi respect bordering on reverence. And he laughed a lot, these days. Even Almeira had lost her initial animosity altogether and treated him with the fondness of a long-lost cousin.

But in the nights, sometimes, Paean lay awake listening with unease to that sound – or absence of a sound – that made her think of an animal in pain. Poor Morrigan! If she could only reverse the damage that had been done to the alien! It felt hardly fair that a creature who had saved her life several times over – no matter how contrived – should have to suffer like that.

Sometimes she woke up from it in the wee hours – and noticed that her Federi wasn't there. It made her uneasy. Was he out hunting for that beast on his own? What about his back-up? Or was he maybe elsewhere? Then she scolded herself for not giving the man enough space, and determinedly went back to sleep.

*

The Solar Wind was making its way through blue waves in the southern Atlantic. It was hot, mid-summer, coming up to Christmas. The Captain and the crew had always been in the habit of observing the old seafarer's tradition of a festive meal and a round of drinks on Christmas Eve. That was, of course, before the trusty chef had been replaced by someone whose entire repertoire of gourmet food consisted of sashimi…

But Shawn had chatted with Ailyss about the necessity to "do" Christmas the right way. He had talked Ailyss into talking Sherman and Captain into observing every little detail of tradition, from the very colour of the candles to be burned for which day of Advent, to the collecting of tree decorations and tinselling. Accordingly, there were weird little touches of festivity aboard the ship.

All this tradition suited Jon Marsden to a T; he loved the very detail of it. Ailyss had to smile about this as she tried to focus on the message she was composing.

Two huge hairy arms folded around her from behind.

"What are you up to?"

The Irish spy girl smiled and closed the message on her wrist-com.

114

"Nothing."

"Ready to go?" asked Wolf. "Shawn's ready and waiting."

She shook her head. "Not going to pick any Christmas trees in Romania today."

"But you said you wanted to drop in on Federi and Paean," objected Wolf. "Be nightmarish and disturb them on their honeymoon. And now?"

She turned and linked stares with the nuclear engineer and his beautiful green eyes.

"No, Wolf. Not going to Romania. Definitely not taking Shawn!"

"Why not?"

She sighed. In for a penny…

"Look, Wolf, this is strictly between us, see? Federi has contacted. He's on the trail of the Unicate. The hounds are all over Romania, apparently. He wants to clear the Unicate up, this time."

"Federi's always chasing the Unicate," commented Wolf. "It's a compulsion. Captain fixed all that!"

Ailyss shook her head gravely. She had been the one to heed Paean's frantic communication to sort out the slaughterhouse in Dublin, calling in Las Village to rescue survivors. She had been the one to divide the surviving sewing ladies into Unicate *Others* and normal impoverished Dubliners. The former had been taken to state hospitals, where Ailyss was certain they would receive preferential treatment anyway… that part of the riddle refused to make sense, what were they doing in a factory? … and the rest of the girls had been taken to Las Village medical emergency centre. Under heavy surveillance by the armed forces. Because the Space Base didn't have enough medical facilities.

"The Unicate is far from fixed," she replied darkly. "I'm with him, Wolf. I'm going to help him."

Wolf stared at her in dismay. "Listen, Ailyss," he said, upset. "You're not doing this alone! I'm coming along! You might just need that extra pair of untrained fists."

Ailyss smiled. "Wolf, we've got a team on the job. Wouldn't want you getting yourself hurt. This is in fact a job for assassins, not untrained fists."

"A whole blooming team? Does Captain know?"

She smiled again. The young engineer was not someone who'd leak a secret; she decided to tell him a little bit.

"Captain's behind it all," she said. "Don't ever underestimate your Captain, Wolf Svendsson."

The sound of boots on the companion ladder made them both glance up.

"Everything ship-shape, Svendsson?" asked Radomir Lascek cheerfully.

"Perfect, Captain," answered Wolf, snapping to attention.

"No cause yet for a new invention?"

"Captain, I'm improving the field of the teleporters to be kinder to the human bio-electric field," replied Wolf.

Radomir Lascek gave him a searching glance, and nodded, satisfied. "That will come in handy. Make sure Ailyss gets the first one – and Federi, and Paean!"

"Thanks, Captain."

"Well done, Wolf." Radomir Lascek threw a last glance around the machine room and ascended the companionway again.

"To complete our previous conversation," said Wolf, staring after him, "how are you actually contacting Federi? I've been trying to contact both of them these past two weeks and their wrist-coms have both been left behind! One gets answered by an Irish Mrs Flanagan and the other by a guy called Mihai, in Russian!"

"That's Romanian," corrected Ailyss with a laugh. "Talking to

Federi on the Comet's console. He actually called me first. Thing is, the console isn't always open for coms."

"He doesn't want Captain calling him," said Wolf. "So what's the story?"

"He needs me to check on Dublin. Keep an eye, sort-of patrol that room where there was that passage to Transylvania. Watch for the dogs to return. Check in at least once a day."

"Patrol? Guard?"

Ailyss nodded.

"You've been doing that these past two weeks? And I didn't even know?"

She grinned.

"That," said Wolf, "is what we've got croaches for!" He smiled. "In fact…"

*

Paean peered over Federi's shoulder. "What are you doing?"

The Tzigan was drawing lines in the half-frozen mud near the fireplace, with a stick. She watched, fascinated. He muttered to himself in Romani, measuring connections between the lines and dots with his hands. Eventually he looked up and sat back.

"See, little luv," he explained. "This is what I got so far. Here are the Unicate attacks over the past twenty years. That's since Federi escaped. I'm trying to find a pattern."

She nodded and looked at the random-looking markings. Twenty years was a long time! Every second year or so marked another attack.

"There are hardly any left," added Federi. "It's just Almeira's clan now and four others in the whole country. And as you see these aren't really big clans."

About twenty heads in total, including the babies. No, thought

Paean, not a very big group.

Frightening, if one considered that Romania used to have the largest gypsy population in the world, before the Sixties. According to the Sherman Files.

"What happened to all Romania's Rroma?" she asked in fascinated horror.

Federi glanced up at her.

"Most of them are in the cities," he said. "Most of them are just that – Rroma. You saw, Mihai and Mirela… most of the Rroma work in factories, at sub-minimum wage. It's miserable. The free Tzigany have always been a vanishingly small minority, little luv. We're the ones who got away, who would rather run and hide but keep our nomadic lifestyle and our cultural values. We don't want to be slaves. The Romanian Romany people were already slaves for five hundred years, little luv. Before they were 'given' rights, by the *gadje*. Did you know the word 'Tzigan' essentially means a slave?"

She gasped. "I didn't know, Federi! I'm sorry!"

Her gypsy grinned at her. "They brought us in," he said. "For our skills. Blacksmiths, goldsmiths, musicians, horse whisperers. Bear whisperers, too! We were bought and sold like horses. Did you know that a lot of the metalware in Romania in the middle ages was forged by gypsies?"

She shook her head.

"And it fetched – what you'd call a pretty penny, all over Europe," he added with another proud grin.

She wondered how that tied in with Ireland's 'tinkers'.

"But then, why do the freest of the free still call themselves 'Tzigany'?" she asked, puzzled.

"Free?" he asked back. "Little luv, when we escaped from being enslaved yet again, we vowed to remember where we came from. But nobody is free. Not while there is Unicate." And he turned back to his map. "This here," he pointed with his stick, "is grim."

"Why don't they emigrate?" asked Paean, desperate to find a solution for Federi's Free Tzigany.

"Where to, little luv? All of Europe has got this plague! And for a whole tribe of Tzigany to stow away on a ship to America…"

"One by one?" she suggested.

Federi shook his head. "That's never going to fly, Paean. One Tzigan alone? Gypsies just don't work that way!"

She sighed. Yes, she supposed. Too many kids and babies. Shawn wouldn't have managed alone either.

"Captain legalized Free Tzigany," Federi pointed out. "I told Almeira, and she asked me what he's planning to do about the Unicate dogs." And he got a faraway look and stared in the direction of the mountains. "You know, little luv, I've got to drag that half-dead immortal out…" He stopped in amazement, then laughed. "That blasted well explains why I couldn't get him executed! He's immortal! Poor thing, and now he's not fully functional anymore… an eternity as a crippled piece of juice, lying somewhere in pain… aw rats!"

She nodded.

"If he'd only complied, and not impersonated or abducted anyone," said Federi, "suppose, if he could have obeyed the command line…"

"He mind-controlled whole civilizations!" Paean reminded him. "He demanded blood sacrifice!" Reminding herself more than him.

"He was only toying with us," replied Federi. "Back there in space. He even fixed the time he wasted for us! He's a prankster. And for that, Federi fried him…" He shook himself out of that line of thought. "Got to interrogate him, in any case. Want to know the connection between his hounds and the Unicate."

"I somehow doubt they are *his* hounds," said Paean. "Only he managed to turn into a bigger one." She pointed at the ground. "So what does that tell you? Any pattern?"

Federi shook his head moodily.

For two weeks they had been trailing through the forests now, looking for evidence, anything strange, anything out of place. They had found none, but Federi assured her that the stuff was only biding its time.

Paean sat down next to him.

"You know, if there were a sort-of alert system…"

"What do you mean?"

"Some or other panic button a tribe could push, and it would call the Solar Wind."

"Or Las Village," completed Federi thoughtfully. "Or more likely, Federi! Should give each tribe a wrist-com. But Paean – the challenge is to find these four tribes, they're scattered all over Romania."

"Maybe Almeira knows," suggested Paean.

"That," said Federi, "was going to be my next question to her." He shuddered.

"What?" asked Paean.

"There is of course a fast way of putting a stop to it," he said. And looked at her. In those dark eyes she read pure frustration. She shook her head.

"Too many," she objected. "You tried that in Dublin."

"That's the problem. We're right at the source. It may be thousands."

*

Peter Piper opened his eyes. Everything was still hazy and his mind was very sluggish. His insides felt as though they had been run

120

over by a truck; his head felt as though it were inflated with water.

The first thing he took stock of, besides these details, was that he was alive. It came as a surprise – he had thought himself dead. Then he was surprised about the way he felt about still being alive. He was angry! There was no surge of joy. Life hadn't been what it should have been in a long time; he had no hope that this was suddenly going to change.

The next thing that registered, slowly and with effort, was that he wasn't actually in familiar surroundings. Up to this point he hadn't really cared where he was; now it puzzled him.

He couldn't remember why life was such a pain. But not being able to remember – that was it! They must have lobotomised him! He didn't wonder who "they" were. He didn't care. With a sigh he closed his heavy eyelids and wished he could go back and be dead again.

*

In the middle of the night, Federi was suddenly awake. Paean was sleeping peacefully in his arms. A skinny layer of neo-nanomer fabric divided them from the icy outside, surprisingly effectively. But the sounds of the night still came in through the wall of the gypsy tent as clearly as though there were no divide.

That blasted Morrigan was at it again! Howling and agonizing! It was doing that every night now, or possibly all the time, but at night things got quiet enough that he could hear it… He'd really have to put the creature out of its misery. It was making the whole country uneasy. And it wasn't even *in* Romania, strictly speaking…

They had been with the Tzigany for two and a half weeks now, and Paean had slipped into the customs and habits of the Free Gypsies, and into his arms with such a natural ease, it left him speechless. He couldn't imagine his life before he met her, anymore. She was in there somewhere, as though she had always been that essential part of him. He gazed at her sleeping face, still unable to fathom his luck.

He hadn't made too many inroads on his investigation of the Unicate here; neither had Ailyss, in Ireland. When Paean was otherwise occupied, Federi tended to nip up to the Comet and exchange notes with the spy-girl. He didn't want to break the little songbird's illusion of a perfect honeymoon too much, but he couldn't just abandon the mission. They were really staking out those dog-men, waiting for the attack. But so far all that had come to light was a bunch of dead-ends in his thinking. There was no pattern to the assaults. And nights the darned Morrigan stole his sleep with its tele-pathetic lamenting.

Oh hell, tomorrow he'd look into it. With a sigh he buried his face in Paean's lush hair and focused on getting back to sleep.

*

Mrs Flanagan surfaced from her sleep. A spinster of many years, she had a habit of sleeping soundly. But nobody could stay asleep with that dreadful hammering on the front door!

It sure wasn't going to be Saint Nicholas, she thought ironically as she slipped into her warm dressing gown and slippers. They sometimes called her awake like that when there was a birth, or a death, or a child lying seriously ill. She paused before turning the key. She suddenly had a horrible sense of foreboding.

The O'Hara baby was due to be born. She couldn't let an irrational fear hold her back now. She opened the door and gazed out into the dark and wet night.

"Mrs Flanagan," said the well-combed young officer, holding up a letter, "unfortunately I have the unenviable task of making you aware that your rent is overdue by four months now."

"My rent." Mrs Flanagan nodded slowly, forcing herself to breathe steadily despite the fear that screamed through her. So this was it. In the middle of the night! Had she ever thought it would be different? They had been moving people out of Molly Street for almost a year now, ever since that day Annie died. The excuse was always the same: The rent. She didn't doubt for a second that each family that had been evicted, had fully paid their rent and had had no clue what hit them.

They usually stuck to the daylight hours, but why had she thought they would come for *her* by day? They must know that she was crafty! They wanted to give her no opportunity.

"My rent is up to date, for your information," she mentioned, more out of indignation than belief that it would make any difference.

"Mrs Flanagan, please don't resist," said the officer sweetly. "You'd be putting me in a very difficult situation."

She peered at him. Nice polished smile; young, straight man, beautiful posture, eyes slightly *Other*, as Paean would put it. They'd sent him straight from Headquarters, she knew. Like the stuff that had come looking for the children the day Annie had passed away.

The study! If they found that, who knew what havoc they could wreak?

"One second," said Mrs Flanagan. She left the perfectly good young man standing on her doorstep and moved the two steps towards her study door. She found the button on the door frame and activated it, for the first and last time.

There was a massive short. The entrance to the study lit up in a blinding flash. Mrs Flanagan was flung backwards. When her head stopped fizzing and she could look up, the door was gone and there was only wall.

"What was that?" asked the young policeman from the door.

"Electric short," said Mrs Flanagan, still a bit dizzy. "I tried to switch my mains off to save electricity. Something must have been damp in there."

"Don't worry about the mains," said the man. "Just come. Head office will take care of the rest."

"Do I get a moment to get dressed? I'm in my nightgown!"

"Mrs Flanagan, it would cause me a lot of trouble to explain these delays at Head Office."

Mrs Flanagan sighed and accepted the young man's nonchalant arm. Cavalier to the death, she thought. There was no way to avoid it, no point in stalling. She followed the man into the truck.

*

Federi listened. There was silence. The howling had stopped. Had the poor creature finally breathed its last?

But that didn't feel right. The psychic silence was intelligent. As though the Morrigan had realized that it was transmitting, and had decided to stop. He shook his head, worried, and his hand wandered reflexively into his sleeping wife's hair and combed through the wild curls. Why would the Morrigan consciously stop transmitting its pain and grief? It could only mean one thing – the blasted creature was feeling better and was in a position to make such decisions!

He listened intently into the silence. Something was wrong, wrong, wrong! He tried to gauge what it was, whether it was the Morrigan. But although the immortal seemed awake and alert, no threat came from that angle at present. Then where?

Were the blasted dog-men on their way? He reached for his semi-automatic and lay in the dark, tense, waiting and listening.

*

The Doc checked into the infirmary. She peered at all the displays of Peter's vital signs on the instruments; she adjusted the drip and placed a hand on his forehead to gauge his general condition.

That gesture might be less accurate than the temperature sensor. But apart from calming the patient, it gave her information all the vital signs machinery failed to. She suspected it had to do with a patient's bioelectric field strength and structure, and that the human skin had not yet been studied to completeness and held, and also communicated, a wealth of subliminal information. But she would have found it hard to verbalize; so she usually told people it was only a habit.

Peter Piper was recovering. This pleased Doc Judith. His eyes were still closed; but his spirit didn't feel absent any longer. The ECG also indicated more brain activity. He was certainly out of his coma.

She frowned and glanced again at that ECG. Those were beta waves! According to this he ought to be awake! But there he was, with his eyes closed, sleeping peacefully... ah, no. He was awake! He was faking sleep! She shook her head, finished her check and left. Why should the young man fake sleep?

His eyes followed her out of the room, she could feel it. She shuddered lightly.

*

Mrs Flanagan was shivering too as the truck rattled on and on along the Irish highways. The young man had been so sweet to let her sit in front, in the cabin next to him; which made very little difference except to her comfort.

She had tried to get to the com Paean had left for her, by begging time to get dressed. She hadn't succeeded. Now that she needed it most, the wrist-com lay uselessly in her room at home.

The lanterns with their cold blue halogen lights passed overhead, illuminating the road just enough that one couldn't say it wasn't lit. No moon overhead. Mrs Flanagan marvelled at how one took in such details when one knew the end was close. She would have liked to see the moon one more time. She had paid the Earth's satellite no attention these past months, barring the rare occasions on which the full moon had risen spectacularly. Then she had wished that Annie Donegal had been there with her to enjoy it. Annie had been a special friend, if Mrs Flanagan had any friends at all.

At least Annie had been spared this terrifying ride to the slaughterhouse, she thought, and then stopped herself. Poor Annie! How scared must she have been as her end drew near? How helpless must she have felt for her children?

Crazy thoughts started to surface. What if Annie wasn't in fact dead? What if the Unicate had taken her away, not to the mortuary for cremation but to some facility where they revived her? What if they had turned her into a mindless Unicate brain-slave? Mrs Flanagan shook her head at these creepy thoughts. Annie was dead, period. The Unicate didn't need brain-slaves, they were a race of...

And there was that horrible block again, that no-go area. Mrs Flanagan knew that she knew the truth about the Unicate. But a block had been installed in her mind, from early childhood. She wasn't even allowed to think the truth!

9 – Mrs Flanagan

"Federi?"

He turned and glanced back at his young wife in the gloom of pre-dawn.   She had caught him red-handed getting armed to the teeth.

"What's wrong, Federi?"

"Going after that blasted Morrigan!"

"You need two," said Paean.

"Two?"

"Teleporters. But it's not a good idea, Federi! We all four of us were toast, last time we tried it."

He nodded. "I'm meeting up with Ailyss."

Paean stared at him, upset. He sighed.

"We've bin through this, little mockingbird. You are my only treasure. Keeping you safe, anna bottle!"

"You're na going to kill him!"

"He's in pain, little luv. It's unkind to leave him there forever. And I've got to find out about those blasted dogs."

"You don't want me to mediate?"

"And have him mesmerise my wife a second time?" retorted Federi. "Have him show you everything Federi can never be for you?"

She rolled her eyes and turned away from him. "So that's why you're going to kill him. Fine. Do what you have to!"

Federi cast her a doubtful look, finished arming himself and left the tent, as silent as his nickname, Shadow.

So, jealousy! After all that they had together, he was still afraid she'd fall for the larks of an alien shifter. Which she had, she reminded herself acidly. Enough to cause Federi a lot of heartbreak.

She sighed and hugged the pillow Federi had insisted on organizing for her. It was sad that he couldn't trust her; even sadder that he had a point. She guessed it came with being married to an assassin: Everyone who was perceived as a threat, was done away with.

And then she had to smile and shake her head at herself. She was being unfair. Federi was not like that. The reason he insisted on going after the Morrigan was because that creature was the force behind Dana's onslaughts on Captain. She consciously reminded herself of the mind-bending and extortion, and the demands for human sacrifice. Perhaps Vlad was really just a prankster, but a prankster with teeth, and – one forgot this – as alien a species to humans as the Great White that had nearly made a meal of her Federi in September. No, Federi was indeed right to finish that job.

But what gave her a twinge, was that he took Ailyss with him instead of her. *She* was his back-up, tried and proven, for wailing! She had given up her freedom so she could back him up!

Her moonbag bipped softly. She dug the spare wrist-com out of it that Shawn had organized her, with Wolf's help and without informing Captain – or Federi, for that matter. An unprimed com without identity, one that would only register on Captain's systems once it had been primed. Captain couldn't break her honeymoon with that. Or call them back from the mission.

"Shawney!"

"Pae! Are you okay?" came the voice of her little brother. She laughed softly. Her feelings must have transmitted to Shawn.

"Fine, Shawney. Where are you?"

"In the Crow's Nest," he said. "Wish you were here, I've got this new idea for a Christmas song, a tropical Christmas song totally

129

without snow, and I need your creative input… Don't know what weather you guys are having, but here the whole sea here is full of light… Aw sis, it's beautiful!"

"Where is 'here'?" she pushed. And missing him, and Ro, and the sea and the salty breeze, and the Solar Wind, became like a physical presence.

"Cape of Storms, Pae. Captain's making us sail around the Cape of Southern, makes us fly the storms, tells us that's all we lazy lubbers are good for. We're headed for Durban Port. That is after Captain checked out the Island Base for Ro and Rushka."

"Can't he leave what's well alone?" snorted Paean. "You guys using the Lolita coils?"

Shawn laughed. "No, we haven't warped to New Dome and back. We're sailing – mostly."

She grinned. "Mostly," she repeated.

"It's Sherman," he enlightened her. "At night, when it's his shift, he takes the Solar Wind up on her magnetic drives and warps her a little bit further. I'm sure he's worked out exactly how far she must fly every night. In the morning Wolf gets on the bridge and checks the coordinates and we are way, way further than we should have been, logically, if Sherman were sticking to Captain's rules! We skipped Panama completely – again."

"And what does Captain say?"

"Nothing," said Shawn with a grin. "And he also says nothing to having to eat sushi three times a day. I just can't get the idea of cooking into Lyr's head. Captain is in a very good mood. He keeps asking how many days to Christmas."

"Shawn," she asked suspiciously, "what have you done to Captain?"

"Not to Captain," said Shawn. "To the Solar Wind! We're getting her ready for Christmas!"

Paean gaped. She hadn't expected that! "And whose idea was that, if I may ask? Surely Captain doesn't 'do' Christmas every year?"

"Mr Marsden tells me that usually the crew pop a champagne bottle and have a few toasts and a nice dinner," said Shawn. "They used to shower the prin- er, I mean, Rushka with gifts because she was the kid aboard. But they haven't done in a year or two."

"So who thought of it this year?"

She could almost hear his broad grin. And she could nearly see the Solar Wind, decorated with tinsel from mast to keel.

"Shawney, you naughty boy! Trying to drive Captain round the bend?"

He laughed. "Only need a tree still… this is the first Christmas…" his voice went away.

A second later Paean was there in the Crow's Nest with him, hugging him tightly.

"It's okay, Shawney! Me too, I know…"

Christmas was a nasty one. She had tried to forget that it existed; and she had nearly succeeded. Her honeymoon – dreamtime with Federi – was designed for large amounts of time to slip by unnoticed. She'd thought it was a new life. But now that she was back aboard, she realized the time limit on that holiday…

Mother had pulled out all the stops last year, knowing it was going to be her last; battling bravely against the terrible fever that robbed her of all her energy and putting together a beautiful Christmas for her children one last time.

Next March would be a bad one, too. Then it would be a year.

*

Federi and Ailyss stalked through the ruins of the broken Dracula

131

castle. The Morrigan was close, but not there. It was once again on the other side of a wall, through a portal or something. On its own planet, Shrn. The difference between the two planets was worn thin here at the old ruin.

"We have to lure it out," said Ailyss.

Federi held up his hand for silence.

Nothing but silence. The hush of snow falling; first snows of the year.

Ailyss studied the Tzigan pensively. He had become wirier, sharper if that were possible. He moved even more like a nocturnal predator than before. And there was an element that he was losing. The easy familiarity from the ship was waning. He paused before answering, as though English didn't come as naturally now; and his Romanian accent, which had always been there if barely noticeable, had become stronger.

His smiles did come more easily, as though Paean were the exact medication he'd always needed. There was no more depressive edge to everything he did. But an edge there was – a sharp, analytical edge that dissected everything and everyone, with his searching stares, his sharp lookout, his careful responses and his knee-jerk second-guessing. Fully rested, he was a lot more intense, his mind honed to a razor edge to complement the lightning-fast instinctive reactions. Only two weeks in wild Romania, she thought. It was enough for him to revert to the feral assassin she had been so afraid of.

But the Morrigan was a solved puzzle! It shouldn't bother him so much! This time she had brought a third teleporter. If two fields had nearly killed the alien, three would – and this time she would make sure that neither she nor her colleague were inside those fields. They hadn't had a choice the last time.

And a lure? She smiled. Simple! Her mind reached out as she

closed her eyes.

Morrigan!

There was silence. A loaded, waiting silence.

Come now, Morrigan! Come out. We want to talk to you!

Another silence.

"He's close," whispered Federi.

Ailyss continued calling the alien telepathically, trailing through the broken ruins. Five minutes later she returned to where Federi was staring at the ruins, willing that entrance to be there again.

"He knows we're here. He's hiding." She shrugged. "Pointless, Federi. We might as well go home and wait for him to strike."

"Nimic!" growled Federi. "I injured him, so badly that he howls through all the nights. Not leaving it like that! Poor thing needs to be put out of its misery!"

"So what do you propose?" asked Ailyss.

"We wait. He's a prankster. He won't be able to resist trying to pull one on us. We stake him out, and when he sticks his nose out of his intergalactic crevice, we zap him!"

*

Wolf glanced up from the new croach chip he was constructing. The equipment nearly dropped from his hands in astonishment. Perched in her favourite spot atop the port-side drive was…

"Paean Donegal!" He moved around the console and gathered her into a hug, his beard splitting into a huge grin. "How are you? Has Federi finally decided to return you to us? Can we have you back now?"

She laughed softly. Wolf studied her critically.

"Why are you back from honeymoon early?" he challenged, getting serious. "Did you two fall out?"

She shook her head. "Just checking in."

"Liar!" Wolf shook his head and picked up the croach chip where he left it off. "I can see that it's not alright!"

"Where's Ailyss?" enquired Paean lightly.

"You know where Ailyss is! Helping Federi trace down the Morrigan!"

"And you're not on the team?" asked Paean.

"Listen, Pae," said Wolf. "I think they're barking up the wrong tree. The Morrigan is dead. According to my calculations that field ought to have torn anything apart that had a molecular density smaller than Uranium. That sticky carbon definitely! Think I'd have let her go alone if I had thought that there were any risk to her?"

"I think you're wrong," said Paean with a shrug. "But they're not being team players, so who knows..." She smiled brightly. "Shawn says the Solar Wind still needs a Christmas tree. You game?"

"After lunch," replied Wolf. "Hang, it's tough with neither Rhine Gold nor Federi aboard. All that raw stuff! I'm craving some good old Federi-style fish and chips."

"You're looking healthy though," she commented.

"Yeah, well..."

Paean smiled and saluted and headed to the steps.

"Where are you going now?" asked Wolf.

"To make some decent lunch for you guys."

~

Wolf was wrong. She hadn't come back aboard because she wanted to stop the honeymoon. It wasn't even a honeymoon; not intentionally anyway. It was a mission. But they didn't know this.

She was here because Shawney needed her. And not only Shawn, it seemed! At least the ship hadn't come apart at the seams the way it had before the croaches. But even they couldn't take over cooking decent meals. She scowled. Why actually not?

The plan was only to cook them all some good lunch, and then take Shawn back with her to the gypsies, introduce him… visit with him until night fell in Romania, and bring him back to the ship. This could be done practically every day, or every other day… her little brother needed her close in this time of remembrance.

The trick was to keep it away from Captain. Or to get his permission, she thought. Why not? Surely he wouldn't cancel her honeymoon out of arbitrary randomness?

She scowled as she felt the Lascekian magic catching her unawares again. She and Federi had officially quit! Captain couldn't tell them anything at all! Not even Federi could. She was her own free agent.

~

Lyr cropped up in the galley door and lifted his nearly invisible eyebrows in surprise.

"I see you are making food!"

"Yup!" Paean glanced up at him and smiled. The tall gangly Atlantean smiled back, with too many irregular merrow teeth.

"But you're not going to spoil things by cooking them," he presumed.

"I am," said Paean. "The crew wants a bit of a change from the whole-food diet. Come, have a seat, Lyr! Can I give you some vegetation to decapitate?"

"Vegetation has a central nervous system?" asked Lyr, puzzled. Paean laughed and pushed the potatoes his way.

"They even have eyes, sometimes," she informed him as she picked up a peeler and showed him how to go about it. The next ten minutes, while she quickly fried up enough fish for the crew, she watched how the tall man struggled to get all the skin off that first potato he had picked up.

135

"Practice makes perfect," she chirped eventually and sat down across from him, picking up more potatoes and pulling a Paean on them. Those potatoes didn't know what was happening to them. A bit in the same line, thought Paean with a grin, as comparing Dana and Perdita playing poker.

"How's Bridget?" she asked.

"I haven't gone to check," said Lyr. "Why did you move our daughters to Dublin Psychiatric, incidentally?"

"It's a place where they will be taken care of," explained Paean, thinking very fast. "The psychiatric ward looks after people who are not adjusted to life. They get fed there, and if they behave well and don't get aggressive, they get to walk in beautiful gardens and speak to other Irish people – Gaelic, I should say – who can nearly understand their language. So we figured it would be the best place for them."

"Besides," added Lyr with a little pointy-toothed smile, "Bridget attacked the Solar Wind. Locking her up is the logical solution for your Captain. It is kindness – in the old Atlantean tradition he would not have let her live."

Paean scowled. She suddenly wondered about the wisdom of her own decision, not to take Lyr to Dublin as well. But he seemed to be very fond of his youngest daughter, Rashni, and otherwise no danger to the ship – so far.

"And you? Don't you feel angry at Captain?"

Lyr shook his head.

"Morrigan treasure," he uttered with disgust. "I saw the damage it did over the centuries. I hope that they never find it, and that its memory is scrubbed out."

"They did find it," said Paean. "Only they don't understand. The treasure is a planet just like Earth."

Lyr was quiet for a while, struggling with the potato.

136

"So what is your Captain planning to do with it?" he asked then.

"Plant it," said Paean. "Make it habitable."

Lyr nodded. "It's moot," he said pensively. "Earth will never be replaced. Even Dana of New Dome found that her planet is not satisfactory."

"Not replaced," corrected Paean. "He means for it to be another place where people can live. He likes creating peaceful places."

Lyr shook his head gravely but didn't comment any further.

"You don't miss Bridget?" asked Paean.

Lyr shook his head once more, never looking up. He was winning – the potato would have to surrender any moment now. "Bridget has spent the last two thousand years thinking only three thoughts. Her treasure, revenge on Dana, and physical gratification. Now that she knows about the Solar Wind, all she can talk about is how she will torture Radomir Lascek to death for taking her treasure, and Federi for destroying the Central Crystal. I believe we have won our freedom back by that evil Crystal being overthrown. No, Bridget is well stowed. I spent many years mourning my little Nimue," he added quietly. "Now that I see she is alive and thriving, I want to stay near. It will be fun to raise my grandchild."

Paean nodded. She had spotted it even back in Dome. There was no love between Bridget and Lyr. And everything else had merely been a diversion for Bridget.

There was surprising gentleness in Lyr, she mused. His whole character seemed composed of one principle: No hard feelings. Refreshing to have someone like that on the Solar Wind, even if he had merrow teeth.

*

Peter Piper opened his eyes. He felt better. A lot better! He could actually feel his limbs!

These past few days he had recovered more by the hour. The ship doctor had added something into his drip that made him feel fantastic. Perhaps she thought that by putting him on happy juice she could make him positive about the ship?

What she had enabled him to do without realizing it, was make his plan. He didn't wish himself dead anymore. It was much, much simpler than that. This was the turning point; his big break in life.

Peter Piper had been born under bad circumstances which had got worse. From an abusive childhood in the inner-city dumps, eking out a living by working for a beggar boss, he had worked up his way with patience and some cunning into the docks; and as a deck hand, into the seafaring circles and eventually into Adamson's service. The only reason he was working for Adamson, was the fact that the guy had a daughter. Peter Piper knew what a price such a young girl could fetch at the right dealer in Korea. And that was possibly the only reason, too, that he hadn't yet helped himself to a healthy portion of her – damaged goods fetched smaller prices. And of course, that the whole rest of the crew, huge, strong sea bears, were protecting her with their lives. He hoped that she hadn't been dealing out favours to them, the little slut – and that she wasn't damaged goods anyway.

So the plan so far had been to wait until Adamson and his trade – which was shady in any case, so the man had to watch his back from the police – made it to Korea, where Piper had a contact; and then to disappear with the girl, and once the trade was done, without the girl. He'd worked it out. Other girls had fallen for his charms. Not this one; but he'd catch her by the very loyalty she showed the other shipmates. He'd tell her that one of them – perhaps that moron Derrick – was badly hurt and needed her help, and rush her off into the harbour town, into a trap where his contact could help him immobilize the brat and get her to her eventual master.

But he'd already hung around on the bleeding Walrus for five months without Korea ever being on the charts, no matter how often he suggested the place for a weapons deal. Adamson only listened to himself. And the other mates looked after Mindy as though she were their younger sister.

The Solar Wind had more than one young girl aboard. He had hacked into the console in the infirmary, which these stupid pirates had left unguarded, believing him to be comatose. And he'd gleaned a view of most of the ship. He could page from cabin to cabin.

There were at least three girls; if he included Mindy, that made four, though Mindy seemed to have injured her back so badly that he doubted she'd fetch the full price now. Then again he was sure there was a niche market specifically for handicapped young girls.

His winnings quadrupled – not a bad deal. However he also knew that there was no way he could influence the Solar Wind's Captain. The man seemed even more unbending than Adamson.

So he had delved a bit deeper into the console – and had suddenly understood about the Solar Wind. This was the Freedom Ship, whose Captain had organized the peace negotiations between Unicate and Rebellion, badly denting trade for Adamson and co.

But not for him! He had contacts in Ireland who would pay handsomely for the kind of information he could sell them. The Donegals, all three, on this ship! At which point, suddenly, the console had shut down and he'd been unable to switch it back on.

Of course Radomir Lascek was a wily old bastard. On his head, the IRP had quite a price too. And Piper had no illusions that Lascek would cotton on within half a second what he was up to, if he tried to influence him by suggestions.

So it should never get that far. He was past trying to influence commanders on their own missions. He'd do better than that. He'd deliver the Solar Wind to his contacts in Dublin on a silver platter.

He listened intently for steps in the passage. There were none. He got up out of the infirmary bunk – something that had become easier by the day – found his small cache of personal items, and crossed the passage quickly, darting from doorway to doorway.

*

Mrs Flanagan followed the officer down the passage through the dark building. This was a Unicate mound; one of those Headquarters structures. The steps from the front door had led down underground, which was where they were now, moving along long tiled passages. There were small lights lining the passages along the floor, casting a dim glow, but the metallic colour of the tiles reflected a lot. Occasionally Unicate officials – mainly female – in their grey uniforms crossed the passage from doors into other doors.

As Mrs Flanagan trailed through the construction, the whole scene held an eerie *déjà vu* for her. She knew that she had been inside one of these before; she also knew that this was in the fenced-off part of her memories, that bit of her childhood where she couldn't go. What puzzled her was why the Unicate would get their victims right into their Headquarters buildings before killing them. That struck her as odd, when the organization had every opportunity to kill people wherever they liked.

Radomir Lascek had overthrown the Unicate and brought Freedom – a nice dream. She didn't even realize she was shaking her head. He was after all just another figurehead. The activities of the Unicate had stayed unaltered, at least where Molly Street was concerned. She didn't believe for one second that this was a different establishment from the one that had murdered Annie Donegal.

140

A huge double-door opened to an office-like room, where a semi-circle of leather-upholstered high-back chairs surrounded a luxurious executive desk. The nice young officer ushered her inside and closed the door behind her. She glanced across the room, wondering about the functions of those lamps and panels of what looked like buttons. And wondering what that huge heap of dirty clothes was doing on the massive boss-chair behind the desk. Until the chair swivelled around and the heap fixated her with large, watery-blue eyes.

"So you have come at last," said the heap, rising cumbersomely from the chair. Its face was pasty and vaguely female; its hair, red. Its body was so obese that Mrs Flanagan had to force her mind into a frame to think of this being, too, as human. It lumbered across to the panels and activated one. "Do have a seat, Mrs Flanagan."

Mrs Flanagan sat down on the leather high-back that had been indicated to her. A torturer's chair, she thought, lame with fear, watching how two pod-lights detached from the ceiling and circled her like flies. Mrs Flanagan wasn't a coward; but this display left her frozen rigid, terrified. She had no idea what torture the Unicate had invented, or copied from the cruellest of the cruel.

The two round spotlights settled left and right of her head, and in perfect synchrony they emitted a blinding flash.

Mrs Flanagan stared at the Unicate woman in horror, her sight clearing slowly from the flashes.

"Now that that is taken care of," said the creature and sat down again on her oversized office chair. "Tell me everything!"

Mrs Flanagan screamed hysterically. She couldn't stop. Her memory block had just been removed.

10 – Peter and the Wolf

"What's this?" asked Paean.

"Observe," said Wolf. "But if you abuse it, I'll take it away from you again!"

Paean studied the brand new wrist-com Wolf was holding out to her. It included a teleporter. "Brilliant! How did you get it that small?"

Wolf grinned. "Not a Svendsson for nothing!"

Paean grinned back. Heck, she was proud of this chosen brother of hers!

"There are only two of these," said Wolf. "The other one is for Ailyss."

Paean nodded, thinking about croaches and wrist-coms and teleporters. Wolf and she – they were a great team.

"Put it on," urged Wolf. "Try it out!"

She removed her temporary wrist-com and put this new one on. It still looked a bit funny – all prototypes did – but she could count on it being waterproofed, and most of all, functional.

"This one is unprimed, too?"

"It's unprimed," smiled Wolf. "Wouldn't want to be the reason for ruining your honeymoon!"

"Wonder where Mr Marsden is," she said lightly and pressed the button.

Wolf smiled. He was very proud of himself for finding a way of making the field on this teleporter gentler.

~

Oasis. That was the name of the place. Paean grinned more as she caught Michelle's baffled look. This was a super-long-range teleporter!

Michelle was planting the new planet with the help of Keenan Quinlan, Space Base, and countless volunteers of the Miami gypsies. Shawn, the rascal, had promised them a share in Dana's treasure if they did. The little pirate, thought Paean as she smiled and waved greetings at Alejandro and Rosalita, and at Keenan. He didn't even know yet if there were a treasure beyond the planet itself!

And Shawn was the one who only put in his appearance at odd times, when the Captain or Perdita wanted to check on the Oasis. Because he was on the Solar Wind, flying storms and getting her ready for Christmas. He was also quietly coordinating the croaches, so that he didn't need to scrub any heads.

Shawn had also established a colony of croaches on Calypso. Wolf had added an 'engineer' into their numbers, a croach whose name was Leonardo, whose sole function was to build AI chips for all new croach babies and install them. Oasis had its own processor; their intelligence slotted into that. It wasn't an artificial intelligence itself, but at least that way they were highly programmable. And Leonardo contacted Wolf all by himself when parts ran low.

Oasis, the camp on Calypso, was a village of caravans which Jon Marsden had painstakingly purchased from somewhere in England. British quality, he had commented back then. Paean saw how the British quality was already beginning to rust around the wheels from the chronic damp sea wind; and how the paint was already sand-blasted off the roofs by the relentless desert land wind. Compounding caravans, or even tents like those of the Tzigany, would have been better, she thought.

Wind shelters had been erected for the trees that lined the outskirts of the camp, so that the wind didn't kill them before they could grow up. Jon Marsden had brought in large trees, selected at random from Earth's arid regions – Eucalypts and wattles from the Australian Outback, Koker trees and giant Baobab from Ovimba in Southern Free, even mangroves to dip their roots in the clean estuary water of the lagoon where the River Dana flowed broadly into the pristine sea.

A tall figure emerged from one of the caravans. Paean flew at her with a stormy hug.

"Perdita!"

*

Wolf glanced up once more at the movement, expecting to see Paean pop back in. And froze.

"Stick'em up," said Peter Piper from behind the Kosaka cannon. "Put everything down – nice and slow – good! Now you contact that muck-sucking loser you call a captain, and tell him to hand over the ship to me. Or you lose your nuts, scumbag."

*

Radomir Lascek glanced at the console that beeped.

"Captain," said his young engineer matter-of-factly. "Peter Piper here says that he is taking over the ship. He's got me at gunpoint. I think he means business."

"Peter Piper?" asked Radomir Lascek, baffled. The last that he was aware of, Peter Piper was lying in the infirmary. Comatose. Lascek paged through the Solar Wind's sensors. "Give me an angle, old ship!"

There was of course no response. He snorted at himself. The Morrigan had conned them all into believing that the Solar Wind was actually sentient and had a personality. What had that alien actually wanted the ship for? With an impatient grunt he hacked manually in the console until he found the camera in the machine room.

The Captain whistled through his teeth. That was not at gunpoint! That was at the loaded end of a blooming missile gun! Gunpoint could injure and with sodden luck, kill a man. But this – poor Wolf stood no chance!

Teleport in, shoot the assailant? But if Piper pulled the trigger in his death throes, Wolf was gone anyway.

"He says you have two more seconds to decide, Captain." Wolf's voice sounded a bit strained now. Lascek activated the ship com.

"Piper, come to the bridge. She's yours!"

Although he felt murderous anger at the look of glee on that hooligan's face, he couldn't disagree with his own decision. Losing Wolf... losing any of his precious crew was not an option. Had never been. He'd have to allow the man to take the console, wait for the right moment...

Was Adamson behind this?

And then something really odd happened on the camera. Something red flashed into existence behind Piper; blinked and flashed out of existence again. And reappeared seconds later in front of him, knocking the missile gun out of his surprised grip. Something metallic flashed at the invader's throat.

By the devil, the girl took risks! Lascek found his hands trembling with adrenaline as he switched the Solar Wind on autopilot – manually – and made his way to the bilge rooms. That blasted Kosaka could have minced her – or Wolf; or both!

~

"Sorry," said Paean as Peter Piper crumpled to the ground in a spray of arterial blood. "Nobody points a frying Kosaka cannon at Wolf." She turned and stared at Wolf, suddenly white as a sheet. The huge engineer caught her in a bear hug before she could collapse on

146

the floor. He looked rather grey himself.

"Thanks, Pae. Thought I was croach kibble there for a seccie!"

Paean's knees went to jelly. She found her favourite cabinet to sit down on. The Captain came down the companion ladder.

"Paean Donegal!"

"Demonos," she whispered.

"Paean Dee," agreed Radomir Lascek, placing a huge hand on her shoulder. "Precious Donegal Magic! If ever you earned a medal, today you deserve two! Thank you for remembering your Solar Wind family and coming back aboard!"

"Thanks," she muttered. "Not technically aboard, Captain. Just checking in. Federi and I..."

"Of course, my girl," replied Lascek with another grin. "You are welcome at any point, but currently not on the crew. I know."

Paean nodded absently. And stared at the bloodbath.

"He was my patient," she said tonelessly. "Why..."

Not so long ago she'd stitched this man up with Doc Judith in an endless operation, pouring every bit of Donegal Magic into him that she had available, trying for his survival. And now she had killed him.

"You realize of course what this means for Adamson and Derrick," said the Captain, staring pensively at the casualty. "They're a liability now. Can't keep them aboard."

"But Captain, why not?" asked Paean, shocked. Derrick still needed medical care!

"Because we don't know if Adamson is behind this," replied Lascek. "And if he is, he'll have every reason to deny it and try again. By the Law of the Pacific I should terminate both him and Derrick."

Paean shook her head.

"But – Mindy? Captain, surely you can't... Captain Adamson is

147

Mindy's father!"

"That's why I'm not going to apply the Law of the Pacific," said Lascek gravely. "I'll put them ashore instead."

If Federi were aboard, he'd do it differently, thought Paean. He'd probably interrogate both Adamson and Derrick. But… Federi wasn't aboard, now was he? He was being a team spoiler back in Romania. Hunting down a lethally wounded alien just to finish a job.

"What about Mindy's back?" asked Wolf with a frown. "She needs to stick with us because if her bridge fails, she collapses! That's happened several times now! If I'm not there to fix it for her, she'll be in a wheelchair!"

"That's a problem," said Lascek.

Paean stared at them both with huge eyes… and teleported out.

*

The world spun slowly back into view. She was lying on a rocking bunk, staring up into a magical forest of gemstones and small artworks, suspended from the cabin's ceiling. And Wolf hovered over her, with Doc Judith in the background, both looking very concerned.

"Teleporter malfuncted," she muttered.

"No, it didn't," disagreed Wolf. "It did exactly what it was supposed to. You tried a leap that was out of range. I've built a safety feature into the new teleporters. If your target is out of range or moving out of range faster than you can reach it, the teleporter reroutes the leap to a place of safety. In your case that is Federi's cabin."

She nodded. "That means that Shawn is out of range? But the range is from here to Calypso!"

148

Wolf nodded, concerned, and moved aside so that Doc Judith could check all Paean's vital signs. And the nausea hit the redhead like a wave.

"Hell," she muttered, studying the blood on her hands with revulsion. She hated being an efficient killer. It had been a split second; Peter Piper had gone down before he even had a chance to pull the trigger. Knowing this didn't help though. She was slime, that she could cut down a man that quickly and coldly.

The blackout hadn't been from trying to teleport. It had been from adrenaline overdose, and revulsion at her own action. But to explain this to Doc?

"Shawn's taken Mindy off the ship," she said. "I've got to fetch him back!"

"Off into space?" asked Wolf quizzically. "Where on Earth would he take her? You'd have reached them on Calypso."

"Dome," said Paean with conviction. "He's taking her to New Dome. I'm sure of it."

"Then there is no problem," replied Wolf. "Perdita's jets have Pluto Base programmed into them by now. Jeannie went into detail about this. From Pluto Base someone will probably take them to New Dome."

"But Dana's on New Dome," fretted Paean.

"That's not a problem," said Wolf, "because so is Johnny Anyhow. Besides, Dana quite likes Shawn."

"And Auntie Katie is on New Dome," added Paean.

"Ah," said Wolf. "That might present a problem."

"He can't take Mindy off the ship," agonized Paean. "Her bridge will slip! She'll be in pain!"

"We'll retrieve the two of them," said Wolf calmly. "No problem, Pae. But please don't go teleporting off right now!"

"In fact," added Doc Judith, "my girl, I'm giving you a bit of sedative, and then you sleep, understood?"

Paean stared at her in desperation. The Doc drew up sedative in a syringe and injected Paean with it. The warm wave of drowsiness was too much to fight against.

"Okay, Doc," Paean managed to mumble before she was washed away on that wave of comfortable oblivion. Her last thought was that Federi didn't know where she was.

*

Federi glanced south, where behind the clouds, the sun was probably at its zenith now. The falling snow blocked that out and gave an impression of timelessness. It was a strange world, thought the Tzigan out of context. The clouds and the snow were only a thin layer of atmosphere over the planet's surface, beyond which the sun was shining as always... space had warped his Earthian perspective forever.

They had been staking out the Morrigan for two hours now. A new plan was needed.

"You go and get Wolf, Ailyss," suggested Federi. "You can get some Christmas trees in the meantime, for the Solar Wind. How many does Captain need? See, there are lots of good ones in these mountains! I'll wait here. I'll call if he sticks his flat nose out. I'll flatten it some more for him." He scowled. "The Morrigan, not Captain," he added.

Ailyss snorted. Captain's large, piratical hook nose could hardly be called flat! And the Morrigan didn't technically even have a nose.

"Thanks, Federi." She teleported out. Federi sighed and studied the rock paintings naughty Tzigany children had drawn on the old ruins. He recognized some of them...

In summer he'd sat here idly practising his slingshot. And

playing on Falco's violin. Nobody ever came here. The Unicate had pretty much sealed off all tourism, worldwide. The birds had been lively and even some of the wild creatures had come to investigate. The universal principle of music, he recalled thinking. He had been twelve. And he'd never aimed his slingshot at a living creature... highly ironic, considering what he'd turned into. This country did strange things to him, made him a child again, and at the same time it made him more himself. And now snow was falling, lightly, persistently, and a carpet of white dust merged in the distance into a white blanket. The bare trees and their branches caught some flakes here and there. Some more of this and Transylvania would turn into a wonderland... a nice present for his Paean. He smiled to himself and thought of her with sharp longing. Couldn't even be away from her for an hour or two...

Ailyss teleported back in with Wolf. Federi glanced at his friend. The engineer looked as though he'd just gone through the Valley of Death, trying to be fearless. Federi smiled.

"What's new, *Vyusher?* Seen a few ghosts?"

Ailyss relayed what Wolf had told her.

"I turn my back," she added angrily. "Can't leave you alone for a second, can I!"

"It was fine," growled Wolf. "I was fine. Nothing did happen, and it wouldn't have either. Captain had already relented. The guy had no reason to shoot me."

Federi's skin crawled. So there had been a situation on the Solar Wind! A blooming life-threatening one! And he, the ship's guardian demon, had not been aboard! He was proud of Paean, but horrified nonetheless. But hell... the situation was averted, the threat had been cut down with uncanny efficiency, and if Captain wanted any officers to make his decision for him concerning the rest of the Walrus' crew – well, not him, he was officially on leave!

151

He wanted to fetch Paean back, hold her tightly. Steal some of that toxic magic from her; know that she was alright. But she was asleep; sedated by Doc. He could see her in his mind's eye, vividly, where she lay sleeping in his bunk, her lovely hair feathered over his pillow. The pull to teleport into the Cabin of Dreams and watch her sleep, as he'd done so often, was overwhelming. But... she wouldn't even know about it, and there was a job to finish here, and tonight... well, tonight was another story.

He borrowed Wolf's com to contact Perdita, and instructed her to follow Shawn and make sure that the boy reached New Dome safely. She agreed and promised to report back when the two runaways were settled. Federi nodded as he handed Wolf's com back. Perdita was efficient. She was the best to look after anyone in space. Shawn and Mindy would be alright.

"Go get a Christmas tree," he encouraged Ailyss and Wolf. "There are choice pines and deodars around the back of this mountain."

He watched them go.

Bait, Ailyss had said. A lure. Well, they were! He set his wrist-com on alert, dug his teleporter out of his pocket, switched his gypsy radar on high – that button was beginning to respond better – and waited.

*

"Sure this is the right way?" asked Mindy, worried.

"Dead sure," said Shawn. The Lolita coils of the Comet had been activated; Pluto should be warping into view any moment now.

Mindy was in pain; her bridge had slipped. But there was no way he was going to allow her to stay on the Solar Wind and Captain to cut her down.

The Solar Wind herself had alerted him to what was happening there in the bilges. He had to admit that by now his sister's mindset wasn't comprehensible to him any longer. She seemed to have mutated into a different species after marrying Federi. It had been a gradual process, so gradual that he'd missed it – but by now she could coldly cut down someone instead of negotiating, in a split second.

Captain was probably going to execute all the survivors of the Walrus now. He'd clapped Paean into chains for only teleporting. This kind of hostile act against the Solar Wind was not going to go unpunished. But Shawn wasn't going to allow Captain to chain down or maroon Mindy, any more than he was allowing him to execute her. Mindy's best chances now lay with Dana – they had to have some sensible remedy on New Dome for a broken back!

Pluto Base warped into view, and the Comet switched automatically from the Lolita coils to the much smoother Perdita drives. The jet started communicating with the base.

"Voilá," smiled Shawn. "All organized, see?"

*

Federi followed Ailyss' and Wolf's trail. He had given them a head start, so that they wouldn't suspect he was following them. Their footprints were clear in the new snow; ideal. He could hear their soft chatting in the distance. Sounds carried in this quiet.

They had taken him literally when he said the other side of the mountain, he thought with amusement. Perhaps Wolf and Ailyss were overdue a holiday too, with romantic walks in the wintry countryside.

There was silence, suddenly. Federi hesitated and listened. This didn't feel right. He kept following their tracks.

153

A little further on he spotted something blue lying between the trees. He approached it with apprehension, his hand on his gun. It was a human shape in a pot-blue parka. Neither Wolf nor Ailyss owned such an item. As he came close, he saw that the figure was dead. Nobody alive was that still in snow. He bent over it and moved the hood out of the way to see who it was – and recoiled. The figure's face was gone, replaced by one bloody, frozen mess. The parka had been ripped open, and so had the man. Something's lunch.

Federi straightened out and took a few steps back to examine the tracks. Ailyss had certainly found this guy. The two sets of footprints milled around the corpse before carrying on. Why hadn't she called him? Where the hell was she?

He looked for bear prints. Or Morrigan prints. Or anything. The fallen snow complicated the tracks. This fellow had been like this for a while. There had been wind and rain obscuring tracks, and now of course the snow. Federi realized what his chances were of finding any clues. He left the scene and concentrated on following the footprints of Wolf and Ailyss.

Footprints that suggested that they had run. They were being too darned quiet. And then the footprints stopped. Cut off across a straight line, like magic. Like the dogmen's prints back in Miami, and in Vlaşta.

Federi frowned. This explained their silence, anna bottle! He stepped across the line and fell through the trapdoor.

11 – The Mystery of Molly Street

It was old Sherman who had been knocking, apologetically but persistently, on the Assassin's Cabin's hatch. And he had entered, as Paean battled her eyes open against the residual gradient of sedative, and now he was looking for a place to sit down.

"Sherman," she mumbled. "Is everything a'right?"

"Sorry to waken you up, dear child," said Sherman. "I don't know anyone else who can help me with this, and that's no exaggeration. Do you know, about your old teacher, Mrs Flanagan?"

Paean nodded, worried. She had a nasty feeling about this conversation. And a few sentences later she had it confirmed.

She teleported. And walked up the steps on Mrs Flanagan's porch and knocked on the door.

Sherman had been in the process of suggesting someone to go along with her; but she had teleported out before he could complete the thought. Who in any case? Federi was in Romania stalking an undead immortal. So was Ailyss. And Paean wasn't going to ask Jon Marsden, who was on bridge duty according to the schedule but was actually on Calypso; or worse, Captain... who might just forbid her to go. Captain couldn't leave the ship in any case, because he had Adamson and crowd to deal with. And Sherman – he was too old to teleport, she thought. One single teleportation might kill him. She wasn't taking the chance.

In any case nobody knew Dublin the way the Donegal Troubles did. She had her escape routes all over the town.

There was silence. Paean knocked again; waited. The silence stretched. Mrs Flanagan wasn't here. Something bad had happened.

She checked the time. Three in the afternoon. She tried the door. It was unlocked. Paean opened it silently and entered the house warily, thinking of Nemiscau. The door closed behind her with a quiet "click", as it had done all those years.

The air inside the place was stale. And something was different here. Paean glanced around. And then it hit her.

Where the study door had been all these years, there was only wall. A huge Victorian-style painting hung in the place that had been the time portal.

Paean investigated but found nothing around that painting – no switches, levers, electronic devices of any kind... it was an honest painting on an honest wall, but it had got there by dishonest means, this she was prepared to bet her treasure on.

She trailed through the rest of the house, softly calling for Mrs Flanagan, looking for her in the kitchen, the bedroom, trying not to panic. The door to the bathroom was open, so she peeked, after all it was possible that her old schoolteacher had fallen and was incapacitated, needed medical help... all sorts of scenarios played themselves out in her mind, in the hope that her and Sherman's hunch was wrong. But Mrs Flanagan was nowhere.

This was very dark. Paean returned to the place where the study used to be. Could Mrs Flanagan be in there, stuck in the time pocket as the portal collapsed?

*

The baying was worse than at the Cape colony of seals. Federi rubbed his head, waiting for the stars to clear. Baying, and clamouring, and growls; and bursts of machinegun fire.

It had been a nasty fall. As the fog cleared, he found himself at Ailyss' feet. She was standing above him, her feet planted apart by shoulder width, mowing down something with her gun. Wolf was in the picture too, holding a handgun and potting off one shot after another. And the victims of Ailyss' fire – huge furry beasts, some half humanoid…

"Nobody said my name," mumbled Federi incoherently. "This doesn't make sense!"

His gun had found its way into his hands by now and was pointing itself at the many monstrosities, and shooting them down without mercy, too.

They were in an enclosed rock crevice. How so many hounds could find their way in, was a mystery to Federi. Until he saw them emerging straight out of the rock. Portals. Dammit!

The bodies were piling up around them. It felt to him as though he were mowing down a whole tribe. A pack. A family. And a rash of goosebumps ran across his hide.

"Stop!" he yelled. "There's got to be another way!" He fumbled with his teleporter. But that was pointless. And the trapdoor through which he'd fallen, was overhead – far above them, at the top of the rocky pothole in which they were trapped.

None of these hounds were wearing uniform. They were not Unicate hounds. And the Unicate hounds in Miami had all posed as officers… they had been working for the Unicate. These had more in common with wolves than with soldiers.

Ailyss wasn't holding her fire. The hounds were still pouring in. And then suddenly another presence melted out of the rock, zinged around them a few times in a show of electricity, and shaped itself into a huge black hound straight from hell, flickering in and out of reality. It turned and growled at the hounds, and they stopped in their tracks and whimpered…

Even projecting an illusion proved more than the Morrigan could maintain. He watched dismally how his illusion flickered, and then disappeared. The hounds were puzzled for a moment or two, and then they refocused on their prey. Some advanced on him, too. This was going to hurt.

The Demon dropped his gun onto its strap and two blades came out, one in each hand, spinning smoothly.

"So!" he shouted. "You worthless hounds are going to attack an injured creature?" He danced forward, advancing on the surprised werehounds. "Just because you can?" Those blades lashed out, first one, then the other, darting forward and withdrawing, and resuming their spinning. Where they had visited, ears were nicked, noses bore slashes and started bleeding. The hounds yelped and cowered where the blades flashed at them, and the surrounding werehounds started backing away too.

"You stinking lot of carrion eaters," shouted the Demon, clearly enraged. "That's right: Back away! Scoot, you jackals! Back off!"

Those shifters seemed to respect his blades. The Morrigan knew that they were cowards; but they didn't understand death. The gunfire had meant nothing to them; seeing their companions go down had only fuelled their anger. But pain they understood. Something he personally was in part responsible for. They whimpered. When a few more ears and tails started getting nicked by those spinning blades, the first ones turned tail and fled. Cut in their sensitive faces? This would hurt them a long time. He watched in admiration how the Demon managed something Ailyss had failed to do with her gunfire: chase the whole mangy lot off.

"And don't you come back!" he yelled after them. "Or this juggler is going to cut your tails off!" And he turned to the Morrigan.

The creature that had been Prince Vlad once, tried disappearing into the ground too. The Demon was in a killing mood, was he? But instead of using the blades to cut him to shreds, Federi knelt down next to him and inspected him critically.

159

"Vlad," he asked, "what are you doing here?" He reached out and touched the Morrigan's raw hide. That hurt! Vlad lashed across the gypsy's hand with an electric charge, making him withdrew it quickly.

"Sorry," said the Assassin, unbelievably. The same man who had got him into such a state. The Morrigan lay pulsing, trying to ignore the deadly burn of the sticky carbon. He'd meant to warn Demonos against Anthrim the Red; because the dragon was a greater threat than Federi. Anthrim was bad news. If Anthrim had turned his greedy gaze towards Earth...

But... why should he warn the Demon? If Anthrim destroyed Federi, that sorted that for Vlad. Except that he'd then have to deal with Anthrim. And his blue furry spy. And there was no guarantee that he was dying fast enough. Anthrim could still make his death more miserable for him. But worse, much worse...

Who'd look after his werefolk for him? Who'd stop Anthrim from eating them all?

~

Federi glanced at Ailyss, as puzzled as she was.

"So why did you come, Vlad? Why did you try to protect us?"

The Morrigan's voice came as from far away, in a hoarse murmur.

"So kill me, Demon! And then die in this werefolk trap!"

"Did you create this trap?" asked Federi.

There was far-off laughter. "No, you simpleton. Every shifter in the universe knows how to open a portal. They don't need the Morrigan for that!"

Federi drew a sharp breath. "They *all* know how to?"

"It's a basic shifter skill," rasped the far-away voice. "Very few shifter species are too dim for that."

"So can you open a portal home for us?" asked Federi.

There was silence as the alien seemed to consider. And then, "If I do, will you kill me?"

Federi ground his teeth. "Dammit, Morrigan, you've just tried to save our lives. Hell, you can be difficult! I think I might let you live… under certain provisos…"

"Then I won't open the portal," came the far-off answer. And the voice trailed off. But the puddle was still there.

"Wait," said Federi, confused. "Let me get this right. You *want* me to kill you?"

There was no answer.

The three of them stared at each other.

"What now?" asked Wolf.

"I'd say, let's get him to the Solar Wind and take it from there," suggested Ailyss. "We've got Michelle, and Itzak, and maybe Paean who could help. Doc is pretty inventive too where biology is concerned. Because we have to find out what this guy knows."

Federi sat back and looked up at the small patch of sky that was visible over the crevice. Blue sky. Then again, of course this planet had oxygen. So like Earth, it could have fooled him.

Two universes, perpendicular to each other. Two sets of juxtaposed stars. And the shifters being able to move freely between the two. No teleporter could get you from Earth to Shrn. But they merely stepped through a portal… that they all knew how to open…

And the other creatures, humans and so on, had no idea how to open a portal, and didn't even know it existed! Who was higher up in the food chain?

He touched the once-coruscating surface of Vlad's protoplasm. It was dry, like a membrane. Dry and cool, like a beached octopus. This time, no electric charge whipped across his hand. There was no electricity left in this poor creature.

"Ailyss," he said, "I'm afraid we're too late. He's dead."

161

"Paean will be pretty upset," she observed.

Federi nodded.

"Federi," Wolf put in, "I'd like to try something. We should try to get him onto the Solar Wind. He's got sticky carbon, he'll be easy to locate if he should get out of hand..."

"He's dead, Wolf," said Ailyss.

"Want to try to revive him," said Wolf. "Got a few ideas."

Federi took off his parka and scooped the alien up with it. In the end, Vlad didn't weigh all that much. Twenty, maybe thirty kilo... incredible, that such a small blob of protoplasm had held whole civilizations in check. He handed him to Wolf.

"You go pour him inna bucket in the in the infirmary," he said. "'s no harm trying to get him back alive, what do we know? We can always chuck him overboard if he starts stinking too much." He turned to Ailyss. "Gun ready? You back up Wolf. I'm going to open a portal. Then you go through, and straight to the Solar Wind, no detours. Got your teleporter? Good! Don't wait for me, under no circumstances."

"You're going to open a portal?" asked Ailyss quizzically.

"Observe," said Federi, and straightened out.

He took out both his knives once more.

"Come and get me!" he yelled, throwing his mane back in a show of bravado. "I'm here, you worthless pack – come and get Federi! Federi Demonos! Lunch, anyone?"

It worked like a charm. And the first Unicate hound that descended on him, was grabbed by the scruff of his uniformed neck, and forced at knife-point to open a portal back to Earth. Ailyss lifted her gun and mowed down all other Unicate hounds that came pouring into the trap, giving Federi space. And then the portal was open, and Wolf pushed through it with the dead Morrigan wrapped in Federi's parka, in his arms. Ailyss followed him, including him in

162

her teleporter field, and they vanished.

Federi kept the semi-human officer at knifepoint as he dragged him out of the portal by his neck fur. He growled at the other Unicate hounds.

"Follow me and I'll kill him," he warned. "And then I have two hands to give you pain…" The Demon echoed menacingly in his voice, promising that he'd enjoy the process. The other Unicate hounds backed away, wary. They were blasted cowards.

Federi slapped the Unicate dog over the nose with the flat side of the Stiletto. The creature yelped.

"And now you close the portal again," the Tzigan growled. The hound complied, terrified.

"Your name is?" snapped the Assassin. The hound whined. "You know I can tear your throat out as fast as cut it," warned the vicious predator that Federi had turned into, baring its teeth. There was still some mutant in there, too. For a second, Federi had to grapple with that blasted mutant and her suggestion that fresh blood would be welcomed and had been missed. It reflected in his eyes. Just a memory, Federi, just a memory!

"Vostovic," yowled the hound. "*Sunt* Vostovic!"

Federi stared at the creature's eyes, trying to rationalize what he saw.

So: Vostovic. You have a human name. And you're not like that… measly pack of Vlad's, over there on Shrn. You're uniformed. You're in cahoots with the freaking Unicate. He stared deeply into the shape-shifter's eyes. Not a very good shifter. Unicate *Other*.

Trying to understand this. Shrn's wild hounds had nothing to do with these – as little as humans had to do with the *Others*. Shrn's hounds were basic predators, probably with a bit of intelligence. These here were… hybrids of a sort. Unicate creations. They obeyed orders, clearly: They had his name programmed into their psyche. But they had certainly also inherited the shifter cowardice of their Shrn ancestry.

It must be easy to be a coward if all you had to do was shift into another shape. Nothing could defy you, everything was terrified of you. Yes. It must not need great reserves of courage for that style of hunting. Until suddenly, one day, you met a quarry who turned around and terrified you.

So what had made the Unicate pick such a whining, cowering species for their basic fighter material? Why not clone something more forceful? Horses for courses, he thought. It didn't take much to intimidate a gypsy. Inwardly he cringed in embarrassment for his people. Running and hiding. The basic survival kit of the meek, the peace-loving.

They would not have got it right in Southern Free! And to shape the boy Federi into the man, the Assassin, had taken terror and hardship, and sharp training by *gadje* assassins and mentors. It had taken surviving the hounds, and surviving Southern Free's sharp customs. There was no time to shape his gypsies into people who'd shoot first and run second. But he supposed, giving them guns was a good start.

The hound was whimpering like a puppy in his grip. He realized that the Stiletto was pressing into the soft of the thing's throat, threatening to prick the skin any moment now.

Ha! And that jackal would be whining much louder in a second! He whapped the flat side of his blade across the hound's nose once more. It left a shallow double cut and drew a yap of pain.

"So, Vostovic!" he ordered. "Go back to Shrn. Spread the word that Federi Demonos is alive, and is coming for all of you! I'll cut you into small strips! You'll be enchiladas! You've savaged your last gypsies."

"*Milă,*" yelped the dog.

164

Something in Federi snapped. *Milă?* – Mercy? Had they shown the gypsies any mercy? With supreme self-control he stopped himself from cutting the dog down right on the spot. He fairly shoved it away.

"Run, you jackal," he yelled after it. "Run, or you'll be goulash! Hot goulash!"

A portal opened and absorbed the hound. Federi chased after it, to make sure that the portal had once again been deleted. No others came storming. He shouted his own name, over and over, shaking in rage. No hounds came investigating. Not even a wet nose peeped out of a portal anywhere.

"*I'm* the top predator around here," he yelled at them, irrationally angry. "*I'm* in charge of Earth's food chain! You'll wish you'd never met me! I'll clean you off *both* planets!" And he fell silent. He realized that he was shivering violently where he stood in the new snow.

Almeira approached with a warm Tzigan mantle for him, and led him back to the tribe.

*

Paean trailed through the little house, trying to find any kind of evidence of what might have happened. And she did find it, in the bedroom; but it only hit her after a while.

She found her old wrist-com lying on the bedside table. But more tellingly, the bed was unmade. This was very untypical of her old teacher who was a neatnick despite being a hoarder. Everything she hoarded had to be exactly in its correct spot, and was looked after flawlessly. To have an unmade bed – could only mean that she had been surprised by something in the middle of the night.

That left too many options, especially with the closed time portal.

165

Paean went back to the Victorian painting, and ran her fingers over the wall where the door had always been… and found a slight elevation of the wallpaper. She took out her small pocket knife and peeled the wallpaper away, and found a button, and pushed it…

Electricity fizzled across the painting. And a hologram sprang to life over it, showing the scene from outside the front door; Mrs Flanagan in slippers and her nightgown, at the door, talking to someone who was behind the camera; a blinding flash as she reached for the study door, and the door disappearing; and then, the old lady meekly following the invisible person outside.

Paean shivered. Her worst fear had been confirmed. The Unicate had come for Mrs Flanagan.

There was a sudden commotion out in the street. Paean lifted the curtain cautiously and peered out of the window. There was a truck parked across the road. Some of the neighbours were arguing loudly with a young Unicate official who was trying to convince them to get into the back of the truck.

Paean left Mrs Flanagan's house and moved towards the vehicle, using the Tzigan invisibility Federi had taught her: To appear so unimportant as to escape notice. As she approached, she heard phrases like "for your own good" and "relocation to a better place".

She hadn't met these neighbours yet. Clearly the neighbourhood, which had been static from the time she was little, had changed drastically in these past nine months. But they looked like Molly Streeters alright – albeit Molly Streeters without Paean's loving guidance. Their clothes were tattier and they didn't have that defiant air of poverty pride that Mother had taught everyone. But they had to have met Mrs Flanagan!

"'scuse me," said the redhead, barging in on the heated argument.

The young Unicate official turned and stared at her. Clearly surprised that here was someone audacious enough to interrupt a

Unicate officer. Not scared anymore, thought Paean with a vicious smile, her left hand wandering into her pocket. Dart gun, teleporter, Paean Special. All in place. And of course her wrist-com was a new teleporter.

She ignored the young officer's demand for identification and turned to the family. The mother, run-down and slightly rounded, defensively clutching a baby to her. Dark hair showing a few grey threads although she couldn't be past her twenties yet. Paean summarized. Four children. Yup, anyone who had more than one ended in Molly Street, she supposed.

"I used to live here," she said, touching the baby that stared at her with frightened eyes. "I'm Paean. You people have any idea what's become of Mrs Flanagan?"

"She was evicted," said a boy, who looked about ten.

Paean stared at him, shocked. "Evicted? When?"

"Two nights back," said the boy. "Kaitlin saw it."

So the Unicate had come for Mrs Flanagan, two weeks after she and Federi had left havoc behind in Dublin. She'd been on honeymoon, enjoying herself, never sparing a thought...

"She was evicted for owing several months' rent," confirmed the Unicate official scathingly. "Terence O'Lynn took the call. Said he found her rather amiable and cooperative. Terence is soft where that is concerned. Sweet spot for the underdog. Loser in the making, if you ask me." He scowled at her. "And I've asked you for identification, beggar!"

Paean eyed him with distaste. "Mrs Flanagan was always up to date with all her accounts," she replied scathingly. "It's a foul excuse and you know it! And I'm Paean Demonos."

She watched with satisfaction as a ripple of unease went through the young officer at that name. She literally watched him piece it together. Demonos – a name that boded bad luck for the Unicate.

But – Paean? It didn't work. The Demon was male, and had some weird gypsy name. The girl had to be bluffing – but she knew too much. Paean got a very small, satisfied curl in the corner of her mouth for the effect she was having.

Was he an *Other*? No – not this one, she thought, he came across more – a bit like Johnny Anyhow, or possibly even Ronan; but with a huge load of bully in him. The narrow escape from poverty was still written all over him, in his immaculately polished uniform and the patronizing attitude over this family here; and the scantily concealed pain at being in such surrounds.

That Unicate official had said that Mrs Flanagan had been compliant. That meant that they had indeed evicted her. At least she wasn't locked into her own study, without food or water or a hope that anyone could save her. And better: This young fiend knew where she was!

Paean reached out to the frantic young mother.

"Trust me," she mouthed. "Calm them down, it will be okay. I used to live here." She turned to the official. "Let me go along," she demanded. "I'm from this neighbourhood. I just want to help them get settled in."

"Then come, Paean Demonos," said the official with a sudden evil grin.

Paean flashed him a defiant smile and climbed into the back of the truck, calling the toddler and the five-year-old to her and beginning to tell them a story.

~

The truck rattled along the pot-holed Irish highway. There was very little light here in the back; basically what came in through the crack above the door and a few rusted holes around bolts that had got tired. The baby and the toddler had fallen asleep. The young mother had introduced herself as Cora Murphy, and her children as Séamus,

168

Skye, Aine and Siobhan. Mr Murphy was a no-go topic; Paean knew too well about that.

Now that the smaller ones were asleep, Paean told Cora parts of her own story, as briefly as possible. And then she leaned forward and explained her plan to Cora, in a hushed voice. The young mother agreed instantly, snatching with both hands at any plan to escape the Unicate.

Paean turned and trained her teleporter, through the metal of the truck's loading chamber and the glass of the cabin, on the genetic signature of the Unicate official and stored it. She wanted to go wherever this truck was going! Then she told the two older children to hang tightly onto their mother. The baby was already in Cora's arms; and little Siobhan, the two-year-old, was asleep on Paean's lap, which was just as well. Paean included them all into the teleporter field and vaulted with them up to the Space Base. Bringing Itzak refugees.

*

"Whoa!" The truck nearly went off the road. Patrick steadied it just in time. "How the hell did you get in here?"

The girl smiled. "Once again, I'm Paean Donegal," she said and extended a hand. "And you are?"

"Patrick," he said, confused. "How did you do that?"

"I'm a ghost," she said with a grin.

Oh no, she was not! Patrick didn't believe in ghosts. But she might be one of those uncanny ones that ran around in the Mounds… he studied her critically, then scarcely prevented the truck from derailing again. No, she wasn't one of *those*. There was none of that weirdness in her eyes.

"If you are planning to do that a lot, maybe I should drive?"

volunteered the girl.

"You are one cheeky girl," commented Patrick.

"So where are we going?" she asked.

"Who did you say you are?" he asked sharply.

"Paean Demonos," she said.

"You said, Paean Donegal!"

"My maiden name," smiled Paean. It was time to scare the Unicate.

Patrick peered sharply at her, for a good few moments. The truck started veering again. He pulled it straight in the nick of time. Paean's hand was on her teleporter, ready to activate it. Of all Unicate dangers, being in a motor accident was not one she'd considered.

Paean Donegal, thought Patrick. The names of the Donegal children were emblazoned in fire across all Unicate trainees' minds, in the first two sessions. Top priority; these three must be found, and brought in. And the name Demonos was up there in another file, also as a red alert. There was only one Demonos – nobody else kept such a vile name. Besides the Donegals, Federi Demonos was the only other case of such an escape, a dangerous enemy who had got away. The case file was much older, but never had been closed; and recently, the name had thundered through all alert systems, various times. The latest was not two weeks in the past. Federi Demonos was most definitely alive, and was actively triggering the system.

"So you are married to…?" he asked.

"Federi Demonos," said Paean with a cheeky grin and her hand still on the teleporter, watching how electric fright zipped across Patrick like a whip. He got a wild look and glanced about fearfully. Oh yes, he knew about the Romanian hounds!

She waited for them. She'd teleport out. He was Unicate and had been on the point of taking a whole family to headquarters; he deserved his fate. But the hounds didn't arrive. This puzzled her quite a bit. It took Patrick a good few minutes of clenched jaws and sweat beading on his freckled forehead, to relax into the knowledge that the hounds were not coming.

"Don't say that name!" he commanded angrily.

"What, the name of my husband? Federi Demonos?" she teased, watching his tension and anger build. "You'd not say that if you knew him. He's actually a very nice guy."

Paean Donegal and Federi Demonos, married! Perhaps she was lying about that, but there was no doubt she knew him. It was in her voice. What a union – made straight in hell!

But, what a find for him! Patrick wasn't a good poker player. He started smiling.

"And you love him very much?" he probed.

The girl looked out of the window. Aha.

Yes, it was definitely his lucky day. All he had to do, was take her to his commander… he started considering what he'd do with the reward money.

"So what's the idea, evicting Molly Streeters?" asked Paean idly.

"You were a Molly Streeter, weren't you?" he asked back with a cold smile.

"Indeed. Why do you evict them? You know very well their rent is all up to date, and if it weren't, it would only be the problem of the landlords."

"The landlords are the Unicate," said Patrick. "I'm working towards a cleaner world."

Paean studied his face which had acquired a fanatical glow. He was not a Unicate *Other*. What was he doing, working for them?

"You see, Paean Donegal," he said, "the ideal population size for this planet is half a billion. The Unicate has already been highly efficient decimating the population back down to two billion. But there are still too many useless poor around!"

"Useless poor," echoed Paean, astounded.

"You are where you put yourself in life," he explained. "It's only rational. You go and have seven children, you'll be poor, and you'll be useless to society because you'll be so busy raising them that you can't do any normal job anymore."

Federi, my love, thought Paean, we'll have seven children. I don't want a normal job.

"So the jobs you do to feed your children aren't useful?" she asked. "And what about the jobs the children do?"

"Once they are old enough," said Patrick. "They'll be under-educated because they have to go straight to work, they can't carry on with school to the degree of education that would be a boon to society."

There was something weird about that logic. On the surface one could nearly think he made sense. But…

"And wouldn't it help to fix the schools instead, and educate the children while they are small?" she prompted.

"Poor children are no good with that," replied Patrick. "They're stupid to begin with. It's genetics. Their parents were stupid."

"Ah," said Paean, "so that is genetics?"

"That is genetics," said Patrick reverently, the shine of zeal all over his face.

"And so the children of the poor – they work in factories, and they learn how to fix machinery, and how to wash floors?"

"Exactly so," he agreed.

"And these jobs are useless?"

"Drones could do them," he said.

Except that there were no drones, thought Paean. There had been, before the Unicate came. She'd read about it in the Sherman files; so much had been roboticized that was now done by hand again.

She thought of poor Ronan, and what his options would have been. It had worried her, back then. Ha! Luckily Ronan had fallen into the butter, because all the opportunities he wouldn't have had by remaining in Dublin had been opened for him by Captain. Because Captain could spot a bright light when he saw one.

"And are there no other jobs open for them? The military? The Unicate police force?" she prodded, trying to imagine what Ronan would have tried if things had run differently. "Marines?" He had been eyeing the marine as a career choice.

The look she earned for that was pure hatred.

"A lot of rabble gets into such positions these days," he spat. "It's disgusting."

"So I take it you're from a wealthy background," she said with a sarcastic little smile in the corner of her mouth. "Then why are you doing the Unicate's dirty work?"

The truck screeched to a halt as Patrick hit those brakes.

"I don't hit girls," he snapped. "But I could kill you for this!"

Out of context, Paean thought of the Pendle witch hunts. This was religious zeal. Fanaticism. It wasn't aimed at purported witch-women; it was based on another superstition entirely.

"Patrick," she said, "The American president Abraham Lincoln was from a super-poor background. So were several of the greatest lights of Europe. Money gets used to control people's lives, but it doesn't control their spirit."

The truck rolled back onto the road and continued its way.

"That's the kind of soggy mish-mash they feed people so that it sounds politically correct," said Patrick. "Look at statistics. The problem is always the poor. They are a drain on resources."

"You still sending money home to your mother?" she asked.

Patrick glared at her. "I've stopped that long ago. She's made

173

her bed. Must lie in it now."

"And she lives in Molly Street?"

"Don't be ridiculous," he snapped. "If she lived in Molly Street, I wouldn't have been eligible to do this work."

"There are many places that are poorer than Molly Street," mentioned Paean. "Do you service them all?"

Patrick clamped his jaw shut and drove. She could nearly hear his thoughts. He was taking her to headquarters. No point in arguing with her.

"You've been a bad son, you know," said Paean, her voice low and far-away. She saw a shiver going through Patrick and realized that she'd sounded just like a Manya.

"You be quiet," he said, but he sounded afraid.

~

The truck rattled on, over country road. Patrick was quiet, battling with his own demons. This witch-like girl was right. He'd betrayed his own family. They were poor; they were filth. His mother had more children than was healthy for any woman. And she poured love on all of them equally, which meant that there was precious little love for each one of them. In the tiny bit of time she had with them, when she wasn't working herself to a standstill in the factory, and it was never enough – never enough. Seven children ate a lot. Which was why he'd taken the best job he could, as soon as he could. It had been pure luck, and incidental connections, that had landed him the job with the Irish Rationalists. At first it had been great, being able to send all that money home and allowing his mother to finally buy some first-hand clothes for his youngest sister, and an extra year at school for his nearest brother, the third oldest. And he, the second, had managed to pride himself a breadwinner. His oldest sister was lost – she'd already opened her legs for some useless bum who had some or other menial job at the docks, and so her life path was predestined. Bairns one and two were already there, and three was on its way. The misery perpetuated.

He had coached and guided his younger siblings, imprinting on them not to have children. The family had to get out of the mire first! Ha, he'd still believed that they could! And if other impoverished families had to be sacrificed to the Unicate to help his own move up, well, too bad for them.

But when his next sister, his favourite sister, had also fallen for the mud of the slums and some beggar boy of a clerk-in-training, he'd given the cause up for lost. He blamed his mother. Seven was too many. How could she have been so stupid?

And so he'd abandoned them all to their fate. The IRP was right. Poor people were what caused the problem on this planet. With fewer of them around, there'd be more resources and less misery for everyone.

"Why?" asked Paean.

He blinked. "Why what?" He hadn't said anything! Was this Paean Donegal, the one the Unicate feared so much, really that powerful that she could read minds? He eyed her uneasily as the truck cut through the slashing rain and sleet. A few poor trees were huddling in groups next to the soaked country road.

"Why are we going to Limerick?"

Had he said Limerick? How did she know?

"Those road signs," she pointed out with a smile.

Oh. Rationalist, Patrick, he called his own thoughts to order. There was no such thing as a mind-reading witch.

"We're basically going to Limerick because that's where the IRP's headquarters are. We operate from there."

"The IRP?"

She was going to die. He might as well tell her.

"The IRP is the Irish Rationalist Power. You as an Irishwoman ought to be a proud member of that party. We are what keeps the country sane. We see to it that poverty is kept in limits."

"I see," she said. As though she really saw. Her voice had that hollow, echoing quality. For a second he thought that he could see, too, what she saw. See clearly.

"That's not the headquarters," she said. "The mound."

"No."

"Oh." She glanced outside. Something like a flame streaked alongside the truck for a second and was gone again. Trick o' the light. "I think I might be on the wrong truck then," she said.

Patrick grinned. Oh no, she was on the right truck!

"Don't worry, love," he said sarcastically. "You're exactly where you are supposed to be. And you will see the inside of a mound, fret not. All will happen in its own good time."

*

Federi sat at the fire, huddled in the grey gypsy mantle that had belonged to Jehan's uncle, and carved patiently at a piece of leather.

Machinegun fire killed those dogs. But it didn't intimidate them – maybe because they had no concept of death. He needed something more vicious, and less lethal, so that they could get away and spread the word. To injure, but not to kill. The idea of having their tails cut off had frightened them – much worse than being mown down by Ailyss' gunfire, collectively.

Besides, he had a dual problem. The hounds of Shrn were not his fry. They had nothing much to do with him. Yes, sure, they sortied out on hunting parties and set traps for humans and probably, other Earth animals – and had probably, since the dawn of time. One more wild predatory species. Who cared? He needed them to fear humans and stay away. It wasn't in him as a Tzigan to destroy a whole

176

species.

But the Unicate dogs were a different story. Them he was going to erase. They were unnatural to begin with. They were some sort of foul hybrid, and he had no idea what the Unicate had done to create them. For that, he needed to find their source, and attack them at it, to finish them off.

But first he needed space. They too had to fear him. He couldn't risk them coming pouring in their huge numbers when he was off guard. This was an ever-present risk here in Romania, and a risk anywhere in the world whenever someone got it into their heads to shout his full name. The Unicate had installed some or other trigger based on the sound signature of those two words. The trigger was everywhere. He'd avoided it in Southern Free by using a pseudonym, Shadow. Even the name Federi was not to be spoken there.

And so he was preparing himself a weapon for this. The neosilk ropes didn't have enough weight to fulfil this function; not even if he attached scalpel blades to their tips, like he was doing with the leather strips. He was creating a whip; a vicious one with several long leads. A cat-o-nine-tails, of sorts. With a long reach – about two metres. And with those razor-sharp little blades on the tips, as improvements. An assassin's cat. He was grinning grimly to himself. A cat to discipline dogs.

Those blasted dogs didn't understand death. But they did understand pain!

And if by chance that accursed Morrigan was still alive and dared to step out of line aboard the Solar Wind, it too would feel the whip's bite!

He didn't realize how his face had changed; how little was left of Federi the entertainer of youngsters, the babysitter of princesses, the hopelessly smitten slave of one young redhead. His features

177

were sharp now, angular, merciless; his teeth grinding without him realizing.

The Unicate had tangled with Falco. Now they were getting Federi as punishment.

12 – Terence

"And what is that?" challenged Doc Judith.

As per Federi's instructions, Wolf poured the Morrigan's body into a bucket and placed it on the deck in the infirmary.

"The Morrigan," he said.

The console screen for the vital signs monitor sprang into life.

You brought him to me? I could kiss you! wrote the Solar Wind.

Wolf glanced, and chuckled. "I doubt you could," he commented. "Welcome back, old ship."

But he doesn't look alive, said the ship.

Perdita chose that moment to check into the infirmary.

"Shawn and Mindy are safely stashed," she reported to nobody in particular. And glanced at the puddle of dead liquid lightning. "What! You must be joking!"

"Was Federi's idea," said Ailyss, who was checking Federi's parka for any residual sticky carbon.

"Actually it was yours," Wolf pointed out. "Federi went along with it. Wonder what's with him, he doesn't seem very decisive today."

"I can't be aboard for long," said Perdita and teleported out.

Wolf glanced at Ailyss.

"She's skittish these days," he observed.

"Ever since the rescue of the Walrus," said Ailyss. "As though she wants to avoid being aboard at all. It's odd."

Wolf and Ailyss checked that the Morrigan-puddle looked stable, and then left Doc in charge.

"They bring you aboard," said Doc Judith to her probably dead alien patient. "And I have to decide what to do with you?" She tried connecting vital signs monitors; but there was nothing to connect to, and certainly no trace of any vital signs.

That lot of protoplasm would start stinking, she realized. Like a dead, metre-large oyster. But… first she should keep it in here to pacify Wolf and Ailyss, and potentially Federi if he decided to stop in.

It was Christmas Eve. Captain was going to call back – or fetch back, if he had to – Federi from the gypsies any moment now.

She left the infirmary with a sigh. There was nothing she could do for the dead alien.

*

Perdita directed the Probe to Pluto Base once more. She had escorted Shawn and Mindy to the base without their knowledge; then she had revealed herself and piloted them to New Dome by Interstellar Leapfrog. She had negotiated with her sister-dearest, whom pregnancy and attachment to Johnny seemed to make slightly soggy. It suited Perdita; it made Dana easier to influence. So Shawn and Mindy had been allowed to move into two rooms at the palace for the time being, instead of being forced to take up residence with Uncle Séamus and his horrible wife. Mindy was in extreme pain a lot of the time; so Dana's personal medic, Aoiffe, had been called in to see what she could do.

As a matter of fact, backs weren't any closer to being fixed on New Dome than on Earth. In fact that solution with the bridge was the best they had seen so far. Backs didn't readily get broken on New Dome, with its peaceful citizens and their sedate lifestyles. And in any case Danaan women had slightly more flexibility than on Earth…

181

She had turned around and fetched the Comet back from Pluto Base and tugged it back to Earth. The youngest Donegal was a pirate too, she decided. To commandeer his sister's essential jet without a backward glance…

Pluto warped into view. Perdita docked the Probe and availed herself of an Interstellar Leapfrog again. That old magic was kicking in again: She didn't have to prove authority, merely be herself. They all respected her.

She had to hand it to Federi. The man was brilliant. Retrieving the Morrigan and sending it back to the Solar Wind – in severely disabled format! The teeth of that old villain had been pulled. But if the alien should recover to a point, it could be useful – for opening portals and various other things. And if it never did recover, if it had indeed died – at least the Solar Wind had started talking again.

She scowled. The blasted Solar Wind had talked, anyway! She had been the one to alert Shawn and Mindy to the situation with Peter Piper. Mindy had made it quite plain that she wasn't mourning that particular Walrus survivor – she mainly recalled how he'd always leered at her when he thought nobody was looking.

*

The truck rattled over bumps in the road, rain seeping down incessantly. Icy rain, as befitted this time of year. Paean scowled. It was Christmas Eve, here in Ireland. She refused to think back to last year; instead she simply absorbed the impressions, as one who now stood outside of that tradition, by means of her family having fallen apart.

Apart? Oh for wailing! She snorted in disgust at her own stint at self-pity. It had not fallen apart! She and Ronan had grown up, married; and they were both looking after Shawn, and all three had

182

found the Solar Wind family.

The truck drew up in front of a grey office building.

"Say thank you," said Patrick as he cut the engine.

"Why?"

"I brought you straight here without first having fun with you."

"Pig!" she exclaimed, incensed. And didn't manage to prevent in time that Patrick clipped handcuffs around her wrists. He did it so fast and so deftly, she realized he had a lot of practice. And she – was out of practice. She'd had such a wonderful, relaxed holiday with Federi that she had lost touch with reality. She thought of him with longing and a bit of desperation. Handcuffs made her feel vulnerable.

Patrick stripped off her wrist-com – the new one with the teleporter. That was when she started panicking. Her whole plan hinged on the teleporter! Could she reach her other teleporter, the older one in her pocket? Not without drawing attention, and it would cost a struggle.

Patrick marched her around to the back of the truck, and opened its hold. And gaped in shock.

While he investigated the case of the missing hostages, Paean tried to reach for her pocket. She found that she couldn't. Not quite. It would take a spectacular twist, and a grab that would most certainly draw Patrick's attention... and if she was too slow and he took the teleporter away from her, she was really marooned.

Nor could she get to any of her guns. The best she could do... there were tricks on her headscarf, that she had put on this morning, before calling Shawn and leaving the gypsies. She searched for her lock-pick, and located it, and a small bead which she detached from the scarf, and then Patrick was confronting her and she very quickly had to hide her tricks in her hands.

"What have you done with them, witch?" he accosted her.

"Nothing," lied Paean. "What do you think? How, would you suggest, should I have got a whole family of people out of the locked trunk of a moving truck?"

Patrick glared at her. She knew that he knew that she was at the root of the disappearances; but he couldn't prove it, couldn't even figure out how she'd done it, so that was that.

"Come," he ordered brusquely.

She bit down an ironic smile as he shoved her roughly towards that dark entrance. She was in a much worse position than she had planned – and it was her own fault. How was she going to negotiate this one?

Inside, there were long passages leading away and down. Paean knew, as many did, that the Unicate liked their offices and headquarters underground. She also knew, as most didn't, that it presented part of the mystery of those Unicate *Others*, and that she and Federi would have to get into some of those mounds sooner or later. The thought was a bit freaky; but right now she was not inside one. This was simply an office building.

Patrick led her to one of the offices, and knocked on the door, and entered after they heard a grumpy sound from inside.

"Commander Bryce, Patrick Calahan reporting back!"

"Are you bringing the fresh material?" asked Commander Bryce. "Where are they?"

"No, Commander. I bring you Paean Donegal."

There was a frozen silence as the commander studied Paean sceptically.

"Paean Donegal from Molly Street? We've been scouring for her for months now! You sure this is her?"

"She admits that she is," said Patrick with a sly smile, keeping the rest of his trumps close. "Commander, we can check it on the system."

184

Bryce hacked a few fast codes into the console. And he stared at the photo of the Donegal Troubles, taken at a gig, and at Paean's face. The girl looked older, more mature, slightly gaunt… but yes, it was certainly the same face!

Bryce grabbed her roughly by her handcuffed wrist and yanked her forward towards the touchpad of his console. And he forcefully opened her right hand. She counted her lucky stars that she was hiding the tricks in the left hand; and then, as he placed her hand on that touchpad, she felt the needle-prick and inhaled sharply.

Was she being drugged? But by all looks of things, her DNA was merely sampled and fed into the system. It came up with a perfect match of the DNA taken at her birth – like all babies that were born in a clinic.

"It's definitely her," confirmed Bryce, calm and businesslike just as Patrick was starting to look very excited.

"That's not all," said Patrick gleefully. "What did you say your married name is, girl?"

Paean clamped her mouth shut. Her teleporter was out of reach, as was most of her artillery. Her hands were chained in front of her; if she tried picking the locks they'd see her.

"She said," Patrick completed for her, "she's married to Federi Demonos."

Bryce's scalp prickled.

"You don't speak that name, imbecile," he warned. "You know what happens when people do!" And he reached nervously for the gun in his belt. Patrick lost his self-assuredness and ripped out his own gun, too, waiting.

For several moments, nothing happened. He relaxed a little. Bryce snorted.

"Patrick, you have Paean Donegal there. Everything else is unconfirmed!"

185

"Yes, sir!" Patrick cleared his throat. "So by when can I expect the reward?"

"I'll give you your reward," said Bryce and lifted his gun.

Paean smashed the prototype bead to the ground with all her force. Her lockpick slipped out of her hands in the process, as there was a blinding flash of light, and a crack like an explosion; but in the five seconds Bryce's eyes took to recover from the flash, she had managed to twist far enough to grab hold of her teleporter, include Patrick in the field, and teleport. Not fast enough; the shot reverberated...

~

"What on Earth, Paean?"

Doc Judith watched how Paean bullied the still shape of a young Unicate officer onto the prow-side infirmary bunk with her hands cuffed.

"Don't ask, Doc," replied Paean flatly. "Brought a replacement for Peter Piper."

Doc Judith took a closer look. "Good heavens!"

The bullet stuck in the bone of Patrick's forehead. The teleportation had stopped it from penetrating; nevertheless the young man was out cold.

Paean held up her handcuffed hands, with a plaintive look at the Doc.

"Oh Paean! What did you get yourself into? I thought you were sleeping! You're not even supposed to teleport!"

"But Doc, they've abducted Mrs Flanagan!"

Doc Judith scowled and gestured to Paean to follow. She led the way to the machineroom and dug in one of the cabinets.

"I remember it was here somewhere..." She fished a small apparatus out of the cabinets and attached it to Paean's left handcuff, and activated it. There was a wheezing noise, and a pop, and the handcuff jumped open. Doc Judith broke the lock on the other side, too. Paean took the broken handcuffs off and put them down.

"Don't get caught again," warned Doc Judith. "Don't take such risks!"

"Okay, Doc," said Paean. She went back to the infirmary, retrieved her new wrist-teleporter out of Patrick's pocket, armed herself with some essentials and reversed her last leap.

*

"Paean Donegal!" exclaimed the Captain, the second time today. "What on Earth have you brought me now?"

Paean dropped the unconscious Bryce at Captain's feet, via teleporter. She looked up at her Captain with puppy-dog eyes.

"IRP," she said. "He's a Unicate-dealing hypocrite. He's the one behind the disappearances from Molly Street."

"One of those *Others* Ailyss and Jon speak about?"

She shook her head. "No, this one's human, Captain. Don't ask me. I'd vote for insanity."

"IRP!" repeated Lascek with a frown. And he keyed the abbreviation into the console.

"Thanks, Captain," trilled Paean and teleported out.

"Paean!" called Lascek, but then his attention was absorbed by this IRP. It was amazing. The girl herself was leading him closer to unravelling the mystery surrounding her story.

She should not teleport so much! But he'd chained her up for it – and it had very nearly cost him two key crewmembers. Hopefully she had by now recovered; hopefully her and Federi's honeymoon had been enough time out that they could return to the ship. If not, he'd have to give them a bit more time, that was all. And he needed to tread lightly with her while she thought she was not on the crew.

All he could hope was that Wolf was making inroads with his research and development on the teleporters.

*

Perdita teleported into the infirmary, and shot the golden bullet into the hide of that heap of protoplasm in the bucket.

It couldn't harm. You never knew if it could help. Blackmailing it out of Dana had been dead easy – the raider was distracted.

And then Perdita spotted Patrick, on the life support apparatus, and bent over his face to have a closer look.

"My word!" She felt his throat for a pulse. The pulse was still there. But it was a matter of time, the chances of him surviving that...

Golden bullets wouldn't help, in his case. Not that she was about to waste any on an unknown in a Unicate uniform. She teleported back out and turned the Probe back towards Calypso.

Captain – Radomir – had said that everyone should be aboard tonight, as he wanted to light a Christmas tree, like the olden-day navies had done. She wondered what good it should do. Such niceties had never been part of the Sancho household; large winnings or pickings off raided ships had usually been celebrated with a huge drinking and drug party, and its inevitable wake. She had hidden during such times. The same had gone for birthdays, especially the birthday of the old man, and as time went by, the oldest son's too. The women had never celebrated their birthdays. Women, in the Sancho household, had merely been slaves.

But – Christmas? She didn't get it.

And then she smiled. The chances were that Captain was trying to establish a culture of civilization between all the mad scrambling for survival and politicking. It also tied in with the Ceilidhs. He probably had the right idea. What differentiated humans and made them human.

*

Jehan came to sit down next to Federi.

"Your wife has left," he commented.

Federi nodded grimly without looking up from fashioning his cat. "Captain's orders. It is Christmas Eve. He ordered us to be back aboard today."

Jehan nodded too. "You don't worry when she leaves you like this?"

"She doesn't leave me," said Federi. "No. I'm not worried. She's safe on the Solar Wind. I'm worried how to keep the stuff away from you people that I'm about to call. Jehan, I need you to round up all the men, pick up the machineguns I've organized you, and follow me." He stood up. The Cat-o'-Nine-Blades was ready.

"What's the plan, Federi?"

"A bloodbath," said Federi. "But not human blood. Not this time!"

He waited for Jehan to call the men together and get them armed. They had all faithfully taken lessons with him, in self-defence, guns, and not hesitating. It would be alright.

He led the four down the slope, well away from the camp, towards a small clearing in the forest. He stationed them in strategic positions, up in the trees, in a circle around the clearing. And then he put himself in the middle of that space, planted his feet firmly apart, shook back his mane, took a deep breath – and called the Unicate hounds.

They took even longer to respond than back at Cassandra; but eventually they did come. And they descended, as was their habit, in

189

a pack out of portals surrounding him.

The Cat danced into action. In his left hand Federi had the singing Stiletto, spinning in lightning colours. None of the hounds dared approach him from the left. But they got an immense talking-to by the Cat as they tried to get inside that circle of dancing scalpel blades around the Assassin.

Federi laughed as some of the hounds tucked their tails in and fled. And one dared approach him from the left.

The Cat whipped around that hound's neck, switching hands with the Stiletto in a flash. Federi pulled the hound closer.

The Unicate variety of Shrn's hounds looked more like a human and less like a beast. Federi stared at the thing's eyes and recognized another one of *those*. His conjectures seemed to be gaining weight.

"Haven't yet had enough?" he asked. "Still want to play?"

The dog-man-creature yelped.

*

Paean touch-activated the console in the IRP man's office. It was on voice-command.

"Molly Street," she put in. A directory of files sprang up, giving her choices. She paged through, trying to find one that made sense. Eventually she found a list of evicted families. She activated "search" and asked for "Mrs Flanagan". And became aware of a searching gaze from the open door.

She glanced up.

A young Unicate *Other* stood in the doorway, studying her. She iced and ripped out her gun, and looked again at his face. A gentle, almost bland face; by every other circumstance a nice young man, but he was an *Other*.

"Hello," he said quietly, and held out a hand to her the way one charms a wary stray cat, "I was hoping I could get to meet you."

"Many hope for that," she replied brusquely, then started feeling stupid for being so aggressive. She lowered her gun.

"I'm Terence," said the man. "And I know who you are, and I will not speak your full name in here, because it triggers the system. Will you walk with me?"

"Where to?" she asked warily.

"To a place that is less observed," said Terence. "I want to discuss a truce." He smiled. "Parley, I believe you pirates call it?"

Paean had to smile. She got up and followed Terence the Unicate *Other* out of the office building.

The Unicate headquarters were odd. There was absolutely no indication that they were anything other than offices, albeit underground. She had somehow expected – more. Something more sinister.

Terence walked with her to where the road came to a T-junction, and picked a table for two at the roadside café that had made its nest there. He hailed a waitress and ordered cappuccino for Paean, and tea for himself.

"Tea?" The redhead pulled a face.

"I like tea," replied Terence with a smile. His light-blue eyes with the *otherness* in them could have been sweet but for that alien element. "It's the Brit in me."

"You're British?" She blinked. Smoke and mirrors! The man was an *Other* – did he think she couldn't spot that?

"My genes are British-derived," he said. "Paean, you are looking for answers. And you are feeling lost, and alone. Your brothers have left you to sort it on your own. Your husband – whom you adore, I know – he is on his own mission. When is he not? You are tired of fighting and it is Christmas Eve, something that means a lot to you. You are longing to return to a year back, or better, two years back,

191

when everything was still fine..."

"Terence," said Paean pointedly, "that tack doesna work with me. I'm my own best psychologist, thank you. So let's cut the Sanskrit, shall we? Why do you want to talk to me?"

"Because I want answers too," said Terence. The order arrived, and he watched as Paean accepted her cappuccino and took a careful sip, half-closing her eyes.

"You want answers," she said with a nod. "That's rich! You hold all the answers I'm looking for, Terence. What answers could the Unicate possibly want?"

There were fine goose-bumps crawling up and down her arms. Here she was, parlaying with a Unicate *Other* instead of shooting at him. She had to be so careful now. But in a certain way he was dead right – she was alone in this. Federi was messing with the Morrigan and other stuff. And Romanian hounds – which Terence was not, or she could call herself Paean Dee no longer! – the Romanian hounds were a huge mystery. They didn't have anything to do with the blasted Unicate – but then why had they hunted and killed Federi's family? Those dogs from Shrn were simply a predatory alien species. She'd be extremely surprised if she found Vlad's dogs being political. They were too primitive. But then what were some of them doing in uniform?

Captain should probably be dealing with Terence instead of her. That was it, she decided. She'd bring him to Captain. There was nothing that indicated that Unicate could teleport. On the contrary; if they could, the Donegals would never have escaped.

But first she had a load of questions. She studied his face – open, honest, young... those eyes with their *otherness* that had nevertheless seen too much, that slightly haunted look, a bit like that Johnsson guy who had died at the Ice Base...

"Terence," she said, "what is it that a Unicate *Other* would possibly want to know from a mere human?"

"Mere human," he echoed her with a cynical little smile. "Paean, you short-change yourself, and all of humankind. Humans are not 'merely' human. They are, like other dominant species, highly versatile, an absolute biological wonder. And then, besides that, it is on record that you yourself, and your brothers, are more than human... you are Founders."

"Ha," pounced Paean, "and could you please enlighten me to what you mean by that?"

Terence smiled and took a sip of his tea. "I really have no information at all. Founder lore isn't documented anywhere. Legends are all we can go on. And the legends are vague, and contradictory. But let's take this step-wise. I have a deal to suggest to you."

"A deal?" pushed Paean. This was highly unusual. Why would a Unicate *Other* want to deal with a human?

"Yes," said Terence. "You won't believe how limiting it is to grow up in the Mound, and then as a male! My life's path is laid out, when I feel I could be so much more if I could have your kind of freedom. So I propose the following. I know where Mrs Flanagan is."

Paean grabbed his hands. "You know? You could take me to her? You could help me rescue her? ...She's alive?"

Terence nodded, and smiled. "Positive to all that. Paean, I was in fact the one they sent to collect her. I'm so tired of doing such things... the poor old lady! She was very compliant, and I tried to be very pleasant while taking her to Head Office, if that helps you at all. I tried to prepare her nicely, but I have to warn you, Paean, they will have traumatized her. With luck, if she was compliant with them too, it may only be emotional trauma, and you may find someone who can help her deal with it."

193

Paean nodded. "Doc Judith," she made a mental note.

"In exchange," said Terence, "you take me to your Captain Lascek and explain to him that I would like to have a chance to be part of his crew."

Paean sat back and stared into vacant space. This was a lot.

He was a defector. From the Mound. And he'd grown up in the Mound. This would take her time to digest. The Mound was where Unicate *Others* were raised?

Something else niggled at her.

"So… you don't have a problem with poverty and resources and children and all that, like the IRP?"

"The IRP has nothing to do with the Unicate," said Terence. "We marvel at their strange views. But the Mound has a deal with them, they bring fresh hostages…"

"What happens to those hostages?" asked Paean, thinking with dread of families, babies…

Terence looked troubled. "They are… turned into Unicate, if you get my meaning. It was what the Toll was for, too, back in the Sixties. To grow our numbers."

Paean scowled and shook her head. He was saying more than he was saying. She had to think of Vlad and his evasiveness – and suddenly Vlad felt like a friendly entity compared to this lot.

"You guys are human mutants?"

"Not mutants," said Terence. "You won't pick up a genetic difference. We are one hundred percent human. This is how I can be British."

It explained why the only difference one saw, was the slight *otherness* in the eyes – and then again, nothing physical you could pinpoint. This was why some didn't spot it at all, and some merely found the Unicate *Others* a bit uncanny. It was all – in the head!

"Brainwashing?" she guessed.

Terence shook his head and got to his feet. "Come, Paean. Let me show you."

"You're leading me into a trap," she growled.

"No. I'm helping you rescue Mrs Flanagan, and then you'll take me to your Captain?"

Half pleading. A broken wing. A man who really didn't want to be any longer what he had been born to be – or changed into? Paean's heart melted. Could he be rehabilitated? If someone could tame a Unicate *Other* and turn him back into a human, it would be Captain, she realized.

Highly dangerous endeavour though!

"Terence," she said, "I'll have to be straight with you though. I'll have to turn you over to Captain in handcuffs. I will mediate, tell him exactly what's going on, and why you are aboard, but then he will decide what to do with you. If you can live with that deal, we can do this."

"That sounds fair," said Terence optimistically.

"Terence," she warned, "he might decide to kill you on the spot! Because you are Unicate."

He shook his head. "Your Captain is a fair man, Paean. I'm pleased you can see yourself doing this. I only need a chance to meet your Captain and plead my case."

She nodded and allowed him to lead her back up the road towards the offices they had just left. It only occurred to her on the way that he hadn't paid for the beverages; only afforded the waitress with one steely stare. It spooked her a little. But – he was Unicate. Used to working differently.

Somehow, the Unicate men were abused. She was intrigued. It would be a good idea to have him aboard; everybody would be able to pump him for inside information. Perhaps, perhaps in fact it could be the beginning of something really big… a truce with the Unicate.

195

13 – Morrigan

The Morrigan stirred.

Consciousness seeped back in. Electricity flickered across his iridescent hide. He was feeling better. The sticky carbon had ceased vibrating.

He opened a tentative sense organ for sight, in his general plasm, and peered out. He was in some sort of container; a very restricted one. A bucket, he realized. And above him, perched on the infirmary bunk, was Perdita with a bottle of something in her hand.

Somehow that bottle looked about as painful as Federi's teleporter.

"Morrigan!" she greeted him. "Welcome back! You are indeed immortal, aren't you?"

"You gave me Brurite," replied the Morrigan. "How did you know that that was the only way to save my life?"

"I didn't," said Perdita. "Shot in the dark, Morrigan."

He was silent for a moment.

"I'll reward you greatly, Perdita," he promised then.

"The only way you can reward any of us," she replied pointedly, "is by being a team player, being one of Captain's loyal crew, and subjugating yourself to Captain's command. There are rules. And if you don't stick to them, Federi can delete you as surely as he organized you aboard."

"Federi brought me aboard?" asked the Morrigan, surprised.

"Not personally, but he ordered it," said Perdita. "Ailyss and Wolf brought you and poured you in here. I think you owe all of them."

"And you," agreed the Morrigan. "For the Brurite. So they got out of the trap?"

"That story I can't tell you," said Perdita. "Wolf and Ailyss came back aboard. I didn't see Federi. I don't think he left Romania."

"Or Shrn," added the Morrigan pensively. If the Demon had been torn apart by the werefolk... he'd have to check. He might have to rescue Federi. But he was in no state to do so; he doubted he could even leave this bucket. He put the eye out on a stalk and looked around. "Where is Paean?"

"Out doing her own thing," said Perdita. "Morrigan, there have to be rules of conduct. I understand who you are and where you came from, and yet I used to fear you. You need to be somewhat human."

The Morrigan groaned.

"Dearest Boudaceia, there is no way I can take any shape right now. Bucket suits me. I'm tired!"

"Shape is not so critical," she replied. "I'm talking about character. Let's start with a name. Nobody is going to worship you or be enslaved by you. You're a crew member. Give me a name."

"Vlad," said the Morrigan.

Perdita scowled, puzzled. "A bit short perhaps?"

"No," said the Morrigan. "Vlad is good. Prince Vlad the Impostor. It's who I've always been – centuries now. Since the real Prince Vlad passed away. And he *was* Romanian," he added. "I met him. Great guy."

"Fine," agreed Perdita. "Vlad then. Next rule. You don't speak into people's heads."

"Aw!" exclaimed Vlad.

"No," insisted Perdita. "No mind-reading, no changing people's thought patterns. No intimidating, no ruling and bullying."

"Influencing?" asked Vlad hopefully.

She shook her head. "Largely, no. You'll have to discuss these rules in great detail with Federi."

The Morrigan sighed. "As long as he stays friendly." And he closed his eye-on-a-stick again.

"Catch some sleep," said Perdita and got up from the infirmary bunk. "I can't be aboard long." She lifted her gaze to the electronic eye in the corner of the infirmary. "Solar Wind, keep an eye on him! If he moves out of this cabin, alert me on my com!"

Yes, Perdita! came the answer on her wrist-com. Perdita nodded, content; and she teleported out.

~

Solar Wind!

Morrigan! By the Stars, am I glad that you are alive!

The Morrigan felt like laughing aloud; he felt like crying, too. None of it was viable in his bucket format. Human? Perdita had no idea.

Why should I need to leave the infirmary? he asked. *You're right here!*

He applied force of flow, and sloshed against the side of the bucket. It fell over, and he ran out, and in under the bunk Perdita had just vacated. And he extended one long, thin tentacle and reached for the Solar Wind's electric point.

The Solar Wind yelped in surprise, electronically. All her screens went fuzzy for a second, and righted themselves again. And that was all… except that nobody would get sense out of her for a while.

*

Terence led Paean back to the place where the truck was parked; but then he moved across the street, to another entrance. An unassuming entrance, looking a bit like a warehouse.

200

Oh! Paean understood. Where he was now leading her, down these half-lit, bare tiled passages lined with office doors – that was the real mound.

He had warned her that there was no way in except for the official entrance; and they would have to improvise to get out. Paean wasn't overly worried about this; it was simple. She'd teleport all three of them out. One single leap. But of course she kept this close. The handcuffs and Patrick were still fresh in her memory.

Terence led her to an office door and knocked.

"In," said a voice. Terence pushed the door open and led Paean in.

"Your Majesty," he said, "this is Paean Donegal. She requested to be with Mrs Flanagan."

Paean iced, her stomach turning. She kicked herself for being off guard twice in such a short timespan. He'd blithely talked her into handing herself over! Her right hand closed around her spare teleporter in her pocket; her left hand around her right wrist. She stared at the enormous mound of human flesh that turned slowly on its swivel-chair and looked at her from a face layered with fat. This was the hugest human shape she'd ever seen in her life – and it spooked her worse than Dahlia from Nemiscau.

Those watery eyes were flat. There was nothing remotely human in them!

"Paean Donegal! How delightful! Finally we have our hands on the precious Founder genes! Terence, my faithful servant – take her wherever she wants to go. Who would deny her?"

Paean couldn't tell who was more relieved to get out of that room – herself or Terence.

~

Long, dim passages. It was cool here underground; the small

201

insufficient lights like evil orange eyes. Paean tried to see if they were bioluminescence or some sort of chemical.

"Focus!" hissed Terence. "Memorize the way, Paean! If you have to return alone you must still find it!"

She glanced at him in surprise. She had actually not expected that she'd be returning, after her name had been shouted across the system like that. Her fingers caressed the teleporter in her pocket, and the second one on her wrist was a great source of security, too. Without those, she'd be lost now. Guaranteed.

Memorize the path. Well, it couldn't hurt. They had done two left turns and one right, passed how many doors – och, it was hopeless, she was already lost. Some assassin, she scolded herself. Lucky that it wasn't that critical.

"We're following the orange double-lights," whispered Terence. "Stick to that and you'll be alright!"

She focused on the lights, mainly to subdue the fear that had started building. It was right – in the passages branching off this one, the lights were a slightly different shade. It was the only visible difference between the passages.

"It's the human factor," said Terence. "Humans are easily disoriented underground, so we have to colour-code where we go."

She shivered slightly. Why then build the mounds underground in the first place? There it was again. He was trying to tell her that the Unicate was purely a human movement; and yet he differentiated them from humans. Indoctrination alone couldn't account for this. And that *otherness*… was it really only a kind of insanity induced by brainwashing? Large pieces of the puzzle had suddenly gone missing again. She was determined that Federi would interrogate Terence thoroughly – with her listening.

Eventually they turned down a passage with red lights, and then into one with purple lights…

Paean was now shivering constantly. They were deep, deep in the bowels of the Earth. The air here was stale from being so far underground, and damp, and cool. The passage sank lower, and then it opened into another passage with even darker lighting, barely visible now. And this passage was lined with prison-like cells; and from these, eyes followed Paean. Yellow glowing eyes; and others. Some came across as hungry and demented, and some, pitying, but all followed her in silence. It made her flesh crawl.

Yellow eyes, like Dahlia. Some of the Unicate had those. Certainly those genes were nowhere human! And these prisoners – were they really vanishing lizards? Not prisoners but beasts? Why such darkness? It wasn't set up for humans at all anymore, down here!

Terence led her to one of the cells and unlocked the huge barred gate. And motioned her to step inside.

She stared at him, aghast. Her gun came out, nearly subconsciously. His finger went to his lips. Were those yellow-eyed monsters guards of a sort? She stepped warily inside the cage, which was not much more than a hollowed-out cave out of the ground; expecting the Unicate *Other* to slam the gate behind her and imprison her. But he didn't. He stepped into the cell with her.

In the far corner on the floor huddled a figure covered in hair. Paean didn't see enough. She reached into her moonbag and took out a tube of bioluminescence and cast some green Paean-light on the scene. It looked like a scrawny old woman, hugging her legs, forehead resting on her knees, and her long grey hair unkempt, falling across her face and knees to the ground. And what had looked like fur, was a threadbare blanket.

Paean crouched down to her and put a hand on her shoulder.

"Mrs Flanagan?"

The figure looked up. It was Mrs Flanagan. But now that she

was half-starved and half-crazed, Paean could see something more in her eyes. She recoiled a bit.

"I'm sorry, Paean," said Mrs Flanagan hollowly.

Mrs Flanagan was one of *those*! Too late! Paean folded her arms around her old teacher's neck and cried.

"So they caught you too," said Mrs Flanagan finally. "Oh Paean, I had so hoped that you would escape! All three of you!"

"They didn't catch me," said Paean. "I'm here to free you!"

Mrs Flanagan smiled tiredly.

"You discuss this right in front of your guard? Hello, Terence!"

"Mrs Flanagan," acknowledged Terence. "It's true."

"So you are..." started Mrs Flanagan uncertainly.

"Rescuing you," said Terence. "This is not the best place to talk about it. Let me work on a plan to get us out of here."

"Already have the plan," smiled Paean and activated her teleporter.

The screen flashed twice, and nothing happened. And an error message appeared on the screen. Destination out of range.

Paean paged through the destinations on her teleporter and saw them disappear one by one. Everything was out of range! She ripped her older teleporter out of her pocket. That one didn't even bother to give information, beyond "not available".

"Everything's out of range!" she gasped quietly.

Terence took a closer look at her teleporter-com. And he fiddled with it, and tried to activate it...

"What's it supposed to do?"

"Take us out of here!" replied Paean. "But..."

"It works on sublatronic frequencies?" asked Terence.

Paean nodded. "I think so." She really had no foggiest idea how the teleporters worked.

"Then it won't work – all communication devices fail in here," said Terence.

Paean stared at him. All sorts of things were milling in her head. He'd brought her in here, even announced her… aw rats, how stupid she had been to trust him like that! He'd had a plan to get in, but not out. He himself was not in danger, on the contrary. He was at home here.

"Make as though we're your prisoners and you have orders to take us somewhere," she instructed.

Terence looked at her – frankly, he looked scared bloodless.

"Terence," she urged, "remember your objective! If you want to be a pirate, you've got to be tough! None of us are scared little girls. We're all survivors. Got to do this for yourself!"

He nodded, looking unconvinced. "Paean, we can try. If they catch us…"

"They won't!" she hissed. "Lead the way, Terence the Brave!"

He smiled wanly at her and helped Mrs Flanagan to her feet. She was very weak. Paean supported her on the other side.

Terence was right; this wouldn't be enough. She dug in her moonbag and located her perfume dispenser, and puffed a few puffs into the air. And then she had to go down and immunize both Terence and Mrs Flanagan against her virus to wake them up again. This gave her immense hope. Both were Unicate *Others* – the one more recently than the other, to be sure – and both responded to the virus. The rest of the Mound would fall asleep too. Back on the ship she'd have to clone another immunotype, as fast as lightning; no problem.

"Good heavens, what on Earth was that?" asked Terence as he rubbed his eyes in shock, coming to from the immunization. Mrs Flanagan was surfacing too; but badly disoriented. Which was perhaps just as well.

"It'll be alright now," said Paean. "Let me do this again: Lead the way, Terence the Brave!"

No eyes followed them this time. They were all sleeping.

*

"Federi!" Radomir Lascek grinned hugely and clapped the gypsy on the shoulder. "Welcome back aboard!"

The Free Gypsy smiled, a bit at odds. "Well, thanks, Captain! Where is Paean?"

Lascek studied Federi. The man was in a bit of a mess; his shirt was bloodied and could do with a good wash in general. He didn't look injured, himself; but he had clearly been in a scuffle, with something furry. And it had come second.

"I think you should maybe clean up before she sees you," Lascek pointed out with a smile.

"But, Captain, she's not on the ship! She's out of teleportation range."

Radomir Lascek scowled. Paean was off the ship?

There was a new, vicious weapon coiled around the Assassin's left shoulder. The Captain studied it in astonishment. Federi had always been into clean efficiency, not pain! This was a nasty development.

"What's that?" asked Federi, shoving the unconscious, tied-up form of Bryce with his foot.

"Hostage," said Lascek. "Paean brought him."

"Alright. What's been going down here while I was sorting out the gypsies?"

"Federi, you might be interested in something Paean has peeled open," said Radomir Lascek. "Ever heard of the IRP?"

Federi glanced at the information the Captain had on the console. Irish Rationalist Power? He scowled. "She's out of teleportation range, Captain. I think that's urgent? Where was she last? Can I get a low-down of her movements?"

"Last with you," said the Captain, scowling.

"Negative, Captain! She hasn't been in Romania since this morning early."

Lascek frowned and peered over the blue sea. Never as blue as at four in the afternoon; never this particular shade of tanzanite except here in Southern, off the Durban coast.

Who knew where the girl was by now? Federi was right. This was critical. Radomir Lascek activated the internal ship com.

"Will everyone who saw Paean today or knows about her whereabouts, come to the command deck, on the double!"

It was a small conclave that gathered on the narrow command deck before the bridge. Radomir Lascek put the Solar Wind on auto-navigation and joined them.

Wolf; Lyr. Dr Jake – though he asked leave to return to the machineroom right away. He had only seen Paean briefly, when she was talking to Wolf. Perdita. Doc Judith. And old Sherman Dougherty.

"Captain, she made lunch," said Lyr gravely. "She didn't stay long though."

"I plead guilty," said Wolf, hanging his head. "Captain, I gave her a new teleporter-com. The teleporter has a fuzzier field and is a lot safer than the conventional ones. But it also has a longer range, all the way to Calypso."

"The one you were constructing earlier? Do you have another one?" asked the Captain.

"Ailyss does," said Wolf, and called her. She scouted to Calypso and came back.

"Bad news, Captain. She's not on Calypso."

"And Pluto Base…"

"Is not quite in range, Captain," smiled Wolf. "There's a difference of a few orders of distance."

"The Comet?" asked Lascek and corrected himself, glancing at the jet. "Right here. She hasn't taken that. She hasn't charged off into space."

"At least," breathed Ailyss.

"She's hiding from me," growled Federi. "She was angry about me hunting down the Morrigan."

"She'll have seen Shawn," said Lascek. "Why isn't Shawn in the meeting? Where is Shawn?"

"Not aboard, Captain," reported Perdita. "He escaped with Mindy when he heard that Adamson was to be put ashore. I arranged him into Dana's safekeeping on New Dome. That way we know where the two are. Doc Aoiffe is tending to Mindy."

"Well done, Perdita," said Lascek, smiling – and then scowling. "Dana and safekeeping don't belong in the same breath!" And he frowned at Federi, too. "What's this about the Morrigan? I thought he was dead!"

"He's much better," said Perdita. "He's aboard, Captain. In the infirmary. Federi ordered Ailyss to bring him back aboard."

"He saved us from the shape-shifting wolf-dogs of Shrn," Wolf mentioned.

"Hold on," said the Captain. "The Morrigan is back aboard?"

"The Morrigan is back alive?" asked Federi, with eyebrows sky-high. "Will have to brief him! If he steps out of line…" He touched the Cat-o'-Nine-Blades. Radomir Lascek experienced involuntary pity for the immortal.

"Poor Morrigan is dead," said Ailyss. "We poured him into a bucket, Federi. There was no more life in there."

"Correction, my girl," said Perdita. "He has been very much

revived. I gave him a Brurite bullet to chew on. We can do with him as an ally."

Lascek gaped at her.

"Captain," said Sherman Dougherty, and launched into a fit of coughing. Lascek studied him with concern. These coughing fits had started after the Solar Wind's return to Earth, and had only got worse. The chronic smoking couldn't be helping; but Sherman was too old to break that habit.

"Doc," prompted the Captain.

"I've been looking at that," replied Doc Judith. "Emphysema. I'm trying to find cures in the Files."

"Brurite wouldn't do it?" asked Lascek.

"We could try, Captain," replied Perdita. "It acts mostly on the filtering organs, and the heart and brain. But I guess it can't hurt?"

"Right. Captain," Sherman tried again. "Concerning Paean. I should plead guilty, too. I alerted Paean to the sudden silence I had from Mrs Flanagan. She went off to investigate."

Federi teleported out.

*

He stood in the street and listened. All quiet in Molly Street. There was no indication of anything strange going on. He walked over to Mrs Flanagan's house and opened the unlocked front door. That in itself was ominous. He trailed through her house, noting that the time pocket had been closed. Wondering if he could force a Romanian hound to open it again for him. Listening for impressions.

Captain had said something about Paean investigating the situation in Ireland. That hostage. And the IRP. Federi teleported back aboard.

"Captain, what about that hostage?"

"There's another one in the infirmary," Doc Judith pointed out. "Young Unicate soldier with a bullet stuck in his forehead."

"Gosh! And he lives?"

"He lives," she confirmed. "Barely, on life support. Federi, you did hear what happened with Peter Piper?"

"I got this jumbled report," growled Federi. "And I understood you sedated her, Doc?"

"I did. She slept. A full two hours."

"Two hours?"

"It wasn't valeriensis," said the Doc. "I prefer the medications I know."

Federi nodded. "Captain, may I revive that hostage?"

"Go ahead, Federi."

*

Bryce opened his eyes. There was a moment's complete confusion. He had no idea where he was; but the floor was unstable, in motion. And a sharp-looking terrorist was hovering over him, with a war bandanna and a dirty shirt splattered with blood.

"Alright," said the vicious-looking man. "You're facing the Demon. The Bane, if you like. Federi. And you'll tell me now where Paean fished you out of."

"What?" groaned Bryce.

"Demonos," snapped Federi. "You are facing Federi Demonos. The descendant of Falco the Traitor. *Hai shala?*"

"The name," muttered Bryce. "Don't speak the name! It brings the hounds, don't you know?"

Federi Demonos tipped his head back and laughed; wildly, madly.

"I can't wait," he announced. "Your name is?"

210

"Commander Bryce," replied Bryce, trying to rally some dignity. It wasn't easy, lying tied up on the ground like this. "Leader of the IRP." He was actually facing the Bane! The man was shorter and scrawnier than he had imagined. But twice as mad.

"Fine," said Federi. "That makes sense for now. So where did Paean take you from?"

"You really are connected," said Bryce, astounded. "You and Paean Donegal."

"Married," said Federi Demonos, and suddenly there was a cold knife tip at Bryce's throat. "You'll tell me now where she found you."

"In my office of course," replied Bryce, swallowing. Supernatural powers? The man who owned a sharp enough knife, didn't need such.

"And that is in…?" prompted Federi with strained patience.

"Limerick," said Bryce and gave the address.

"What the hell business," asked Federi dangerously, "does Limerick have with Molly Street in Dublin?" And he was suddenly not there anymore.

Bryce watched the surrounds nervously, waiting for the hounds.

*

It was dark in Limerick. Rain and sleet came down relentlessly. Christmas, thought Federi fleetingly. Dark, wet. He'd rather organize it for Paean in Romania, now that it had snowed.

Bryce's offices were right across from the Unicate mound. Federi scowled. His teleporter showed Paean out of range. But he had a distinct idea… aw hell, little luv! Did she really believe she could rescue Mrs Flanagan right out of a Mound? Federi took his viral spray in one hand and his stiletto in the other. Her teleporter

211

was clearly blocked by something. He'd have to get her out manually. Stealth was the way now. He stole into the dark entrance and immediately moved out of the light.

He had been inside a mound once. The time when he was fourteen, when he'd rescued that thankless traitor of a girl. With the help of a guard, who, if he thought about it now, had been one of *those*. Only *those* moved in this mound anyway. He kept to the shadows.

He thought of the Hub in America. Was it a mound like this one? These Headquarters buildings were all over Europe, but not in the capitals. Always in slightly smaller towns, in unexpected places. Almost as though...

He had thought that Unicate only had a peculiar way of building their headquarters underground because of the nuclear fallout of the Sixties, and then those offices had become establishments. But now that he'd been away from Earth and realized that life in space was not only a possibility but a definite fact, those childhood speculations didn't seem so way-out anymore. The Unicate was an alien species. Falco had sold the Earth out to aliens.

But how did they then manage to look like humans? Were they all shifters? The Romanian hound he'd had by the scruff of its neck was a Unicate *Other* – but not in the same sense as Anya or Jack Miller. The only detectable *otherness* was in the eyes. And then, not for everyone to see either. And it was a shifter too, as though it somehow did come from Shrn after all...

Paean would have to collect a teeny tiny piece of *Other* and run it through the Genitron to figure out what was going on there. In fact, that might be a very neat way of finishing that plague off once and for all. It had worked famously on the mutants.

He slunk from shadow to shadow in the half-lit passageway with the clean tiles, wondering whether the Cat-o'-Nine-Blades would mean anything at all if these *Others* decided to mob him. Whether they would be braver than the Unicate hounds.

A soft voice called across to him from one of the doors. He glanced up – and looked straight into the eyes of the fattest thing he'd ever come across. She beckoned him into her office.

Federi Demonos entered and closed the door behind himself.

"You know who I am," he said with a soft smile. "May I ask who you are?"

"Queen Rhyn," said the creature. "We have been waiting for you."

From all sides Unicate *Others* encircled him. Federi eyed them and wondered if he should pull his machinegun trick now.

*

Paean scooted ahead and sprayed virus, and Terence followed, carrying Mrs Flanagan on his back. The old teacher looked confused and afraid; she said nothing. Terence's eyes were darting all over the place.

"We're nearly there," said Terence when the passage lights changed to orange. "Keep courage, Paean, we're doing well!"

And then her virus ran dry. "Blast," she whispered softly and dug in her moonbag. More? She had more vials of lyophilised virus, but no more water to shake it up and spray it. And she had darts, but they got one person at a time.

A soft whistling started up.

"They've discovered us," said Terence. "The mound itself is aware. We've had it."

The whistling changed pitch. It turned into a war cry, unanimous out of many mouths. "Traitors! Fugitives!"

Paean took out her semiautomatic and waited for them to come closer. Terence was unarmed, she realized with a sudden chilling certainty. He was only a worker here.

Well, hell! "Hang onto Mrs Flanagan," she instructed. "Stay behind me. The virus is everywhere there!"

The Unicate descended on her, streaming out from side passages and trouping down the main… Paean aimed into the mob and mowed a few of them down, but they kept on coming.

They seemed to have no concept of death, she thought as her gun rattled. They stepped over their fallen comrades and kept on advancing; unarmed, workers like Terence, but they could still tear her limb from limb if they came too close. And it was nearly as though… they couldn't care if they were mown down. It frightened her; it made them seem somehow brain-dead.

She held her fire for a second to wipe the cold sweat out of her eyes, and listened. Was there an echo in this place? Machinegun fire from the front too? She retook her shooting and watched how some of the ones she hadn't hit, became disoriented.

They were too close now, and too many. She hadn't had time to practice Federi's machinegun trick, really. They were pressing in on all sides. Paean ripped out her razor-sharp dagger and launched herself into the mob.

"Imaya!" she yelled the first battle cry that entered her head.

The machinegun fire came closer. From behind the mob. She wondered if she and Terence and Mrs Flanagan were going to be mowed down. Then there was a flash of light, and a trail of fire whizzed around the room several times, scattering the Unicate. It streaked away down the main passage again as fast as it had come; but none of the Unicate remained standing, except for Terence.

And one more person. Paean peered into the dim passage over the many motionless Unicates. The man with the machine gun. She sheathed her dagger and flew to meet him, and threw her arms

214

around his neck.

"You're here! Federi!" she squealed. His arms went around her and she clung to him, the world once again complete.

She introduced him to Terence. And to Mrs Flanagan, and then laughed in confusion. Federi had already met the old teacher!

He narrowed his eyes and peered at Mrs Flanagan through the darkness. "Paean, I don't want to be strange about this, but…"

"I know," she sighed. "Came as a surprise to me as well. There are things I must tell you. But not here."

Federi studied the young Unicate *Other* with deep suspicion, shouldering his gun. He listened to Paean's explanation, and gave it thought.

"You want Captain to deal with him?"

She nodded.

"Come," he said. "The Solar Wind's got Christmas on. Don't want to miss that!"

"We've got to get Mrs Flanagan into the infirmary," said Paean urgently. Christmas could jolly well wait! "And we got to get Terence to safety too, Federi, he's on our side…"

"Course," said the Tzigan. "Come! Follow me! Just tell me one thing, little luv. What the heck was that vanishing lizard doing in here?"

"That was Imaya," said Paean. "Don't know why she came, I just wanted to call her name, it made me feel braver."

"She sorted this for us," said Federi. And he scowled. Imaya had done for them in the Mound what the Morrigan had tried to do in the werefolk trap. Somehow it was an incomplete feeling, having a powerful alien bail one out of one's messes.

It also raised some pointy questions. He had been under the solid impression that the vanishing lizards were Unicate. But if that were the case, why should Imaya have defended them?

215

He glanced at Terence, then at Mrs Flanagan. "Come!"

"Sir," said Terence. "I can't believe I'm speaking to you in person! Never thought I'd have that luck!"

"How is that lucky for you?" asked Federi's silver tooth.

14 – Christmas

Federi gazed at the many lights in the rigging, and the huge Christmas tree that Shawn had organized. Cor! Jingles acquired a whole new meaning! The tree was fastened to the main mast. Like a hostage, thought Federi. And he corrected himself. It wasn't nice to have such thoughts about his young brother-in-law's best efforts at Christmas. Shawn had dug the tree out with roots and all and organized a pot for it, all with teleportation. Lights sparkled in it, illuminating thousands of glitzy things. Federi gazed across them to port where the countless little lights of Durban Harbour glittered slightly to the south, and the more sparse lights from private houses twinkled straight across, over at Durban Beach. They lay anchored outside the bay. Captain didn't like the harbour much and found it perfectly sufficient to teleport the small distance as needed. Ironic, thought the gypsy. After all the effort of navigating here the old way.

The crew of the Solar Wind was gathered on the deck, partially to bring the ship into harbour; but to a large part to have a look at the whole rigging full of lights. He was at the rail; Paean was leaning against him, secured by his arm, and she was fast asleep. Poor little luv. Shawn had decorated the whole Solar Wind for her, and now he wasn't even aboard.

That, at the very least, needed to be fixed! He ought to discuss it with Perdita.

Terence was on the deck, observing procedures with undue fascination. Federi eyed him with suspicion. Sure, it was a good idea to have a Unicate *Other* aboard for questioning – which he'd have to organize, anna bottle; but what was a less great idea was the

Other observing all the Solar Wind's secrets!

Bryce was chained in the bilges, where Wolf manned the drives. Dr Jake was going to take a shift later on. Patrick from the IRP and the Morrigan from planet Shrn – Earth's sister planet – were both in the infirmary, supervised by Luigi; and Mrs Flanagan – another *Other* – had been tucked into the second infirmary bunk. It could safely be said that they had an infirmary full of Unicate and aliens.

Adamson and Derrick were still aboard – they were going to go ashore tomorrow. They had withdrawn to the cabin temporarily assigned to Adamson, and whenever Federi checked on the system, they were holding a heated discussion about the subject of Mindy having been abducted, and the Captain's duplicity. A conversation he ought to monitor! He had instructed the Solar Wind to record it all and copy the entire debate to Luigi's mobile memory chip, so that he could have a good look at it later.

Terence, Bryce, Patrick, Adamson, Derrick and Vlad! Federi shook his head. Fraternizing with the enemy was a trend on the Solar Wind that was getting out of hand. But he had to plead guilty – he had brought half of them aboard himself, and the other half had been brought – via his bad example – by his Paean.

And where were Captain's decisive orders to stop that nonsense and put them all ashore? Captain seemed quite happy to go along with all that. Federi glanced at the bridge, where Captain and Perdita were holding a conference. Should Jon and Michelle not be fetched aboard from Calypso? He could do so with a single teleportation there and back.

The Christmas dinner had been sushi, served out here on the deck, seeing that the night was balmy. Federi didn't think he'd survive long on the Solar Wind. Lyr was historically an enemy too! One should never unleash an enemy in the galley.

Durban's lights sparkled to portside. The Solar Wind lay docked.

219

Federi took it all in, mute, thinking of the gypsies in Romania and how easily Paean had slipped into their rhythms. Thinking of Paean.

It really didn't matter where they were; the Solar Wind, the Tzigany, the Unicate mound… as long as he could hold her close like this and know that she was his. He would never allow Captain's infernal commands to come between them again.

Sherman Dougherty came over and leaned on the rail too.

"Noisy bunch," he commented with a grin and a puff on his pipe, and nodded in the direction of the crew. And coughed. He went into a spasm of coughing that had him doubling over.

Federi grabbed hold of the veteran; a second later Paean was abruptly awake and by Sherman's side too. "You alright, Sherman?"

"Can't live forever, y'know, my lass." He shook his head and grinned and stopped coughing.

"Get you some Christmas punch, Sherman," muttered Federi.

"Noo, Federi, leave it. Alcohol makes it worse."

"How long has this been going now?" asked Paean, concerned.

"From the time you two left the ship," replied Sherman. "Don't look at me like that, Paean! In the sixties everyone still knew that if you smoke you end up drowning in yer own juices."

"But then why do you?" Paean was upset now.

"Let it go, wee girl," smiled Sherman. "I'm an old man, don't you know? Hundred and fifteen years. How's that for you?"

"Sixteen," said Federi softly, gazing at the incredible light display in the rigging. "Sherman is exactly a hundred years older than you, Paean. He was born with the millennium."

"Congratulations, Federi," laughed Sherman and coughed a bit more. "You've just managed to make me feel a thousand, not a hundred!"

"Well, it's Christmas," snapped Paean. "Can't a few more people decide to kick it on Christmas Eve?" And she turned abruptly and left, heading belowdecks.

"I'll still have a couple of weeks," the old man mentioned after her back. "You guys have been such amazing friends! My life has been so blessed!"

Federi stared at Durban Port and said nothing.

"Doesn't handle death very well, does she," commented the ancient mariner.

"Who does," muttered Federi through his teeth.

~

Paean stomped in through the infirmary's door, muttering angry monologue to herself, working very hard on restraining those tears. She was furious. Mother had had no choice about dying. But Sherman had been killing himself slowly all these years?

Mrs Flanagan was sleeping. So was Patrick; Paean checked both their vital signs, and then she stepped on something and nearly slipped.

"Oh hell! What's this?" She checked under the bunk, and shrieked.

"Your husband organized me aboard," said the Morrigan defensively, two stalk-eyes sticking out of his general goo.

"Really?" She started to prime the teleporter on her wrist-com.

The console beeped once. *He actually did, Paean,* wrote the Solar Wind.

"And you'll say anything to have him close," snapped Paean. "You're a liar and a traitor, Solar Wind!" Rats! Mrs Flanagan was stirring, disturbed by her shriek.

"Actually, Mistress," peeped Luigi from the console, "he did. Earlier today."

"Wolf hasn't enabled lying as a function for you, has he?" challenged Paean.

"No, Mistress. We wouldn't see the point. I doubt he would

either."

"Right!" She glared at the Morrigan who was flowing cumbersomely out under the bunk. And she looked again. "You're injured! How can you be injured? You're a liquid! Heal yourself this instant!"

"A liquid with a biofield," said the Morrigan. "That biofield along with my semi-solid molecular structure was severely disrupted by your sticky carbon and double teleporter field."

"Clearly it didn't kill you," retorted Paean.

"It was killing me," said the Morrigan. "Then Perdita fed me Brurite in pure form. And the Solar Wind is reviving me."

"The Solar Wind? How?"

"With an exchange of energy." The Morrigan peered uncertainly at her, forming two skyward reaching eyebrows above his stalk eyes.

"So, lovely," bit Paean. "You who are a mind-controlling, manipulating fiend get to live, and ol' Sherman Dougherty who's been nothing but sweet all these years, gets to die!"

The Morrigan's stalk eyes formed question marks. "Sherman is dying?"

"Yes! Quit squinting, blast you! 's not funny! Drowning in his own juices, now isn't he! And didn't he bring it on himself? But who's left wi' the heartache?" She performed another unnecessary check on her patients and left the infirmary, heading for the lab.

~

The Morrigan considered. So the Founder girl, whom he regarded with the same jealous protectiveness as a diver does the find of a rare black pearl, was breaking her heart over the mortality of the oldest human crew member.

Federi's actions and decisions puzzled Vlad immensely. The man was a walking contradiction. But Paean was simple to understand. She was all heart. Even her laser-sharp intelligence was directed and subjugated by her emotions. It was her greatest problem; and her most endearing quality. He wanted to reach out and comfort her; the Founderling's heartache echoed loudly across the universes. Mortality was a human condition.

But it didn't have to be! Vlad gathered himself up from the floor and put on his Dracula suit. He winked at Mrs Flanagan who had surfaced and looked quite horrified, and he flowed to the outer deck. Even while in human guise, he still came across slightly liquefied.

"Feeling better, Morrigan?" asked the Captain as the alien stepped onto the deck. "Coming to celebrate Christmas with us? Like some Shiraz?"

"How does Shiraz celebrate?" asked Vlad, puzzled. "Does it have a biofield too?"

"How is your injured biofield?" asked Wolf.

"Practically restored," said Vlad. "Twinge here and there still... will be good as new in the morning!"

~

Federi watched from the rail. As long as the blasted alien kept in line... the Cat-o'-Nine-Blades was in the Cabin... maybe he should ask Wolf to add mini teleporters on the tips...

"And how did you manage that fast recovery?" he asked suspiciously.

"Perdita gave me Brurite. And the Solar Wind is restoring my bioelectric field."

"The Solar Wind? How on Earth?" asked Federi, baffled.

"Making love."

Federi gasped. Sherman developed a nasty coughing fit.

"Vlad's medicine," he managed to say between laughing and wheezing for air.

"Ah," said Vlad with a diagnostic glance at the Solar Wind's veteran. "I see what Paean means. Not very conducive to survival, not at all!"

He reached out and placed one tentacle on Sherman's shoulder. The old man's water-blue eyes flew open. He took a cautious breath, and another… and emitted a surprised little noise. "I can breathe!"

"While we're at it," said Vlad and kept the tentacle on Sherman's shoulder.

Federi saw how wrinkles became less deep in Sherman's face and his yellowed old hands unbent and straightened, losing the arthritis that had started plaguing him after all these years.

"Vlad, are you working an illusion here?" challenged the Tzigan.

"I don't think he is," replied Sherman. "I can breathe! Can't even remember when breathing was this easy!"

"What have you done, Vlad?"

"Increased his life span," said the Morrigan nonchalantly. "Corrected the mistakes in his biofield. People live that short because they don't know any better."

"Uh-huh," said Federi intelligently. In his books hundred-and-sixteen years wasn't exactly a short life.

"He has four more centuries to enjoy now," said Vlad. "I've observed Dougherty. Someone who gets that much joy out of being alive ought to live forever!"

"Four more centuries!" gasped Sherman. "How am I going to live through all that?"

"I could reverse the changes," offered Vlad helpfully.

"Oh noo, thanks, I think I'll keep them!" With a huge grin, Sherman relit his pipe. "If I keep smoking, how long before I need my next treatment?"

"Give about twenty years," said Vlad. "You shouldn't smoke, Sherman. It upsets the crew."

And then Federi's wiry hand was on Vlad's shoulder, and activating a nerve point, the function of which Vlad only understood now. His knees buckled and he grinned, baring his Dracula teeth. He tried liquidizing and found that the Demon was behind that grip, commanding his psyche to stay in solid shape.

"What now, Demon? Are you not happy with me restoring health to your friend?"

"Very thankful. You're going to enlighten me," said Federi with an amiable smile. "What precisely have you done to Sherman? Is it one of your Morrigan tricks? Is this how you subdued the entire population of Atlantis?"

"Essentially," admitted the Morrigan.

"And now you're trying it on the Solar Wind?"

"No, Federi! I wouldn't dare!"

"Just to reverse the changes when we stop dancing to your tune?"

To his own embarrassment Vlad whimpered. Federi let him go with a feral grin, and the alien melted to the deck and lay there in a coruscating puddle.

"Don't forget," warned the Tzigan.

I know, replied the Morrigan inside his head. *You have the power to terminate me.*

"Don't use telepathy!" snapped Federi. "Don't you dare intrude in our minds! The crew's minds are sacrosanct! I won't allow any alien-worshipping!"

Vlad formed himself back into his humanoid shape, this time careful to remain more liquid on the inside.

"And now you tell me exactly what you did," demanded the gypsy. "On pain of being thrown off the Solar Wind. I'll force you back through the portal to your home world if you don't cooperate. I'll use Romanian hounds to open the portal and lock it behind your scintillating bum."

Vlad explained hastily. The changes he had made to Sherman ran deep; as deep as his DNA and his very cell structures. He had basically refreshed the blueprint, erased time-caused mutations, restored and improved the telomeres – the cellular clocks – raised the cellular defences, raised the entire metabolism, both cellular and overall; and restored Sherman Dougherty's biological energy field to the youthfulness of a toddler.

"And how did you achieve all of that?" asked Federi.

Bioelectric energy fields, explained Vlad. The whole functioning of a living organism rested on electric fields. By working with those fields in enough detail you could change the actual molecular patterns.

Federi nodded and stared out to Durban Port. He should fetch Paean and show her that Sherman was fine. And then of course…

"Come with me," he commanded.

*

"Paean."

"Hi, Perdita," said the little redhead listlessly, not looking up from the lab's console.

"Merry Christmas," said Perdita.

"Yeah…" replied Paean. "You too…"

"Except that you don't look as if it's merry for you?"

"It's not, anna bottle!" exploded Paean. "My mother died this year, I'm missing her. My little brother has escaped to another solar system, and my older brother isn't even aboard. I have some precious friends and two are dying. How's all that merry?"

"Who is dying?" asked Perdita with a scowl.

"Well, Mrs Flanagan – we don't know if she's going to make it, after her encounter with the Unicate; and o' course old Sherman! Smoking himself to death, now isn't he?"

Perdita sighed. She had seen too much drug abuse at the

Sanchos to be ignorant about emphysema. She too was observing Sherman's symptoms with worry. On New Dome, nobody smoked; and you didn't get emphysema from burning incense and working with essential oils. So there wasn't a cure for such lung diseases; they didn't occur. Blackmailing help out of Dana was moot. Lung disease was an Earth problem.

She couldn't help about old Sherman. But she could do something else for the young Freedom Fighter.

"Come," she invited. "Let's take a flight."

*

"What hey?" Federi stared at his wrist-com. On there, Paean was announcing that she and Perdita were fetching Shawn back. His teleporter came out at warp speed, and he leaped after the Probe.

It was a hell of a long jump. Black icy space surrounded him. This time he was sure he had miscalculated – he'd end up in Nirvana.

And then there was a bubble of warmth and oxygen surrounding him, and he perched atop some sort of airborne animal... a scaly dragon, he decided. It was an illusion; his mind playing out its last cards. Interesting card trick though.

The dragon turned its head and squared a pupil at him.

Don't do that again! scolded Vlad, straight into his head. *Should ask Captain to take your teleporter away!*

Oh! Not an illusion.

No telepathy! warned Federi.

Vlad chuckled without sound. *Then there is no way of communicating. Pay attention, Demon! You are still in deep space! See that?*

Federi had to admit that the Morrigan was right. This time he had indeed miscalculated; taken a risk that was too great. And once

227

again – by the cheese in the Milky Way – his blasted Assassin had rescued him, by means of the Morrigan!

Not complaining, he said, just curious. *Why do you keep on saving our lives?*

That is indeed a very complex question, agreed the Morrigan. *I have various ulterior motives, if that puts you at ease. Goodwill is the least of it.*

Federi snorted. Right. So he'd better watch his back. And he didn't even have the Cat on him.

How do you manage to keep the oxygen in deep space? he asked, fascinated.

Intergalactic travel, said Vlad. *Morrigan are a space species. We take our atmosphere with us.*

Federi nodded. He couldn't pretend that he understood.

Space species have two options for their atmosphere, explained the Morrigan. *Either they carry it inside themselves, like the Arachne and the Gargantuans. That means they have to have very large bodies. Or else they create enough gravity and magnetosphere around them to trap the air in a bubble. That's us Morrigan. And a few others. Then of course you get some that don't need atmosphere at all...*

Federi's hair stood on end. He didn't want to hear more. A few months back Earth was rather a lonely planet, and now it wasn't even a matter of how many alien planets there were; space itself was overpopulated...

You take horrible risks, Vlad pointed out. *I'm curious too. Why do you do it?*

Morrigan, replied Federi tiredly, *I'm her supervisor. Day, night, regardless. You have no idea what hard work that is. You won't believe where I pulled her out of, earlier today.*

Where?

A Unicate mound, Vlad. A blasted Unicate mound.

A shudder went through the Morrigan.

Is she mentally unstable? he asked.

She's sixteen and believes she's immortal, said Federi. *Comes to the same thing.*

And now, where is she off to?

Probably just fetching Shawn from New Dome.

The Morrigan-dragon gave two beats with his powerful wings and the stars fused into a tunnel. Warp speed acquired a new definition.

*

"Federi!"

"Ah," said Federi, breathing a sigh of relief, "Perdita!"

The Golden Honey glanced at him and returned her attention to the flight console of the Probe. Paean crawled into his arms and found her comfort spot. The Morrigan relaxed on the floor of the jet in a puddle of flickering light, exhausted from the action.

"We're fetching Shawn back?" asked Federi.

Perdita grunted an affirmative.

"And Mindy," added Paean.

"There's a pickle," said Federi thoughtfully. Not releasing his wife. "What to do about Mindy Adamson?"

"Has Captain not changed his mind yet?" asked Paean, irritated. "Bout keeping Captain Adamson aboard?"

"And he's not going to either," replied Federi and found himself a chair to sit on cross-legged. Paean released him and returned to her own seat.

"Can't say that I'm easy with all those enemies aboard and us off the ship," he mentioned.

"Federi," said the puddle of lightning from the deck of the jet, "are you worried about Terence?"

"He's Unicate, anna bottle!" replied Federi. "But he's just a part of the problem."

The Morrigan vanished.

*

Terence was a Unicate *Other*. He didn't spook easily. Yet something about this ship crept under his skin and gave him the willies. He felt as though there were eyes watching him, from every corner. Unseen eyes. From every crevice. The walls themselves. As though the ship had a personality. And quite like the Mound, an unfriendly one. And unlike the Mound, unfamiliar, too.

But since a few minutes back a whole dimension was added to this feeling of unease. He kept having the impression of someone following him. Or something. When he turned, he always thought he saw something move in the corner of his eye, and always, there was nothing.

Terence was a Unicate *Other*; not given to superstition or irrational fears. In fact, rationality was programmed indelibly into his deepest psyche. Being aware of this, he was by now convinced: There was something not right aboard the Solar Wind.

*

Vlad considered what Federi had said, and also what he hadn't said. Federi was alone in this.

Terence was an easy project. Vlad had asked the Solar Wind to keep him updated of the man's every move; and he was content that he'd spooked the beheebees out of the Unicate *Other*. But Terence

230

was not the only enemy aboard. So Vlad decided to do a round, just like the Assassin, and check on all the Solar Wind's enemies.

Lyr was traditionally an enemy of the Solar Wind too. Vlad checked on him, finding him in the galley polishing knives. Lyr – one of his own unbending subjects.

The fish-man looked up, and his white merrow teeth were exposed in two long rows as he grinned mirthlessly at the Morrigan.

"Morrigan," he acknowledged.

"Atlantean," Vlad returned the greeting. "What are you up to?"

"Trying to prepare a meal that will satisfy the crew," said Lyr with a sigh. "The cook is aboard, but he doesn't seem too interested in lending a hand."

Vlad chuckled softly.

"If you are going to try with the Solar Wind what you did to Atlantis," said Lyr casually, "you may find that you are out of your depth."

"You're only so cocky because you know you are protected," returned the Morrigan.

"Not quite accurate," said Lyr and sucked the eyes out of another fish before glancing at it lovingly and filleting it the traditional way. "I don't care. I didn't care before; I care even less now that my daughters and wife are in a facility for maladjusted people. You caused that."

"I gave you endless life spans," said Vlad.

"The illusion of immortality," smiled Lyr. "Regardless, Morrigan. Your day is fading. Your era is over. Nobody on this ship will worship you. They already have a deity. Radomir Lascek."

"My era," said Vlad with a smug little smirk, "is only beginning. Don't worry, my loyal disciple. I shall not be exacting worship or any other form of torture. I have much more interesting things to do."

231

"Such as?"

"Making love," said Vlad grandly.

Lyr shook his head and grinned wryly. "Ha! Right! Love."

"You didn't get too much of that, did you?" pressed the Morrigan.

"I had that duty all the time," said Lyr. "It gets boring very quickly."

"You're very jaded," commented Vlad, surprised.

"Not nearly as jaded as a certain immortal who designed the demise of a whole civilization out of mere boredom," retorted Lyr.

"Hostile, too," added Vlad.

"What do you expect?" Lyr got up and fetched another five fishes, still squirming, out of the bucket in which they had been caught, and killed them with quick, efficient flicks of their spines. And he paused and stared at the alien with his huge, light-blue eyes. He became completely still. Vlad's pupils squared in surprise. By the very force of his stillness, the Atlantean was mesmerizing him!

"Morrigan," said Lyr softly, with his deep, gentle bass voice, "let me say this very clearly. I have never been afraid of you, nor shall I ever be. You can play your mind games with others, but not with the fallen Emperor of Atlantis. I'm watching you. If you put a tentacle tip or the thought thereof anywhere near my daughter or her husband, or if you do anything fissshy…" he drawled the sibilant dreamily, "to anybody aboard, you shall find out things about me that you wished you didn't know. Your mind games are at an end."

The Morrigan blinked himself out of his trance.

"Don't worry, Lyr," he said. "I'm technically on your side. The Demon is also keeping a close watch, if that makes you feel better."

"Federi is mostly not aboard," Lyr pointed out. "I am."

"I understand. I shan't underestimate you, Lyr." Vlad smiled and wandered out of the galley.

"You just did," Lyr replied softly to himself and returned to the filleting of fish.

*

The Morrigan slunk back down to the lower deck. Staying in the Vlad shape was quite a new experience. He had deliberately shifted his body back into a fully human state, with all the correct nerves and juices. For millennia he had copied the external shape of a human body for impersonation purposes. Or any other species, for that matter. But now he was curious. He wanted to experience things the way a human would. And this body generated surprising combinations, odd sensations and feelings.

He checked into the bilges, and was sorely tempted to shift his guise to look like Federi when Dr Jake glanced up – and glanced twice, surprised.

"Oh," he said. "I thought it was Federi! Who are you?" And his hand hovered over the console; ready to hit the alarm.

"Prince Vlad at your service," said the Morrigan with a flawless bow. "I see Captain has not briefed any of you. I'm back aboard, after nearly dying in a place opposite Romania. I'm the Morrigan."

"You are the Morrigan," replied Dr Jake, his hand still hovering. "Our Space Crawler?"

"The same, Doc," said Vlad.

"So you are basically an interplanetary prankster," said Dr Jake. "Correct?"

"Accurate, Doc. May I add, a highly intelligent predator."

"That is to intimidate me?" asked Dr Jake.

"No, Doc. If you recall, your own younger colleague programmed a substance that proved to be nearly my death."

"Sticky carbon," said Dr Jake.

"Rendering me quite vulnerable to attack," said Vlad.

"Morrigan, it doesn't help. I don't have such a thing as sympathy," said Dr Jake with a dry smile. "I take it the Captain knows?"

"He is in the picture, and agrees," said Vlad.

"Then that settles that. What are you up to now?"

"Checking on the enemies aboard, for Federi," said Vlad.

"Good. Keep it up. If you find one stepping out of line, eat him."

"That would be breaking the codes, Doc," said Vlad. "Federi absolutely forbade me to make a meal of a human."

Dr Jake nodded, already half-absorbed in his programming again.

"Then carry on, marine," he dismissed the Morrigan absently.

~

Vlad checked on Bryce, lying chained up between the crates. The man had been doused with more sedative, the Solar Wind informed him. The easiest way of keeping a prisoner under control. The Morrigan flowed back up the companionway and along the deck, returning to the infirmary.

Patrick was comatose. He was another case Federi had worried about. Vlad checked the young human and placed a tentacle across his forehead. It was a miracle that the man was still alive. There was a lot of damage. With bioelectric tentacles Vlad rerouted arteries and veins, made a biological drainage pipe from the man's brain into his stomach so that the pressure and excess blood could drain. He removed the bullet and reconstructed the skull, liquefying all bone fragments that had shattered into the soft brain tissue. And then began the much more intricate work of repairing the damage to the central nervous system itself.

Patrick wouldn't be able to think all that clearly when he came to; but at least he would live. A silent bonus was that he wouldn't turn into an enemy. He couldn't. The brainpower was now lacking. He wouldn't be a liability though; intelligent enough to clean cabins. As long as the croaches didn't get too frustrated with him.

And Vlad turned to the other bunk and peered at Mrs Flanagan, who was still sleeping, too. Yuck – another Unicate *Other*. She was exhausted, and she was old; but Unicate had their own regeneration patterns, and he wasn't about to make it easier for them. He feared the Unicate, because they were a force he didn't quite understand. He knew that they were more powerful than he, and he was thankful that they couldn't breed in his universe. It stood at right angles to their possibilities.

They could trespass into his world though, they had found a way. They had stolen a few of his werefolk, when those were on a sortie to Earth for some food. And ever since then, he had some weird werefolk that came and went, but didn't act like werefolk and couldn't stay on Shrn for overly long. He had no way of catching them.

Hamlin and infestations! Hamlin's rats had nothing on what Falco Demonos had brought upon the Earth!

And then the Doc stood in the infirmary door, staring at the Morrigan.

"So you're feeling better, space crawler?"

Vlad smiled, baring some Dracula fangs.

"Are you messing with my patients?" asked Doc Judith suspiciously. "No scaring them!"

"This one is a Unicate specimen," Vlad pointed out. "I hope you're aware of it?"

Doc Judith shuddered.

"Pancreas," said Vlad out of context, remembering. "Federi asked me to fix someone's pancreas. Who would that be?"

"You do that kind of thing?"

235

"Certainly! Have a look at your other patient!"

Doc Judith looked. Patrick's bullet hole in his forehead had closed up. He was breathing more easily, sleeping.

"So you're medically inclined?" asked Doc Judith with a fascinated smile. "Can you be trusted?"

15 – Christmas Eve

The Probe docked at the Pluto Base. Perdita got out and demanded a Leapfrog to be readied. The little cadets fell over each other trying to comply. Perdita took the opportunity to chat to Sulis, and make sure that everything still was as it should be.

There was something niggling at her, causing her some deep unease. Something she was sure she had forgotten about. She'd have to go and patrol the outskirts of the solar system a bit, when everyone was back aboard who needed to be.

Paean took Federi aside, to the ornate, open gates that marked the entrance to the living quarters of the base. The Danaan society, as much as they were space-going, were into intricately wrought metalwork and delicate paintings of maidens in forests. Judging by the artwork, men hadn't featured in the Danaan society for a long time. The art couldn't quite be compared to the lewd posters at Deep Base.

"Got something for you," Paean said quietly, and watched those gypsy eyebrows as they arched enquiringly. "Was going to give it to you tomorrow, at the gypsies, you know… but…"

"But now you don't think we'll be at the gypsies tomorrow," Federi completed for her. Guiltily. He knew too. Captain had them both back, despite their mission that they needed to complete.

"I'm sorry, little luv," he began. She shook her head.

"Here," she said and dug in her pocket. "Close your eyes!"

Federi closed his eyes, and she pressed her gift into his hand. He looked at it in surprise, studied it from all angles.

Paean took the ring out of his hand again and positioned it on his left ring finger. He grinned at her, lost for words.

A wedding band. She had organized him one! He removed all the other rings from his hands – he did go through phases when he liked wearing some looted treasure, but he supposed he didn't need to anymore. And he stuck them in his pocket and studied the ring. Nearly expecting glowing letters. No, wait – it had to be put in the fire for that.

The ring was of platinum and had strange, Celtic markings on it, in some black opalescent material. He knew there were no gemstones that could be moulded into writing or runes. He looked closely at the markings.

In a very curly handwriting, it was an F and a P, joined by an eternity symbol.

"Kitty made it," said Paean with a grin. "She said she'd never forgive me if I asked anyone else. Paid her in shipwreck treasure."

So Kitty had made quite a bit out of the deal! Ha!

"What's the black material?" he asked.

"Star dust. It was all over the Comet's outsides when we came back to Earth. Ailyss helped me collect it with an electromagnet – it was trapped in that shield of the Comet, that…"

"Kovalski shield," completed Federi. And he grinned mindlessly. "So you write our names together in star dust?"

"Didn't have a birthday present for you," she said. "Lost track of time. We were at the gypsies."

He stared at her, touched. And he drew her into his arms. And kissed her convincingly.

"Lovebirds," said Perdita behind them, "excuse me, the Leapfrog is ready."

*

239

Paean marvelled at the green planet as they disembarked at the interchange, and an airborne transport took them to the palace. She didn't know what she had expected of Dana's civilization, but the vast amounts of greenery, the floral art, the topiary in the gardens surprised her. The architecture was calm and lovely; everything had soft curves and muted colours.

This was an exclusively female society, she remembered. And why had she thought that they were all forward and bossy like Dana? Why should they not all be celebrating their femininity instead?

"This place makes me fidgety," Perdita answered her unspoken commentary. "And so does the colour magenta."

Paean grinned and nodded. There was a lot of magenta between the muted greens and pinks.

The White Palace was another matter entirely. The two little castle guards stepped aside hastily when they saw Perdita approaching. They peered curiously at Paean and suspiciously at Federi, whose quick eyes were everywhere. He was taking in everything as fast as he could. Paean knew what he was doing, probably instinctively by now: He was charting the place in his mind and looking for quick escape routes, should it become necessary. Federi never just walked into a place.

Perdita demanded an audience with Dana; kept it extremely short, and had Shawn and Mindy before her in no time at all.

"But..." said Shawn.

"Captain's orders," said Perdita. "Shawn, you are still a Solar Wind sailor. You are contractually bound, my friend. And Mindy is in pain. Did you hope Dana could cure her back?"

"We don't exactly break our backs here on New Dome," Dana commented from the sidelines.

Paean bit back a snappy response. It was Bridget's monstrosity that had caused Mindy's broken back, not Dana's. Not that Dana's monsters were any better – or for that matter, Perdita's... or Paean's, she had to think with a dry grin. Her own monsters were the worst.

"Captain isna going to execute Mindy, if that's what you're worried about, Shawney," she said.

"But he will put her ashore," objected Shawn. "And then who will be looking after her back?"

"Captain isna going to put her ashore either, now is he?" retorted Paean.

"Shawn," Federi intervened, "if Captain decides to put Mindy ashore, we'll take her to the gypsies in Miami. And make sure that Cassandra calls Wolf every time the bridge slips."

Mindy looked as though she were being brave.

"I think the sooner she's back aboard, the better," said Paean. "You're being selfish, Shawn!" And with that the matter was sealed. Shawn allowed himself and Mindy to be led back to the Interstellar Leapfrog.

*

Perdita left the Solar Wind behind once more; the fourth time today. It might be Christmas Eve, but that didn't mean anything to the nasty feeling in her gut. She promised herself not to take long; she wanted to be back for Christmas morning.

She put the Probe into warp for a small moment – the drives that she hadn't managed to construct on Earth, despite her best efforts, because they contained materials that were not available on Earth – and leaped with the small shuttle to the outskirts of the solar system. Outskirts, what a joke! She calculated her distance from the sun, and kept a steady orbit. She had long since tweaked the Lolita drives to be able to modulate down; this gave her a much smoother mode of travel than Dana's weird Salamanca drives for which Captain had opted.

She'd kissed Radomir lightly and promised him she'd be back soon; but this couldn't wait. If Perdita hated one thing, it was a feeling of uncertainty. She couldn't tell where her feeling of unease came from, but it had assaulted her six times today; every time she approached, or left, Pluto.

Nothing but space, as usual. She smiled at the way little Shawn had got protective of Mindy Adamson. And she shook her head, too, and wondered what history Federi had with the deceased Angelina Carter. None, knowing the gypsy. From what she'd gleaned about him from various crew members and staff on the bases, he'd been a sealed case file until Paean had appeared on the scene.

Radomir didn't know that she was patrolling the Solar System. She wasn't sure what he presumed; possibly that she was checking on the bases, or the gypsies, or her own bases... which were on her list, too, but not for tonight. Nothing urgent wanted to catch her attention there.

She turned the console lights to minimal, and touched the console, activating some Sherman files with the most beautiful music on Earth. Suitable for Christmas Eve. And she sighed, and relaxed.

*

Bryce peered through lowered eyelids. The machine room was empty. This was his chance.

Christmas! The fools! Did they think that the leader of the IRP could be chained up with measly electronic handcuffs and metal chains, and then be left alone so they could celebrate Christmas? Idiots the lot of them. It only proved once again how evil people indulged in magical thinking and sloppy mental processing, and how

242

the truth won out, of necessity.

He managed to press the button on his wrist-watch that sent a massive electric discharge – for its size, and endured the excruciating pain as the electronic handcuffs opened with a pop. They were well and truly blasted.

There were many strange things wrong with the Solar Wind, he had discovered from his unprivileged position on the deck of the bilge-rooms. He could see the black bilge water sloshing a little at the bottom of the bilges, through the grill on which he lay. He wasn't insane enough to believe that there lay the way out! He had never been on a ship before; but this had to be the very bottom, and down there was only solid wall. And pumps for the water, he hoped.

People had been coming in and out of here; scruffy-looking pirates with beards; sleek-looking girls and women who were clearly expecting. What was this ship, a secret breeding station for rabble? And the man who'd brought him his food, had too many teeth altogether, and overly sharp ones. And the food was raw fish.

Well, the Solar Wind with her scaly crew was going to be history within the next three weeks, he thought as he sneaked up the companionway to the lower crew deck, found the nearest empty cabin, opened the porthole and dived down into the green waves of Durban Bay.

*

Vlad! Help!
Solar Wind, my love. What is it?
Bryce has escaped.

Vlad peered telepathically through the Solar Wind's sensors. *Ah.* The prisoner in the bilges. *Is that bad?*

Federi will have a conniption, the Solar Wind confided. I was

243

supposed to watch!

And why weren't you, my love?

You know why not!

Vlad smiled smugly. Of course he knew! Multitasking was a fine feature in artificial intelligences. The Solar Wind was good at it – or had been, up to the point where Vlad had started with his sensory overload. It was cute to see how the highly efficient girl lost her focus because of him.

Vlad called a croach closer.

A tiny croach. It was the size of a standard roach. Without his ability to see biofields he wouldn't have been able to differentiate.

"And who might you be?"

"S.I. Lucy," whispered the miniscule creature.

"S.I.?"

"Special Issue, sir," whispered the croach. "Wolf designed me for special missions."

"You're going to be more special in a second," said Vlad and reached into the small creature's biofield.

Wolf, the highly efficient genius engineer. He waterproofed everything. But clearly it hadn't occurred to him yet what a good idea it was to waterproof these little cyborgs. Or perhaps he hadn't yet worked out how.

"You are now an amphibian, for sweet and salt water," explained Vlad. He took his leave from the Solar Wind, slipped out under the infirmary bunk on which Mrs Flanagan lay sleeping, and flowed along the deck, taking little S.I. Lucy with him.

*

There was no way, thought Bryce, that they would see him today. The water was very salty and green in the dawn light. He dived deep

– he had won championships for diving in the past, it was a speciality of his. The waves were warm; much warmer than anything he had ever encountered on the coasts of Ireland, but it worked for him. His breath lasted longer that way. He pushed on through the murky water, aiming for that fishing trawler he'd seen.

Something huge brushed past him. Something as smooth as silk, and as large as a submarine. He gaped. A Great White! Mindless panic rushed through him. He had heard of their habit of brushing against their prey just before they attacked. He struggled towards the surface as fast as he could. The way up was endless! He had gone too deep! Nobody would know if he died down here, swallowed whole by this terrifying prehistoric predator!

The shark circled and returned; suddenly a huge maw of teeth was staring at him. Bryce lost control of all his intestines.

The shark snapped its jaw shut.

"Yuk!" it exclaimed. "Filthy human! Try to contain yourself! Others have to *breathe* this water, you know!"

Bryce was past mindless panic now, and out the far end. He battled against his convulsing lungs and his cramping stomach as he tried to get to the surface. The shark turned and dealt him a whack with its tail that left his ears ringing – but it propelled him all the way to the top. Bryce gasped for air and screamed and thrashed. The shark grabbed him by his shoelace and pulled him back down under water. It turned until it was squarely facing him, and then it grinned.

"You know of course that nobody is ever going to believe you," it said gleefully, turned and vanished into the depths.

Bryce struggled to the side of the fishing trawler and battled up the rungs. He climbed over the rail onto the boat with shaking limbs and awful trousers and grabbed the nearest crewmember by the shoulders, half leaning on him and half collapsing on the deck.

"Great White," he gasped.

"What?"

"Great White Shark in the bay!"

"Oh!" The Southern Frisbean gazed speculatively across in the direction of the swimming beach. It looked like a seal colony right now. It was a Southern Free custom to overpopulate the beaches on Christmas Day. The fisherman shrugged. "Don't swim behind the shark nets. Use the swimming beach. It's got safety in numbers. The buddy system. You feed the shark your buddy."

16 – 72-hour Christmas Day

Federi opened his eyes to gaze into the bluest eyes he'd ever seen. He drew Paean into his arms. It didn't matter where they were; at the gypsies or on the ship, as long as they were together.

"Merry Christmas," she murmured.

"Whatever that means, little luv," he countered and kissed her. She freed herself, just a little.

"No," she said sternly, "Federi, we're going to have family traditions, okay? That's important, especially for the kiddies."

"Kiddies," he smiled.

"Well, in the future!" she replied, blushing. "Didn't your family ever celebrate anything?"

"We celebrated," said Federi, his eyes glazing over. "Gypsies celebrate. We celebrated every occasion we could get an excuse to celebrate. Singing, dancing, bonfires. Music. Can't tell you how often Federi was called on – 'play us something, boy' – ha, you should know! We celebrated birthdays, and we celebrated weddings and special achievements, and every saint's day from every religion we could get our hands on, and…"

"That's not celebrating," said Paean with a smirk, "that's a lifestyle!"

"Wise-nose!" he countered with a grin, but it faded. "Little luv, these days gypsies have nothing to celebrate."

"I thought you were mentioning rather too many parties for the sedate life I just experienced at the gypsies," she said.

"It's the Unicate," replied Federi, scowling. "Those bleeding hounds. Takes all the celebration out of life."

247

She nodded thoughtfully.

"We're sorting that, though," she pointed out. "Right, Federi?"

"Right."

"We're going back today?"

"Tomorrow," said Federi. "Can't quite abandon ship yet."

"But we can check on them today, right?"

He peered critically at her.

"Little luv, what are you getting?"

"Just – I have an uneasy feeling about us not being there."

"For us or for them?"

She listened at the ether. "Both," she said. And scowled. There was more. She couldn't pinpoint it.

Federi got up out of the bunk in one swift movement and started getting dressed, and arming himself. "We're going back right after breakfast," he promised.

"Breakfast," smiled Paean. "That's great. Let me just check on breakfast. Wonder what Shawney's organized."

"Shawn wasn't aboard to do the organizing yesterday," Federi reminded her. "It's most likely going to be sushi."

She dressed, got armed up and left the cabin.

Those blasted Unicate werehounds! Federi strolled down to the infirmary to get a grip on the Morrigan. He peered in through the door, and found Mrs Flanagan still asleep, and Patrick with no head wound, but still out as well. And a tentacle touched his shoulder. He spun round.

"Ah, Vlad."

"Federi," acknowledged the Morrigan. He was in the shape of Prince Vlad the Impostor again; Federi was beginning to get used to him in that guise. With the exception of the left hand, which was a tentacle. Just to remind people that he was indeed an alien. Mind conjuring!

"Vlad, I have a question."

"I heard your vibes challenging me from the other end of the ship," said the Morrigan.

"Exactly. You have werefolk on your planet. And they seem to respect you. Now, they respect me too – or at least, my whip. But I can't be everywhere. I need to know that they will not attack the gypsies while I'm gone."

"Federi," objected Vlad, "it's Christmas! You want me to be away from the Solar Wind on Christmas?"

"Since when do you celebrate Christmas?" asked Federi, baffled.

"Since the Solar Wind does," replied the Morrigan. "But if you like, I'll go check on them – only, I must know that it isn't a trick of yours to kick me off the ship."

"It's not," said Federi shortly. "Check on them for me. Be so kind. Tell them that if they as much as nibble on a human, they'll be demon kibble."

The Morrigan sighed dramatically.

"In fact," demanded Federi, "take me along. Then I can know that you're doing it the right way."

"If they still listen to me," replied Vlad melodramatically. "When, oh master?"

"Right after breakfast," decreed Federi. "We'll teleport together." And he dismissed the Morrigan and went in search of Paean, who had gone in search of Shawn.

Vlad the Impostor flowed into the galley. He found Ronan there, trying to coax Rushka to eat something.

The girl looked terrible. Vlad looked more closely. As the daughter of Dana she shouldn't be capable of looking that sick. Something was definitely not right, and it had to do with that bulging stomach…

He walked up to her and placed his tentacle on her shoulder.

"Hey!" protested Ronan. "Who the hell are you and what are you doing with my wife?"

Vlad's pupils turned square; he grinned horribly, growing more merrow teeth than Lyr could ever hope for, and momentarily allowing his eyes to bulge. The early light spilling in through the portholes dipped and there was a distant rumble of thunder.

"Who am I?" he asked. "I'm the Morrigan! Cringe, human!"

Ronan went down as far as the bench, and sat down next to Rushka. His spine was straight; "cringe" had been a direct command to his bone marrow, but he was a Donegal, blast!

His gun came out; not as fast and as reflexively as his sister's would have, but out it came, nevertheless, and it took sharp aim. Unwavering despite the Morrigan command.

"So what are you doing to my wife?" he demanded angrily.

"Helping her," said Vlad quietly. "Hush, proud Donegal mage!"

Another order directly to his limbic system! Ronan snapped his mouth shut and watched in concern, lowering his handgun. What had the Morrigan meant, calling him a mage?

Doc Vlad diagnosed, and shook his head in disgust.

"Princess Rushka," he said. "Crown princess of New Dome, and my loyal s…"

Federi had entered the galley and had come to a complete, quiet halt.

"Loyal what?" he demanded softly.

"Royal nothing," replied Vlad. "She is the princess of Dome. Federi, give me some space here. Rushka is ill, very ill. It's the worst case of foetal cannibalism I've ever seen. They are eating her alive, taking everything out of her that she has. She won't live to full term – and neither will her babies."

Federi stood rooted to the spot, staring at his foster sister of many years. Flying stars, she was going to die?

"But, why?"

"A bad combination of the human and Danaan genes," said Vlad. "It expresses fully only in the second generation. Seeing this I must presume that Dana didn't have too easy a time expecting Rushka, either."

Federi didn't respond to this. He wouldn't know.

"She won't live to term?" he asked, horrified.

Vlad solemnly shook his head.

"Vlad, can't you do something about it?"

The Morrigan considered.

"I could," he said. "But it's a lot of adaptations. You'll have to be sure of this."

"Better than see my little sister die!"

"Go ahead, Morrigan," Ronan put in.

"Rushka?" asked Federi. "How about you – are you alright with the Morrigan making changes in your body? If they help you with the twins?"

"Go ahead," groaned Rushka. "Sure it's safe?"

"Safer than the alternative," said the Morrigan. He placed his tentacle back on Rushka's shoulder and concentrated.

Federi watched how colour returned to the Princess's cheeks. And he relaxed a bit about what Vlad was doing. Rushka slumped forward, resting her head on her arms on the Ironwood table, and released a deep sigh.

"Feel so much better," she murmured. "Just want to sleep!"

Paean came across Shawn on the deck where he was fussing with some of the decorations that had blown loose in the gentle breeze in the early morning. He turned to her and accepted her hug and her Christmas wishes.

"You know what bugs me," he said, "Mrs Flanagan. She doesn't talk at all. Pae, she's a Unicate *Other*! I canna believe that of our Mrs Flanagan! I don't know what's going on."

"She's gone through hell," said Paean. "Give her a bit o' leeway, Shawn."

"She was never a Unicate anything," Shawn objected.

"We didn't know how to spot Unicate *Others* back then," Paean reminded him.

"Sure, but she was never creepy," said Shawn.

"She's na creepy now, either," replied Paean.

"That's," said her little brother, "where I beg to differ from you, Pae. She's creepy. She wafts around the Solar Wind's passages and doesna recognize me. I asked her questions about her old home and she just looks at me funny. I don't think…"

"What are you suggesting?" asked Paean.

"That's na Mrs Flanagan," said Shawn in a half-whisper.

Paean stared at him for a long moment, his message sinking in.

"Then we've still got to rescue her," she pointed out. "Then she's still in there, in the Mound! If she's still alive…"

"You're na going back into that Mound!" shot Shawn. "Not over my dead body!"

"I only need a teeny, tinsy bit of her, Shawn," said Paean. "Of our Unicate *Other*. Just a blood sample. To find out what I can clone against the Unicate. Then I put my virus into the mound and I just walk in and find the real one." She shuddered. "Course, Shawney, you know what else this means? If you're right, that is?"

"I'm right," said Shawn with rock-solid conviction.

"It means that Terence set it up so he can be on the Solar Wind. He's even organized himself a backup. No wonder nobody stopped

252

us in that mound! Here I was thinking the man was actually helping us…"

"It means that we'd better let Captain know," said Shawn.

Paean nodded. And it all started looming, a whole overwhelming day. Captain. He'd be giving her orders, she'd never get to anything else she had planned.

"But Shawney, I've got to check on the gypsies first. Got this feeling. All isn't right there. Coming with me?"

"Alright," said Shawn. "But if you think I'll be shooting anyone down the way you did that Peter Piper…"

Paean groaned. She felt absolutely awful about that bit of honed reflex.

"If they're threatening to kill the gypsies I will be shooting them down," she said firmly. And she teleported to the machineroom to arm herself with a Kosaka cannon additionally to the full arsenal she was already wearing.

Radomir Lascek hadn't slept a wink. He watched his crew on deck from the bridge. He'd given up walking in small circles like a tiger, either. Perdita hadn't returned.

He had tried locating her via wrist-com and teleporter, and had failed. She was out of range. This meant in all probability that she was doing some deals with Dana on New Dome; but it also meant that he was uneasy. She should not do that, blast! It was putting his patience on trial in a way it had never meant to be tried.

Something honed in on the Solar Wind; something like a shimmering black seagull. It approached the bridge window like a falling brick and came to an abrupt halt just outside the volcaniplex. And stared at him, hovering.

Paean teleported with Shawn to the Space Base, and begged some polar gear for him from Itzak. The husky man had a soft spot for her since the first time he'd set eyes on her, back at that doomed place, the Ice Base. He organized the gear in record time. Paean made Shawn put it on.

"It's cold in Romania," she warned. And she looked up the location on her wrist-com teleporter. Wolf had copied all the data from her older teleporter to her new one in the night; he'd allowed her to take her new wrist-teleporter back when she'd needed it for picking up Federi's ring from Kitty Murphy. But he'd retained her older teleporter. He didn't want her to use that one anymore, because of its unsafe field.

They found themselves in Romania, in the snow. Paean brought the Comet closer via the remote function Wolf had programmed into the new wrist-com.

"This is the middle of nowhere," Shawn pointed out.

"This is, reversing the last leap from the gypsies," she countered as she looked around. And her heart sank. "You're right, Shawney! They've left."

This was what she had been worried about. This was why she had wanted to return here earlier.

She and Federi had only been gone for a day, anna bottle!

She studied the fresh snow that had fallen. It covered any tracks there might have been to give them clues. She paged through her teleporter's options, but she had never trained it on any of the gypsies; she'd relied on Federi to be around.

"You sure they were here?" asked Shawn.

"Course. Shawn, this is how they do it. They leave without a trace." She walked to where the small campfire should be and scratched aside the fallen snow, and brushed the leaves underneath

254

away too, and then some earth… "There! You see?"

Coals. The campfire had been right here.

"Wonder why," she muttered.

"Maybe they didn't feel safe without Federi around?" asked Shawn.

"Likely," replied Paean. "He armed them with machineguns, Shawn. What can go wrong?"

Shawn went completely quiet. He closed his eyes and listened.

Paean followed suit. Now that she concentrated, she could hear it too: The baying of hounds.

"Which way?" she whispered, and Shawn pointed north, downhill. They scrambled down the slope, Paean keeping her Kosaka gun ready.

At some point suddenly there were tracks. Fresh tracks in the snow, of people – a whole tribe. And as abruptly they vanished across a line.

"If I had Federi's courage I'd call the dogs now and force them to open the portal," said Paean.

Shawn walked across the invisible line and disappeared. Paean lunged after him – and stumbled headlong to the ground, because the ground was at ninety degrees to reality, and so was gravity.

The baying and noise was terrible. The gypsies were defending themselves and their children with the guns Federi had provided; but there were a lot of hounds and no Cat-o'-Nine-Blades.

"Shawn, get back!" screamed Paean, motioning her little brother towards the portal. The werefolk had discovered them both and were bearing down; fell hybrids in Unicate uniforms. Paean shot a few Kosaka missiles into the foremost few, while Shawn escaped behind her out of the portal, back to Earth.

The snow of Romania greeted him face-first. He activated his com. This was out of their league. They needed Federi.

Federi's com registered out of range.

This was bad. Shawn tried the whole Solar Wind, one by one; all registered out of range except for Ailyss, Wolf, and Jon Marsden.

He tried to link into the Solar Wind's console with his wrist-com, as he'd done many times while helping Sherman with the early shift – and found that the ship, too, registered out of range.

He called Ailyss on his com. Within a split second she was standing next to him, and Wolf with her. They were both not exactly dressed for the Romanian winter, and were rather surprised about all this.

He explained the situation in the briefest words he could find, but before he had finished, Ailyss had dived into the portal. Wolf emitted a growl and lunged after her; so nothing was left for Shawn to do but follow.

He didn't own a personal gun yet, but it was a quick thing to take one off half a Unicate hound that had been felled by one of Paean's missiles, and work out how the thing worked. His sister was by now on the ground; but she was still shooting at everything that had a uniform. She had run out of Kosaka missiles, but was using her Paean Special. She looked injured. He glanced and saw blood...

Ailyss was mowing down Unicate hounds with her submachine gun. Wolf had his pistol out and was aiming, and shooting, and aiming, and shooting, and every time he shot, one hound went down.

The pack of hounds was now decimated enough that the survivors caught fear – finally – and fled.

"Shoot," cursed Paean, looking at the slaughter.

Jehan rounded up the gypsies and then came over to her as Almeira took over counting heads and checking injuries.

"You got hurt, shay?"

256

"Not to – speak of," grunted Paean, trying to get to her feet. Her left leg had been mangled. It hurt like burning hell; but that was because the situation was over.

"Everyone survived?" she asked anxiously.

"Everyone is fine," said Jehan. "We've got a few injuries too, nothing that will go bad though, it's winter…"

"On your ally," retorted Paean. "Taking you guys to Las Village! Not taking that risk again!"

In the next few minutes Ailyss, Shawn and Wolf teleported the gypsies to the Ginavian rescue village. Doc Vera had all sorts of stuff to say but started on the repairs immediately. Eventually only Jehan, who had stayed with Paean to protect her if the dogs should return, was left.

"I think I had better stay and look after Paean," he informed her little brother and her surrogate brother and her chosen sister. "If Federi is not around, who will protect her?"

Wolf stared at the guy, gobsmacked.

Shawn grinned. "She's got us," he pointed out, "but you're very welcome." He loaded his sister into his teleporter field and teleported with her to Marge's place. Ginavis was still Europe; the uncanny hounds could pop up there, too, searching for her. But they never came to Southern Free, or so Federi had promised him.

Marge nearly fell over when she saw the small group of Solar Wind crew and the single gypsy.

"Oh my word! Paean, you're hurt!" She bustled them all inside and helped Paean to the closest guest suite. The surprised couple that was currently in there, was moved to a different suite.

"Shawn, can you teleport me to town to get a doctor?" asked Marge. "It's so much faster than driving there!"

Paean looked at them all with eyes strained from not screaming in pain, and passed out.

17 – Vanished

Voices. Paean heard them in the half-dark, through the open door, coming from the other room.

She lay in pain, studying her surrounds, trying to remember what had happened. She was tucked in under a furry blanket, in a solid-feeling bed, in a room with a lot of wood and raw face-brick walls. Animal skins decorated the walls like tapestries, one here, one there. The place smelt musty, and rich, and of a country that was somehow closer to the earth than Ireland.

Marge's place. She was at Marge's. Shawn had taken her here with the teleporter. And her leg hurt like hell. She couldn't get those weird, wild *Other* eyes out of her head, the hound that had attacked her just as she had chased Shawn back out of the portal to fetch Federi.

Where was Federi? Why wasn't he here? Shawn had brought Wolf and Ailyss. That was good, but…

She lay wondering for a while, her brain too cloudy to think properly. She had pulverized that hound with a Kosaka missile, it had been extremely messy. But those eyes…

She tried moving her leg and groaned. It felt tight, and hot. She sat up and moved the blanket aside, and looked. Her thigh was bandaged. Someone had looked after her.

Where the hell was Federi? She'd have expected to wake up to those dark, unfathomable gypsy eyes studying her, in love and anger – that she had got herself injured. He wasn't in the habit of budging from her side when she was hurt. This was strange.

She reached for her wrist-com to call for him, and found that

258

someone had removed it. Ah! Blast! Overprotective after all; the wrist-com had a teleporter built in. She dug in her pocket for the other teleporter and found that gone too, and also found that she had been thoroughly disarmed.

That was Ailyss. Federi would never leave her defenceless like this! She rallied her powers to get up and find out what was going on, and just as suddenly, her energy deserted her. She slumped back into the pillows and lay listening.

Of the voices carrying over from Marge's lounge, she recognized Wolf's gruff Neanderthal statements; Ailyss' quiet but loaded commentary; Shawn's bright voice; there was also Marge, and some other voices that she didn't recognize; and then Jon Marsden's quiet, polite input.

Jon Marsden. In her mind's eye she saw Federi perched cross-legged on one of Marge's lounge chairs, carving away at something. Observing everyone and not commenting. She took a deep breath and got up.

Her leg ached to the extreme, and she needed to hold onto something to stabilize herself. She made her way from wall to door, holding onto whatever she could grab hold of, and inched her way through the short bit of passageway into the lounge.

"Paean!" Jon Marsden got to his feet and helped her hobble to one of the rustic chairs. She thankfully sank down in it.

"You shouldn't be out of bed," said the First Mate.

She studied the gathered people. The first thing she missed, and by now this was almost as bad an ache as her leg, was Federi's dark eyes. He wasn't here! Shawn, Michelle, Ailyss, Wolf who was looking very worried, Jehan from the gypsies, and Lucy, the daughter of Marge. And some elderly, balding man whom she did not recognize but who had an air of authority about him. And a vital

259

signs probe around his neck...

"Where's Federi?" asked Paean.

"That's the problem," said Jon. "The Solar Wind has disappeared."

She started scrambling to her feet.

"Stay seated!" commanded the First Mate.

She stared at them all, frightened. "How can the Solar Wind have disappeared?"

"We were ashore in Durban Port when Shawn called us," said Ailyss. "The Solar Wind is gone, she isn't in the harbour, there's no trace, all the coms are out of range and so are the genetic signatures."

"Anyone contacted Dana?" asked Paean.

"That's the first thing we did when Ailyss alerted us," said Jon Marsden. "Right after she helped you with your tiff with the werehounds."

"Jehan," asked Paean anxiously, switching to Romani without a moment's hesitation, "the gypsies?"

"Your Las Village team helped move them to Ginavis," Jehan reminded her. "There aren't too many injuries, nothing as bad as yours anyway, and that is thanks to Federi arming us with guns. We must be the first *familia* that shoots back."

"Why did you leave the campsite?" asked Paean.

"Almeira could hear them," said Jehan. "She thought packing up and moving would help us get away from them. But we walked right into their trap."

"They open their flying portals wherever they want," said Paean angrily. And she went quiet. Those eyes haunted her. They weren't like the eyes of Dahlia, but the *otherness* was in them anyway; but along with that there was the wild, alien element too that she had seen in Vlad's were dogs that had chased her.

Those hadn't worn uniform. These had.

And she understood. The uniformed werehounds were as alien to Shrn's native werefolk as the *Others* were to humans. The Unicate had invaded Shrn, too. She had to warn the Morrigan!

If he wasn't the reason for the Unicate... no; that was Falco.

They were all staring at her. She returned to the present.

"This is Dr Swart," said Marge, introducing the balding man with the friendly smile. "He stitched your injury."

"Pleased to meet you, doctor," said Paean shyly.

"You too, Paean," said Dr Swart. He had the same Southern hemispheric accent in his English as Marge. "You must speak up when you want a painkiller, because that injury is quite deep. Your muscle has been torn. You can expect it to take a few months before you start feeling normal again, and you're always going to walk with a limp. Luckily we caught it early, so the risk for infection is small."

She went quiet. To be disabled was not part of her agenda!

So the Solar Wind was missing?

"What does Dana say?"

"Dana has mobilized her fleet," said Jon Marsden. "She takes a very serious view on this. They are looking for positron traces of the Solar Wind around the portal at the Interchange."

"Positron traces!" gasped Paean.

"Pae, everything leaves a positron trace," said Wolf. "It's part of the nature of the universe. It doesn't mean that..."

She breathed again.

"So we're assuming that the Solar Wind has gone off into space?" she asked.

"What else would you presume?"

"Shrn," said Paean. "The Morrigan might have opened a portal to Shrn and abducted her there."

"You're right!" said Ailyss, getting to her feet. "We can check that! That should explain how we can't access her." She activated

261

her teleporter and disappeared. Wolf winked out a second later, following her.

"They're going back to the werefolk trap!" exclaimed Paean. "They'll be eaten!" She started getting up.

"It's Ailyss," replied Jon Marsden. "Stay put! She won't get hurt. She knows what she's doing."

Paean sat down again, worried. She'd have to rely on that.

"How did you get back from the Solar Wind, sir?" she asked Jon Marsden, suddenly puzzled.

"I wasn't on the ship," said Marsden. "Michelle and I were on Calypso."

She nodded. It was like this. Jon and Michelle, and Ronan and Rushka, and Rhine Gold and Rashni could all have their space and their time off. But she and Tzigan? And because of that, now Federi had disappeared with the ship.

"Sis, Ro and Rushka are on the Solar Wind too," Shawn answered her thoughts. "I'm very worried!"

Ailyss and Wolf reappeared.

"The teleporters don't detect them on Shrn, either," said Ailyss. "Nor do the coms. But…"

"Exactly," completed Paean. "The Morrigan knows how to make walls against transmissions."

"Exclusionary portal fields," said Wolf. "Probably driven by tachyolytic standing-wave radiation."

"Tachyolytic…" repeated Shawn.

"A tachyon is defined as a particle that can travel faster than light," explained Wolf.

"Ah," said Shawn, "so, all of us!"

Wolf grinned. "You're right," he said. "We all fit the description. We're all tachyons. It has been long disputed that they exist," he added.

"They don't," said Paean bitterly. "Tachyon physics is voodoo."

"Coming from you, sis," grinned Shawn.

"You're saying we're all fictitious?" asked Ailyss with a smile.

"Look, the teleporters work on positriolic interactions," said Wolf. "But Shawn is right, they turn us into tachyons."

"Don't we have to be sub-nuclear particles for that?" asked Shawn.

"Or in wave form," completed Ailyss.

"The frying coms don't work on vitriolic interchanges," snapped Paean. "How can he block the coms? If I catch that Morrigan! Why would he do that? We saved his iridescent hide! Or was all of that a show too? – Ow!"

"Back to bed with you," ordered the doctor. "You shouldn't be up, and you mustn't walk on that leg at all."

Wolf and Ailyss helped Paean back to her prison-room. Which it was, anna bottle! Paean was furious.

"Then can you guys at least be in here and discuss what's happening in here? 'm not a bleeding invalid!"

"You are," said Wolf with a pitying grin. "It's your turn, sister."

"And that's why you took my teleporters away?"

"You need bed rest, so that you can heal," said Wolf earnestly. "Doc Judith is off the planet. We don't have the Solar Wind's facilities with us."

Paean nodded in resignation and crawled back into Marge's guest bed and allowed Ailyss to cover her with the furry blanket. It was warm; but her thermostat was out of order, because the blanket felt good. She only realized now that she was actually dead tired.

So the Solar Wind had gone off into space; or else the Morrigan was keeping her captive on Shrn. If the latter was the case, she could count on it that Federi was working on solving the matter. She thought of the whip-o-nine-blades and wondered how the Morrigan would respond to that. Pointless: The shifter would simply liquidize. What they needed to do, was ask Wolf...

Wolf wasn't on the Solar Wind; he was here. The Morrigan had certainly picked his moment! Federi was on his own. This might take a while.

She had to try to find an answer from this end, she thought as Dr Swart injected her with a painkiller and probably, sedative. The pain in her leg let up over the next few seconds and wonderful warmth enveloped her.

Maybe after another bit of sleep some answers would come.

Jonathan Marsden whistled softly. Leila crawled out of Paean's pocket and reported in with her tinny voice.

"Yes, master?"

"You sit here and guard her," the First Mate instructed. "We know that she doesn't like being restrained. If she tries to get up or leave, immediately inform me on my com, understood?"

"Yes, master," replied Leila. "Master, a conflict of priorities arises. In the first place I need to report to Paean as she is my primary mistress. If she gives me a direct order to the contrary, it might overrule your orders, sir."

"You must place higher priority on her personal safety than on her orders," instructed Marsden. "My orders are for her personal safety. Hers don't always take that into consideration, given her immature status."

"Yes, master. I have set your current orders to highest priority, not to be overruled," replied Leila.

"Good girl – er, roach," said Marsden and left the room, leaving the door open by a crack. He would be monitoring Paean too. He owed it to his best friend who had disappeared into nowhere. Jon Marsden didn't easily show emotion; but the disappearance of the

Solar Wind struck him as very sinister. A black dog he hadn't seen in a long time, had slunk into his psyche and found its spot by his feet, ready to trip him up. He'd have to be careful.

The chirping of a nightjar woke Paean up. It was such a foreign sound, so warm and summery, as opposed to the wintry silence of Romania or the ocean sounds on the ship. She looked around and found her bearings. She hadn't moved from when Ailyss and the doctor tucked her in. Her leg felt stiff and ached dully; it was the ache that had fetched her back out of troubled dreams as much as the nightjar had.

The nightjar chirped again – right on her pillow. She blinked, and spotted a roach. She sat up like a flash, and stared at the tiny insect that was eyeing her back.

"Mistress Paean Demonos," it whispered, "I have an urgent message for the Morrigan and need your assistance in finding him!"

Paean glanced at Leila who sat on the small side-table next to her bed, apparently dozing.

"You're a croach?" she asked the foreign little insect. "Or are you a shifter from Shrn?"

"I'm S.I. Lucy, mistress," whispered the creature. "Special issue service croach, prototype, designed by Master Wolf."

"What are you doing dealing with the Morrigan?" asked Paean in apprehension.

"Mistress, Master Vlad sent me with the prisoner Bryce to monitor his movements and report back to the Solar Wind," said S.I. Lucy. "I wish to make my report but the Solar Wind does not register on my teleportation system."

So S.I. Lucy had a teleporter built in? Paean was impressed. And then the message sank in.

"Bryce? But Bryce is captive in the machine room…" So blast, the prisoner got out! She shivered slightly. "S.I. Lucy, we are working on locating the Solar Wind. In the interim, please report to me."

A momentary hesitation; then, "I find that I have no security codes to the contrary," said S.I. Lucy, "therefore I shall report, but when the Solar Wind is located, I shall report again."

"Spiffing," replied Paean. "Go ahead!"

"Mistress, Prisoner Bryce escaped but Master Vlad intercepted him and planted myself as a spy device," said S.I. Lucy. "I recorded the movements of the prisoner back to Limerick, by means of a fast airborne transport of the Peeping Tom type. He contacted the Unicate military and such a transport was sent to collect him. However he had to move off the coast of Southern Free to achieve the meeting. In Limerick he used the data he had collected from the Solar Wind's processor to locate all the bases. He has also stolen a teleporter, but it is clear that he doesn't know how to activate it; he believes it merely to be a data device and has copied the locations listed in its history, onto his own data storage system."

Paean listened to this with growing horror.

"Which teleporter did he steal, S.I. Lucy?"

"Mistress, the identity chip of the teleporter identified it as WT-2 06."

Wolf-designed Teleporter, second generation, sixth handset. The one she had been using, before this new one! So Wolf had left it lying around in the machineroom, probably intent on fiddling with it and improving it… and now it was in the hands of the enemy!

The implications sank in. She felt very cold suddenly, despite the balmy summer night.

That teleporter had every last one of Captain's bases on it; and by tracing her and Federi's movements, the location of Vlaşta, the co-houses in Miami, the place where the gypsies had camped…

Had she been at the Deep Base? She strained to remember. She had certainly been at Kango Base, when she'd cloned the antidote to the Unicate virus, but… that might have been with a different teleporter, as the Doc had taken her teleporter away after the showdown with the Morrigan. So… with luck the places on that teleporter were limited to where she had been with Federi after she left the ship.

Could Bryce get around to all those places? And round up hostages, and feed them to the Unicate the way Molly Street had been done! Evacuate and relocate… She had to find her old friends! This was impossible! Maybe Mrs Flanagan knew more? No, she wouldn't, she was a victim herself. Terence? He would, she thought. He could perhaps lead her to all her old friends and neighbours the way he'd led her to… a fake Mrs Flanagan… what if Shawn was right?

Right now she urgently had to get to the bases and warn them, maybe even evacuate.

"S.I. Lucy, can your teleporter take me to places?"

S.I. Lucy did a calculation. "No, mistress. Master Wolf has not yet found a way to enhance the protopositriolic field on such a small porter engine sufficiently to take cargo."

"Mistress," came Leila's tinny voice from the side-table, "I have Mr Marsden's orders to report if you move away from the bed."

Paean blinked in surprised indignation. "What? Leila? You are mine – I can override that!"

"Sorry, Mistress," came the peeped reply, "but Mr Marsden has set the priority of his orders to highest order."

"Really!" She thought about it, quietly fuming. How dare Mr Marsden? Leila was hers! "So if I as much as move out of bed…"

"I'm under orders to report you," confirmed Leila. "Very sorry, Mistress."

Ha! Very well then!

"Oh, I'm not moving anywhere," said Paean innocently. "But you, Leila, are going to fetch me my wrist-com from Wolf's room."

"Mistress, Wolf's orders are not to allow you near a teleporter," said Leila. "He also asked me to call him if you get up."

"Nice," said Paean. "How must I go to the toilet?" She saw her moonbag lying on the small table next to where the croach was crouching, and she picked it up and dug in it. And she noted with satisfaction that her bandanna was in there, and slung it around her head; and discovered that nobody had messed with her first-aid kit and biochemical arsenal. Good!

Now, if she knew the engineer…

"Fetch me Wolf," she ordered. And she picked S.I. Lucy up and stuck her in her moonbag.

"Mistress," objected Leila, "Mr Marsden told me to keep you under observation."

"Then contact Wolf on his com, you dense insect," snapped Paean. "Tell him that I'm escaping!"

"Mistress, you cannot escape! Keep your personal safety in mind!" peeped Leila in distress, and accessed Wolf's wrist-com.

Paean huffed impatiently. Being kept prisoner again by this ratty bunch of pirates! A plan was forming in her mind about how she was going to get around. It didn't exactly include a wheelchair. She removed a fishhook from her scarf, picked up Leila and touched that tiny sensitive electric spot behind the croach's neck delicately with the end of the fishhook. The croach's chip reset itself. She stuffed Leila into her pocket. It would take time to reprogram the croach, but better that than have her betray her to Mr Marsden. These pirates were dense. There were lives at stake!

Wolf staggered in through the door, groggy from sleep.

"Paean, you can't…" Her dart found him, and the huge man

crumpled to the floor.

"Sorry, soul brother," she muttered as she crawled to his unconscious shape and dug her wrist-com/teleporter out of his pocket. Just as she had presumed. He'd kept the thing on his person for safety.

If he'd only done that with the other one too, she thought as she teleported to Las Village.

*

Mihai got up and opened the tent-shack's flap.

Outside was a motorcycle, with a *gadchey* in a parka on it. He looked closer and realized it was Federi's young wife.

"Paean! Come in! It's cold!"

By now she was fluent enough in the Romanian Romani not to have to wonder about what he was saying. And fluent enough that she could get her message across.

"Mihai, wake up your wife and your children. I have to move you guys right now!"

"Why?" he asked, baffled.

"The Unicate is coming!"

That was enough to fire the man into action. In seconds, he had his wife and both sleep-logged children by his side. Paean included them all into her teleporter field and teleported up to the Space Base with them.

Itzak was in the Common Room, making coffee as she and the Roma family materialized, with Paean on her motorbike. He nearly dropped his mug.

"Paean!"

"Itzak, you've got to help me," she begged. "Huge crisis. One of the Unicate guys who are on our case has got hold of a teleporter –

269

and it's got all the locations programmed into it!"

"Major security risk," muttered Itzak.

"Including Cassandra's gypsies and the co-houses," added Paean.

"Right." Itzak activated the hot-line to Deep Base from the panic button in the lounge. "Pierre, come in!"

Pierre Hougaardt's voice came seconds later. Itzak warned him of an impending Unicate attack, and asked him to help.

"Can I bring them all up here?" asked Paean frantically.

"Sure," said Itzak. "Get Las Village to help, Paean. They are used to emergencies."

"Shukar." She teleported out.

In the next thirty minutes Paean rounded up Las Village and with their help evacuated the co-houses, the Miami gypsies and Kitty Murphy. Itzak and Little John, with the help of whoever arrived, took the fugitives into Space Base and made them comfortable. Emergency blankets came out, cabins were assigned, and people who couldn't go back to sleep, gathered in the lounge.

Paean rounded up the last of the bricklayers and on-site helpers who had been building the co-houses, and included them into her teleporter field. Here in Miami it was only dusk. Christmas Day had gone by in a coma for her. As she and the remaining few teleported to the Space Base, the co-house site exploded behind them. She felt the same hot wave that had marked her blowing up the vessel with Dana's mutants.

So, worse than hostages! Bryce was going around bombing! This was terrible.

She had warned each of Captain's bases of a potential onslaught, and they had armed up. Her motorcycle had caused quite a bit of stir wherever she went; but it was her key to retaining her dignity. She needed to do this sitting down, but not in a wheelchair!

She checked in on the Kango Base, which was empty as predicted, this time of the night. And a hand gripped her shoulder at that precise spot that caused muscular collapse. If she hadn't been sitting on a motorcycle, she'd have ended on the floor. She turned.

"So, you little pirate," said Ailyss angrily. There was no humour left in her. Jon Marsden was standing behind her. "Tracking you down is a nightmare! Wolf said you mustn't teleport, and how often have you teleported now? Twenty times in a row? And you shot down Wolf so you could get your teleporter back! That green bug always gives him a hell of a headache, Paean!"

"Ailyss, the Unicate has got our location," said Paean frantically. "I had to rescue and evacuate people! Should see the co-houses, the blasted Unicate has bombed them!"

"What?"

"See for yourself," said Paean. She pulled S.I. Lucy out of her pocket and handed her to Ailyss. "S.I. Lucy, please repeat your report to Ailyss!"

The special issue croach repeated what she had told Paean. Ailyss and Jon listened with dark frowns.

"The teleporter Bryce got is the one I had at the gypsies," added Paean when S.I. Lucy was finished. "The only other teleporter that has the same locations is this one."

Ailyss pocketed S.I. Lucy. "So he blew up the co-houses? Paean, that doesn't sound like a Peeping Tom. Even they don't fly that fast."

"I know," replied Paean, her face contorted in worried wrinkles. "It means he's figured out the teleporter! We've got to take it away from him again! And what if he finds Shawn?"

"Good that you've organized yourself a wheelchair," said Ailyss with a quick glance at the motorbike. "Give me your teleporter!"

"But Ailyss…"

271

"Give it to her!" commanded Jon Marsden sternly. "Paean, you're in breach of direct orders. You dealt with this completely wrong! You should have sent S.I. Lucy to me and let me take care of it all."

Paean handed over the teleporter to Ailyss, and the spy gave her a different one.

"Take yourself back to Marge and tell them all to get armed," she said. "We're dealing with an arsonist."

"Ailyss and I will track down Bryce," said Jon Marsden. "Go warn Marge now, and then you stay put and wait for us there!"

"Yes, sir," said Paean resignedly, and teleported herself back to Southern Free to wake up the others and apologize to Wolf.

All the bases had armed guards by now; the staff was taking turns. Las Village was also guarded; possibly better than most, with ex-Unicate marines and Danaan petites.

Paean and her motorbike landed in Marge's lounge. The doctor and Marge were sitting there discussing; and Wolf also sat there holding his head. He barely looked up. Jehan sat on one of the high-back chairs, looking uneasy.

The doctor got up to look at the motorcycle. "Nice machine! Paean, what are you doing? You should be in bed!"

"Marge," said Paean, "there's a crisis. Can you get someone to guard the house? There's an arsonist with a teleporter going around blowing up everywhere Federi and I have been."

"Shit," groaned Wolf. Jehan was on his feet.

"I'll wake up Richard," said Marge and left the lounge.

"I was working on a data device on the Solar Wind that tracks every teleporter's movements," said Wolf glumly. Paean rolled closer with her bike and reached out to touch his shoulder.

"Wolf, I'm so sorry! There was no time to explain. You know, Bryce has blown up the co-houses?"

"Shit!" Wolf groaned again. "Any good news, sister?"

"Apart from that Ailyss and Mr Marsden are taking care of the situation now," said Paean.

"You call that good news?"

"Well, Wolf, I warned all the bases and evacuated the co-houses – and also Mihai's family, just in case," she said, glancing at Jehan. "Wolf, could you organize me my Genitron from the Comet?"

The nuclear engineer got up and left the room without a further comment. A few minutes later he was back with Paean's Genitron.

"Sister, if you hadn't been the force behind me keeping my leg I wouldn't forgive you now for that green bug," he informed her. "Don't you ever do that again! You use up your friends, you know that?"

She bit her lip and got off the motorcycle and found herself a spot in one of the rustic arm chairs. Wolf stuck the Genitron in her hand.

"No idea what you want with that," he said.

"First of all," she said and fell silent, focused on programming.

During their time at the gypsies Federi had finally had time to write her the hack that allowed for the Genitron to plug into the console of the Comet, by remote communication. He'd also had the time to copy the Sherman Files into the Comet's console; Sherman himself had helped him with this. And Federi had made a point of stealing a fair supply of nucleotides and enzymes from Perdita's base and stashing them in the tiny ice box of the small fridge that was built into the Comet's drinks cabinet.

She thought of Federi, and her thoughts shied away. She didn't want to pursue the possibilities of what had happened to the Solar Wind. If she started wondering about it, she might not recover...

273

She glanced up and met Jehan's eyes. He was sitting with the machinegun Federi had organized for him, across his lap.

Marge had woken up her son Richard, who was staying over for Christmas. He appeared in the door now, with a hunting rifle.

"Come, Richard," said Wolf. "Let's go guard the premises!"

Jehan got up and accompanied the other two men out of the house, into the dark outside. The doctor came over to Paean and watched what she was doing. She explained briefly how the Genitron worked.

"Illegal apparatus," commented Dr Swart.

"Doktor, don't go there," laughed Marge. "Everything these pirates do is illegal. I had no idea what I was taking on when I first took Federi into my home." And she fell silent too. She didn't want to explore the possibilities either.

Because they might just lead them all to the conclusion that the Solar Wind had been bombed into subatomic particles by Bryce and company.

Paean asked Marge to call Wolf in, half an hour later. She had put the Genitron on warm, cloning her remedy at the rate of Federitic pancakes. It was ready now.

"What are you going to give me now?" asked Wolf suspiciously. "More poison?"

"Something that mops up the poison out of your bloodstream," said Paean. "Should make you feel better quickly."

"I'll live," growled Wolf, but he held still so she could inject her experiment into his vein. "I hope," he added with a lopsided grin.

"Wolf, that machine you were working on to track people's movements," she said. "Is there any way you could try again, maybe with materials sourced from Space Base or so?"

Wolf thought about it. His bushy eyebrow bunched into a knot.

And then he lightened up and teleported out, leaving her alone with her Genitron. Paean smiled. And then she frowned and wondered.

If the Morrigan had set S.I. Lucy to track Bryce's movements, it was unlikely that he had abducted the ship. At least, it wouldn't make sense. Not from a human logical aspect anyway. Unless he'd removed the ship to protect her from Bryce… but then, why shield her from the remaining crew?

But Bryce had stolen a teleporter. He'd know how to track them even on Shrn, being a blasted Unicate man. Unless the Morrigan shielded her.

But Federi would have found a way of escaping that, by now. That Demon was a lot more powerful than Vlad, at least that was Paean's impression. Then again the Morrigan had been rescuing and healing people. Maybe he really wanted to be in their good books? Which left another, much more frightening possibility.

They'd had two Unicate *Others* aboard the Solar Wind. She'd been thinking in the line of blood samples and virus, just before the Solar Wind disappeared. Could it be that the Unicate – Terence maybe – destroyed the Solar Wind to prevent her from this?

Bryce was suddenly in lounge, holding an old-fashioned chemical grenade.

"Freeze!"

Paean reflexively ripped out her gun and prevented herself just in time from shooting his head off; instead she shot his knees out under him. The man went down, roaring in pain. He ripped the safety pin out of the grenade and fiddled with his teleporter. Paean lunged for the grenade and grabbed at it, and hurled it out through the open window, hoping desperately that Jehan and Richard were in another part of the garden. She regretted now not having shot his head off. The grenade exploded with a huge blast, shattering all the windows.

Two trees outside caught fire; there was a hole where a third one had been.

And powerful hands grabbed Paean around the neck and throttled.

"Head Office has a price on your head," commented Bryce in vicious satisfaction, "but they have a smaller price on your dead body, too. I don't need all that much money. This is so much more fun!"

She kicked, panicking, unable to breathe. She realized vaguely that other people were entering the fray, battling to get Bryce to release her. He was an enormously strong man. Marge and Lucy were no match for him. Paean's vision started blackening out. And then the whole huge weight of the Unicate man collapsed on top of her, forcing what rest of air had been in her lungs, out.

Hands prised his fingers off her neck, and bullied his heavy hulk off her. Her lungs grabbed a huge gasp of air, and she coughed spasmodically, recovering. And looked.

Marge, Lucy and Shawn were there; the doctor was coming in at the lounge door and Jehan and Richard were bursting in from outside.

"Fire!" shouted Richard.

And Jon and Ailyss materialized in the lounge.

"There he is!" exclaimed Ailyss, pointing at Bryce's hulk on the carpet.

Shawn was kneeling down at his sister's side.

"Are you alright, Pae?"

"Better, thanks," she rasped, finding her voice back. It sounded funny. Her throat would be sore for days, she knew. "Did you kill him?"

"Just darted him," said Shawn.

"Good thinking," she lauded.

"Cause he's still got to tell us where the heck the Solar Wind is!" said Shawn angrily. "So we can't kill him – yet. Anyway I'd like to torture him over a small flame. 'e doesn't deserve a quick death!"

Ailyss locked handcuffs around Bryce's wrists; Jon Marsden teleported out again.

"Fire," said Jehan to nobody in particular.

Moments later Las Village was swarming over the property, fighting the flames.

Paean stared at Bryce. Something was nagging at her; a detail...

Ailyss picked up the teleporter and pocketed it, and disarmed the man. The doctor and Shawn helped Paean get back onto a chair.

"He got out of electronic handcuffs last time," she pointed out to Ailyss.

The brunette glanced at her and pulled S.I. Lucy out of her pocket, and gave the special issue croach a detailed instruction in a subdued voice. S.I. Lucy teleported away and returned ten seconds later with some Magiseal tape, the kind with which Itzak and Little John secured the connections around mobile parts in space. The tape had a way of bonding with the molecules of the substances it was stuck to for longer than thirty seconds, forming a compound.

"Ooh, evil," commented Paean with a satisfied little grin as Ailyss wrapped the tape around Bryce's wrists. And then, the spygirl used the Magiseal tape to crudely tape up the wounds in Bryce's legs where Paean had shot him. They were large wounds; those submachine guns blasted big holes. That he hadn't passed out purely from pain was an indication of his brute willpower.

"If you really want him to survive, you can't let him bleed to death," she pointed out.

Shawn studied his sister disapprovingly, where she lay on the floor, propped up on one arm.

"Sis, I know you had to do all this," he said, "but now you keep still, okay? Give your leg a chance to heal."

"Shawn," said Paean, "in principle I agree. In practice, if there's something I need to rescue, I can't let an injury slow me down."

"You're so stubborn!" exclaimed Shawn. "Now what if you end up walking with a limp for life?"

"There's a Morrigan aboard the Solar Wind," said Paean. "He can fix injuries. He fixed Patrick – did you see that?"

"And…" Shawn sighed. "Pae… if the Solar Wind doesn't come back?"

"Then I don't care if I'm lame for life," said Paean angrily.

18 – Werewolf

Birds chirping manically. Paean opened her eyes to peer into the dawn from behind a throbbing headache. She couldn't sleep any longer; couldn't even pretend to. She peered outside into Marge's garden.

Where the fire had raged very briefly last night was a blackened wound; and a crater where an old tree had stood. She felt very bad about that. She had always loved trees; and the way Federi treated them with respect, they had become nearly sacred to her. And the grass and flowers were trampled where Las Village had invaded to kill the fire.

She found two crutches that Wolf had left next to her bed, and hobbled on them to the kitchen, helping herself to some water and painkillers from her moonbag. The willow bark powders worked quite fast, as usual. She stared out into the misty dawn, her mind blanked out with missing Federi.

Yesterday she had woken up wrapped in his arms, as she had got so used to. At the deep end of one of his unfathomable gazes, his eyes like pools of black water without a bottom. Like hypnotic portals into the world of his soul; you could see in but you couldn't go there. Yet she spent most of her dreamtime in there.

She closed her burning eyes for a moment, recapturing that feeling. Some of the suppressed tears escaped. She hobbled back to her room on her crutches, checking on all her resources.

The motorbike was still parked in the lounge; she was pretty sure of that. She doubted that Marge had had time to clear up after all last night's escapades. Leila was sitting on her bedside table, but when Paean called to her, the croach didn't respond. Intelligence chip reset, she remembered. And S.I. Lucy came awake as she dug in her moonbag.

"Lucy," she whispered, "how do I get Leila's intelligence reloaded? Wait, I think I know." She dug in her pocket and located the elderly teleporter that Ailyss had forgotten to take away from her again. Or perhaps Ailyss was just fed up. This was distinctly possible. "Donegal Troubles," she heard her Captain's voice, on Samoa in the house of Benita D'Araujo. "Poor Federi – the blasted Donegals were just too much trouble!"

Well yes, perhaps they were, she thought angrily. But then again she, Paean, had a long record of rescuing the Solar Wind out of scrapes. Case in point, today. She was going to find where the Morrigan had stashed the ship, and bring her home.

She teleported into the Comet with Leila and connected her into the console by Red Dot. The lights of understanding came back on in the little servant's eyes. Paean stuck her into her pocket, dressed herself in her polar gear with parka, lined Arctic pants and boots, strapped an empty backpack on her back, and teleported back into Marge's lounge. Her motorcycle stood parked there. She registered its console chip on the teleporter and considered herself lucky that it had one, albeit a small one. There had been others that had been more basic – just heavy-weight bicycles with solar drive. This one had two beautiful features. Firstly, it had more than solar drives. It had a fuel drive that roared. It had after all been stolen from the police office in Sabie. And secondly it had a coordinates-based console map that could take you to anywhere on Earth – with the help of a teleporter of course! You picked where you wanted to go on the map, found the coordinates and keyed them into your teleporter. Handy.

And then she mounted her motorbike and teleported back to

Romania, to Dracula's castle. She was going to find those portals, and if it were the last thing she did!

Ice and snow greeted her, and darkness. No dawn yet. The day broke significantly later here, as it was winter. She let the teleporter sniff for genetic signatures, and followed the trail that was days old now, of her Federi. Her motorbike was on solar drives, so it moved stealthily for now; she was thankful about the broad tyres. It was a heavy-duty, cross-country bike as the police used to find criminals that thought of hiding in the forests around Sabie. It could handle stony slopes and muddy banks and didn't sink away too badly in the snow either.

She could of course call the Romanian hounds to open the portal... but for that, she felt she didn't have enough resilience. If they ate her before she could free the Solar Wind out of Vlad's clutches, what was the point?

There was a dead person lying face-up in the snow... or at least, the side was up that should have had a face. The man was deep-frozen; she circled him twice with her bike, undecidedly. He was nobody from the Solar Wind; nobody she knew. She pressed on, following the genetic signature traces.

"Mistress," hissed S.I. Lucy, just a second too late.

Paean, mountain motorbike and all, crashed through the portal to Shrn.

Ouch! That hurt! Paean waited for the stars to clear as she gripped her aching leg. Once she could focus again, she dragged herself up and checked that her motorbike was still functional. It seemed to have sustained no damage; the rugged bike seemed to be built for such opportunities.

She checked on her teleporter for genetic signatures. Her disappointment was not entirely unforeseen though. It had been a long shot; and of course, if Vlad was keeping the Solar Wind inside a bubble in his castle, none of the crew would register anywhere on Earth or on Shrn.

Alright then: Plan B.

"Lucy," she instructed, "locate me the closest werefolk that are not wearing uniform."

The Special Issue buzzed off her hand and headed out of the rocky hole. A few minutes later S.I. Lucy was back.

"Located them, mistress."

"Now feed the coordinates into my teleporter," said Paean. Rats, she really had to push Wolf to put a strong enough teleporter into the Special Issue that she could take passengers!

"Done, mistress."

"Thanks." Paean activated her teleporter and took out her submachine gun in the same movement.

A blink later she was in the midst of a pack of werefolk, motorbike and all.

Her arrival caused panic. Several werepeople wet themselves in fright. Paean lifted her gun. And she recognized a huge golden werehound, and smiled.

In his eyes she saw recognition too. The leader growled an order to his pack. The werehounds gave Paean some space. The leader approached her, his beautiful amber eyes studying her with deep suspicion. He morphed into a semi-human shape, still covered in his lush golden fur, including most of his face.

"What do you want?" he growled. Paean blinked in surprise. The thing spoke English! His speech was laced with wild noises, but she could understand him.

"You can talk?" she gasped.

"I can speak your language," corrected the werehound with an angry snarl. "You can't speak mine. Does this mean that you can't talk? Primitive human!"

She nodded. "Sorry."

"What do you want?" barked the hound. Even in humanoid, bipedal shape he was still more wolf than anything else. "If Shrn hadn't forbidden us to kill you, you would be a small snack, Paean Donegal!"

She digested this.

"Shrn? The planet has forbidden you to kill me?"

"The planetary Keeper, you idiot human," snapped the werehound. "The Morrigan of Shrn!"

"Vlad," she said, comprehension dawning. "Prince Vlad."

"In whatever guise he chooses to meet you," said the hound impatiently.

Vlad was the planetary Keeper of Shrn? Wow! This changed the angle of things. She needed to use every inch of advantage she had on the Morrigan, now. She took a breath.

"It's your planetary Keeper I'm looking for," she said.

"What do you want from Shrn?" growled the hound.

"That is between him and me," said Paean, suddenly fed up. "If you remember I'm his favoured human companion. You will take me to him."

The werehound's neck hair bristled and he growled angrily. "You do not speak to Grww like this! I am the Great Leader of all the Tribes here!"

"Great Leader," said Paean sarcastically, "your tribes don't seem to obey you! They still attacked me yesterday!"

Grww stared at her, taken aback. He sniffed; then he came closer to her and her bike, and sniffed her, and located her injured leg. Paean held completely still, frozen stiff with fear. She remembered how sharks went into a feeding frenzy when they smelt blood.

Grww investigated the bandages by smell, then also sniffed suspiciously at the bike. Paean nearly hiccuped with relief when he moved out of her personal space again.

"You're scared," he grinned at her. "Last time you were so scared you shed water."

"Last time I was your quarry," she replied, working on a steady voice. "You're dangerous and unpredictable. I'm used to great predators, I only don't like them quite this close."

Grww smiled and licked his nose. A second later Paean realized that he was embarrassed.

"It wasn't the tribes that hurt you," he observed. "I smell Unicate *Other* all over you. The tribes wouldn't dare to disobey me – or Shrn."

"Unicate *Other*?"

"It's Earth's fault," snarled Grww. "That blasted Prince of Earth, as he called himself – that Falco. He brought the Unicate. Before that, Earth and Shrn both had peace, and we had ample hunting grounds, but now – we have those creepy *Others* that pretend to be werefolk and that cause trouble with Earth! Werehounds have never yet collaborated with puny humans! We're a Free People! We are nobody's slaves! But the Romanian IRM – they control those *Others* that look like us but are Unicate."

Paean listened in fascination. Free People. Grww said it with the same pride that swung in Federi's voice when he talked about the Free Tzigany, and the inhabitants of Southern Free.

"You are a proud people, too," she observed with a smile.

"We are," said Grww, grinning.

"And because of Falco, you have been hunting for Federi?" asked Paean.

"We hate him," said Grww. "His ancestor and his people brought

284

the Unicate."

"And so you killed his baby brothers, and his kid sister and his parents?" asked Paean, suddenly bitter.

Grww gazed at her from his large golden eyes.

"We don't hunt babies," he said with disdain. "It's against our pride. It was his own Unicate monsters that slaughtered his tribe."

His own... Paean shook her head, seething.

"They eat our babies, too," added Grww in a growl. "A messy death on that Falco Demonos! They steal them in the night, and they use their Unicate portals to get away."

"And you can't make portals..."

"We can make portals, you mucus-brain," snapped Grww. "You don't understand the first thing about portals, do you, stupid Earth girl? Every shifter in the universe can make a portal. But we can't follow them into their mounds."

Paean shivered.

"Grww," she said, "I wish you'd see that we're on the same side. Federi and I have been hunting Unicate for months now. He shoots them down. We've even been inside a mound..." She shuddered again. "Grww, I have to speak to the Morrigan. He is the only one who can help."

"Shrn won't go near the Unicate," said Grww. "You're hoping in vain."

"The Morrigan won't go near the Unicate?" asked Paean, not overly surprised. Vlad was a bit of a coward. If she were technically immortal she'd also be one, she found herself thinking. Not risk her life in a Unicate mound for a foreign species. He was simply not martyr material.

But something of that didn't want to gel. "He's the Keeper of Shrn and the Unicate targets his werefolk but he refuses to confront the Unicate?"

285

"He is tied by laws," said Grww.

"Which laws?" challenged Paean.

"Intergalactic laws," said Grww.

Paean gasped. "You're a planet-bound species but know more than humans about intergalactic things?"

"It's easy for a simple mind like yours to mistake planet-bound hunters for primitive," said Grww smugly. "You don't even know how to open and close portals."

"Beautiful," retorted Paean. "So which Intergalactic law forbids Vlad to interfere with the Unicate?"

"How should I know? I'm not a planetary Keeper," said Grww. "I don't deal with the Intergalactic Council."

Paean paused. The Intergalactic Council. So there was a governing body of sorts, similar to what Captain had established on Earth? She stared at the golden werewolf, and his pack which was around... some of them had lain down and gone to sleep; some had disappeared on business of their own; a few were listening intently, occasionally scratching behind a pesky ear. And in the lush green forest – as pristine as that in Southern Free, at Marge – there were colourful birds and monkey-like creatures flitting about.

So there was an Intergalactic Council... which made laws...

"I need to speak to Vlad in any case," she said. "He's holding the Solar Wind and all her people. We are the core team of Earth fighters against the Unicate, Grww."

The werehound considered.

"By your honour as a Founder," he said then, slowly, carefully. "If you swear never to turn against the werefolk of Shrn, we can join forces."

"Grww," replied Paean, as cautiously, "as long as no werefolk attack me or mine, I shall not lift a hand against them. But I cannot make an oath and then stand by and watch your werefolk eat my humans."

Grww considered.

"We enjoy the taste of human meat," he said, "but this is important. There is enough other food around. So be it. No wereperson of Shrn shall hunt or eat human again. If one does, his life is forfeit and you, or any human or shifter can kill him at will."

Paean beamed. This was so much more than she'd ever hoped to achieve. Peace with the werefolk!

"Done," she said. "Consider it a contract!"

"If you break the contract you are my next meal," warned Grww.

"Guess that's how these things work," agreed Paean. "Could you please take me to the Morrigan now?"

"If you can keep up," grinned Grww. He morphed back into a wolf and loped off. Paean started her motorbike and roared after him on fuel drives.

19 – IRM

By the time Paean returned through the portal that Grww had graciously opened for her, she had taken stock.

Powdered rats on that Morrigan! So all along, he was the planetary Keeper of Shrn, with the duties of helping his werefolk develop into a civilized people; and instead he'd found it more important to mess with Earth's humans? What a pirate!

He wasn't at his castle. Grww had tried calling him, from all angles, without luck. Paean's teleporter had definitely also shown him absent. Neither was the Solar Wind present, nor any of the crew.

Paean set her jaw and made her way to the small village she knew about, that Federi had mapped for her on their honeymoon.

Four villages, Vlaşta, Verda, Sat Gri and Niciuna, not too far from the old Romanian town of Tirgu Mures. On her Southern Free heavy-duty mountain motorbike she roared into the small town, looking for the poliţia. If nothing else, to report the person who was lying dead in the snow. Someone must have been missing him!

She didn't have any specific plan of action anymore. She had achieved a pact with the werefolk – the real werefolk, not the Romanian Hounds. At least Grww and his lot would not be hunting gypsies anymore. But now, to get a grip on those hounds…

She knew where to start, blast! There was a trail leading from an Irish factory – a desolate place where her mother had worked – to Vlaşta, where Federi was born, more or less. A trail of Romanian Hounds; and a trail of IRP. She was going to ask the blasted poliţia to their faces what the connection was. And if they all then turned into Romanian hounds and converged on her – well, she'd teleport out.

And... there was another thing, about Vlad.

There was a higher authority! Higher than the planetary leadership, which was officially Captain but in reality still the Unicate – those deep levels. The higher authority was a council of intergalactic sages. This was good; they needed to be alerted regarding the Unicate, maybe they would know how to take care of it. And Vlad knew how to contact them.

Vlad had vanished with the Solar Wind.

Vlad was an immortal, blast him! Not even a double teleporter field and sticky carbon had finished him off! He'd be back, she'd have to count on that. And when he returned from wherever or whatever, she'd beat him into submission about taking her to the Intergalactic Council.

Ailyss was suddenly on the motorbike behind her. Paean nearly fell off from fright.

"You can't keep still for a second, can you," scolded Ailyss. "Where to now, Madame Red Ant?"

"The poliţia," said Paean. "To report that dead person in the snow. And the attacks on the Tzigany."

"You want to contact the police?"

"Yup."

"You're nuts," said Ailyss. "I'd better supervise."

"Suit yourself," said Paean. And she half-turned, concerned. "Ailyss, is Wolf feeling better?"

"Yes. You've redeemed yourself this time, little red devil." Ailyss gave her a half-hearted grin. "But Federi is still going to skin me for allowing you to hop around like that when you're injured."

Paean locked her jaw. If they ever saw Federi again. Her rescue mission to Shrn had turned out empty-handed.

The man behind the counter was very fat and looked half asleep. The arrival of a motorbike with two young girls on it had rattled him out of his trance; but now that Paean was reporting on the werefolk attacks on the gypsies, his eyes were closing. Paean fought down her annoyance as she perched on her motorbike. The man had put down her complaint as "trouble with Rroma people", which was as unfair as it was inaccurate. A blonde fuzzy creature fluttered around the office, clearing away files and moving cups around until the police chief barked at her to stop fidgeting, at which she disappeared into the back of the police station.

"It's not Rroma," Paean repeated with strained patience for the third time, "it's Tzigany. Free gypsies."

"Tzigany, eh?" The fat man yawned demonstratively, leaned backwards and called into the station. "Demus! You here?"

A tall, thirty-something man with a merciless crew cut emerged from the back of the office. His grey eyes studied Paean and Ailyss for a completely still second.

As merciless a crew cut as she'd inflicted on herself and her brothers when they had escaped Dublin. But there was something else. Something in this man reminded her of Johnny Anyhow – and more, of that Johnsson Ailyss had had a shine on, down at the Ice Base.

Yes, Johnsson. Exactly. She glanced at her chosen sister and knew that Ailyss had made the same connection. It was the eyes. As though they had seen a lot... and weren't telling.

He wasn't an *Other*. But he knew how to spot them! Paean was sure of that.

"We're talking about attacks on Free Gypsies," she said calmly.

The man, Demus, eyed her with that focused stillness of a stalking predator. And his internal double tried a clueless front.

290

"Trouble with Tzigany? I didn't know we still had any!"

"Not trouble with," said Paean pointedly, "attacks on! Tzigany, you know. They used to be illegal. Now the new World Constitution protects them." She set her jaw once again. Captain Radomir's constitution. And who was going to enforce that, if the Solar Wind didn't miraculously reappear?

She would, she decided. She'd mobilize the Admiral. And then she, and Ailyss, and Jon Marsden would make sure that the Constitution was enforced.

"Would be right up your creek, Zoltan," said the police chief. "You like these obscure cases."

"I like all cases," muttered Zoltan Demus. "What's with the Mythical People?"

The chief pointed to the file. "Couple of werewolves lured the Tzigany through a portal onto another planet and savaged them there. Out of our district, wouldn't you say?"

"Portal? Planet?" Demus' eyebrows furrowed. "Werewolves? What is this?"

The fat police chief packed up laughing. "Clearly a hoax, Zoltan! Can't you tell?"

Zoltan Demus shook his head. He didn't get it. What would be the point in a hoax?

Ailyss glanced at Paean, and smiled at the officer. "Call it a hoax if you like. It's not. There's another interesting thing we found," she mentioned. "Go around this mountain, the left-hand side. About two-thirds to the top you'll find a dead man in the snow."

"What?" Now she had the police's attention.

"Come!" she invited, beckoning Zoltan Demus along.

Zoltan indicated for them to wait for him in front of the police office. Paean's motorbike negotiated the couple of steps carefully, slowly, on solar power. She didn't want the ratted thing to go keel-up.

The officer arrived in a heavy-duty bush-bashing vehicle with snow chains. Paean, with Ailyss riding pillion as before, led the way. They arrived at the blue-parka'd dead man as the snow began to fall again.

Zoltan got out of his van, forgetting to close the door. He crouched down at the dead man and gaped in horror at the missing face. Ailyss also got off the motorbike to have another close look at the victim.

"Bears," said Zoltan eventually, after a long silence. "This was a bear. There have been attacks in these mountains. We've even seen prints."

"Right," agreed Ailyss, nodding. "Bears! Of course!"

"Bears!" snorted Paean. "Fine. Officer, you want to tell me what you know about the IRP?"

Zoltan gifted her a long, hard stare.

"Who are you?" he asked eventually.

"Paean Demonos," said Paean, getting her teleporter ready. "Founder, daughter of Annie Donegal, and wife of Federi Demonos." She glanced about wildly, waiting for those blasted hounds.

None came.

Could it be that Federi had intimidated them so badly with his blades weapon?

"Paean Demonos," said Zoltan quietly, with a grin. Paean could see how he noted Ailyss' hand on her submachine gun. "The IRP has a price on your head, but not nearly as much as the IRM has on your husband's."

"And you're a member of theirs," snapped Paean. "I should shoot you now!" She felt Ailyss' hand on her arm, calming and restraining her.

"He's not one of those," the spygirl pointed out. "Hold your fire, Paean!"

"The IRP is a human association," retorted Paean. "Right up to…" She turned back to the policeman. "What's your association with the bleeding IRM?" she demanded. "Officer Demus?"

"An infrequent one," said Zoltan Demus, peering up at the grey clouds that were losing snowflakes at a faster rate now.

"It's illegal now," said Paean angrily. "The IRM and the IRP both are now unconstitutional." And then suddenly the fight was out of her. "You'll be happy to hear that Federi is gone," she said, her voice dropping along with her energy levels.

"Gone?" repeated Zoltan blankly.

"He disappeared from the face of the Earth two days back," said Paean quietly. "There's no finding him. Chances are he was pulverized in an explosion by the IRP." She turned her motorbike and took off along the slope at a breakneck speed, disappearing in the whirling flakes.

Zoltan Demus stared after her, then glanced at the other girl who had now missed her lift.

"I think she's only facing up to it now," said the dark-haired beauty sadly. "Officer, not a word. Federi Demonos was a great man, and a good friend. Not a word!"

"I wasn't going to say anything," replied Zoltan, feeling oddly sad for the loss of these two young girls. Even if it meant the death of one of Earth's greatest crooks. "And you are?"

"Out of here," said the girl and was suddenly gone.

Zoltan Demus recovered from his moment of shock. She had been a hologram, projected by some or other device that Paean Demonos had dropped. The device must have self-destroyed, there was no trace of it. The police themselves used such devices on

293

occasion.

He turned to investigate the "werewolf" activity.

Of course he knew about the "werewolves". Wild predators that looked like nothing logical. They were coming over the borders too often now. Portals? Planet? He was prepared to believe anything by now, seeing that he had no better alternative explanation. And that stuff that had reported in at the IRM meeting, that one time... stuff straight out of the nightmarish Wars of the Sixties, if documentaries were anything to go by... he had his own theories, concerning labs and illegal splicing of species, but his theory was as difficult to prove as a garbled account by a teenager of portals and magic.

But if Federi Demonos had been demolished – how was it he hadn't heard about it? For twenty years the IRM had scoured the Earth for the man. If he was dead, why hadn't the news burned through the IRM like wildfire?

Paean Demonos? Demonos had taken a young teenager for a wife, in keeping with Free Gypsy custom? Then even if the report of his death were true, in all probability she carried the next generation of Demonos! She had to be retrieved.

Zoltan scowled. Yet something held him back from jumping into his truck and following the clear trail of the small motorbike. So the IRP/IRM now had two compelling reasons to lay their hands on Paean Donegal. But he didn't share the superstition of that organization, that the old gypsy curse of Falco Demonos crawled through the generations. The whole line of attack of the organization suddenly felt suspect to him. Psychic powers? Demonic attributes? Primitive hogwash...

All this was off the records, he thought as he documented the details of the werewolf-mauled unknown civilian. This attack would enter the file system as yet another bear attack. And the youngsters who had reported it would remain anonymous. But he was going to start his own investigation.

"Didn't you give the officer a bit much information there, Paean?" Ailyss approached the younger girl where she sat curled up, her head hidden in her arms. The parka's hood disguised any sign of life. Snow fell on Paean's shoulders and back; she was sitting in a mound of more snow, under an ancient plantation pine. And she didn't answer Ailyss.

The spygirl crouched down and put her hand on Paean's shoulder. And the little redhead lifted her tear-streaked face from her arms.

"Ailyss," she said in a low, despondent voice, "my mother was murdered. My husband was murdered. My older brother and my sister-in-law and my little nephews were murdered. The whole family, wiped out. I'm lucky I still have Shawn, but you know... how long before they come after him again? I have a mission, and I won't stop until I either accomplish it or die trying."

"You sound like Federi," commented Ailyss and bit her lip.

"Yes," said Paean with icy sarcasm, "I sound like Federi. Odd, ni?"

And Vlad teleported in and put a tentacle on Paean's other shoulder.

"Top o' the morning to you ladies!" he said brightly.

"Vlad!" exclaimed Paean and Ailyss in unison, and Paean gripped his tentacle. "Welcome home, Vlad, where's the Solar Wind?"

"Back in Durban, where she started," said Vlad with a grin.

Paean trained her teleporter on Federi's genetic signature. And found it still out of range.

She paged through everyone. Ronan and Rushka were back, apparently. So were a number of the crew; but Captain, Perdita and Federi were still missing. She jumped up and teleported.

"Vlad," said Ailyss, "what happened?"

Vlad took a breath.

"And where the hell is Federi?" demanded Paean, teleporting back in and collapsing on the ground. "His genetic signature doesn't register."

"Paean!" exclaimed Prince Vlad. "You're injured!" He placed a tentacle upon her injured leg.

"Thanks to your werefolk," she snapped, but caught herself and said more gently, "actually not thanks to your werefolk. Thanks to the blasted IRM Unicate Hounds. Got a new mission, Vlad. And you, as Planetary Keeper of Shrn, are going to help me!"

Ailyss stared at Vlad in surprise. The Morrigan cycled through a few rainbow colours.

"Aw," he said. "The embarrassment! My secret is out of the bag?"

"The Intergalactic Council," said Paean. The Morrigan winced. "You'll take me to them," pushed Paean. "They must help Earth get rid of the Unicate."

"Blast," said Vlad. "Paean Dee, the last time an Earth human spoke to the Council it was Falco Demonos. It was not what I'd call a success story." He peered at her, mimicking bushy eyebrows.

"Then again Falco Demonos didn't exactly manage to negotiate peace with the werefolk either, did he," Paean played her trump. "And Paean Demonos did. Maybe I'm better at negotiating?"

"Better than Falco?" asked Vlad with an overdone raised eyebrow. "What? You made a deal with the werefolk?"

"That Grww is such a big teddybear," said Paean with a grin.

"Grww who nearly ate you last year?"

"So people change," said Paean with a shrug and noticed that the constant pain in her leg had eased away. "Hay!" She got to her feet. "Wow! You fixed my leg!"

"Go slowly," warned Vlad. "The molecules are just very patchy at this point and the morphic field around the new tissues is still young and uncertain. It needs a good few days to stabilize, so be careful anyway."

"Thanks, Vlad!" She smiled. "But now tell me, where is Federi?"

"He should be entering our atmosphere with an intergalactic Gargantuan vessel any time now," said Vlad. "I'm wondering what's taking him so long. Maybe it's the alien console."

"So what happened?"

"We followed Perdita into space," said Vlad. "Captain got a message that she'd been abducted. Ronan has brought the Solar Wind back and Captain, Perdita and Federi are returning on the alien vessel."

Paean snorted. "Really, that Dana!"

"Wasn't Dana," said Ailyss. "Remember, it was one of the first places where we checked?"

"'fraid Ailyss is right," said the Morrigan. "It was no human abduction this time. It was Moozils." He scowled. "Which are a slave species to the Rapacins, in other words they were raiding for the Rapacins. That is in any case not right," he commented. "Earth is a sanctuary! They can't raid Earth yet. Paean, regrettably you are right. This needs to be brought before the Intergalactic Council."

20 – Moozils

Federi crept along the oesophagus. It had taken him a while to make the connection that the inside of the giant space creature these Moozils were using for a spaceship, was of course insides! Guts, and anatomical structures. Somehow those aliens had managed to preserve it so it didn't stink too badly. To Federi it still smelt like death, but his problem was that his radar was as alert to the psychic side of the smell as his nose was.

He had left his silver Perdita-spacesuit on the bridge and was back in plain clothes, without oxygen mask, only keeping the head torch on. Clothes could be washed; but it was a pain having to get past the suit to his various weapons. His reasoning was that if Perdita was alive, she was able to breathe whatever air was in here. And indeed the air was breathable. Vlad had tried to convince him and Captain to let him carry them through space unmasked and without protective suits; the electric bubble he was making around them was enough to provide both air and the right temperature, he had said. Captain didn't trust the Morrigan, and so both he and Federi had got into Perdita's fair-weather raincoats, Federi keeping mum about their real function. But he'd suspected that if Moozils ate humans, the chances were they breathed the same kind of oxygen, too. He'd been right.

Hold the bridge, Captain had said. Right after which the ship had made a sideways turn and vaulted through a portal. They could be anywhere now. It was maddening.

The Solar Wind had warped away out of Southern Free when Captain had received a message – the equivalent of a Black Box –

from Perdita. Captain had given him thirty seconds – thirty seconds, for wailing – to get all crew belowdecks and seal up. People on shore leave were left ashore. And at the very moment at which he'd tried to call his Paean back aboard, she'd registered out of range.

In retrospect, he should have teleported after her; but in practice the count-down was drilled so deeply into him that his well-trained body had overruled all thought and forced him through the insane routine in exactly thirty seconds. Not that he could have teleported to her, if he thought about it logically. She was out of range.

But he knew exactly where she'd gone, anna bottle! Where he himself was off to, as well – the gypsies! And her registering out of range was very bad news. It meant most likely that she'd gone over to Shrn…

… where the Morrigan wasn't around to protect her!

He had grilled Vlad on this; the shifter had assured him that he'd issued a limbic order to the werefolk that they were not allowed to eat her. Limbic orders couldn't be disobeyed. At least, he'd added, not by werefolk.

Federi hoped that Vlad wasn't underestimating the werefolk the way he'd underestimated the Solar Wind's crew.

He'd tried various times to touch Paean via telepathy. The question was, was she not paying attention, or was she dead – or was he imagining the whole effect? There was zero feedback from her.

Telepathy! The frying console of this alien vessel supposedly worked on telepathy. Captain had left him, Tzigan, in charge of the alien vessel and gone off to look for Perdita in the depths of the thing's intestines. Somehow the whole passage was imbued with some or other metallic substance that made the guts teleportation-proof. Accidentally. Unless, he thought, the creatures had met Dana and her technology before; in which case it was less likely to be accidental. He needed to find out what metal they used, so he could

299

use it too!

When telepathy hadn't worked, Federi had tried psychology on that jolly console, and extortion. Nothing. The "craft" had doggedly stayed on course – away from the portal back into the Milky Way.

Vlad had originally helped him get aboard; back there in the Spiral Galaxy. He had given him and Captain, fully dressed in Perdita's pseudo-space suits, a lift to the eyes of the Gargantuan, which were really portholes of sorts to the control room; the only part of the whole vessel that wasn't proofed against teleportation. It couldn't be; coating the portholes with metal would blind the vessel.

So he and Captain had teleported in and shot down the alien holding the bridge – a fuzzy animal looking a bit like a koala bear. It felt wrong, like shooting down cute teddybears, but Vlad had pointed out that teddybears wouldn't abduct humans in order to feed them to their masters – and that the masters were anything but cute.

Captain had gone ahead in his search for Perdita; he'd given the orders that Vlad should take the Solar Wind home, and that Federi should follow him with the alien ship, seeing that the console – according to Vlad – worked via telepathy. And Vlad had obeyed and warped home with the Solar Wind… while Federi, unable to follow, watched helplessly as the bleeding alien vessel was pulled sideways through a portal into another galaxy.

He wasn't at all sure that this supposedly dead alien was in fact really dead.

Aw, for the stink in aliens! Federi saw it clearly. The Morrigan may even have set it up. One slick move to get control of the Solar Wind and get rid of the Demon and the Captain!

Another unsuspecting Moozil came past and met his fate. Federi thought back to a Rebellion Schooner. These Moozils were intelligences too. Further advanced than humans; a space-going species. And – which made it feel so unfair – only about the size of

300

red panda bears.

Vlad had explained the set-up. Ha! If Vlad were to be believed! He had told Federi and the Captain that Rapacins, a comparatively planet-bound species, sent out slave species to "fish" on lesser developed planets for prey. The Rapacins were a Rosetta species. They had long since devoured every last life form on their own group of planets; abducting prey from other planets was all that remained for them.

Federi deduced from this that the chances were that they were currently in the Rosetta Nebula. Not that he had any way of telling.

If they were planet-bound, how could they control other species? Telepathy, Vlad had explained. A much-used functionality all over the universes; only some species had not yet evolved its proper use, and others had forgotten and the facilities had deteriorated. Species whose telepathic abilities were underdeveloped had a bad time up against species like the Rapacins who were master mind mages. Humans had better shape up, the Morrigan had added, because there was a lot of stuff out there that liked controlling the minds of weaker species.

And that was of course why Federi's bit of telepathy was too little to control the Gargantuan back onto an Earthbound course. Something else was overruling his telepathic command. Little point in staying on the bridge in that case.

He'd lost his way into the bronchi just now, proving that this Gargantuan had been a gas-breathing organism. From outside, its head had looked like that of a giant hawk, with a ragged beak and five huge eye sockets. Its body was shaped almost like a mammal, with a long, flat tail and two pairs of flippered hind legs and one pair of front legs stretched out in death. It was covered in silver scales and sealed with some or other substance. And now he was at the end of the oesophagus, and the passage narrowed and tied off with a

301

gastric valve.

Federi touched the valve experimentally. To his surprise it opened in response, into a small hollow chamber. The stomach, he presumed. The chamber was empty. He squeezed through the valve and into the stomach; the valve closed behind him. A nasty suspicion raised its hand. Federi touched the stomach valve again; it failed to open. Rats. He didn't like having his escape route cut off. He swore and felt his pockets for solutions.

An explosion in space was a scary thing at best. Even a little one like this. He had his rebreather mask back on in case oxygen started leaking out. The valve was blown apart; so was the whole passage. Federi grabbed onto whatever he could get hold of – small protrusions all along the wall. They were soft; they didn't hold his weight long as the intestinal passage tilted and flopped down into the darkness. Federi slipped slowly but unstoppably to the ragged opening in that small pre-stomach. The other end of the passage hung somewhere below in the dark, smouldering ominously.

Arww rancid hell! He braced with all fours, stretching his arms and legs out as far as he could to prevent the inevitable fall; but the soft gastric wall stretched with him, and the villi which he was holding onto, tore away… for a horrible second he spiralled into the dark abyss, the only point of reference those glowing ends of the other side of the passage. He crouched reflexively, putting hands and feet out in the direction of the fall, and landed – softly, like a cat, to his surprise – in fluffy material. He sank away in it and panicked, struggling to make space for himself to breathe. And he reached into his back pocket and pulled out one of Paean's magic green tubes, and twisted it to break the inner seal, and shook it to activate it…

The material in which he'd landed, looked pink even in the dim green light. It looked like fibrous pink filler. He was, this he could be fairly sure of, on an intercostal muscle of the animal, but the

302

muscle had dried completely and been coated with this deep pink fluff. Which smelt slightly synthetic. Like factory.

Great. He looked into the hollow darkness above him, and remembered. The mutant had been on one of these before. And right on cue, his mutant senses started kicking in. The darkness wasn't quite as dark. He could see grey shapes of things. The giant, dried-up organs of the poor mummified creature. The convoluted mess that was the intestinal passages; where the Moozils had their whole ship works; passenger decks, cabins, and all. And he'd exploded the oesophagus, right at the first gastric valve.

He tried to find the passage again and saw it dangling somewhere close by, with its opening to the floor. The abdominal wall, he thought. Well, whatever.

There was no getting back into those passages. He thought about it. Teleportation-proof, but not sturdy enough to withstand fire. Now, if he could find the place where Perdita was held captive, from outside, and cut a hole into it... or if he could set the whole thing on fire and wait for her to drop out of wherever they held her...

He activated his com.

"Captain, what's the situation?"

"Found her," said Lascek.

"Could you give me a signal?" asked Federi.

"What kind of a signal?" came the answer. "What do you mean?"

"I have no clue," growled Federi. "Had hoped you'd have an idea, Captain. Can't figure out where you are."

"Well, after the first short passage I went through four pockets before coming to this main one," said Lascek. "Just keep going down the passage, you'll get there. We're inside the Gargantuan's digestive tract."

"I know," replied Federi, and shut off his com. He unwound his newest rope from his middle and added a drop of glue to its loose end, and attached one of his rings as a weight – the ones he had taken off this morning when Paean had presented him with his One Ring. And he flung the rope as high up as he could, wondering whether he should ask Wolf to create small missile-engines for his rope ends. And remembering the croaches. Actually Luigi could be asked to… he patted all his pockets. Negative. Luigi was on the Solar Wind.

The rope stuck to some or other bit of digestive tract. He pulled sharply at it to test it – and it came flying back down.

Arww, rats! He retrieved the rope-end, ring and all, and found that it had indeed stuck to a piece of guts – but the latter had come off with it when he'd tugged.

This was a bad scene! He stared up into the cavernous darkness, and activated his com again.

"Captain, could you please lead Perdita out of the stomach you are in, and along the passage back to where it ends?"

"How, Tzigan? Those valves are one-way doors!"

"By explosion," said Federi. "Only way, Captain!"

"You mean, I explode the valve open…"

"Just be careful, Captain!"

Not too long after that there was a muffled crack, and a flash high up in the intestines. And more of the stuff came tumbling down, and with it, Captain and Perdita.

Federi stalked over to them, through the deep fluff.

"Where's the Probe?" he asked.

"No idea," said Perdita.

"Tzigan!" exclaimed Radomir Lascek, dusting himself off. "You knew what exploding that valve would cause!"

"Was the only way to get you to do it, Capt'n," said Federi sanguinely. "Got to find a way to get back on the bridge now."

Out of the passages, Moozils came charging. They had strange weapons on them that looked like nets.

"Stay away from those," warned Perdita. "They shock."

"I know," said Federi before he could stop the mutant. Perdita gave him an odd look before taking out her dart gun.

"Darts do nothing to them," Federi pointed out.

"Bullets in space are dangerous," she replied.

Federi took off the whip-o-nine-tails. "Let's see if the werefolk whip talks to them." He whipped the air. The Moozils disappeared – into the deep pink fluff. "Aw rats," cursed Federi. Those creatures moved fast. One bit him in the ankle. "Bloody ow!" he exclaimed as his knife sank into the Moozil.

This deep fluff was dangerous. These creatures were vicious. His laser pen came out without first negotiating, and a small flame ignited at its other end, and Federi set that to the fluff…

The inferno lasted a full three seconds, then the stuff had combusted, at a surprisingly low temperature. Too low for Perdita's glorious hair to catch flame. But the Moozils, who had been in the middle of the fluff, were stripped of fur. Naked they looked frightening, in the low glow of the Captain's head lamp. They also looked pretty angry.

"Now," announced Federi, allowing his whip to dance. "Can you see me now? Don't come close!"

Perdita glanced at Radomir Lascek.

"Vicious," she commented as Federi's whip danced around the three of them, creating a protective perimeter across which the Moozils didn't dare to trespass.

"That's why I don't like him going off to the gypsies," growled Lascek. "When he returns it's back to square one, taming him."

"'s a pleasure, Captain," commented Federi with bared teeth, never slowing in the display of the whip. "'s meant to buy us time. Any idea what we do next?"

21 – The Intergalactic Council

"Wait for m…." Ailyss' call tapered off in an exasperated shrug as she watched Paean atop the Morrigan, who'd assumed the shape of a huge space dragon, warp away into space. She sighed. "Can anyone tell me when I can catch the next Morrigan?"

Silver dragon wings beat through the star tunnels. Vlad thought with trepidation of that Council Member he had to face. Anthrim had demanded that he kill the Demon. There was no way he could; he'd tried, before. And by now, Vlad had no incentive to kill Federi. The man had spared his life and returned him to the one place in the universes where he most wanted to be; the Solar Wind.

There were Twelve on the Intergalactic Council. There always had to be twelve, for balance. But seeing that they were all immortals, the original Twelve were still the same. Of them all, Anthrim headed the Council in most decisions, even though Vlad had the idea that some of the members were more powerful.

Stars warped by so fast that they turned into tunnels. Vlad scoured the place for Anthrim. In matters of Earth being breached by aliens, the Council Leader was probably not going to call a meeting of the whole Council but sort it out himself. Vlad mulled. Rapacins. Those were very bad news. The most voracious species in the Rosetta Nebula. If they had discovered Earth and raided her once, that was most likely only a sortie to test the response. This would be why they had targeted Perdita – the most important person to the planetary leader. They wanted to see what his worst response could be before expanding their hunting grounds. Vlad skirted the edges of a beautiful supernova to treat his young passenger to a first-class view, and heard her gasp in amazement.

And she gasped a second time. This time, it whipped across Vlad's biofield like the sting of a Cosmanta. She wasn't even aware of her Founder voice, was she?

"What's wrong?" he asked.

"Federi's in trouble. Deep trouble!"

"He should be touching down on Earth any moment now," said Vlad. "If he hasn't already."

"Something's pulling on his mind," she replied. "Something's trying to hypnotize him."

Vlad increased the pace back to warp speed. Something like a flame streaked past him and disappeared in the void. He blinked. A Founder illusion?

He could practically feel the wave of frustration and despair from Paean. Here she was, stuck in an atmospheric bubble in the middle of deep space, completely unable to rush to the help of the Demon.

"Paean," he said, "we'll hurry up. We won't let anything happen to your Federi, alright?"

Because, and to the pits of hell with Anthrim's orders, he didn't think he'd survive the mourning vibes of a Founder from up close. That would be worse than a double teleporter field.

It didn't leave him too many options with the Council leader. He'd have to play poker, as he'd learned from Wolf and Old Sherman when they thought they were playing against Dana, or Johnny, depending.

*

Federi was nowhere near touching down on Earth. He stared into the psychic eye of his opponent. A faceted eye, in an armour-plated,

308

triangular face. With mandibles. For some irrational reason he had to think of Queen Rhyn.

The Unicate, too, were insectoids! At least in their patterns of living in a hive under the mind-control of a single queen, and reacting to chemical messages. His discoveries about the were folk had simplified things, at the same time as complicating them. The Mound was a central concept. He'd have to keep that in focus. Nemiscau, Dahlia, the Hub… radioactivity… these were all puzzle pieces that he felt were very close to falling into place. They tied in with the mounds. And what about those fire lizards?

The creature he was facing now, had things in common with Queen Rhyn. Not her exterior, which was huge and insectile. But her thought patterns. They were fairly simplistic, but shrewd. Eat, mate, breed. And a thousand little schemes, some highly intelligent and intricate, to lure or catch prey, enslave species, find new planets to raid… Raid, yes, he thought. He'd like to spray Raid at her.

This Queen was staring at him, a satirical smile on her mandibles. That was just the shape of her face, thought Federi with irritation. Mandibles couldn't smile! But sentiments could! She knew that she was in complete control of the ship, directing it closer. She didn't mind particularly about the killed Moozils – she and hers would have eaten them sooner or later anyway, and today was just fine. And she was allowing him to wrestle her for mind-control of the ship the way a bully would allow a toddler to wrestle a door open, just to push it closed despite the younger child's best efforts. Federi understood this, and it irritated him.

Humans, a weak species. Yes, he'd always known it. Gypsies looked down on the *gadje* for being weak. How often had Federi looked at his own people and the way they suffered and struggled, and wondered who was the loser in the equation! Looking at the Unicate, all human beings, *gadje* and Gyp alike.

But to have some primitive eat-mate-breed species overrule his psychic powers...

It had taken Perdita's bag of tricks, with a tiny floating device that neutralized gravity and slotted into the console's grid system, to take them back up to the bridge of the Gargantuan. Federi had silently blessed the fact that not having teleporters had led Perdita down such diverse avenues of R&D. Because inside the Gargantuan the teleporters were useless. They had been teleportation-proofed, probably as a result of a previous encounter with Dana, or someone like her.

But Perdita didn't have anything with which she could make the steering more accessible. Telepathy it was, unfortunately. And that meant staring into the psychic visage of that ugly insectoid apparition.

*

Ronan scowled at the blue sea. Jon Marsden had ordered him to keep an eye on the Solar Wind while he did a routine check of the ship. Things were rather chaotic; Captain was not aboard, he hadn't yet returned, so Jon was considering returning to the coordinates with the Solar Wind and going after Captain.

There was a lot of lazy action in Durban Port. The sun flickered on the blue waves; yachts sailed out of the harbour mouth for a day at sea, and larger ships came and went. Everything so peaceful. And Rushka was sleeping, exhausted from the pregnancy and finally capable of relaxing after the Morrigan had balanced her system.

There was something about the whole setup that bothered Ronan. From what he'd gathered from Jon Marsden, Paean had apparently left with the Morrigan, to look up some or other Council. Off into space on the back of a Morrigan, as though the blasted thing were a

Shetland pony!

And her distress call hit him.

Ro! Ro, help!

Oh hell! If she was in deep space, how could he help her?

Ro! Can you hear me?

Oh, he could hear her quite plainly. He had been hearing her every time she called, in the past months; but he'd been ignoring her, hoping that the connection would fade. He was married now, and he resented her having psychically intruded on his most intimate moments with Rushka, down at the Ice Base.

But the connection hadn't faded. And today he suddenly didn't think losing it was such a good idea. Yes, she'd drive him nuts the way she was permanently leaping into trouble with both feet first. But somehow this was different.

He closed his eyes and focused. His aura grew like a dark-blue mantle around him. Putting on his big brother cape.

What's wrong, Pae?

He could nearly hear her sigh of relief as the connection was established.

Federi's not back yet, is he?

No.

Ro, you must help him! He's stuck in space, and he's up against some or other big creature. It's bending his mind and it plans to eat him. All of them. Captain and Perdita, too.

Shards. This was bad news!

Give me a seccie, sis. I'll see what I can do.

Don't take too long, came her panicky response.

Ronan opened his eyes. This was how it had often been, in times of great need; they could be far apart, the three of them, but they were communicating as though they were in the same room.

So Federi was in trouble? Up against some massive space

predator. That would explain why the three of them hadn't arrived back yet. He had to tell the First... wait.

Jon Marsden would never get it together in time. Ronan was also tired of giving away the leadership. Jon was on the ship so seldom now, someone really needed to step into the position of First Mate. Had Captain known when he'd started training him for an officer?

There was only one person Ronan could imagine confronting a huge space predator and winning. He activated his com.

"Dana, report in! You have to help here."

The LD com was relayed to the Pluto Base by various Wolf- and Perdita-tricks, from where a message was dispatched to the White Palace on New Dome. It took a few minutes; during which Ronan could tangibly feel Paean's stress. She was oscillating between him and checking on Federi.

And then there was an answer, relayed by Sulis, in Gaelic.

"Pluto to Earth. Young commander, you do not speak like that to the Empress of Dome. She demands to know what you'll do for her if she listens to your request."

Ronan bristled. The woman was a psychopath. Her little underling had no idea!

"The real question," he said, "is what will happen to New Dome if she doesn't."

*

A dot on the left of Federi's field of vision drew his attention. A red dot. Outside the Gargantuan. Seconds later a small round, magenta spacecraft attached itself to the Gargantuan skull. A blink later, Dana popped into existence next to him, scanning the gathered crew.

312

"Radomir!" she purred. "And sister dearest! What a lovely surprise! And Demonos!" She smiled.

"Dana!" growled Lascek. "Where there's trouble, I should know you can't be too far!"

"Come on, Radomir! This is the Rosetta Nebula! My playground! A surprise to find you caught by the Rapacins!"

"You know about Rapacins?" asked the Captain.

"Oh, for the green on New Dome! Am I a Space Goddess, Radomir?" She glared at Perdita. "Didn't ask *you*, girl!"

"Wasn't going to grace it with an answer," replied Perdita with a smug smile.

"So, Federi," said Dana, placing a dainty, manicured hand on the gypsy's shoulder. He hadn't said anything so far, his eyes fixed on that terrible planet ahead, and his full focus on that insect. "Mind-wrestling with the Rapacin Queen?"

He failed to reply. Formulating an answer would be enough to lethally break his focus.

"So what made you drop in?" asked Radomir Lascek.

Dana laughed. "I was in the neighbourhood," she explained. "Thought I'd check what a Gargantuan was doing being towed in by the Queen herself."

"How were you in the neighbourhood?" challenged Lascek. "In space there is no neighbourhood!"

"Aw, alright," Dana relented. "Ronan called me. All the way to New Dome. He didn't have to, the silly boy. Didn't have to frighten Sulis. I was checking in on our Co-houses in Miami. You know of course that those have been bombed into the ground?"

"What?!" exclaimed Lascek.

"Exactly. I instantly contacted the Solar Wind, and she told me that all of you responsible folks were off the ship and in space on your way to becoming a Rapacin meal. That fitted in neatly with

313

Ronan's garbled account of Federi playing with a large predator."

Federi snorted, but he failed to shift his focus from the Rapacin queen. The co-houses bombed... what more bad news? But if he didn't win this battle, they could all meet again on the other side!

"Rhine Gold and Rashni?" Perdita asked urgently. "Are they safe?"

"They're fine," said Dana. "Turns out that Paean vacated all the bases, just before they were bombed. Makes me wonder what she knows! Very odd, I must add. Why should the Rapacins target Earth?"

"Because we're a fairly defenceless species," said Lascek. "We don't have their technology – or whatever you'd call it. They raid us because they can."

Federi peered out through the eyes of the Gargantuan, to where a red planet had come into view. The planet was in fact covered in burning gas. Federi was surprised that anything could live on that. But... what did he know about aliens? And what he was about to find out, would only last long enough until the Rapacin Queen's digestive juices had found their way to his brain... He tried to access the mutant's memories and found that this was one place she really hadn't been yet. Presumably any mutants who had ended up on the Rapacin worlds had been eaten without a trace. It was beyond the scope of Dana's bioengineering. If it was done by dousing the prey in chemical juices, he could understand how no cells had managed to escape.

That Rapacin Queen was roping the ship in, but she was doing it against a gradient of Demon. Still she was by far the more experienced mind mage. He was quite curious how the Assassin would cope with her. Would he still manage to get away – or was it like with Dana's mutants, the outer limit reached?

"So to conclude, Ronan was rather persuasive," said Dana. "He promised me more babysitting." The luscious space raider took Federi's hand, turned it palm-up and placed a small, smooth apparatus in it. He blinked his stare away from the planet and looked at her in surprise.

"What's that?" he asked.

"Pocket hypnotron. Use it. Demonos – I wouldn't dare, myself, against her. But you have the Demon. In connection with the hypnotron…"

Federi smiled.

"If it doesn't work, I've got a stronger one aboard," she added.

"Thank you, Dana." She had just endeared herself to him. He was ready to believe that she could actually be liked. In fact he was ready to kiss her feet.

"Of course you'll fix the thing with the Co-houses once we're home?" pushed the raider.

Federi sighed. He'd almost forgotten. Nothing was for nothing with this one.

"Course." He switched the little apparatus on and focused on the Rapacin Queen again. And smiled. That little machine had latched onto his brain. He thought of the portal back to the Spiral Galaxy.

The Gargantuan veered from its course and turned back.

A hellish screech tore through Federi's psychic perception. The Queen wasn't a good loser.

The lights of the portal faded behind them. They were back in the Spiral Galaxy. The Rapacin Queen's psychic pull didn't reach as far as this. Here, she only had the power to be a nightmare.

"Can I have my hypnotron back?"

The Tzigan smiled. " 's a useful little apparatus."

"It's mine, Demonos."

315

"Then again I'm a pirate," smiled Federi.

Dana pouted and frowned and stomped her foot. "I lent it to you to rescue you and your crowd from the Rapacins! Now give it back!"

Federi's eyebrows shot up and he smiled sweetly. "Seeing that you're asking nicely." He handed the hypnotron back. Rats! It would have come in handy in the fight against the Unicate. "When we're back on the Blue Planet, could you lend it to Wolf so he can copy the design?"

"What? And have you all own hypnotrons? You've got to be joking!" Dana smiled at them all, waved and teleported out. Seconds later the magenta spacecraft detached from the Gargantuan and flashed away into space.

22 – Breach

The Solar Wind lay docked at the Space Base. In the lounge of the base, Captain's inner circle and added officers were gathered; including everyone who had additional information. Captain Radomir Lascek paced before his gathered crew, his boots making deep solemn prints in the overly plush carpet.

He had debriefed everyone by now; Ronan, who had disclosed that he had a psychic link with his sister – not really a surprise, after all Paean was pretty well-connected; Ailyss, with her tale of Romania, Southern Free, the bases, and all that had happened; Itzak – who had taken in a host of Romany fugitives who refused to get settled in because they felt uncomfortable in cabins.

Jon had had his bit to add about Paean's gross insubordination and her spectacular injury. Dr Swart had been fetched and questioned about this in detail, with Doc Judith sitting by, listening carefully. She had to be ready to take over the care of Paean's injury when the girl returned. And Shawn sat in, merely to witness and take note of everything that was discussed.

Eventually Federi had spoken up too, in a low, exhausted voice, about retrieving Paean out of a Unicate mound, and the strange fire lizard who had flattened the remaining Unicate workers so that they could get out. He'd told his tale with deep misgivings; Captain had said, no disclosing to aliens, and yet Perdita sat in this meeting.

And now Captain was pacing, like a tiger, studying each of his allies and crew in turn, and shaking his head, and agonizing. They all agonized with him.

"How does it fit together?" he growled. "What is this Intergalactic Council? How do we know that Paean will be back?"

"Radomir," said Perdita, "the Council is literally that. They are twelve space creatures; all of them immortals. Their function is to regulate the universe, just like you and the Admiral regulate Earth. They lay down the law, so that powerful predatory species don't simply raze everything in the universe. The Morrigan was right to contact them. The Rapacins had no right to start hunting on Earth."

"Why not?" asked Lascek.

"Earth is a nature reserve," said Perdita. "Before a civilization becomes space-going, the planet is off-limits for raiding species."

"We're space-going," said Lascek gravely. "I'm cursed to hell. I should have left things the way they were."

"We're not space-going," countered Perdita. "That's exactly the breach. A single craft doesn't mean a planet has emerged."

"Emerged?" asked Lascek.

"From its primitive darkness," replied Perdita with a grin. Federi snorted in disgust.

"So I take it that Dana has had many little talks with the Council by now," speculated Lascek.

Perdita laughed. "Dana avoids the Council like poison."

Federi looked up from honing the blade of his woodcarving knife.

"Did you say, the planet is off-limits for raiding aliens?"

"For all aliens, technically," said Perdita. "Vlad is also in trouble if it is ever discovered how much he's meddled. Interfering aliens are also in the wrong."

"… and the Unicate?" he asked, his eyebrows arched.

"I don't know," said Perdita. "Logic dictates that they are wrong too, and the Council should move against them. But they haven't yet, so I don't know."

"All we can do," stated Radomir Lascek, "is wait for Paean and the Morrigan to return. We'll take it from there. In the interim I want an investigation into all our bases, and the co-houses."

*

The passage through the star tunnels slowed, and a white planet came hurtling towards Paean. And Vlad slowed the descent and dived into the atmosphere.

"Ice world?" asked Paean, recovering her poise after Vlad's madcap dive. She had promised Federi that she'd skydive for him every day if he needed her to. Her words seemed to be coming back to haunt her.

"Crystal," replied Vlad. "Pure white quartz. I'm hoping to find Anthrim here."

She heard the unspoken part in his voice. Actually he was hoping never to find Anthrim.

"Vlad? What's wrong with Anthrim?"

"Nothing," he said with an embarrassed laugh. "We don't... necessarily agree on everything."

"Such as?"

"Territories, hunting grounds... taking an active part in the development of an undereducated species..."

"Such as humans..." elaborated Paean with a grin.

Vlad touched down on the rim of an enormous canyon. There were volcanoes on the far rim; and the whole ground was red, a huge mountain range lying below them. Paean marvelled and wondered if Calypso had such features. Vlad threw his dragon head back and released a sound like a fog horn. Paean nearly fell off him with fright.

And the whole ground of the canyon started moving. When the

319

whole mountain range had reared up, Paean recognized it for what it was. An enormous space creature with a ridged back. A dragon.

"Paean, forgive me," said Vlad. Something buzzed around inside her head like a fly, and her ears popped, and suddenly she could hear much more clearly. With her second hearing. "Had to do that," apologized Vlad at a whisper, "even though it breaches your man's orders. You need to be in on this conversation, and though your native Founder telepathy is pretty good, it won't be enough for this style of communication. I increased the electric emissions from your third eye – that's the area around your pineal gland in your brain, for your information – and strengthened your interpretive pathways."

"Thanks!" Paean nodded. As long as he hadn't rewired anything except that; such as, her obedience pathways…

"I wouldn't dare," said the Morrigan in her mind. And the enormous red dragon stretched and turned its ocean-liner-sized head towards them, fixing both with a huge green eye.

"Shrn!" it bellowed, in telepathy, into both Vlad's and Paean's heads. "You took your time! Have you accomplished the mission? Have you done as I told you? Do you have good news for me?"

Shrn scratched behind his left dragon ear with his left dragon hind talon. And then he repeated the procedure on the right.

"Not quite," he said. "Hasn't that blue furry nonsense relayed to you? I was quite dead."

Anthrim laughed heartily, and loudly. Thunder rolled; rock slides crashed into valleys.

"That is not why we are here," said Vlad.

"But it's what I'm interested in hearing about!" replied Anthrim. "What seems to be the problem?"

Vlad deliberately misunderstood him.

"The problem is that Rapacins are now raiding Earth. This is a first-rate breach."

Anthrim inclined his head to change the angle from which he was fixing Vlad with his dinosaur stare.

"Rapacins," he repeated thoughtfully. "That is indeed a breach. Earth is not yet emerged, is she?"

"Not as a civilization," said Vlad.

"And yet, a group of Earth humans transgressed into the Rosetta Nebula," said Anthrim. "The Rapacins can be forgiven for misunderstanding."

Paean scowled. Whose side was this dragon on?

"Sir," she ventured.

"Maiden," the huge dragon replied, in a voice like distant volcanoes. "Is there something you would ask of the Council?"

"I'd like to know," said Paean. "Do I understand this right? An unemerged planet has a right to be protected from alien invasion?"

"That is the Intergalactic Law," said Anthrim.

"Right," said Paean. "In that case the breach reaches much further back than the Rapacins. The past sixty years, Earth was not emerged, but we are infested by an alien species that has taken over everywhere and is decimating humankind."

"Really?" asked Anthrim with keen interest. "Which species is that?"

"The Unicate," said Paean.

Anthrim inclined his head. Paean realized that he didn't have many expressive options with that reptilian face – it looked old, wise from a certain angle, and above all, predatory. His bone structure was to blame.

"Young Earth maiden," he said, "the Council does not interfere in political matters within unemerged civilizations. The Unicate is a political group."

"They are a bunch of aliens," corrected Paean.

"They look exactly like Earth humans," said Anthrim.

321

"But they are aliens," replied Paean, exasperated. "I don't know how they do it, they imitate us precisely…"

"Can you prove it?" asked Anthrim.

She stared at him in frustration. "Falco Demonos called the -"

"Ah, Prince Demonos," said Anthrim. "Falco Demonos, Prince of Earth. A troublemaker. He asked the Council for help as humans on Earth were laying waste with their nuclear weapons and he couldn't seem to stop them. We obliged, something we have learnt never to do; but nuclear waste is a serious problem for many life forms, and we felt the need to intervene on behalf of all that were not human, on Earth. We instated his peaceful if strict leadership for him; the Unicate. Once the leadership was in place, Prince Demonos was not content any longer and started making endless trouble."

"Because they are aliens!" exclaimed Paean, her fuse growing very short.

"Whether or not the Unicate is an alien organization remains to be proved," said Anthrim with dignity. "But it is a moot point, as she is there by intergalactic agreement."

Paean shook her head but fell silent.

In the past few months she had dealt with too many treacherous, two-faced people to miss the implications. The Council was backing the Unicate. Captain would have to tread very lightly if he wanted to survive.

But then again… maybe it was only Anthrim. That might be it. Why was the Morrigan dealing with him, instead of a more approachable Council member?

The Unicate, 'she'. This gave Paean food for thought, especially in the light of Terence and Queen Rhyn. The Unicate was essentially a female organization – this much she and Federi had already discovered on the mission. But… she had to stop that track right now, because in all likelihood Anthrim could hear her thoughts clearly.

"Shrn," the great dragon turned back to Vlad, "I issued an order. When will you locate Demonos, and bring him to me?"

Vlad lost his dragon shape and turned into an amoeba, just for the effect of giving the dragon a huge grin. Paean heard his telepathic command to her clearly: Hold tight!

"Never," he said. "The Demon is out of my league; he killed me once and I refuse to give him a second chance."

"Then die yourself, weakling!" thundered the dragon and opened his huge maws.

Paean's submachine gun came out in a flash.

"Stand back!" she yelled. "You shall not touch this Morrigan!"

There was a moment's shocked silence as her words reverberated across the galaxies, huge as the Law. The most surprised was Paean herself.

The dragon studied her with suddenly much keener interest.

"Who are you?" he demanded.

"Paean Donegal," replied the redhead, noting with satisfaction that her name, too, caused ripples.

Anthrim raised a huge claw and scooped her up with that, and eyed her with utter curiosity.

"Paean Donegal," he said in wonder. "One of the last surviving Founders." He blew an experimental flame at her. But before it could reach her, a tentacle snatched at her, and she was ripped away, and then she was in a teleportation, and in warp...

"Hold tight!" snarled the Morrigan. "I told you to hold tight! Thanks anyway for your solidarity. You could have got yourself killed!"

"If he'd eaten you, I'd have been next anyway," she pointed out, clinging to the tough hide that had reformed under her, for purposes of being a dragon. "And even if he hadn't – how would I've got back home?"

"The Council now knows that not only Demonos has survived, but Paean Donegal, too," said Vlad acidly. "You shouldn't have told him!"

"But… what's the Council got against Founders?" asked Paean, baffled. "Why was that dragon trying to fry me ?"

"Not the Council," said Vlad as the stars fused into tunnels again. "Anthrim. I was wondering about him."

"What I don't understand," said Paean, "is why my voice was suddenly so… imposing."

"You're a Founder," said Vlad with a grin. "You don't even know how powerful you are, do you? You three Donegal Troubles."

"But – we're not powerful," objected Paean. "Sure, we have this link to each other… why can't I do the same on Earth?"

"Quartz world," said Vlad with the dragon equivalent of a shrug. "It amplifies all psychic events."

So much for the Council, thought Paean. Earth would have to sort out their own Rapacin problem. And she had the means. All she needed, was a teeny tiny piece of Rapacin. She wondered who'd fetch it for her.

*

"Wolf!"

"Whoo!" The nuclear engineer jumped with fright, and grinned broadly. "Paean! You're back!" He clapped her into a bear hug. "You went off without waiting for Ailyss! She was hellishly worried. You naughty girl!"

"Aw," laughed Paean, peering around the Solar Wind's machine room. So the rest of the crew had discovered that the Solar Wind

324

was back, and had taken their places. "Wolf, you're not angry with me anymore?"

"Angry!" snorted the engineer. "The kid saves my life various times over, and then she steps out of line once... C'mon, Paean, get real. But next time, don't you dare!"

"Won't," she promised. "Wolf, I need a pocket genitron. How fast can you build me one?"

"What? Bang, whiz! I can pull that kind of stuff out of my sleeve! Hold tight, Paean Dee! First I've got to take one apart! Wonder if Doc will allow it."

"There's the spare from Kango Base on the Comet," said Paean. "But I need something that runs a bit warmer and a bit faster and more efficiently. I found I needed one out there in space. A Kosaka cannon wouldn't have taken care of the guy I was facing."

"Sounds ominous," said Wolf. "Maybe you'd want to mutate him with a gene gun."

Comprehension failed to dawn in her eyes. Wolf laughed and moved over to the console, and with a few touches he opened a page in the archives. "Have a look! They used to take DNA and wrap it around gold and other metal grains, and shoot it straight into the organisms they wanted to change."

Paean stared. "How inefficient is that!"

"Apparently it was quite efficient," said Wolf. "When you started messing around with genetics, I thought I'd better read up to keep you out of trouble. It's astounding how much gene cloning was going on hundred years back."

"But – how would the genes find their exact spot in the DNA of the organism?" she asked.

"They didn't. Didn't need to."

"That's what I mean! Messy! Inefficient! Can't imagine all the mutants and monsters coming out of that."

325

"That's partially what those Sixties were about," said Wolf. "They started that with food, but soon they were onto improved animals for organ harvests, and war clones, and all sorts of other unspeakables…"

"Ew," commented Paean.

"I've just been commissioned to build a combat croach," said Wolf, returning his attention to his work.

"A combat croach?" Paean grinned and shook her head. "Not for the Rapacins?"

"Would you like to face them in open combat?"

"I have no idea," said Paean. "What do they look like?"

"Like Death," said Federi from the companionway.

Paean turned into a motion stripe. She was in his arms in less than a split second. Angles of molecules shifted back to the way they were supposed to be. The world was whole again as she clung to him, laughing uncontrollably.

"There you have it," commented Wolf with a grin. Federi grunted and clamped Paean tightly to him.

"You're back," she hiccuped. "You're alive!"

Federi laughed softly. "And so are you, right?"

"Thanks to the Morrigan," she said.

"No worshipping of aliens!" he warned.

"Federi – how did you escape that thing you were wrestling?"

"With Dana's help," he said. "She lent me her hypnotron. Or we'd have been a messy goo by now, being slurped up by Rapacins. They have no teeth, you know."

"No teeth? So you were up against a toothless threat?" asked Paean, incredulous. "What was the danger?"

He laughed again. "They've got mandibles instead. They're insects. They use acid."

"Ooh," shuddered Paean. "And you want to fight them with croaches?"

"Those are insects too," said Federi with a smile. "I suggested explosive, but I don't think the whole Sancho empire has enough to sort out that lot!"

"Blow up a planet," said Paean thoughtfully. "Need Dana for that, I suppose."

"Dana helped us get away," said Federi. "But she made it pretty clear that it's a temporary fix. She doesn't want to get involved."

"Ha!" growled Paean. "It's a crisis to humanity! She's got a duty!"

"Duty, Dana," said Federi pensively. "Somehow those two words don't want to line up." He released her just a little bit as the Solar Wind's failure to rock made him reach for the handrail. And he gazed at her. "You stick with me now, understood? I couldn't believe it that Captain managed to separate us yet again! And at such a critical moment! Needed you with me."

"They were mauling the gypsies," said Paean.

"I know! You caught that just in time. We need to find all the remaining tribes and rescue them too. I thought I'd intimidated those blasted dogs well enough…"

"How did they know you wouldn't be there?" asked Paean with a scowl.

"Anna bottle! And that's not all! So the Rapacins attack and distract the Solar Wind away from Earth, and the next thing the IRM bombs all our bases out?"

"Not all the bases, just the co-houses," said Paean. "I think we caught the rest of it in time, too."

"Jon reported," said Federi. "You and Ailyss were hopping around in Romania and the next thing, Vlad takes you off into Space? What were you thinking, little luv?"

327

"I forged an alliance with the Werefolk," she said proudly. "But Federi, the Unicate Hounds are definitely not werefolk…"

"I know, anna bottle!"

Paean could tell that the alliance bit hadn't registered.

"And that Anthrim… Wolf? How far is that pocket genitron?"

Wolf snorted.

"Go shoo, you two lovebirds! I'll bring it when it's ready! Still busy with the croach. Which is for the Moozils, incidentally. Not the Rapacins."

Federi peered at her, too.

"What Anthrim, Paean?"

"Anthrim from the… Oy, I've got bad news for you, Federi Demonos, Prince of Earth!"

The double-take the Romany did, was spectacular. Wolf stared at the two, startled.

"*Who* says that?" snapped Federi, enraged.

"Nobody, I figured it out myself. Stands to reason, if Falco Demonos…"

"Falco the Traitor! Prince, my horse's backside! Svendsson, come along, Assassin's Cabin! You two were plotting something to visit on the unsuspecting crew anyway."

"Federi, you go," said Wolf, pointing to his project. "I can't. Got to finish constructing this stuff."

"Right," said Federi grimly and marched Paean up to the upper crew deck. There was no further word out of him until the door of the Cabin of Chains closed behind the two of them.

"So," he snapped, "first thing, Paean Demonos. You arrive back on the Solar Wind and you first check in on *Wolf?*"

She gaped at him, speechless. They stared at each other for a furious few seconds, then Federi's frown cracked. He laughed out loud and pulled her back into his arms. "Get the message!" he told her as he kissed her.

She smiled. "Och Federi, I missed you!"

"From the second you left the gypsies…"

"I know," she sighed. "Nothing but trouble. Should never have stopped our honeymoon! Federi, I forged an alliance with the werefolk."

"You what?" He made her sit down on the bunk, then found his own comfort spot there too, cross-legged, leaning against the bulkhead, for once nothing in his fidgety hands. "Tell me everything, little luv."

She talked. About everything, even about rescuing Mrs Flanagan out of the Mound – "oh, but you were there, of course…" – and Shawn's suspicion that the person they had rescued was not actually Mrs Flanagan. Federi scowled at this but didn't interrupt.

And then she was telling about her encounter with Anthrim.

"Really bad news, Federi. The Unicate is legal. And the Morrigan is too scared of them to protect even his own werefolk from the invasion. Federi, we've got to help him!"

Federi blinked. Help the Morrigan? … again?

"Anthrim – the Intergalactic Council," said Paean and took a breath. "Morrigan and I went to see the Intergalactic Council about the –"

"Wait!" Federi held up a hand. "I've heard something weird like that in the meeting, few minutes back. So there's an intergalactic council?"

"But yes," said Paean impatiently. "They make the Intergalactic Law! They see to it that it is kept, and they deal with people who…" She came to a halt, and stared at Federi, and started giggling. "I think I know the right man who must deal with them!"

Federi grinned. "This Intergalactic Law. Let's see… is it more a set of guidelines?"

She laughed. But then she got serious again. "Federi, but really now. Those twelve intergalactic sages – immortals, you know…"

"Twelve?" asked Federi thoughtfully.

"Can I get to my point please?" asked Paean, half in irritation. "'bout the Rapacin breach. 'parently the Rapacins have no right to invade. But the Unicate does! There's a contract. They're legal."

Federi swore.

"Apparently that Prince of Earth –"

"Let's get this straight," snapped Federi. "Falco Demonos was a human. A gypsy. My ancestor. The Prince of Earth is the Devil. *Finis. Basta.*"

"But Anthrim called him the…"

Federi started laughing. "Oh, *Anthrim!* I see! Alright, little luv, let's keep the illusion going then! My respect for ol' Falco has just gone up. He was a real *rom baro.*"

"Got to explain that," said Paean.

"Before the Manya system," said Federi, "gypsy families were led by a *rom baro.* A *Vojda*, or *Voyvote*, depending where you find yourself. A Big Man. Think of Big Michael."

Paean smiled.

"The *rom baro* was also responsible for dealing with the *gadje*," said Federi. "Especially where authorities were involved. Stands to reason that a common trick used by the *rom baro* is to tell the silly *gadje* that he is the king of the gypsies, or the prince, or the president – whichever system they currently believe in. It builds a little respect. Not enough, but better than none."

Paean started laughing. "So Falco…"

"You got it, little luv."

"So as his descendent, you…"

Federi rolled his eyes.

"Guess I'll have to."

330

"And Anthrim is trying to palm them off as humans," Paean added. "Trying to tell me the frying Unicate is actually human."

"Ha!" exploded Federi. "We know whose side he's on, then!"

"But, Federi – what I found out from Terence…"

He scowled at her. Terence was a defector at best, a spy at worst. And Federi had been kept too busy to keep an eye on the Unicate *Other*.

"Sounded to me," said Paean, "as though they are really just humans who were corrupted – brainwashed somehow. He says, that's what the Toll was for, too: To provide more material for Unicate."

Federi glared darkly at her. It was of course possible. It would explain things. Heck, it would explain a lot! Like Johnsson's story, for instance: Why the Unicate made a whole school class of top achievers disappear. Of course: Prime, elite material to 'recruit' into the force, by means of brainwiping.

It meant something more: It meant that Unicate *Others* could be rehabilitated, be made into humans again.

But it failed to explain Dahlia and co, anna bottle! How should ordinary humans suddenly become less susceptible to damage from radioactivity? Why should they actively seek it out? And what about those forsaken fire lizards? And Queen Rhyn? It didn't want to gel, yodiho and so on!

"And, Vlad is the Keeper of Shrn," added Paean. "But if the Council finds out how he's been neglecting his duties…"

"How can Shrn be our problem?" asked Federi.

"Who else should eat the werefolk if they step out of line?" asked Paean.

"Aha! I see!" Federi glanced at the porthole, and the darkness of the Space Base's bay.

Shrn was not their problem. This should be obvious.

331

But the Intergalactic Council was. Being the top of the ladder had begun to feel so natural, any authority that established itself above the Solar Wind felt like a threat. Federi didn't relish the idea of lapsing back into a lifestyle of running and hiding. Because one thing was crystal clear. No Intergalactic Council was going to stop him from pursuing his mission, to eradicate – or then, to rehabilitate – the Unicate.

Nimic! Never in his life was he going to believe that Genevieve, that spooky *Other* that had stalked them all the way to the Hub, was a normal teenager that had been brainwashed. And Anya Miller – the way that woman's dead eyes had stared up at him as she sank away in the depths, as though she could still see him… the way her equally uncanny brother had died, in such a sentient way… Federi had been an assassin for almost twenty years now. He knew what a death ought to look like. And the way those two had died, could only be described as completely alien.

He felt like grabbing Terence by the scruff of his neck and shaking the *Other* until he told the truth. He'd dropped all sorts of confusionary titbits just to mess up Paean's concept of what the Unicate was.

"She," said Paean. "Anthrim referred to the Unicate as 'she'. As though she were one single female organism. In the same breath as saying they were normal humans."

Ah. His wonderful, telepathic, eaves-dropping wife!

"Knew it," said Federi. "There's your answer. If Anthrim calls her a 'she', then that's what she is. He knows more than all of us together including Vlad." Yup: Eradicate it was, not rehabilitate.

Which meant that Terence would have to be dealt with, a.s.a.p. And that Mrs Flanagan… that really bothered Federi. Another frying riddle.

And as for the Rapacins: They would be back. They knew where

332

to find Earth. At least, the Moozils did. That Rapacin Queen had not seemed happy about losing her quarry. If she were an intelligence, as Federi suspected, she'd not only retaliate against Earth, but against New Dome too. He'd have to prime Johnny.

Wiping the Rapacins out and dealing with the Council was now top priority. He pulled his young wife closer and stretched out on the bunk, burying his face in her hair as she made herself comfortable in his arms. He'd just spent two days locked in telepathic combat. He was exhausted. Romanian hounds with and without uniform, a moundful of *Others*, Morrigan, Terence and the IRP spun into a dread vortex with mandibles, hypnotrons and fuzzy red teddybears. With teeth. And blazing infernos. Fire, at the co-houses and in the alien space shuttle.

"Fuzzywuzzy wasn't fuzzy after all," he mumbled as he dropped off to sleep.

23 – Rapacins

The Space Base drifted in its anchor spot, fixed roughly into position by a Perdita grid. Some oscillation was allowed in that grid; it had taken special programming. The huge silver network of passages and nodes glistened mysteriously in the slanted sunlight. From afar, it looked like an iridescent spiderweb of filigreed silver; a fancy doily; a frost flower of incredible fragility.

From inside, it felt safe. Far from the ground and the reach of the Unicate; too far even for military planes to hound and harry the crew.

Radomir Lascek paced along the passages and checked into the cabins that lined them. Paean had brought a host of new people up here, fugitives all. They would have to clone more tobuskies at this rate; the air was slightly stale by now and there weren't enough leaves to metabolize the carbon dioxide levels. He'd have to investigate into more efficient ways of removing that gas. Perhaps he ought to look at lining strategic bulkheads with something to remove the excess carbon dioxide. He should put it to Little John.

There was an enormous crash and a jolt. And the alarms went off. Systematically, valves started hermetically sealing off portions of the Space Base, breaking the large web into many small capsules that could potentially detach and, if the base should be damaged, be self-sustaining until they all had auto-navigated down to the Deep Base.

Radomir Lascek turned and moved like lightning up to the console room, where Itzak was hacking around frantically in the console, and John Whitcombe had also arrived, looking unkempt and woken-up. It wasn't yet his shift.

Itzak motioned to the volcaniplex dome that capped the console room. Radomir Lascek glanced out, and icy dread settled in his limbs, laming him. A voiceless gasp escaped him.

The whole vast expanse around them was strewn, littered, with light points. It looked as though Earth and the Space Base found themselves in an endless swarm of fireflies, all of which evil, and converging on them.

Another jolt shuddered through the Space Base. Radomir Lascek realized that those evil light points were shooting missiles at him.

"Shields up!" he snapped. That was stupid: The shields were already up, their default state was up since Perdita had a hand in his bases. Without Kovalski shields the base would not have withstood that impact. He activated his wrist-com. "All officers: Report to the Space Base for critical meeting!"

He glanced at Itzak who was operating the console. The husky-trainer glanced back; he looked chalky. And Little John was standing rooted to the spot, his eyes riveted on the alien fleet out there.

"The Admiral," said Lascek. "Men, hold the fort. I'm contacting him!" He teleported out just as Perdita teleported in.

She took a look at the skies. "Moozil invasion," she said matter-of-factly, her calm tone of voice belying her shock – and her immediate anger. She leaned past Itzak and drummed some sequences into the console. In a separate window on the console, the Space Base's cannons showed up.

"We need one fighter for each cannon," she pointed out. "Itzak, who in your team can operate a missile gun?"

Itzak made a list of names for her. This was going to be like the Ice Base; but at least this time, nobody was sending him away to

335

look after the huskies.

Perdita teleported out, rounding up her Sancho team as well. She contacted all her bases and ordered the various space cannons that she had stashed around the globe, to be manned and activated. She had armed and shielded the Space Base; but her project of shielding and arming Planet Earth dated back much further. Juan – the imbecile – had been playing with one of her guns, the one in Venezuela; but manning it for its correct purpose was a fast matter.

The ghosts of the Ice Base were with Pierre Hougaardt as he crouched next to the missile gun assigned to him. He'd hoped never to do this again; but working for Captain, one couldn't be a mindless pacifist. Yang Ko was at his left elbow, entertaining him with upbeat commentary; and Johnsson, silent and focused, was there at his right, checking that his aim was good. Ghosts from Ice Base, supporting him.

Jets started checking in from below the base. Pierre recognized the special forces from Las Village; Captain had sent the elite marines and petites in as reinforcements. With relief Pierre registered that this time, their chances were better than back at the Ice Base. Except when he looked at the endless alien fleet... they would wear them down by sheer numbers.

*

Perdita Sancho had done a complete job making the base defensible. Radomir Lascek checked its electronic shield, and its Kovalski shield, and launched two un-crewed probes. He had to gather more information about the enemy.

A burning meteorite hurtled towards Earth, followed by more. Lascek gave orders to fire, and the missile guns of the base were discharged at the Rapacin fleet.

One of the specks detached from the fleet and came plummeting towards the base. Lascek hoped that the Kovalski shield would hold up against such an impact. But the small black craft stopped short of the base, and the next moment, Dana was in the control room with him.

"Radomir! I see Earth is having a patch of trouble?"

He snorted. "You could say that."

"I brought you a fleet," she volunteered with a sweet smile.

He gaped at her. He could kiss her! She pointed to the glittering skies.

"Half of the ships up there are Danaan forces," she announced. "Battle Maidens and Corsairs and Cutters and Wasps, and of course a number of Supergirls. All manned with my petite elite."

Lascek laughed. "Oh, you marvellous woman!"

"Don't mention it, Radomir," purred Dana. "The Rapacin Queen and I have a few old bones to grind. She deleted a whole fleet of my mutants."

"There are no mutants up there currently?" asked Lascek cautiously.

"No. I shan't be bringing those into the vicinity of Earth again soon. Paean's prioid is everywhere. They're too valuable to be wasted like that."

Lascek nodded, relieved. Though he'd have wished those mutants on the Moozils up there.

Perdita teleported back into the control room and spotted Dana. The look that passed between the two, the raider and the terrorist boss, confirmed to Lascek that they were sisters after all. It was a look of understanding, of sudden solidarity in a crisis; and amazingly, mutual respect.

"Dana," said Perdita with a nod and a smile. "Good that you're here."

"Can count on me, girl," replied the Space Goddess. "Your Space Base is well defended, I have to say. Good job."

"You know that the Council has been contacted?" asked Perdita.

"What? Of all the foolish idiocies!" exclaimed Dana. "Whose idea was that?"

"Vlad's," said Perdita.

"Who the hell is Vlad?"

"The Morrigan," elucidated Perdita.

A huge burning missile came flying towards the Space Base and rebounded off the Kovalski shield with a massive crash. But the shield held up.

"The Morrigan?" Dana turned a bit pale. "Where's he now? Thought he was dead?"

*

The cabin juddered. Federi was sitting up in an instant, listening. Paean surfaced, groggy and confused from that too-short nap.

"Wha's that?"

Federi shook his head and got up. He had no idea. At the cabin's hatch he nearly collided with Wolf, who had been on the point of knocking.

"Need Paean in the lab," said the engineer. "For the battle croaches."

"Uh-huh," she replied woozily and staggered after him. Federi shadowed them and stood in the hatch of the lab for a while, until he'd gathered what this was about.

The Morrigan was in there, helping Wolf construct a battle croach against the Moozils. The first generation of croach was already up and running, teleported off into the enemy space shuttles.

338

Some of their offspring had returned with samples of Moozil. Paean was needed to establish what Moozils were sensitive to. And this needed to happen in record time. From what Wolf said, the Space Base was already under attack. This explained the terrible shuddering: She was being bombarded.

Federi recalled the battle before Prime Oil that Johnny Anyhow had given him, and how beautifully Paean had coped, stepping up the cloning by whole orders of speed. He looked at her until her light eyes lifted and returned his gaze.

"'s not simply tweaking valeriensis, this time," she said, her eyebrows in a knot of worry. "This is totally alien stuff, Federi! Look..." and she gazed at the Genitron, and smiled. "Ha! Bananas!"

"What?" asked Wolf.

"The Solar Wind has just determined that banana essence ought to be extremely toxic to these aliens."

"Good," said Federi and left the three of them to it. To have the Morrigan on that team! It struck him as dangerous, unstable – but necessary. He sauntered off towards the upper deck and the Space Base's control room, to speak to Captain.

Wolf recalled a pair of his battle croaches so that Paean could load the formula into their poison genes. Vlad facilitated; Paean doubted that she'd have managed to do the same in such a short time. Vlad also gave the croaches the facility to transfer these poison genes to other adult croaches. Paean made a mental note to ask him exactly how he did this. But she suspected it had something to do with biofields. Out of her league in that case.

*

Radomir Lascek had ordered all his forces to shoot only at the missiles, to deflect them. It was hard to tell which alien spaceships were Moozils and which were Danaan petites. Federi ghosted into the Space Base and had a look into the control room.

"Tzigan!" said Lascek, more jovially than he felt. "Good that you're here! Now you can..."

Federi didn't hear the rest of the order. His overtired body had taken him on a walk out of there, and along the passages.

Everywhere he came across locked valves. The only places that were accessible, were the lounge, control room, arboretum and the core cells, which had gone up first. That included the docking bay, but only because the cut-off valve had been manually overruled so that Captain didn't have to teleport to access the Solar Wind.

So the Danaan and the Battle Croaches were sorting out the invading Moozils. Captain was using missiles as bodyguards for Earth and the Space Base. And the Intergalactic Council had said...

That Intergalactic Council gave him nightmares. Damn! He returned to Captain.

"Federi," Lascek tried again, "a word?"

"Captain," replied Federi, "I have to make an urgent report first!"

"That's," said Lascek, rolling his eyes skywards, "what I'm talking about, Tzigan!" He handed the command of the defence of the Space Base to Perdita and led the way to the Solar Wind's bridge.

"Now, Federi," prompted the Captain, "I'd like your angle on this. You have debriefed Paean by now?"

Federi nodded gravely.

"Seems to me," he said, "that this invasion is critical, but we're not going to win it at this level. Got a mission."

"The Rapacins," Lascek guessed shrewdly.

"Absolutely, Captain. And then, the Intergalactic Council."

Radomir Lascek stared at him in dismay. "The Intergalactic

Council is on your list?"

"Yes, Captain. Got to get into negotiations with them. They're capable of breaking everything for us."

"Federi, say the word," said the Captain. "The Rapacins are yours; I'll take the Council. Whom do you need on your team?"

"Paean," said Federi. "And Shawn."

"Why Shawn?"

"To hold the console of the Comet when Paean and I go into the Rapacin worlds."

Lascek nodded. He sensed that this wasn't the main reason; that Federi's actual agenda was to keep the youngest Donegal under close supervision. And there was this thing Perdita had mentioned, about the Donegals being Founders... whatever that meant.

"Take Ailyss as well," he said.

"Right, Captain. But I can only go when this invasion has been averted," replied Federi.

His Captain's huge hand clapped down on his shoulder.

"Federi," said Lascek gravely, "I must ask you to take the team now. Don't wait until the assault is beaten off – it may never be. I can't take that risk on behalf of Earth. Go now, and destroy the Rapacins. Take a Genitron along. Even if the Space Base is destroyed, at least Earth still stands a chance as long as the Rapacins are eradicated."

"But you need me here to help shoot them down," objected Federi desperately. Scenes from finding the burnt-out Ice Base replayed in his head.

"My friend," said Lascek with a smile, "there are better canonniers than you are. Jon. And Anyhow. Dr Jake, even. I need you to complete the Rapacin mission. For the survival of Earth, my friend."

Federi nodded, feeling dejected. "Captain, I hate leaving the

341

base to fend for itself…"

"Look," invited Lascek and keyed a sequence into the Solar Wind's console. A screen opened, giving a visual of the skies above the Space Base, relayed directly from the base's own CPU. Missiles were flying between the different space craft much more often than they came heading towards the base, or Earth. "Dana's fleet is beating them back," explained Lascek. "She's giving us a gap. Take it, Federi! I can't leave here, or I'd come with you; but you jump through the loophole and get away. Understood?"

*

The Comet fell away from the Space Base amidst burning missiles, leaving the silver filigree structure behind. Federi glanced back at it, worrying. Up there, surrounding Earth in an endless fleet were the Gargantuan vessels, the aliens; and between them, the smaller, more versatile black titanium ships of Dana's fleet, shapes and sizes more varied than a nightmare. Even the Battle Maidens, her largest warships, were dwarfed by those Gargantuans; but her missiles were certainly nothing to be sneezed at. The battle raged up there; by now only half the missiles from the Gargantuans were launched at Earth. The others were definitely aimed at Danaan vessels, and while many of them were deflected by Dana's amazing shields, here and there a titanium ship exploded in a momentary cloud of burning gas.

The gypsy's heart ached for the young girls, no older than a physical nineteen years, that were being sacrificed up there. He found himself muttering an old gypsy blessing to support them, and he hoped that Wolf's battle croaches were going to do their thing really fast. He wished he could have an extra battle croach for every time he'd wished that roaches didn't breed so fast.

342

The Comet had circled the Earth once, by now. There was no getting away from it. The massive fleet had completely surrounded the planet. Federi pulled a face and changed the jet's course. It was all or nothing now. The jet streaked past the fragile-looking Space Base, and up, straight at that enormous fleet. Missiles zinged around their ears; Federi's fingers were dancing a fandango on the console to keep the Comet out of the way of flying rocks of molten nuclear material. The Danaan were shooting at the Gargantuans with meaning; and the Moozils gave as good as they received. Paean cowered on the floor of the Comet, her face covered with her hands. Federi knew that she was thinking of the Ice Base. Ailyss was silent and grim; Shawn as pale as a ghost, trying to be brave and not wince with every missile that flashed past them.

"Technically they shouldn't be burning, in the vacuum," the clever young teenager commented.

"They're not burning," replied Federi. "No oxygen involved. They're just hot. Molten. Nuclear style hot. Like the inside of a star."

"Ah." And Shawn fell silent.

Federi welcomed that. He had a course to plot. He was still exhausted from mind-wrestling that Rapacin Queen; but there was no space for exhaustion now. He had to eradicate her. The Rapacins were the most voracious predators of the Rosetta galaxy. And they did it all by mind control and slave species. Even if Earth and New Dome together managed to defeat the Moozils, they'd be back! He didn't fool himself into thinking that the Moozils were their only slave species; and he wasn't keen on meeting the others.

So the whole thing had to be rooted out. The Rapacins themselves had to be stopped; they knew where Earth was.

How? This puzzled him. They had to have planted some or other spy on the Solar Wind, or the Comet perhaps, or even... on

Calypso… Suddenly that planet had something creepy to it. How could they know what all lay frozen under its ice? Which was practically all melted now, polar caps excepted?

A burning missile streaked past the Comet on its way to Earth. It met something in mid-air and exploded in a spectacular shower of fireworks.

"Wish on a star," muttered Federi under his breath.

And then the Morrigan poured himself into the Comet, like a sudden mountain creek over a drop. He turned into Vlad the Impostor and presented Leila the croach to Paean with a flourish. She looked up and gave him a tentative smile; he responded with a magnificent bow.

"Your data, milady. The Moozil genomic code has been saved on her chip. You can plug her into the jet-board Genitron to produce whatever you like to destroy those Moozils."

Paean smiled, relieved. "Thank you, Prince Vlad!" And she grinned suddenly. Federi glanced at her with suspicion. "So now there are two princes aboard!"

"How…" asked Vlad and put out a stalk eye at Federi. "Ah! Of course! Your Majesty!" And he bowed deeply to the Tzigan.

"Your own majesty, with knobs on," replied Federi, dodging another burning missile. They were nearly out of the cloud of spaceships by now. "Still owe you an assassination over that. You corrupted my wife's thinking."

The Morrigan shrunk to the size of a garden gnome and found himself a spot on the Comet's floor to plop down.

"Federi, you're right," he conceded. "I'm sorry. It was deliberate. We were enemies then. I would never do it today."

"Bet you wouldn't," growled Federi and focused on the path to the Danaan portal. They were out of the enemy fleet by now, with only one or two ships still shooting after them. He activated the

Salamanca drives, which Perdita had installed for Paean so that the Comet had all the options of the Probe, too. They warped away from the space fleet and hurtled headlong in the direction of Pluto.

He'd have to be careful with the Salamanca drives. They accelerated the craft to nearly intergalactic speeds. He worried that he might miss the base entirely. But there simply weren't hours available to do this on magnetic drives alone. A bit more automation of the pathways was required. He'd put Wolf's mind to it.

Federi hoped fervently that when they returned, the Space Base would still exist. But he had to agree with Captain: The time for a counter-attack would never be as good as right now, when the Rapacin Queen thought all of Earth was fully occupied fending off her Moozils.

A tentacle lashed out from Vlad and snatched something out of the air next to Federi's ear. The Assassin stared wildly at the Morrigan. In Vlad's tentacle hung a small, dusky-blue creature that looked a bit like a rat with wings.

"So," said Vlad scathingly. "Still at it, you little plague?"

Paean was right there to defend the small creature. "What's it done wrong? It's so cute!"

"Oh, so you like rats?" asked Vlad.

"I'm not a rat," peeped the small creature, sensing sympathy from Paean. "I'm a Blue Furry Dragon. Mammalian, you know! Highly intelligent creatures, us Furry Blues."

"Anthrim 's intelligence agent," said the Morrigan with an ironic baring of a fang. "Tell nice auntie Paean your name, you little pest!"

"Mischief Maker," said the Blue Furry.

"Your soul name," said Vlad menacingly.

"Furrl," squeaked the small animal.

"Great! Furrl: You are going to stay here with us. You are not reporting back to Anthrim."

"He'll eat me!" squealed the small creature.

"If you do, I'll eat you," said Vlad with a nasty smile. "And I'll make you suffer. I'll eat you slowly, I'll first dissolve one wing-tip, then the other…"

"Mercy!" whimpered Furrl.

"Then don't blink!" ordered Vlad.

"That's cruel," commented Paean. The Morrigan turned to her with a quizzically hyper-lifted eyebrow. It lifted right off his face.

"Blinking is what they call it when they teleport," he explained. "Federi, is there anything on the Comet with which we can restrain his wings?"

"His wings?" asked the Tzigan, baffled.

"Blue Furries can teleport into the seventeenth dimension," explained Vlad. "They can go from one end of the universe to the other in a blink, using interdimensions. The function is embedded in their wings. Restrain their wings and they can't move."

Shawn got up from the spot on the floor he'd been occupying and found the jet-board toolbox. One could see that the jet had been in Federi's care; the box was well stocked. He found electric insulation tape and used that to wrap around the small creature's wings.

"Now he's not going anywhere," said Vlad, content, handing the small creature to Shawn. "Federi, where are we going? Why are you heading to the Domnian interchange?"

"Warn Johnny of the invasion," said Federi shortly. "They'll strike at Dome too, that's a given. And I need the hypnotron. After that, Rapacins."

"Meet me at the portal," said Vlad. "I'll inform Johnny and get you your hypnotron. Don't waste time on that." And he teleported out.

Federi redirected the Comet to the portal through which the Solar

Wind had gone in hunt of Dana's treasure. The coordinates were permanently programmed into the Comet's console.

He had ripped the pathway to the Rapacin worlds from the Solar Wind's log. The portal into the Rosetta Nebula was the same as the treasure hunt portal; which proved to Federi that one could have a portal from one place in the horizontal universe to another without having to hop through the vertical universe. He didn't know what value there was in that insight. He was up against a wall in his own mind; he was jolly ignorant, that was what, and he wished that old Falco, the grandfather he would never acknowledge, could be by his side now and unpack what he knew. Not that potentially having him right inside his own mind was quite such a comforting thought.

The little songbird got off her console chair and came to sit on the floor next to his chair. She leaned against him; his hand sank into her lush curls.

"I'm officially freaked and boggled," she stated.

"Myself, little luv," he agreed without taking his eyes off the void ahead.

"Bad enough the Unicate, and the were folk," she said. "But... all these aliens! You know, Federi – it would be wonderful to tramp through the South American rainforests and discover new species, or see a sloth up close, or an Anaconda... but this? They all bite or sting or want to rip us apart!"

"Anacondas strangle you," Federi pointed out dreamily. "And crocodiles drag you under water to drown you, and then hide your body somewhere. When you've gone nice and soft, then they eat you, portion by portion. Frugal animals, crocs."

She smiled. He couldn't see it, but he sensed it.

"It's different," she said. "We own Earth's animals. Just our own fault if they try to eat us. We're s'posed to be the top o' the food chain."

He laughed softly.

"But all these aliens," repeated Paean. "And that Anthrim ! I didn't know dragons still existed – and that they could be evil!"

Federi nodded. They'd have to deal with Anthrim when they got there. Who knew – it might be Vlad's gap to get onto the Intergalactic Council. Which might be useful. Aargh! He should leave the political schemes to Captain!

"A year back I'd never have believed any of this, now would I?" said Paean.

Federi sighed deeply. "Little luv, when the meteorite hit the dinosaurs, I'm sure there wasn't one who'd have seen it coming. Things can happen fast. What ol' Falco was afraid of. It would only have taken one hot-headed politician in the Sixties to push a button that could have split the Earth in two. Would have been only seconds."

She nodded.

"Let's hope the button was destroyed, not only taken over by the Unicate!" added Federi.

"Federi," said Paean, "don't go there now! Let's focus on the Rapacins."

Federi set his teeth and swooped close to that amazing fleet again, sending a thankyou to his lucky stars that the blasted intergalactic portal, which was close to Earth, wasn't so close that he'd have to dip into the enemy cloud. Still he had to dodge a number of missiles.

Paean woke up from her shallow dozing when Vlad materialized back in the Comet, shimmering mysteriously and starting as a hologram that slowly solidified. The Morrigan presented Federi with a pocket hypnotron.

"Dome has been alerted," he reported back. "Johnny is gearing up the remaining forces. A lot of Dana's forces are in Earth's voidspace though."

"Did you check on Earth?" asked Paean.

"Give me a break, milady," replied Vlad. "I'm only one Morrigan!"

Federi growled something unintelligible through his teeth and then said, "Fantastic! Let's go!"

The Comet vaulted through the portal and clicked into the pathway that the Solar Wind had been dragged along, not two days back.

*

Cabin fever. Paean hadn't seen it before; it was amazing how an inhuman amount of work on the Solar Wind had kept them all from developing it. But Shawn had it now, and Federi was also pretty crabby, and Ailyss had sunk into her own uncommunicative inner world. The only person aboard who was still fun, was Vlad. And Vlad was trying to keep people's spirits up.

She scowled. Weren't they supposed to take tobuskies along to improve the oxygen? But this time, the glowing little dogs had been left far behind.

She thought back to the way the Morrigan had made them all depressed, back on the space roundtrip. Couldn't he achieve the opposite now?

It had been hours. In fact, she'd lost track of time. The Comet's clock still faithfully recorded time... but what did that mean, out here? Yet she was quite sure that if they had been on their way for days, the oxygen situation in the Comet would be far worse. The air conditioning system was slowly feeding oxygen into the cabin while absorbing carbon dioxide and somehow doing away with it. Her tobuskies would have been a nice addition, but Perdita's systems were perfectly adequate.

It was different from when Perdita had taken her on a patrol around the Solar System. The lady had known where she was going. Federi was acting on a hunch, and Paean was altogether uneasy about him finding the way. The only encouraging factor was that they had Vlad aboard.

Federi turned, tearing himself away from his glum staring into the dark void ahead.

They were losing precious time; and while they were out here, the Space Base and Earth were under attack. Federi had no idea how to get news on that battle. It was maddening.

But… he wasn't using all the resources he had!

"Vlad!"

"Yes, Marsther," the alien rasped with a Frankenstein's Monster-voice.

"Quit that!" ordered Federi. "This is no comedy. Listen, Vlad. Do you know a short-cut to the Rapacin worlds?"

Vlad winced. "I'd hoped you wouldn't ask."

"So you do!"

"I know how I can get you there faster," said the Morrigan. "But the trouble is, the Rapacin Queen knows me. She'll know I'm approaching."

"She knows you?" Federi studied him thoughtfully. "Then you could…"

"Forget it, assassin," said Vlad. "There's no way. I'm not immortal by being stupid."

Paean blinked. Was Vlad mimicking Federi? Her gypsy noticed this too, and pulled a face.

"Morrigan, this time, not doing as I tell you is the stupid part," he informed him. "How fast can you get us there?"

"Plus, I need a teeny tiny piece of Rapacin," Paean piped up.

"Noooo!" crooned Vlad. "Spare me!"

"Vlad, it's necessary!" pressed Paean. "You know what I do with small samples of species."

The Morrigan shuddered theatrically. "I nearly feel sorry for the Rapacins."

"Whose side are you on?" snapped Paean angrily.

"Alright, alright, Paean Donegal," acceded the alien. "Anything for the pretty lady!" And he warped out of the Comet.

"Demonos!" Federi hissed after him. "Not Donegal!"

The area surrounding the Comet started to shimmer orange. Stars became stripes and then disappeared; and a few minutes later, stripes reappeared and turned back into stars. The Comet hovered over a planet. Another planet was visible, a bit larger than a star, in the night sky.

"There are five Rapacin worlds," said Vlad, rematerializing in the Comet. "I've taken you to the world with the Queen on it. But we have to clean up all five, or a new queen will emerge."

Federi nodded.

"So now," said Paean, "how about that sample?"

"Furrl can go get it," said Vlad, pulling a face.

In the end it was Federi who went with Vlad and Furrl to fetch the sample. Paean had threatened to go by herself; which resulted unfailingly in the males volunteering, and forcing the small creature along. It didn't suit Paean too well. She had wanted to see the Rapacin worlds.

"You can't trust him!"

Her words rang in Federi's ears. He waited in the dark muddy tunnel where Vlad had positioned him, his Kosaka ready, trying to hold his breath. The acrid stink in here was nearly lethal. On his shoulder sat Furrl, the blue furry dragon; its wings temporarily unbound, but the small creature's soul bound by its name.

Vlad had scouted ahead, to visit the Queen. He had made himself invisible, his thoughts inaudible to Intergalactic Common. He didn't want her army to become aware of him. So Federi was in that tunnel alone.

Paean had wanted Leila to go, instead of Furrl. Or S.I. Lucy. But neither were set up for this mission. Vlad had assured her that they were not resistant to the acid Rapacins carried all over their slimy scales. The trouble with the dragonling was that it could escape into thought space, leaving the gypsy to his fate. Vlad had assured them that its true name was a great lever, by which it was bound; but Federi wasn't so sure.

Well, it wouldn't be the first insectile tunnel he'd be blasting a path out of, he thought with a certain professional pride, and a quietly shuddering memory of the recent Unicate mound. What was it about the Unicate that reminded him so strongly of a hive? He glanced at the small blue shadow on his shoulder. So far Furrl had stayed true, although the little craven was fretting in a solid stream in his highly pitched psychic monologue. Federi's head buzzed from it.

Something dragged closer, like the rasping sound of snake skin on cement. Except that there were smacking, sucking sounds in there too. It stood to reason, considering the deep mud through which whatever-it-was slicked…

It rounded the corner and was suddenly there. Federi understood about the scraping. The maggot face filled the whole tunnel, and its skin scraped against the sides and roof where there were still some protruding rocks that hadn't yet been licked completely round by the acid. A huge white blob, stinking horribly of acid slime. Its head was not yet shaped quite like that of an insect, but it already had razor-sharp mandibles the size of elephants' tusks, and faceted eyes, and a pair of segmented red feelers waving too close to Federi's face.

"Shoot at the eyes," Vlad had advised. Federi lifted his cannon. The Rapacin maggot slurped closer, touching Federi's face with its hairy feeler tips. Liquid started drooling from the mandibles, steaming a puddle onto the floor, which dissolved a bit worse.

Federi shot at the eyes. The whole maggot was ripped apart, exploding in a mess of acid, whitish intestines and hard exterior shell pieces. The debris was flung at Federi with force… Furrl panicked.

"You're back," said Paean, delighted.

"You smell!" commented Shawn, grinning.

"Furrl!" scolded Federi. "Get us back in there and complete your task!"

The blue furry dragon whimpered but blinked with Federi back into that muddy passage. Various smaller Rapacin maggots were already converging on their dead mate. Furrl swooped down over it and ripped a small piece out of its eye with his razor-sharp teeth. His claws dug into Federi's shoulder, and he blinked again, taking Federi with him.

They arrived back in the Comet. The little Mischief Maker spat out the Rapacin biopsy and then emptied its entire stomach contents on the floor.

"Messy critter," commented Shawn, revolted. The little beast was coughing and retching miserably. "And you smell," Shawn told Federi good-naturedly. "'s not like you, Federi!"

"Smart-ass," retorted Federi. "Paean, you'll have to pick your teeny tiny little piece of Rapacin out of that mess yourself." He turned on the spot and made a straight line for the shower cubicle, barely controlling his own gag reflex.

Paean picked the biopsy up with tweezers and placed it into the test receptacle of the Genitron. She felt quite queasy, both from the

353

stench and from watching the blue furry dragon be violently sick like that on her jet's floor. She closed the Genitron's lid. Her fingers played deftly over the buttons, if a bit shakily. Leila sat next to her, waving her feelers in anticipation of her mistress' orders. Shawn retrieved some toilet paper to remove Furrl's mess, and grabbed the small dragon in two fingers to rinse him thoroughly in the basin of the ablutions cubicle.

"I wonder how Vlad is doing," said Paean. Ailyss looked up from her novel.

"Say, what?"

Five Rapacin worlds. She didn't have the luxury of time, that she… hadn't actually had with Dana's mutants either. But this time it was worse. If they took too long, if Vlad failed somehow, the Rapacin queen would discover them and start roping them in telepathically. The only reason she hadn't yet, was because clearly whatever Vlad was doing as a distraction, was working. And Shawn was concentrating very hard on them being psychically invisible; imagining he could shield the whole craft from the Queen's probing psychic tendrils. He had the Hypnotron in hand to help him. Paean hoped he was managing.

That left her practically no time at all. She needed to clone something fast-growing, and vicious. A prioid, in the hope that the stuff spread better and further than virus or bacteria. She scanned frantically over the facts the Genitron was spitting out, and mulling how she could go about this. And then she had it. Inspiration came, like a deep-blue cloud, out of the void. She started developing her weapon at warp speed.

By the time Federi emerged from the shower, Paean was ready with her biological weapon. Shawn had rinsed Furrl down and pensively tied his wings again. Ailyss was sitting by, trying to read a novel. She was Federi's backup; but while he didn't need her, all she could do was be on standby.

Paean glanced up at Federi as he came out of that cubicle, and had to smile. He was wearing one of Perdita's space suits. And no bandanna. His clothes were in a sealed bag. He didn't look like himself.

"We'll have to go in again, you know," she told him. He nodded grimly.

"I think Perdita has enough rubbish bags left for us to change into," he commented wryly.

"My prioid is ready," Paean added.

"Then let's go!" replied Federi and handed her a space suit, too. "Let's hope these raincoats are a bit acid-proof."

She loaded the prioid she had cloned, into darts and spray bottles. Shawn handed her Furrl.

"Don't make me go in there again!" whimpered the little dragon, and started dry-retching again.

"Stop that!" snapped Federi. "You're a coward! Your part in this plot is not a fraction of what Vlad has to do."

"I'm a spy, not a combat-machine!" howled Furrl.

"The penalty for spying is death," Federi informed him. "Pirate Law of the Pacific. So would you prefer to die or to comply?"

Furrl gave in, whimpering pitifully to himself. He blinked with both Paean and Federi into the Rapacin world, right back to where they had just escaped from. About twenty of those larvae were wriggling around in the tunnel, mopping up the remains of their fallen hive mate; all instantly turned on the three newcomers, the fresh wriggling meat, the moment they arrived.

"Traitor!" yelled Federi in fury as he ripped out his submachine gun and shot at Rapacin eyes. Furrl could have touched down anywhere with them; why in the middle of this feeding frenzy?

The only spot in which Rapacins were at all vulnerable was their eyes. Luckily these were quite large. Federi didn't even have to aim before shooting.

Paean sprayed prioid over them. It took only a few moments for the Rapacins, dead and alive, to dissolve and become a slimy, wobbly mess on the floor. The ruckus brought more Rapacins out of the side tunnels; they too fell prey to the prioid.

"We have to get to the other worlds," said Federi.

"Vlad mentioned that they are all connected with each other," said Paean. "Interplanetary space tunnels. How those are different from portals…"

"Let's hope the prioid can cross those tunnels," said Federi moodily. "We'll have to wait for Vlad to take us to the other planets. Wonder how he's doing! Furrl, get us back to the Comet!"

The Morrigan had turned into a huge silver dragon and was circling the last home world several times, gathering courage. His baggage – a small but lethal explosive charge, combining Paean's prioid with good old explosive – was in his talons.

The touch on his mind came.

"Do my aged sensors deceive me?"

"No," replied Vlad with a shudder of revulsion.

"You've come back for me?"

"I'm here," replied Vlad, his scales turning translucent and iridescence running across them. This took more courage than facing down the Demon. "I'm here to break the rules one more time."

"This time," said the Queen, "I'll eat you when you are done."

"Quite the contrary," said Vlad. "I'm here to make sure you'll

356

never stop thinking of me while you're alive!"

"I never did yet."

Vlad shook himself in disgust. He had been stuck in the Rapacin worlds once. Turning into a Rapacin look-alike hadn't helped – they smelt him out, and he couldn't synthesize their particular acrid stink in himself. It damaged his structure. He had escaped into the largest chamber of them all – and had come face to face with the Rapacin Queen.

He wished he couldn't remember how he had sweet-talked his way out of there that time. It had taken him being a major Morrigan to get away with his coruscating hide intact. He had to be crazy to go in there a second time! But – he still feared the Demon more. And he wasn't immortal by loading the dice on the wrong side.

Besides, thwarting that Anthrim of the Council gave him immense pleasure. And the bleeding Council hadn't stopped the Rapacins. For all he knew, they had invited that ever-hungry species to help itself to Earth.

This was one of the worlds on which even Dana's mutants had failed. It wasn't the Raider's first run-in with this species; and so far, she and her girls had survived. Vlad had to hand it to the tough-minded little Atlantean. She was a top-notch space pirate, despite her diplomatic shortcomings. He quite liked the way he could see new angles in people and species from the human perspective. He had stopped viewing Dana and Perdita as his priestesses. That old game had got boring during the space trip.

Half a minute later Vlad was back on the Leapfrog. He simulated Vlad Dracul's shape and threw up in the toilet, then shook his head sadly. "That makes no difference. Just a waste of good food." He got into the shower and turned it on and allowed the hot water to stream between his molecules. Slowly the Rapacin stench dissipated. He wished the memory would dissipate with it.

357

"Mission accomplished?"

"Mission accomplished, Federi," groaned the Morrigan. "She's stew. Should have seen that explosion. Wasn't easy, getting close enough to plant that bomb. That female was immensely wily."

"How did you manage to get close enough?" asked Paean, intrigued.

He gave her a pained look. "Don't go there, Your Ladyship!"

"Well done, Vlad," said Federi approvingly.

"And now the Moozils," the Morrigan said brightly.

"But Vlad," Paean piped up, "we've only pest-controlled one of the five home worlds! Don't we need to do the rest?"

"That prioid will spread," said the Morrigan confidently. "Don't worry. The Rapacins are constantly visiting each other on the different home worlds; it's one wriggly mass of worms. Before a new queen can mature, the prioid will have finished them."

"I thought they are planet-bound?"

"Ha! Yes," said the Morrigan. "There are stunnels…"

"But if the Rapacins are gone, why do we have to eradicate the Moozils too?" asked Paean. "It feels wrong! They were just a slave species."

"They are also always hungry," said Vlad. "And they know where Earth is. Come, Paean. I'll get you a teeny tiny piece of Moozil."

"I'm not happy about this," grumbled Paean. Federi scratched his calf where a Moozil had sunk its teeth into his leg on the Perdita rescue mission. There was an itchy sore, healing at mutant rates, but still too slowly for Federi's liking.

"I'll get you a whole Moozil then," said Vlad. "So you can see for yourself. They are vicious!"

"But you're a Morrigan! Can't you change their genetic setup?"

Vlad got thoughtful.

It had taken him a religion and an artefact to keep the Atlantean civilization under control. And his mind-control had slipped when, after several centuries, he got bored of playing with them.

Granted, he'd changed their lifespan and the shape of their eyes; but that had been a genetic alteration in only a few founders, from where the genes had spread. But to do this in a Moozil population several billion strong?

"You make them a prioid," he said. "I'll see what I can do." And he teleported out.

Paean shook her head and sat down with a pen and neopaper, trying to decide what to do to the Moozils.

Maybe one should turn them into obligatory herbivores. And docile. Very docile. That was actually the easy part. Clone something into their blood that did to them what valeriensis did to humans. Just not completely.

Vlad returned with a pair of Moozils in his clutches.

"Here are your test animals," he said. "Knock yourself out!"

"Need a cage of sorts for them," said Paean.

"They're under mind-control," Vlad replied.

Paean still looked doubtful.

"Oh, alright," conceded the Morrigan and vanished. A few minutes later he was back, dropping a pet carrier of sorts on the Comet's floor and forcing the Moozils into it.

"Where did you get that?" asked Paean, surprised.

"I shaped it out of some organic debris," said Vlad.

"You can create things?"

"Sure – so can you, can't you?"

She thought about this.

*

359

Patrick opened his eyes. There had been a pull towards reality, drawing him out of the safety of his coma. And now there was this yellow-eyed person over him, staring at him with the strangest smile...

"You're coming back with me," said Terence. "Head Office wants you."

It had to be a horrible dream. Patrick squeezed his eyes shut, trying to escape back into the comfortable world of blackness he had been drifting in. But long, wiry fingers like steel talons gripped him, and he felt a queasy shift in reality, and then...

His eyes flew open again. Rain streamed down in the dismal dusk. The young Unicate's talons were still around his arm... Patrick screamed, but it helped him nothing. The Unicate *Other* forced his steps in a straight line to the entrance of that mound that hunched grey and ominous next to the IRP headquarters.

If he could only get to those headquarters... but his boss, Bryce, had shot at him, aimed to kill! There was no safety there either!

Patrick's mind rolled back to endless grey days in orphanages; to roaming the streets after his escape, trying to connect, to belong somewhere. There had been a brief sense of belonging in that small yellow cabin, a false sense of safety. People had cared for him. Paean Donegal had ripped him away from the very bullet aimed at him by his boss. A girl whose family was prosecuted by his own organization; out of whose capture and death he had hoped to make a buck. He thought back disconnectedly to so many impoverished families, ripped out of their squalid existence – a happy loving existence, it struck him suddenly – to become test subjects and die terribly from Bryce's monster viruses, or be handed to the Mound, never to be seen again. Bryce's idea had been to find the "poor gene" and unleash a plague on all the poor in the world, reducing the world's population down to a tenth and raising general wealth levels.

Poor like himself, Patrick thought uneasily. But there was no poor gene. It could happen to anyone. He knew this.

And the Mound? They were "gearing up" one way or the other. Patrick didn't know what they needed poor people for. But he was beginning to think he was on the verge of finding out.

Where was that gutsy Donegal girl now? Couldn't she rescue him a second time? He was white with terror as Terence, his amiable colleague from the mound who had helped him collect so many test subjects, dragged him down the dimly lit passages.

It smelt of mould down here. Patrick thought disconnectedly of a termite mound. And then the young Unicate *Other* opened a door and ushered Patrick in.

"Here he is, your majesty."

A beautiful young woman peered at Patrick from the swivel chair. Her middle was ever so slightly bulging in pregnancy.

"Do come in," she smiled. "I am Queen Rhyn."

24 – Prioid

The Comet hung over one of the Moozil worlds. A lovely blue-green planet, so nearly like Earth.

"Help me, Vlad! I'm stuck!"

The Morrigan bent over the Genitron and analysed what Paean was trying to do.

"Tell me what you're up to," he invited.

"I want to turn them vegetarian," she said. "And docile."

"And infertile," added Vlad. "They breed terribly fast."

"I see. So I've got the docile prioid ready, but I don't know if it will help. How do we get it to all of them?"

Vlad's pupils became square and his eyes focused on infinite as he reached out with one tentacle, touching the Genitron's keypad. The small machine whizzed and hummed as code appeared on its screen. Eventually Vlad released it.

"Time to hit the 'synthesize' button," he instructed Paean. "This machine is convenient! My!"

The Comet emerged from the cold ion cloud silently, like an assassin in the night. Federi steered it towards the waypoint Vlad had given him. The Moozils were restless in their organic pet carrier that Vlad had shaped out of a piece of debris from the Rapacin worlds. The Genitron's display was flashing figures and letters that only made sense to Paean, and possibly to Vlad. Leila had crawled onto Paean's shoulder and was watching raptly. S.I. Lucy, more the dimensions of a normal roach, was hiding in his pocket. Ailyss was still immersed in her novel;   and Vlad was entertaining Shawn

362

Donegal by teaching him mind wrestling techniques. Just as well. Part of the boy's training, thought Federi.

He wasn't going to give too much thought to what they had just done. They had deleted a complete species down to the last bit of DNA – if that was in fact the material Rapacins had used for their genes. It had been a species that had threatened his home planet. As a human he felt perfectly fine about it. He preferred being at the top of the food chain. As a gypsy, no problem. Those Rapacins were monsters. There were no gypsy laws against killing monsters. But as an intergalactic person, a citizen of the Universe… the thought niggled that there might be a responsibility here. He might have overstepped something. He refused to explore it at this point, because for the sake of Earth, they had to do it again – change the genetic make-up of an entire species.

Vlad's idea for the Moozils was brilliant. They would have met the same fate as the Rapacins, except for two things: Firstly they weren't as localized and therefore more difficult to find. The Moozils were a highly space-going species. They were spread all over. But secondly, they were cute. They didn't stink; they were soft and fluffy and they looked like live teddybears. Humans could like Moozils – that was, humans who hadn't already been bitten. Vlad had started to think like a human. That was the best news.

It was of course against the rules to interfere with the natural evolution of a species, the Morrigan had explained. Not that rules had ever bothered him. Federi thought back to the Danaan race.

"Wish I could get an update from Earth," said Paean wistfully next to him. He glanced at her. She looked worried.

"Your prioid works, little luv," he assured her. "By now those aliens should all be dead."

"As long as they didn't bomb Earth out of the sky before they all died," she muttered.

The memory of Ice Base stood written in her ice-blue eyes as she cast him a strained look. Federi grabbed her hand and smiled at her, battling down his own sadness.

"It will be alright," he promised. "We'll come back and they will all be there… we got Dana's fleet fighting for us, Paean. Cheer up! She's been a space pirate for a long time. Centuries longer than we have."

That did cheer her up.

"Anyway the Intergalactic Council wouldn't allow the Unicate to be destroyed," added Federi with more than a hint of acid irony.

Paean smiled. "Now, a prioid…"

"We have to make sure they are genetically not human," said Federi.

"That's the key," she said. "Terence had me pretty convinced it was only a matter of brainwashing, but that mound… Federi, there's something so wrong about that whole thing! It has awareness. Now we know, the Solar Wind is AI too, but… I don't know…"

"The Mound mind-controls them," said Federi. "And who controls the Mound? Queen Rhyn… which means the Mound in Limerick ought to be destroyed. Until a new queen arises." He gazed into space. "Almost as if the actual *Others* really are only mind-controlled humans, but the Mound is the real alien entity."

"We have a specimen aboard," said Paean. "We can test that."

"Two specimens," Shawn put in from the back.

"We're not sure of that," Paean replied.

"Right now I'd like to investigate that contract Falco the Rat set up with the Intergalactic Council," said Federi. "It can't be right!"

"What if it's all legal?" she asked.

He got another sly smile in the corner of his mouth as they approached the waypoint. "You know, little luv, where there are Gadje laws…"

"… there are Tzigan loopholes," she completed with a huge grin. "That's fair, Federi. I'm with you. We'll try it the legal way first."

Behind them Vlad heaved a huge sigh of relief. And a second one. Federi laughed softly.

"Why did you sigh twice?" asked Paean.

"Doubles the physiological effect," said the Morrigan.

The Genitron beeped. The prioid was ready. Paean tested it on the two Moozils.

They stopped pacing and settled down, and went to sleep within minutes.

"Great," proclaimed Vlad. "It works! Let's load it into the poison nozzles."

"Are they going to survive?" asked Paean sceptically.

"Do we have time to worry about this?" Vlad asked back. "Are you doubting your own abilities as a Founder?"

"What the jolly hell is a Founder?" replied Paean with quite some irritation.

"You are," said Vlad. Ailyss stood up silently and loaded the prioid into the Comet's poison nozzles.

"And now, She'nedra?" asked Paean, unsettled.

"Paean, the Morrigan is right," said Ailyss. "Your designs always work; but even if this one has a flaw, we don't have the time to find out. We must get back to Earth. So we have to use it as is and hope for the best."

"But how will we know if it goes wrong?" protested Paean.

"We can take these two with us instead of sending them home," suggested Ailyss. "Then if you notice they are declining, you can start on a solution on Earth and we can come back to distribute it here."

Federi had lowered the Comet towards the planet and was now nudging her into a gentle, close orbit. Paean realized that he was already releasing a fine mist of prioid over the planet.

"And the other Moozils, on all those other planets?" she asked.

"They are in constant exchange," said Vlad. "It will spread, don't worry."

Paean nodded and resigned herself to the way things were.

It took an hour before Federi and Ailyss were both content that the Moozil planet was well seeded. The gypsy adjusted the Comet's course, and the jet shot off into space, first on Salamanca drives, then switching to Lolita coils.

"Home," said Shawn with obvious relief.

Federi grimaced and turned to the two Donegals and the rest of his crew.

"Kids, would it make sense to look for life-supporting planets?"

"Space Base needs us!" – "There's a war going, Federi!" – "We can't just go missing in action!"

"Assassin," said Vlad the Impostor, "I don't relish the idea of meeting the Council either. I also think they are waiting for us. Let's get it over with!"

"I didn't get twenty years to prepare for this one," objected Federi.

"I didn't even get twenty seconds to prepare for your sticky carbon," countered Vlad. "And if you don't know what the Council will do with you, I do know what they'll do with me. They will bite me in halves."

"That's what I'm worried about," said Federi.

"Then what are we waiting for?" asked Vlad, a strange dare-devil glint in his square pupil.

Federi set the Comet's destination to the portal.

The atmosphere on the jet was loaded as they emerged above the cloud of Gargantuan vessels. It still hung around Planet Earth like an evil aura. But no further missiles were flying to and fro. Either the Danaan had managed to negotiate a ceasefire, or the aliens were dead. Or… there was a third possibility.

The crew of the Comet stared at the situation, the burnt-out Ice Base hanging like a ghost between them.

"Where's Furrl?" asked Paean eventually.

"I've got him." Shawn pulled the tiny beast out of his pocket and handed him to his sister.

Paean carefully removed the tape from Furrl's wings and grabbed a Kosaka cannon. "Come on, Furrl! Let's go check if there are any more live Moozils!"

"Wait!" called Federi, but Paean and Furrl had already blinked out. Federi cursed and teleported after Paean. Ailyss took the controls.

By the third leap Federi caught up with the little red dynamo. He grabbed her by the wrist and glanced at the devastation around them.

"Are you insane?"

Dead Moozil remains all over; the floor teeming with combat croaches that ignored the humans completely while they busily ate Moozil and did their math. Multiplications. The Tzigan shuddered, his feet twitching to dance the Cucuracha on that infestation.

Paean looked at him in surprise.

"It's okay, Federi. I'm fine!"

"You had no idea what you'd find! You couldn't even know whether you'd be able to breathe!"

"No, Federi. We did an analysis before we created the combat croaches, remember?"

"Report-back," Federi commanded into his wrist-com. "What's the situation, croaches?"

You guys are back!, came an overjoyed message.

367

"Yes, Solar Wind, we're back. What's the toll?"

No human casualties on our team, replied the Mother Ship. Paean emitted an ear-splitting whoop of glee and hugged him stormily. Federi held her tightly, his ears ringing. Thank the Stars: No casualties amongst our friends!

All alien ships are taken and razed of crew, the Solar Wind continued her report. The Danaan took serious losses, but their situation improved when the combat croaches gained sufficient numbers. Roughly 2.556 times 10 to the power of seven combat croaches at this present moment. I'm currently commanding them into hibernate mode. This will take some time.

"Yoh, that's a lot of croaches!" gasped Paean. "Biomass? Carbon footprint?"

Surprisingly the biomass would not even be enough to populate a small planet, replied the Solar Wind. Despite their size, the battle croaches are lightweight. And a carbon footprint is an outmoded model, Paean. Everything in nature is recycled, every molecule is rewon. Remember that the biomass of the battle croaches was sourced from the biomass of the hostile aliens.

"But they must be using up a lot of oxygen," said Paean.

Correct. Part of the reason they were so efficient was the suffocation effect. The croaches can live in much lower oxygen concentrations than the Moozils.

Paean pulled a face. "So why am I breathing?"

"I'm maintaining an oxygen bubble around you and your partner, Paean Donegal," Furrl squeaked. "Common intergalactic policy when travelling with atmosphere-dependent life forms."

"Ah. So actually there's no air at all in here?"

"'s all carbon dioxide," said Federi, gnashing his teeth. He hated to be at the whimsical mercy of Furrl. "How's Captain doing?" he asked the Solar Wind.

Frantic. You are needed in a very important meeting. Shall I tell him that you are available now?

"One second," said Federi and switched off his com. He pulled his wife closer and kissed her until her ears started ringing too, and her eyes went soft and her knees went wobbly.

"What have I done now?" she asked, surprised.

"You're a genius, little luv. Was your croaches. – Wanted to do this back at Lake Gatun too, you know. Wasn't allowed."

She gazed at him, remembering a meeting in the galley, in the first locks of Panama. Just her and Federi. A sweet friend; a dicey alley, she remembered thinking. And she recalled his response to her coming clean about her valeriensis bug. Laughing until he had tears; now she knew him better, she realized he'd been crying with relief. Calling her 'little luv' for the first time. Talking sense into her; rewarding her piracy with her first bandanna. She gazed into his dark eyes, and slipped her arms around his neck and kissed him back, thoroughly.

"You should have," she told him. "This is for then. Was already halfway…"

Furrl picked that moment to blink them back to the Comet.

"Traitor!" spat Federi, letting go of his young wife and glaring at the transgalactic dragonling.

"Can't leave them alone for a second," commented Shawn with a naughty smirk. Vlad's grin nearly lifted off his face.

Ailyss glanced up from the console.

"What?" she asked.

Federi flashed her a razor-sharp smile. Nice touch, that fake inattentiveness. There wasn't a detail that eluded the young spy; he knew this because she was like himself.

"Mistress," peeped Leila, "there is another craft approaching us at high speed."

Paean glanced at the console and then out of the windshield. The other vessel was a Perdita jet, too. Navigating it was in fact Wolf; next to him Paean spotted another familiar face.

"Jehan!" she uttered, surprised. "What's he doing out in space?"

The intercom activated.

"Federi," came Wolf's bass voice, "so good that you're back! Captain is calling you – they need you in an urgent meeting, but they are on Shrn."

"We read you, Wolf," replied Federi, switching seamlessly from English to Romanian Rom. "Reading your lips in fact! Jehan, what are you doing out here?"

"Making sure that my cousins come back," came the reply.

Federi smiled. It was good to be a gypsy again.

"We're following," he said. "Lead the way!" And then he had to translate it back into English for Wolf.

"I'll get you for that," Wolf replied in Swedish. "Two can play that game!"

Federi laughed.

"Well done, old monster! I must really ask Vlad to enable you for intergalactic telepathy as well."

"No, thanks," said Wolf cynically, and swung away with the second jet towards the portal at Dracula's Castle.

"He won't have a choice," commented Vlad. "Sooner or later I'll have to enable the whole team. You are far too exposed without it."

"Intergalactic telepathy," said Paean thoughtfully. She'd miss the exclusivity of her and her loved ones' telepathic connections.

"It's more a translating function," said Vlad. "You learn to understand what they put out. It doesn't mean that you can see what they are really thinking. Not unless they broadcast it."

"And you can't enable us for that…"

"Sorry," said Vlad. "The Danaan tried;   that's why they

developed the Hypnotron. Mind-control and genuine mind-reading are talents that cannot be reproduced by altering brain physiology."

Federi scowled. Until it suits Vlad, he added in his mind. He followed Wolf's craft to the portal at Dracula's castle. Both craft set down in the snow.

"You're kidding," said Federi and teleported away. The Donegal sibs and Ailyss stared at each other in surprise. Wolf came over from the other jet, through the blizzard. Both were wearing polar parkas by now.

Before Wolf reached the Comet, Federi was back, handing polar gear out to his crew. They each shouldered one of the Kosaka cannons that had gone into space with the Comet, and only then did they follow Wolf and Jehan to the portal.

The warm, humid atmosphere on Shrn hit them like a wall. They emerged in the centre of a circle. Instinctively they moved with their backs together, cannons pointed outwards at the huge creatures that sat gathered, waiting.

"That was low of them," hissed Vlad. "Holding the meeting right around my portal!"

Paean stared at the Intergalactic Council. Of course Anthrim would be too large to lead this trial on the Space Base. He was unlikely to choose Earth; who knew what the repercussions of that would be? And the other eleven Council Members were on average not much smaller than him. There were a number more dragons; some strange shelled species she couldn't place at all, looking like something from an interstellar toy shop; a couple of Morrigan and two or three beings that looked as though nothing except energy held them together. Yes, it made sense that this lot would hold their meeting in the comparative wilderness of Shrn. She wondered whether Grww had been informed, and how she'd explain this to

371

him.

To one side huddled the officers and Captain of the Solar Wind. Radomir Lascek met Paean's eyes. He was frowning terribly. His hand touched his pocket. She got the message. Have teleporter ready. But what would that help, here on Shrn? Teleport to where?

The tallest of the beings of pure energy stepped forward. A plasma, thought Paean. That's what Wolf calls that state of being. She wondered whether he'd be able to design something like sticky carbon for it. The creature was shimmering in various colours; mostly purple, with ultra-violet edges merging into blackness before phasing out. Huge feather-like structures of purple light extended out of its back; wings, Paean understood. What did it need them for? It moved by energy displacement! But she already knew: For intimidation, of course! Be not afraid, puny humans, though I have the power to put out your tiny flame with the slightest touch.

Thought like a criminal, she berated herself. This being was an angel. That was good news. An angel on the Council. No, three of them! There was another in red light, like fire; and yet a third shimmering orange. Three angelic beings. There would be justice. But... was that indeed good? She wondered.

Mother had raised them with firm beliefs and solid faith. In the past nine months since her death Paean hadn't given these half a thought. She hadn't wanted to talk to a creator who allowed for such atrocities. And with time and events, guilt had been added. She certainly didn't want to go up to Heaven now and chat with any Divine or angelic beings, for fear of being catapulted straight to the other place. She only hoped Mother had gone to the Summer Country, not to Heaven...

Have teleporter ready? What did Captain mean? There was no getting away from these!

"Shrn," the angel addressed Vlad. "Lose the disguise. Don't add an insult to the Council to your crimes!"

Vlad the Impostor dissolved and melted into his amorphous shape. Paean caught his wink. Shape-shifting on command was the least of his worries.

"All of it!" commanded the Being. Paean gaped. What did that angel mean? Vlad was being a complete blob!

"Your Mercy," begged the Morrigan, "I have learned and am still learning new ways of thinking by utilizing the neurological and physiological organization of a human brain."

"Lose them!" boomed the entity. "You dare to contradict."

Vlad shifted a bit flatter still. He really resembled a cosmic amoeba now. Paean touched his coruscating skin.

It's alright, Vlad. We'll protect you.

That's right, Federi added in. Be calm.

I don't want to think like a Morrigan now, replied Vlad. Those thought patterns are too predictable!

Don't worry, you're more than half human already, commented Paean. You called Moozils cute.

That was with my human brain! wailed Vlad.

"I am the Archangel Uryel," said the angel. "The Council has been called by Earth, for assistance against alien invasions. Anthrim the Great shall state his case."

The huge red dragon raised its head and blew a fire plume into the blue skies of Shrn. Several bird-like flying shifters got fried and plummeted to the ground. Paean could feel how Vlad was inwardly gnashing his teeth.

Anthrim lowered his face to be on a level with Vlad.

"Shrn, step forward," he commanded. Vlad slithered out of his small group of allies. "You stand accused of – what's wrong with

373

you? What's that on your back?"

The Morrigan's injuries from tangling with his own werefolk hadn't completely healed. They were showing up as slightly luminescent scars criss-crossing his hide. Paean worried about this; it meant that Vlad might be vulnerable to physical attacks. Probably because of her sticky carbon.

"That's an injury," said Federi, never quite lowering his gun. "Shrn risked his life defending us against the Were Folk of Shrn."

"Ah," said Anthrim, training both independent eyes on the Assassin. "It has been a long time, Prince Falco! We have been waiting for you, your majesty!" He bowed low, with his huge head and neck.

Federi drew himself up tall. Paean could practically feel how his toes twitched inside their sneakers. His left eyebrow quivered in a nervous tic. *Your own majesty's fat backside,* she picked up his errant thought. *Damn you, Falco! Now I have to be you!*

This is it, she thought. *Go, Federi! You're my hero! Make them cancel the Unicate's contract!*

"Yes," said Federi softly. "It's been a while, hasn't it, Your Sageness? You have no clue what havoc your little Unicate pets have been wreaking! I demand that we renegotiate."

Where there were *gadje* laws, there were loopholes. Paean could see what Federi was trying. His physical resemblance to Falco and the open possibility that he might be the man himself, came in good stead. It would help to know the actual laws and the wording of the actual contract. Oh, Federi! She kept her cannon ready and wished fervently that Wolf had taken the time to create a pocket Genitron for her.

25 – Trial and Error

Federi stared resolutely into the huge green eye of the space dragon.

"Renegotiate?" Anthrim 's pupils narrowed. He lifted his head and peered at his colleagues. "Explain yourself, Prince Falco."

"You may know that the Lascekian system of justice which we have here on Earth is the fairest in all the universes," stated Federi, noting with a poker face how his Captain pocketed that compliment without batting an eyelid. "In this system, a contract can be contested if either party is grievously unhappy with the result. If the other side proves willing, then the contract is renegotiated."

"And if the other side is unwilling?" asked Anthrim, clearly fascinated.

"Then the side with the grievance turns to a higher authority," said Federi. "And so on."

"And if even the highest authority does not agree that renegotiation is in order?"

"Then there is war," said the Assassin softly. "The winner decides the outcome."

"Ah!" Anthrim turned to his associates. "The fairest in all universes? Your majesty, may I remind you that you came to us with your request in order to stop the wars humankind was waging?"

"Correct," said Federi. "It's been suggested that they would rather have nuclear war than deal with the menace of the Unicate any further."

"The Unicate will not see it that way," replied Anthrim. "She kept her side of the deal. The Unicate brought peace to Planet

Earth."

"Peace," repeated Federi. "Subjugation! Humans are no longer the dominant species on their own home planet. May I suggest that the Unicate broke the contract?"

"How so?"

"By decimating humanity, by controlling us like farm animals, by turning into predators, and us into prey."

"A certain amount of predation was part of the contract," said Anthrim.

What! Federi's falconic eyebrows tried – and failed – to meet. He was deeply convinced that no matter what a rat Falco had been, he wouldn't have allowed for that.

"Predation?" he replied. "Surely not?"

"The Unicate is a parasitic species," said Anthrim. "The contract stated clearly that she could decide herself which measures were needed to control humankind into peaceful coexistence."

"Coexistence," echoed Federi. "With each other or with the Unicate?"

Anthrim bared his formidable fangs in what was probably a smile, and said nothing. Federi glanced at Paean. A parasitic species? So she could – ah! Yes: she could simply help herself?

"Could such coexistence include predation? Parasitism? The contract never specified, did it?"

"Accurately observed," smiled Anthrim.

Aargh! Why did his grandfather have to be legally illiterate! Full marks for bravery, zero for common sense. Federi shook his head. If he himself had drawn up any such contract, he'd have set different parameters! What a mess!

She. The Mound, thought Federi. The Mound and the Queen were one. The Unicate: She. There were countless mounds by now; but he would have to assume that it had started with one. Sixty years

377

for those mounds to replicate…

He'd have to try another angle.

"In Earth law," he stated slowly, cautiously, "if a contract is based on an illegal or unethical premise, that contract is regarded null and void. A contract cannot stand in contradiction to the prevailing law." Out of the corner of his eye he saw how Paean lowered her Kosaka gun and sat down on the ground. Poor little luv. She must be exhausted.

"The Intergalactic Council represents the Law," said Anthrim. "You are aware of this."

Where did I hear that before, thought Federi. His eyes met Captain's. There seemed to be a plan brewing behind that formidable brow.

Well, peaceful coexistence his foot! The Unicate was in no way peaceful. They had been planning another nuclear war; besides which they assassinated people like Annie Donegal who gained too much insight. They had reverted Earth's technology to a pre-airborne era. And what was peaceful about hunting down gypsies – and cloning vicious diseases, for the love of green dogs? Systematic conquering of every last port, every town? Peaceful?

"They breached the contract nevertheless," said Federi. "They initiated military action against humanity. The contract was for peace, not war and domination. Seeing that they broke it from their side…"

"We are the highest authority in the universes," said Anthrim. "Let me confer with the other Sages whether this contract deserves a second look. As for the verdict over Shrn –"

"I champion him," proclaimed Paean, getting back to her feet and subconsciously pointing her Kosaka cannon at Anthrim. "Shrn is our friend! He didn't bring any aliens down on Earth. The Were Folk were disobeying his command. They even attacked him. Nothing

378

but a temporary slip of his authority. He is fully back in control, and a truce has been achieved between the Werefolk of Shrn, and Earth."

"One voice for the Morrigan of Shrn," said Anthrim with amusement. Paean got the impression that he hadn't even heard the part about the truce. "Paean Donegal, did my delegate find you?"

"We found him," said Paean and held up the tied-up little dragon. "He's been well-behaved so far but we're keeping him under observation." Furrl squeaked in fear.

"So I see," said Anthrim with a smile. "Furrl, report back to me after this."

Paean tweaked the little dragon so hard that it squeaked again. "You're not going to," she whispered. "Or you're dead!"

"I speak for the Morrigan too," said Ailyss. "So does my associate here." Wolf nodded.

"Your Sageness, does it make any difference who speaks for Shrn?" asked Radomir Lascek.

"It might impact on how the Council views his actions," said Anthrim carefully.

"In that case Earth speaks for Shrn," said Lascek imperially.

"The Human Leadership of Earth," corrected Anthrim.

"The Keeper of Earth," corrected Lascek.

"The Keeper of Earth has only so far diverted the trial's overall purpose and confused everyone with contractual issues," commented Anthrim.

Federi tried to hide his surprise. By the Morrigan, was he now the Keeper of Earth? Was this a nightmare? Anna bottle!

In fact, the dragon was the one distracting and diverting! How on Earth had a call for intergalactic justice, concerning a Rapacin invasion, turned into a trial for one of Earth's best allies? Brilliant, that dragon! Earning a Tzigan-badge for clouding issues and veering off the topic! The 'Prince of Earth' burst out laughing. The Council members whispered at each other in shock.

"Your Sageness, of course Earth speaks for the Morrigan! He's our Morrigan! Without him our ship doesn't know how to function. On the contrary," he smiled with a silver glint, "the Morrigan of Shrn stands under the protection of Earth!" And he glanced at Vlad and pocketed that ripple of surprise that went over the scintillating hide. Take that, Morrigan!

Anthrim inclined his head. His green eyes narrowed slyly. "Acknowledged, your majesty. This weighs heavily in Shrn's favour. It shall influence the verdict. Of course it also renders your own point void."

"What ...?"

"By showing your supreme authority you have conclusively demonstrated that humankind, not the Unicate, is still the dominant species in charge of Earth. Therefore the contract has not been breached, and stands."

A red haze rose in front of Federi's eyes. Every breathing entity turned into a target with concentric circles and a Bull's Eye. Being bested at his own game was one thing, and he could take a joke; but the consequences of this intergalactic fraud! He raised his Kosaka cannon, wondering if this was what had been pulled on Falco, too. Probably.

Keeper of Earth! Federi knew now exactly what had happened. Somewhere Falco had learnt about an Intergalactic Council. He'd decided to take the problems of the nuclear wars to them, calling for help, speaking for the helpless inhabitants of Earth – the gypsies, and the normal everyday people, and all animals and plants. He had acted as Keeper; so he'd been awarded the title. Like chewing gum on the sole of his shoe. And he'd been tricked into agreeing to the Unicate taking matters "in hand"...

Paean's light touch on his arm brought him back.

It's alright, Federi. She raised her ice-blue eyes defiantly to the great dragon.

"Your honour, we called the Council to get help against the invasion of the Rapacins, not to be judged ourselves. This contravenes all concepts of justice. We shall take the dispute to a higher authority."

Thank you, little luv, thought Federi, his breath hissing through his teeth. And if the Higher Authority doesn't do anything, we'll take it into our own hands, and then, ajuto al fuoco!1

Anthrim bared his ragged jaws. The Archangel Uryel chuckled softly.

"Young female, we are the highest authority in the known universes."

She smiled.

"You're an angel, not?"

"An Archangel," said Uryel proudly. "And the Chosen Leader of the Twelve."

"And you call yourself highest authority? You're not perhaps a fallen angel?"

"The question falls outside our frame of reference," said the being. "Let us reconvene in..." it consulted briefly with Anthrim, "thirty of your Earth minutes. We shall have the verdict over Shrn ready."

The Council teleported out as one, leaving the humans and the Morrigan behind in a rag-tag, seething heap.

Radomir Lascek bore down on the task force, Perdita one step behind him.

"Federi, what's this majesty nonsense?"

Federi laughed grimly. "Arw, Captain, it's a good name for a horse's backside. Falco Demonos called himself Prince of Earth. Was his *hokano baro*, his great joke. They think I'm him. Simple."

381

"Sometimes…" the Captain started.

"The trouble is, Captain," interrupted Federi, "now, the only way I can get them to call the contract off is by letting them know Falco had no claim to that title. And then they execute Vlad, because Earth isn't speaking in his favour."

"They may execute him anyway," said Lascek.

"He's under my protection," growled Federi, thinking of a semi-liquid puddle of misery he'd stuffed into Ailyss' arms to take back to the Solar Wind. "Whatever that means. Not too long ago I had to protect all of you against him! Do you think the Demon stands a chance against an Archangel?"

"That's no Archangel," growled Paean. "I for one am going to seek out the Highest Authority."

"Rash, sweetness," advised Federi softly.

"We have half an hour," said Vlad. "I second Paean!"

"What if the authority you're referring to, doesn't exist, Paean?" asked Radomir Lascek.

"What if He does," added Federi under his breath. "I wouldn't."

"Paean," Perdita tried, "angels are simply intergalactic life forms. They may not be dependent on atmosphere, and they may replicate by inaccurate binary fission, but they are still only another species. Of alien, if you like. Archangels are a sub-species that is larger and stronger. So they consider themselves a better class of angel, hence the snobbery. They all are immensely powerful, they live via electromagnetism. But that doesn't mean that the Creator you are looking for, exists! We have no conclusive evidence for him or her."

Paean nodded.

"Perdita, it's worth a try. If he or she does exist, those angels won't know what hit them. Right?" She moved towards the portal without waiting for a further reply, Vlad shadowing her. Federi gave an angry snort and followed. At a pace. Shawn Donegal ran to catch up.

"Put a word in for your old Pirate Captain," called Radomir Lascek. Paean laughed and gave a thumbs-up. And then she was gone.

"She's barking up the wrong tree," said Perdita. "Chasing after spirits."

"One has to admire her courage," replied Radomir with a smile. "Perdita, importantly, she's bought us time, and she's taken both the Prince of Hell and the Morrigan of Shrn out of the line of fire. Brilliant girl."

"So, now," asked Federi scathingly when the three humans and one Morrigan were once more in the Comet, "how were you going to get to that Highest Authority?"

"I have no idea," said Paean. "But I won't stop until I've tried." She steered the Comet away from Earth in a great arc, and headed towards the Interstellar Exchange. Falling through the void was becoming as familiar as the rocking of ocean under her feet – which she missed, but didn't know how to replace. The Solar Wind chronically seemed to be docked up at the Space Base.

"Do you even know where to start?" asked Federi, nearly amused.

Paean shot him an old look. "I should start by praying. Ow!" She sat down abruptly on the Comet's glass floor.

Federi blinked. "What's wrong?"

"My leg," she gasped and glanced down. Dark blood was seeping through her jeans where her thigh had been ripped by werefolk. "Don't know! Don't understand it! Vlad fixed it!"

"Hell, little luv," exclaimed Federi, dropping to the floor of the Comet next to her to take a close look at her leg.

"Paean!" scolded Vlad. "I told you to be cautious! I realigned your molecules, but the connections needed time to strengthen and regrow! You've ripped it."

"How?" She was white from pain.

"Too much exertion," said Vlad. "You humans never listen!"

Paean cast him a sorrowful glance and passed out. Shawn looked as though he were going to pass out as well. The blood was flowing freely now; it was already trickling down to the Comet's floor.

Federi took out his jack-knife and cut her jeans open from below, like she had done for Wolf in Atuona. He gasped when he saw the wound.

It was a yawning hole; the stitches from Dr Swart were sitting in a neat row next to where the fabric of her tissues had disintegrated. It was a big, bloody, jelly-like mess. The muscle itself looked half-liquidized.

"Never seen anything as horrible as this," he emitted with an accusing stare at Vlad. "What the hell have you done here? Looks digested!"

The Morrigan placed two tentacles left and right of the awful injury. This slowed the bleeding down significantly.

"Federi," he said intently, "it was a very bad injury to begin with. I warned her to keep it still. I had to spread her molecules over a larger area to rebuild the substance. This means that they were further apart, like here," and he pointed at the half-disintegrated muscle, "and the links between them were weakened. It makes it easier for blood and lymph vessels and nerves to regrow. Something like that needs to be kept quiet for two or three weeks – as long as it would have taken her to heal in the way of that doctor who had stitched it; only, my way gives more immediate comfort, no scars and no lasting damage. But if one uses the muscle a lot and puts strain on it as she did, the cells pull apart and reopen the injury.

384

Does this make sense?"

Federi nodded grimly.

"Vlad," he said, "you like Paean a lot, don't you?"

"She's adorable," admitted the Morrigan. "Nearly as cute as the Moozils, and twice as dangerous."

"So you gave her the best healing you could?"

"Of course," said Vlad. "I was only surprised at the depth of the injury."

"Totally honest?" pushed the gypsy.

"Absolutely, Federi! She comes second only to the Solar Wind, Ailyss and Perdita."

"That's fourth," Federi pointed out and opened the jet-board first-aid kit. "Can you spread the molecules across the area again?" he asked.

"Not really," said Vlad. "They are in shock. They are vibrating too fast."

"And the tissue is now too jelly to suture," added Federi, troubled. "What do we do?" He dug in the kit and found some post-op artificial skin bandages. "Can you at least purify it so it won't get infected?"

"That's easy," said Vlad, raised his tentacles and promptly radiated UV light at Paean's injured muscles. Federi picked the stitches out of her skin and pasted the artificial skin over her open wound, leaving only a small drainage fold so that an overload of blood could trickle out. He then located a blanket and covered her with it.

"Poor little luv," he muttered under his breath.

Paean drifted through green undersea tangles, swaying with the rhythm of the warm water. This had to be close to Atuona, she thought. And Federi was somewhere close by, taking underwater shots of sharks. A shipwreck with fifteen skeletons in the bilges...

She surfaced in an air bubble. The bubble was golden from tropical sunlight.

Paean.

Someone was addressing her. She could hear the voice, but not see the Speaker. But she knew Who it was anyway. She flinched. And then, slowly, she recalled the purpose of her mission.

"Good that I found You," she said. "Didn't know I had to pass out from pain first... I've come to beg You to spare the Morrigan from the Council. There's an Archangel on the Council who calls himself Highest Authority, and that just ticked me off..."

You never pray anymore, came the reply.

"I know. I'm sorry. I don't feel I should, I'm a pirate now."

You are still angry.

"No comment," said Paean. "About the Morrigan..."

And married to an assassin. Who calls himself a Demon.

This was beginning to scare Paean.

"Can we please stay on the topic? The Morrigan..."

The Morrigan is a creature of instincts, said the Speaker. He cannot be judged by the same standards as a human. If you beg for his life, then so be it.

"Thank you." Paean smiled. "I knew you'd understand."

About your Assassin, added the Highest Authority.

Paean's eyes filled with tears. Federi was not an alien, a creature of instincts. He was a sentient human being and could definitely be held responsible for all he had done. She wanted to beg for mercy on his behalf too; but she didn't know how to start formulating.

You wish for me to spare him, too, said the Speaker.

Paean nodded.

His record is overloaded, the Highest pointed out.

Paean nodded again.

Why should We not give him what he deserves?

"Because I love him," sobbed Paean. "What's the point of loving someone if they have to die?"

Everyone has to die, said the Voice. But your love has already bought him many years. Keep him out of trouble, Paean Donegal.

"What trouble," she wailed. "It's who he is! Always sorting out other people's messes!"

Karmic trouble. Killing others and self.

She nodded, and sniffed. She understood. "I'll try."

I know you will. You took that sacred duty on yourself months back.

Yes, she had. And then she had taken up guns and joined in the killing. Paean shook her head in desperation. There was too much bad stuff happening. There was no way she could be a pacifist. She wasn't going to push her luck and ask to be spared, herself. For the past, maybe; that couldn't be changed. But not for the future; and not for the present moment, because she wasn't going to damage Donegal Honour by making a promise she knew she was going to break.

We have given each human being the power of Choice, commented the Highest Authority. We do not interfere with how that Choice is exercised. That is the definition of Choice.

And she chose the path of a killer! "One more question," said Paean, fighting down her tears. "Is Mother with you?"

She is on Earth, on a mission, said the Highest Authority.

"What mission?"

Watching over Ronan, Rushka and the babies.

Those tears were streaming again. Mother would never hold those babies on her lap the way a grandmother should! "Why did she have to die?"

Everyone dies, came the over-calm answer.

"But not like that! How could you allow it?"

There was no answer.

"What kind of merciful God allows such atrocities?"

There was silence.

"Are you still there?"

Nothing.

"Do you even exist?!"

Her own words were echoing in her head as she came to, in the arms of her beloved Assassin, with her little brother holding a cold pack against her forehead and the Morrigan of Shrn with his tentacles over her injury. Her face was wet; she was still upset.

"You cried in your sleep," Federi pointed out unnecessarily. "Nightmare?"

"No. I went to look up Highest Authority. And I found the guy."

"It's a guy?" asked Federi.

"More like – something that always answered back. Couldn't see anything. Except a golden bubble."

"So you got answers?"

She tried to sit up but got dizzy and leaned back against Federi.

"I have no idea. In the end, it vanished as though I'd imagined all of it. Probably just a dream," said Paean sadly.

"So we try again?" asked Federi. "Without blacking out?"

"But where would we find access to Him?"

"We'd probably have to die first," said Shawn logically.

"That defeats the purpose," the Morrigan pointed out.

Federi glanced up at the bright lights outside the Comet. "Where are we anyway?"

Vlad got up like a lightning bolt. "Oh hell!" He flowed to the console. "Not where. When. We're a week in the past, and

388

travelling further back at the rate of minus an hour per minute. Four light-minutes sun-wise of New Dome."

"Why the lights?"

"Temporal friction," explained Vlad. "This is a space-time eddy we use a lot for short-cuts. Except that we got drawn into its spiral this time because nobody was steering. Oh, sorry, S.I. Lucy."

"Sorry, Boss," peeped Lucy. "My command facilities were overridden!"

Federi stared at her. That sounded ominous!

"Hear ye, the verdict over the Morrigan who was Keeper of Shrn!"

The Solar Wind's Officers and her Captain were present as the Archangel Uryel opened the session. Radomir Lascek looked around. Wait – they ought to wait.

"Gathered mortals," the Archangel continued, "Prince of Earth, Supreme Ruler, Paean Donegal, and Shrn. Step forward, Shrn, to hear your verdict!"

There was silence.

"Where is he?" thundered Anthrim and belched a huge plume of red flames straight up at the sky. "The coward ran! How can you defend this? Prince Falco! Does his act not tell its own tale?" He looked in the round of humans and expelled another angry flame. "So the Prince has run, too! And Paean Donegal."

Radomir Lascek bristled.

In the first place, this was his home planet – or then, his home set of planets. The Council ought not open the session; he should! He was the host as well as the plaintiff. The accused was by no means Vlad – by thunder, his team had coped perfectly fine with the Morrigan. He was immensely proud of them, especially for managing to subdue rather than kill the immortal, and turning him into an ally.

The Council was breaching all the rules of being visiting dignitaries; and then they tried to bring their exotic intergalactic laws with them?

Not in his territory! He felt a speech coming on. In preparation, he stepped towards the huge red dragon and stared the beast down until it averted its eye.

The point was this: Paean Donegal was his Paean Donegal. The Prince of Earth – hokano or not – was his Assassin. And Vlad – was his Morrigan! He'd deal with this himself, thank you kindly!

"Anthrim the Great," thundered Radomir Lascek. "Archangel Uryel. Gathered Mages and Sages of the Council. It has come to my attention that there has been a series of misunderstandings of intergalactic proportions!"

Silence ruled supreme. They were watching him, mesmerized. Lascek smiled. This was better!

"There seems to be an assumption on this flea-bitten planet," he announced loudly, "that just because a tribe of young Rapacin slaves thought they could invade us, there is a planetary emergency."

He started pacing slowly before the gathered Twelve, studying them one by one with critical, menacing stares.

"There seems to be an idea amongst these measly ranks," he exclaimed, righteous anger vibrating in his voice by now, "that the Leadership of Earth doesn't know how to deal with an amateurish alien raid, and a case of sloppy Keepership from a young neighbouring Morrigan!"

They were gaping at him, mesmerized.

"Let me make one thing crystal clear," said Radomir Lascek icily. "There is Law on Planet Earth. While you are standing on – or hovering over, whichever the case – my ground, you fall under my

Law. And let me be very precise on this. I am the Law on this planet. I create the Law; I enforce it, and I deal with whoever oversteps it!" He planted himself squarely in front of Anthrim. "Anthrim the Great!"

The huge dragon actually appeared taken aback. It backed away a little as it eyed this vicious planetary Leader. It had learned in its long aeons of life that the smallest life forms weren't necessarily the most harmless!

"I did not authorize Paean Demonos and Vlad Dracul – whom you refer to as Shrn – to call for your help. They shall be dealt with for their insubordination. The Morrigan is a crew member. He falls under my command. I shall be the one dealing them justice, not you."

Anthrim's left eye scanned his colleagues for reactions; but they stood petrified. His right eye never left Radomir Lascek.

"If there was an Intergalactic breach at all," continued Lascek, "and that still has to be established, then seeing that it concerned Earth, I shall be the one dealing with the perpetrators. If the Morrigan of Shrn failed in his duties to his wards, which I doubt very much – they look like very well-fed werefolk to me – then seeing that he is on my crew, once again, I shall be the one dealing out a suitable punishment."

There was shocked silence. Radomir Lascek held up his hand to keep it there.

"I did not call this Council," he added. "But seeing that you are all here, and seeing that you find yourselves on my ground, let me show you hospitality and invite you all for some two-centuries-old shipwreck brandy. It's a very precious beverage, reserved for personages of high respect. There shall be no judging and speaking of unnecessary verdicts today. We shall seal our friendship and alliance, as is Earth's wont, with alcohol."

He grinned brightly. A general gasp of relief went through the gathered Council. Radomir Lascek glanced at his crew and found them all grinning broadly.

"You're invited too," he called with a jovial wave of his arm. "Come, my loyal crew, let's celebrate this new alliance!" And he caught Marsden's poker-faced look. The First Mate knew that even the last statement had been made to impress the Council; which didn't mean that he necessarily approved. Good old Jon!

As they all cleared the portal and found a suitable spot to drink to their alliance – the bombed-out crater of the Miami mansions – Ailyss whispered to Wolf:

"It didn't occur to any of them that they weren't even on his planet!"

Wolf grinned back. "What do you mean? Vlad is in Captain's complete control. Why should Shrn not be Captain's planet?"

26 – Time Warp

"Ronan! Are you alright?"

"You," said Ronan, looking up from holding his head in his hands, "are not supposed to teleport." He patted the bench next to himself, in the lush arboretum on Space Base that his little brother had set up. "Sit down, Rush." He shook his head. "I can't believe it."

"Believe what?"

"That crater! Where our homes stood! We only needed the finishing touches, and I was fitting out the nursery…" He sighed, and his head dipped back into his hands. "I've been a bad husband, Rushka. You should leave me."

"What?!"

"Can't even provide a home for our little ones!"

Rushka shook her head. She hadn't meant to take the wind out of his and Federi's sails with the Co-houses; but this development suited her. She hadn't wanted to leave the Solar Wind. Now they had a reason to stay aboard.

Ever since the Morrigan had fixed her metabolism and she didn't feel that sick anymore, she had resumed her original stance of raising the babies aboard. There were empty cabins; one of them could be made into a nursery. One was in fact right across the passage from their own cabin. It had the added advantage that it was in really close audible distance from Federi's cabin; the sleepless Assassin was more than likely to take turns entertaining the babies at night. Keeping them busy peeling potatoes, she thought. One could feel sorry for them when the time came.

"We'll probably go ashore in Anaho Bay for the birth," she pacified her perturbed worse half. "Those little homes are really beautiful, Ro."

"They're small," said Ronan with disdain.

"So? I grew up in a cabin. Even smaller. There's nothing wrong with that."

Ronan nodded and clasped his wife's hand. Good that she took the devastation of their home in her stride.

"There's a communal kitchen at Anaho Bay too," added Rushka. "Just like you guys were planning…"

"I'll miss the gypsies," said Ronan glumly.

"We could also move into the Space Base," added Rushka. "It doesn't really matter, as long as we're together."

The next moment, both came to their feet with a surprised shriek. Enormous creatures popped into existence in the air above the crater and settled down comfortably in it: A huge red dragon; a smaller dragon; three beings of pure light of assorted colours; and various others.

Rushka counted as they teleported in.

"Twelve," she commented quietly. "I think I spot a pattern?"

"The Intergalactic Council," surmised Ronan.

He had his idea confirmed when the Solar Wind's officers arrived just behind the creatures.

"My final decision about Shrn," proclaimed Uryel jovially over his sixth full container of shipwreck brandy, "is that he has been replaced. I have someone in mind for a Keeper for Shrn. While the Morrigan is abdicating, we have to contact the new Keeper as fast as we can so the Were Folk are not left without guidance."

"Who?" asked Anthrim, who was on his ninth crate. Radomir Lascek had started replacing the invaluable shipwreck brandy with less exclusive stuff, home-brewed from Southern Free and procured by Captain Ali, very soon; Ailyss and Wolf were already on their second mission with the African pirate to find more good quality Akkedisbult. They bought it by the truckload; but it got emptied faster than they could keep up.

"Jitanali," said Uryel. "She is ideal. Young, energetic, powerful and honest."

"Female," noted Anthrim with disdain. "But I agree with your idea that it must be a dragon. Morrigan are... unreliable. Sorry, Belarius."

One of the two Morrigan on the Council glanced up from the serious discussion he was having with one of the other angels, all over a lot of alcohol. "What, Brother Anthrim?"

"Nothing important," said Anthrim. "Carry on, I'll update you later."

"Paean!"

She opened her eyes.

"You blacked out again," said Shawn, who was sitting beside her. And hovering over her on the other side was Federi, his dark eyes riddled with stress. For a disoriented moment she thought she was back on a Rebellion Schooner, gazing up into the gypsy's eyes after he'd freed her and Sherman. She reached up and touched his cheek.

The pain in her leg was not funny. It felt as though a freight carrier had parked on it. And then some. She closed her eyes again, trying to escape that pain.

"Stay with us, little luv," rasped Federi's voice, and his fingers brushed the hair out of her face.

She couldn't remember what she had been about to do. She'd had some sort of mission. She opened her eyes once more, only a little, looking for Federi. And she reached out and felt him clasp her hand.

"It's just your leg, sweetheart," he said softly. "It doesn't matter. It will heal, but you must be brave now."

"If it doesn't, I'll be Long-Jane Silver," she said with an exhausted little grin.

"That's fine. I'll commandeer a ship for you," replied Federi, smiling. "Hang in there, little luv!"

She felt him lift her head onto his lap, cross-legged on the floor again. And his long, artistic fingers running through her tangled curls, combing them.

"I want a ship anyway," she muttered. And she slipped away a bit, half-conscious of the swirling lights around them and the cool, hard floor, and the hands playing through her hair.

Her mission came back to her.

"I met him," she whispered. "Highest Authority. He said the Morrigan's innocent because he's an animal."

"What?!"

That reaction from Vlad brought her round, and she had to grin at the shifter. "Dear Prince Vlad, according to the Highest, you cannot be judged to human standards as you don't have the same sense of responsibility. Hazard of your species."

"You were dreaming, Pae," said Shawn with a dry grin. "Vlad can't be innocent. 'e was born guilty!"

"It's not humans judging me," Vlad pointed out. "My, this is fascinating! The human brain is so egocentric that it even hallucinates itself to be the most sentient of all life forms!"

"Who are the most sentient then?" asked Shawn.

"Morrigan, of course," replied Vlad with a grin.

396

Paean chuckled softly. But then she grew serious.

"I failed," she said. "I pleaded for you with the Highest, and you were pardoned. But I can't prove this meeting ever took place, and I don't know how to persuade the Highest to reveal Itself to the Council. Or even to me!"

"I was pardoned?" asked Vlad.

She nodded.

"Then what are we waiting for?"

The Comet leaped out of the space-time eddy and retook its course, back to the Interstellar Exchange.

"You've broken us out of the space-time lock!" cheered Shawn. Federi cast the Morrigan a long, dark stare.

"But I can't prove it," said Paean, her voice dreamy and far-away. She slipped back into dreams.

Federi stared at the still face of his young wife. Freckles outlined like caramel splatters against the too-pale skin. She hadn't had enough sun recently. Of course the weather in Romania had been all but summery on their too-short honeymoon; but after that there had been nothing but trouble.

He so wanted to give her a peaceful, comfortable life, spoil her, buy her a beautiful mansion in the mountains with a view into next century...

She already had that view. That was the trouble. He sighed as he started working some of her curls into thin, long plaits. She was a clairvoyant; and a Founder. Whatever that meant, confound it! And with that clairvoyance she foresaw what he saw too – no way out, no peaceful place to settle. They had to finish the Unicate mission first.

Terence wanted to give the impression that humans were caught by the Unicate, as children even – perhaps that was why Molly Street was such a target – and brought into the Mound, indoctrinated, brainwashed. That the *Others* were truly still human, genetically. And Paean was hoping to negotiate peace with the Unicate, using this knowledge.

Was this what Annie had found out? But – the Unicate, *she*. A parasitic life form. Predation. The sentient Mound.

If he went evacuating and then bombing out the mounds, would that do the trick? And yet... he recalled Dahlia, and Genevieve. Anya Miller. No. There was more. Terence might act like a brainwashed Mound slave; but Dahlia certainly hadn't. She'd acted like a force in her own right, a fully qualified – queen, he thought. The Unicate women were queens! True aliens. Queen Rhyn had had the same insane glint as Dahlia, before he'd mowed her and her royal guard down.

The Mound had a Queen. The Queen was the expression of the Mound. The rest of the *Others* might well be indoctrinated slaves, humans. The Toll! They used the Toll to swell their numbers, enslaving those children. And in the depth of Federi's dark soul sounded a single warning chime – another Death Toll. Wrong. He was getting it wrong.

And the fire lizards?

His mind ticked over. Too much.

27 – New Dome

Federi looked up with another sigh, and blinked. They were at the Interchange – but small official craft like Stabilizers swarmed around the Comet, flashing warnings.

"Paean Donegal, come in," a voice came through the onboard com.

Shawn jumped to the console to reply.

"Paean Donegal is unavailable, but I'm Shawn Donegal, I'm her brother, you can speak to me."

"Perdita Sancho sends a warning," said the young feminine voice. "You must not cross back to the Earthian solar system. You must stay Dome-side and wait for her."

"Okay," said Shawn. "No problem."

"Thank you," replied the young voice, and the com switched off.

Perdita's Probe cleared the Galactic Interchange a few minutes later. She tagged onto the Comet and tugged them after her, heading towards New Dome.

An ominous cloud hung around the planet. Federi peered into the fleet of Gargantuan vessels to see whether any Danaan battleships were visible. They were; but not in their previous numbers. Dana's fleet had been decimated, and the Moozils had taken the moment to hit back at Earth's ally.

"Aw, man!" exclaimed Shawn. "But I don't understand! We fixed the Moozils! They're supposed to be peaceful now!"

"The prioid wouldn't have had time to reach all the Moozil worlds yet," said Vlad. "I didn't think of this."

399

"Foresight's not your strongest point, is it," Federi muttered.

"No," replied Vlad regretfully. "If it were… We Morrigan can plan quite impressively, but we can't really guess at what others are planning."

Federi went quiet, morose. Perdita tugged the Comet down into the space port close to the White Palace. She came out of her jet, Jehan in tow. Shawn opened the hatch of the Comet and disembarked, Vlad flowing out behind him.

"Morrigan," said Perdita. "I think you owe Dana some thanks."

"I do?" asked Vlad, puzzled.

"Her Brurite restored you to life," Perdita pointed out.

"Of course," agreed Vlad. "Of course!"

"As long as you don't forget that," said Perdita sharply. "Federi! What's going on? Where's Paean?"

The gypsy had emerged from the Comet's hatch, looking defeated.

"She's injured," he said. "Badly. Think Dana could…?"

"Dana has more on her plate than I could tell you," snapped Perdita. She studied the gypsy, and peered into the Comet where Paean lay sleeping on the floor, her red hair spilling in all directions like a halo. "Well, I'm sure Dana would," she added and called some young cadets closer. They fetched a stretcher, and Federi lifted his wife off the Comet's floor, brought her down the steps and gently laid her down on the stretcher.

"Moozils?" he asked Perdita sharply. "Are you sure?"

She nodded grimly.

"Then why don't you bring a number of the Gargantuans from around the Space Base…"

"Yes," said Perdita. "It's being organized."

Johnny Anyhow came towards them. He greeted Federi with a

handshake and a shoulder-clap.

"I hear you took losses," mentioned the gypsy.

"How did your mission go?" asked the marine.

"Accomplished. The Rapacins are no more, and the Moozils – they ought to become peaceful, but clearly the message hasn't reached that lot there," and he pointed to the skies. They heard the impacts of missiles in the city, one every few minutes.

"We've lost most of our fleet," confirmed Anyhow with the dogged stance of a commander who, despite dreadful losses, finds defeat inconceivable. "They will rather flatten New Dome than come to an agreement."

Dana teleported in, and glanced at Federi, Perdita and their crews, evidently surprised.

"So you're here?" she asked the gypsy. "And what's with Paean?" She had by now spotted the stretcher.

"Injured," said Federi. "We've come to offer help. Perdita is bringing some battle croaches."

"It would be nice to have something to shield the city, in the meanwhile," Dana pointed out. "Demonos, we've had encounters with the Moozils before. They are vicious. They leave no-one alive. Everyone gets eaten. Seems to me by helping Earth we sacrificed ourselves. Not my usual style."

"Earth won, thanks to you and Paean," said Federi. "The battle croaches are on their way."

"Thank the Morri…" Dana glanced at Vlad and emitted a small shriek. "What? The Morrigan? On *my* planet?"

"I come in peace," pleaded Vlad, his tentacle bifurcated in a Vulcan greeting. "I have been battered, beaten, basted and baked. I…" He peered at Federi, whose hand had twitched and was now instinctively pointing a small gun at him. "What, Your Majesty?"

"Nothing," replied Federi, shaking himself out of that frame.

"Drop the bleeding 'majesty', Vlad! Dana, Vlad is now allied to us. In fact he stands under the protection of..." he sighed and rolled his eyes.

Dana started laughing in disbelief. "No! Impossible! Federi Demonos? He's under the protection of Federi Demonos?"

Once again Federi's hand twitched, this time only to check that his Cat-o'-Nine-Blades was safely wrapped around his shoulder.

"And," added Dana, "Vlad?"

The Morrigan performed a flawless bow, with his nose in fact touching his toes. "Prince Vlad the Impostor at your service, Madame."

"One of his personas," explained Federi. "Where's Paean?" He fiddled with his teleporter, and twitched, and was gone.

"He's twitchier than in a long time," Dana said accusingly. "What have you been doing to him, Boudaceia?"

Perdita pointed at the skies, where a string of new Gargantuan vessels joined the already present fleet. The new Gargantuans arrived and parked between the other vessels, but didn't do anything further.

Dana stared despondently at the skies that were lit with streaks of fire as the Moozils fired missiles at her beautiful planet.

"They already decimated my girls back at Earth," she said bitterly. "Now they hound us home. It is like the damned Moozils to eradicate another civilization completely. They take no prisoners."

"Those are actually your reinforcements," said Perdita. "Call your girls back, Dana. In half an hour the battle will be over. Spare your remaining forces."

"How?" asked Dana suspiciously.

"Paean Donegal," said Perdita, and told her Atlantean sister about the battle croaches.

Dana managed to smile. "Thank the stars, as Radomir would

402

say! And did the Intergalactic Council help in any way?"

"Help?" asked Perdita with a cynical laugh. "They are a major nuisance! Radomir is keeping them occupied and boozed up to the eyelids, or he would be here."

"He's giving them alcohol?" asked Dana incredulously. "Brilliant! The man is brilliant! Alcohol has such a severe effect on interstellar dragons in particular!"

Paean opened her eyes. She half-expected a nightjar to be chirping on her pillow; but there wasn't. She wasn't in Marge's rustic guest suite; she was in a fluffy white princess bed in a dainty white princess room, and the pain in her leg was – different.

"Where am I?" And this time, things were right, because the first thing she gazed into were Federi's unfathomable dark eyes. With smiles in them.

"Hey, little luv!"

She smiled back, reaching for a tendril of his black mane. "Missed you."

"We're on New Dome," Federi answered her question. "I brought Doc Judith for you, between her and Vlad they have been keeping an eye on you. Vlad is good, but according to Doc he still needs quite a bit of training."

"New Dome," repeated Paean. "Why?"

"We were escaping from the blasted Intergalactic Council," said Federi. "Then you developed an emergency with your injury there."

"But Vlad fixed that!"

"But it turned to jelly," replied Federi.

Bits and pieces came back to her. She'd sought out the Highest Authority to plead for Vlad...

"The Council has left Earth by now," said Federi. "They have given Captain three weeks to locate Vlad. The protocol demands that they tell the old Keeper of Shrn first that he's been replaced, before putting the replacement in charge."

Paean smiled. "And where is Vlad?"

"Here on Dome." Federi told her about the Moozil attack, and how Perdita had brought the newly awakened battle croaches, which had fixed the outcome within half an hour. "That was yesterday," he added. "I negotiated with Dana that we stick around here for a while, until your leg is in a state that you can use it again."

"There's something that worries me," said Paean. "Those scars on Vlad. The logic doesn't work out. He's a liquid. There should be no trace of any injury – there ought to be no injury!"

Federi smiled.

"Vlad!" he called.

The Morrigan seeped in through a window, turned into Prince Vlad and got stuck halfway through his bow.

"Oh! Paean Demonos is with us again!"

"She was wondering about your scars," said Federi.

Vlad dissolved into a scintillating puddle. Paean looked for those scars. Not a trace.

"It was a show!" she said indignantly. And she laughed. "Og, you good-for-nothing space crawler!"

Vlad grinned.

"So, whom do they want to put in charge of Shrn?" asked Paean.

"What?" asked Vlad. "They're replacing me? Why doesn't anyone update me?"

"Some space dragon," said Federi. "'cording to Shawn's report, it's a female, Jitanali or something."

Vlad nodded thoughtfully. "She's a good girl," he said. "But I'm not yielding the Keepership of Shrn."

"The Intergalactic Council seems to think you will," said Federi.

"Ha!" snorted Vlad. "That's not how it works! You volunteer for the job! Show that you care and you become the Keeper. You should know."

"I do know," growled Federi.

"'scuse me," said Vlad. "I'm going to find her first."

"Take me along!" piped Paean.

Vlad whipped an ultra-long tentacle around her and her lily-white duvet, and snatched her up and placed her on his back, turning into a space dragon en route and warping out of the room with her. The whole manoeuvre hadn't taken more than a quarter second. Federi cursed aloud and ripped out his teleporter, only to find that the two were already out of range.

"Your leg, Paean!" he snapped at the space where she had been a moment before.

Damn!

He sauntered out of the White Palace, took a cab to the space port, borrowed a small shuttle to the Interchange, warped through, commandeered one of the local shuttles – the personnel on the Pluto Base merely watched him in frozen awe; they knew from Perdita that he was the Keeper of Earth – and warped back towards Earth. He'd have taken the Comet if he'd thought for a moment that Paean wouldn't miss it the moment she returned to New Dome.

28 – Jitanali

By the time he stood before the Mound in Limerick, Federi had picked up a tag.

"And?" he snapped at Ailyss. "What's your point?"

Green eyes studied him critically.

"That's what I was about to ask you, Mr Demonos," said the Irish spy quietly. Federi twitched at the unnecessary calling of his name. He touched the Cat-o'-Nine-Blades that was slung across his shoulder permanently, then remembered where he was and mobilized his submachine gun instead.

"You're going after the Unicate," Ailyss stated needlessly.

"No, I'm picking violets," snarled the Assassin, still keeping his voice low.

"Federi." Ailyss placed her hand on his arm with the gun. "I am not the enemy. Remember we made a pact to help you."

"I'm best on my own," he replied impatiently.

"Fine," said Ailyss, "so am I. But the trouble is, I'm under orders. Both your Captain –"

"Stick Captain where the sun…"

"…and your wife have instructed me never to let you go hunt the Unicate without backup. I'm your backup. Like it or lump it."

Federi fell silent. Caramel-coloured freckles against too-pale, nearly Icelandic skin. And she'd gone off with Vlad into the who-knew-where. And Vlad had admitted that she was high up on his list of favourites – only on fourth place. Couldn't Ailyss rather have backed up Paean?

He shook his head grimly.

"And if you get injured? You're a friend. If they target you, they've got me because they know I'll never leave you to bleed out."

Ailyss gave his arm a squeeze and smiled. "I don't bleed out," she chuckled softly. "Not too long ago you wondered if I even bleed red. Come, Federi. Let's go get them!"

"But you've got to be stealthier than Tzigan," he warned.

She smiled again. "I am, my friend. I am."

Federi grunted and led the way into the Mound.

*

"I've got a child somewhere in this galaxy," mentioned Vlad as he soared through the star tunnels. Rainbow colours flashed past.

"Which galaxy is this?"

"Sanaritana," said Vlad. "You humans call it the Horse's Head. Which is funny, because the Solar Wind tells me there's a gypsy tune that goes, 'the Horse's Head can handle my sorrow'."

"Why is that funny?" asked Paean, confused.

Vlad smiled and shook his head. Morrigan humour, he suspected. He grew an extra tentacle out of his dragon's back, and placed it over Paean's leg. "Your limb still hurting?"

"It'll hold," said Paean bravely. "What does Doc Ju say?"

"The same as your Demon," said Vlad. "She's never seen anything look that nasty without actually being decayed."

"That doesn't sound hopeful," said Paean doubtfully.

"They don't really understand the subatomic bridges between molecules as well as I do," said Vlad. "It will heal, my girl. But you really have to keep it still."

"How long?"

He smiled. "Three to six weeks. The best is if Federi keeps you in bed all that time. Maybe on New Dome."

Paean grinned and shook her head.

"What child of yours lives here?" she asked.

"A Morrigan," said Vlad.

Paean laughed. That was obvious, she had thought!

"Not at all," countered Vlad. "Morrigan mix easily with other species. The whole Shifter Universe is full of our offspring. It's actually rather rare that a Morrigan has a true Morrigan offspring, it means that at some point they must have got on well enough with another Morrigan not to eat each other. Well, not immediately."

Paean shook her head. "You're a weird species."

"So are spiders," he pointed out. "Let's see if we can call her."

"She won't simply eat us?"

"Nah!" Vlad laughed. "That was a joke!"

Paean wasn't so sure about this one.

The next moment her psychic abilities were being flooded.

Child of mine! Vlad was shouting with all telepathic force. *Child of the Morrigan of Shrn! Come out and be seen!*

Paean clung on and waited for the mad descent through the stars to slow until the tunnels separated into recognizable separate star clusters; until these spaced out and they were once again well between myriads of stars and gas clouds.

Child of mine! Vlad shouted. *Show yourself!*

A white speck grew in the distance. Paean peered at it, trying to see it before it was really discernible. It flapped closer, first like a tiny, far-away seagull; the closer it came, the larger it appeared until Paean saw that it was shaped like a huge white Manta ray.

"Ah," said the Morrigan with deep satisfaction. "Here she is. My, isn't she a beauty! And already grown."

Paean had to agree. There was something extremely beautiful about the young female Morrigan.

I am here, sire of mine, the creature called back. *Have you come to challenge me for my home and hunting grounds?*

Not at all, replied Vlad, then switched to spoken language, though Paean was following just fine. "There's someone I want you to meet." They were now close enough that the invisible atmospheric bubbles each carried, could connect into a single larger bubble. Circling each other like a pair of sharks.

"How odd," replied the young female. "Why?"

Vlad smiled. "I don't think you'll understand why. Have you had any contact with other species other than for feeding?"

"Sire, to be frank, how does that concern you? I've known other species to care for their young, but never yet a Morrigan. What would a mouldy old jelly like yourself understand about friendships?"

Vlad laughed softly. Paean grinned delightedly. "She's a teenager!"

"Equivalent of," agreed Vlad. "Child of mine, do they call you by any name or can you take one?"

He got an old look from his daughter.

"A name is a word you make your own, to describe yourself," he supplied.

"Sire, I wasn't born blunt-witted! I know what a name is! They call me Virian."

"Hi Virian," piped Paean, unable to stay quiet any longer. She was delighted about this young Morrigan. "I'm Paean Donegal."

There was a sudden interstellar hush.

"Demonos," she corrected hastily. "I'm Paean Demonos!" What was that – an interstellar hush? It was always dead silent between stars! Sound waves were a gas-based phenomenon!

Vlad indicated to Paean. "See, Virian, I have friends too. This is my little friend. I have more. I want you to meet them."

"Why?" asked Virian.

"Are you jaded?" asked Paean, surprised. "Don't you want to meet us?"

"Because they are fun and intelligent," explained Vlad. "You're going to enjoy them and they'll find you a treat. Do you know the dragon Jitanali?"

"She's a friend of *mine*," said Virian. "What do you want with Jitanali? She's too young to be mated!"

Paean snorted, getting a bit annoyed with the cynicism of this younger Morrigan. Vlad only laughed.

"See, Paean. This is the life of a Morrigan. The only reason they would seek out other species is for creating new types of shifters."

"Speak for yourself, sire," snapped Virian.

"I'm speaking for other Morrigan," said Vlad. "I've learnt better. In fact I want to see Jitanali because I have news for her from the Council! Come, my child. Help me find your friend!"

"What does the Council want from Jitanali?" Virian came back. "Is the Red One looking for a mate? I told you she's too young!"

"No, Virian," said Paean, finally fed up. "Look, I'm a young adult in my species too, but even I find your back-chat a bit much. If my father..." She petered off, then spat past Vlad's head. The old Morrigan ducked instinctively. "Alright, maybe I do understand you, in a way. But firstly Vlad has never been nasty to you. It's just normal for *your* species that the fathers push off early in your lives. No promises made, none broken. Secondly the Council has a great honour in store for Jitanali. But they are stealing it from Vlad. This is not right. We need to speak to her and come to an agreement."

"What honour?" asked Virian sharply.

"Keepership of a planet," said Paean, only catching the shooshing vibes from Vlad after she'd already said it.

"Jitanali is too young for that," Virian answered back.

"My point exactly," cheered Paean. "Now would you kindly lead us to her so we can warn her of this terrible honour that's coming her way?"

Virian looked doubtful.

"Leave it, Paean," said Vlad. "I know where to find our green friend without Virian showing the way. I'd only thought it would be fun having her along."

"Fun," scoffed Virian. "What do you know about fun?"

Vlad warped away with Paean on his back. Virian set off after them.

"What a sour young Morrigan," commented Paean.

"She doesn't exactly have reason to be anything else, to us," replied Vlad.

*

Unicate military uniform was grey. It didn't matter though, because that was not how they recognized each other. Federi was sure of it by now. He in his gaudy joker camouflage and Ailyss in her black skin-tight jeans and polar neck crept along the passages, dodging from doorway to doorway, machine guns ready.

The mission was for that IRP agent, Patrick. Paean had rescued him; the Solar Wind had informed Federi when he'd asked where Terence was, that the young *Other* had taken the agent off the ship.

He'd been meaning to investigate the Mound anyway, following up on what he'd learnt from both Terence and the Intergalactic Council, and see if he couldn't find out how and where they turned werefolk into *Others*. The ship's disclosure had only added direction and urgency to his mission.

He peered into the open doorway to Queen Rhyn's office. It was empty. He'd shot down the Queen, less than a week back. Up at New Dome he had hardly managed to remember; but now it felt like a few minutes back and the terror was as real as then.

The Mound wouldn't have had time to generate a new queen – unless one had been ready for her mating flight just before Queen Rhyn had been shot down. Termites, he thought. And if the young queen matured just as the old queen was killed, didn't the young queen inherit the Mound rather than having to start a new one?

Did this model fit? He slunk along the dark passages, occasionally peering at the shadow that was his accomplice. She was really quieter and less visible than Tzigan. He had to hand it to her. What a power-team they could become!

There were no workers. This puzzled and worried him. Then again, he, Paean and mostly Imaya had decimated the population of this mound. Perhaps it hadn't had time to stock up again – recruit, regenerate, whatever?

Down, down the passages wound. Federi was constructing a mental map of the place. He suspected that Terence had taken Patrick to those damp dungeon cells where Paean had rescued Mrs Flanagan. If Patrick had been taken prisoner. Somehow Federi's radar told him that the fate of the young IRP man was much worse than that.

The lights at the bottoms of the passage were glowing a sinister dark violet by now, and they hadn't encountered a worker yet. The place was deserted. Federi pulled Ailyss into one of the small chambers off the passage and closed the door.

"What's going on, do you think?" he whispered.

Ailyss shook her head and put her finger across her lips. She gestured at the door. Federi slipped back out, checking after a while that she was still following.

Yellow eyes followed them from the cells in the dungeons. Federi scanned the locked-up victims. Many Unicate *Others*; many human victims too. If he freed all the humans…

412

"Hsst! Federi Demonos!"

He stared. One of the prisoners was beckoning at him – an emaciated, wizened female with a wild bush of white hair flying in all directions. He moved closer – and froze.

It couldn't be!

But it was. And she was human. He couldn't detect a trace of *Other* in her.

"Mrs Flanagan!" How the hell? He decided to free her. He was going to take that chance. Paean had rescued a fake. He looked at the lock of the cage.

"You've got to be careful," whispered Mrs Flanagan excitedly. "How did you get in here anyway? Is Paean alright? Thought I'd never see daylight again, thank God you are here…"

He inserted his smallest tool – an Allen key small enough to tighten a chin rest on a violin, or to pick-pocket a fly with. That sensitive little stick dug around in the lock, found a lever, and suddenly the whole lock just came apart and the door opened.

And with it a high-pitched wailing arose. The mound was sounding alarm.

"Take her to the outside," Federi instructed Ailyss. "And up to Space Base! I'm carrying on here! Be quick! Be careful!"

"Gotcha," said Ailyss.

"Bless you, Demonos," said Mrs Flanagan, with tears in her eyes.

"Run!" ordered Federi. Ailyss took Mrs Flanagan into a side passage, her machinegun lifted for action.

Federi waited until someone actually spotted him, then he bolted in the opposite direction. He waited a bit for the pursuer to catch up. Then he dashed down the passage like a March hare.

Where in hell did this place lead? The passages twisted and branched, and he struggled to keep up with the mind map of the place. Deeper and deeper into the Earth they chased him. He led

413

them well away from Ailyss and Mrs Flanagan before considering getting to safety himself or retaking the mission for Patrick and Terence.

It was stuffy and warm down here. The pursuers were only two turns behind him. He dodged into a doorway and closed it behind himself. All the doors had so far led to tiny chambers or offices off the main passage. He turned and looked at the inside of the chamber. And his knees nearly gave way.

Here they all were! He was in the entrance of a huge underground cavern; up on a ledge that led in a narrow path down into the main part. From where he stood he had a clear view from above of the teeming masses of workers relentlessly busy down here. There were other doors and passages leading out of the chamber; he made a mental note of them for escape routes.

This must be the heart of the Mound.

Grey-clothed workers were milling about, collecting large oval objects of an opalescent white, moving them to tiny niches in the walls; or tending to strange-looking creatures that were stuck in similar niches, feeding them. Federi squinted, trying to see those creatures better. They looked like gangly, emaciated – human children! From the roof hung silky-white upside-down pupae of man-sized proportions, with very lively things stirring inside. He had stumbled into the nursery! In the middle of the room a younger version of the old horror he had blasted apart not too long ago, crouched on the floor laying egg after egg, and…

Federi's instincts took over as he spotted the young IRP man Paean had rescued. He raised his machinegun and shot, pumping that alien Queen so full of exploding rounds that she was spread all over the room. The action freed Patrick – or what was left of him. The IRP guy stared at Federi, and then he screamed – a long, drawn-out, terrible scream that fitted with half of him being absorbed by

414

that thing that was now a featureless mess. Federi ran down the narrow walkway and to Patrick's side, ignoring the slaves that converged on him.

"Patrick?"

The half-a-man reached out and ripped Federi's pistol out of its holster. Before Federi could stop him, he turned it against his own temple and shot. He pulled the trigger five times. Federi was positive that by the third time at the latest it was only reflexes in death.

The Assassin stood back, his whole body quaking in shock, staring at the mangled shape in front of him, still seeing the vivid image of what had gone before, and trying to fit it all into a logical picture. And failing. The nightmarish scene would haunt him forever. His psyche was frozen to the spot from overload; he was peripherally aware of the workers converging on him, but couldn't move for the horror.

Federi!

Katya. Thank all the mercy in Romany luck that his young sister, and his baby brothers, had escaped this fate. The queen of a mound absorbed human bodies to derive the material for her vile eggs! Not termites, his mind pointed out scientifically. Wasps.

Federi! Move!

And the damned *Others* were aliens after all! Terence's game of deceit was up. Federi glanced around at the Unicate workers that were all around him. He didn't see Terence amongst them, but the young *Other* could easily be there anyway; there were such a lot of them! They could have grabbed him long ago; but they seemed somehow afraid, reluctant, unsure of how to attack. Workers, not soldiers, he remembered.

Hell with that; they'd worked together to force Patrick into this extremely messy death. Federi's machine gun moved up by itself,

415

and into action as he stepped out of the reach of those hands. He spun in a circle, mowing them down with exploding rounds, a dance of death that was entirely the domain of the Assassin.

A space opened around him as they instinctively backed away from the bullets. Federi transferred the gun to his left hand and kept shooting while his right searched his many pockets and found what he was looking for. He scattered the pellets wildly amongst the Unicate, blasted a path into them and escaped along it to the exit. In the doorway, while the Unicate workers still milled about in confusion, he pulled his flat glass flask out of his pocket and flung it into the room, and dodged through the door.

Behind him the hall exploded in a series of fireworks. Federi pounded up the passageway, retracing his steps and eventually resurfacing in the dungeons. He listened intently. There were footsteps approaching from all sides. Shards! Every way he turned, they came streaming in, around the corners, out of side passages.

Federi paused for a moment. Where was the exit? He was thoroughly lost; but somewhere a whiff of rain and cold air brushed by him, and he decided that there lay the way out. He launched himself directly at a group of them who were emerging from the passage he was hoping to take. His Stiletto came dancing out of his sleeve; his jack-knife jumping out of his pocket, snapping open. The machinegun hung loosely on its strap. The blades danced into the attackers.

They didn't expect such an up-close assault; but these were Unicate *Others*. They weren't programmed for surprise. A parasitic alien species, probably older than the dinosaurs, and they had survived by learning and remembering every trick in the book, probably of thousands of different host species. Was this the first time they were up against humans? Were humans really that unique with their creative thinking? Most older species had well-established

416

survival patterns and styles. He could imagine that some aliens had evolved logical thinking into such a fine art that it became a hundred percent predictable. And...

He had learnt something recently. From the Council. Telepathy was the main means of communication for many intergalactic encounters. And mind control was a way of catching prey.

They didn't back away from his slashing knives. They knew as well as he did that they were many and he was only one; so if they all worked together he could not escape. But there was the uncanny thought he had just understood: They were choreographed into working together. For each one he cut down, another took his place as though death didn't matter at all. Did they even have a choice? Did Terence ever have the choice to change sides? By now Federi doubted it. Queen Rhyn had sent him. Who choreographed them now? Clearly not the Queen – she was dead. He doubted that in these few minutes the mound had had the chance to establish a new queen. The Queen – as he had just seen – was only the reproductive organ of the mound. He shuddered as he recalled how close he'd been to that fate himself – had it not been for his machinegun trick and his fast response of cutting her down and asking questions later, his wise choice of not playing his luck at that moment.

But the Queen was not the brain of the Mound. Or the *Others* ought to have entered a disorganized state of confusion at the point of her death. So the sentient Mound itself was coordinating them. He hoped that Ailyss had got away with Mrs Flanagan. He wished he could call her on the com. But that would be giving her position away.

It was pointless dealing with these individuals. Like ants or termites, each individual *Other* was only a cell in the whole organism – the Mound. He couldn't hope to kill them all – there were too many. He had to deal with the Mound.

417

"Halt!"

His shout got the *Others* to pause in their onslaught.

"I wish to negotiate!"

They all understood English. They stared at him in silence. There was nobody for him to negotiate with, he knew. Not amongst them!

"Step back! I can't think!" He watched in suspense as the whole bundle backed off one step, giving him an arm's length of breathing space. The best proof that they weren't human. A human captor would never have given a captive space on request!

He watched them with wary eyes as he called the Mound in his mind.

Unicate! Mound Rhyn!

The Mound was listening. It had no words; but he got the impression that it could understand the images he projected.

You have human prisoners, thought Federi. *Why?*

The answering impression came. He had seen for what.

Why? Are they food?

Genetic material. It was the way the Unicate integrated into a host species.

The Toll. That had been the function of the Toll. Oh hell, how he wished he could tap into what Falco knew!

He wasn't Falco. He was Federi. All he had now, was Federi. Which was more than most could deal with. He smiled grimly.

Would you like to be entertained? asked Federi, the performer.

Ailyss took a deep breath of fresh air as she and Mrs Flanagan emerged from the mound. She grabbed the elderly teacher more firmly by the wrist and teleported.

The scrawny old Irishwoman had held up remarkably well; it

didn't seem as though being incarcerated by the Unicate had done her much damage. Ailyss didn't buy it. There was something wrong with this one.

They popped back into reality on Calypso, in a desert spot well away from the Oasis. By now the Solar Wind had been stationed at the Oasis, lying at anchor on the shallow waves; Captain however was patrolling the crater in Miami and trying to decide what to do when the Council returned. Well, that was trouble for another day.

Ailyss had teleported into a truly deserted spot; there was no indication in which direction one should stumble across the endless red sand until one would eventually arrive at the only inhabited spot on the whole planet. She let the old woman go and drew her gun, and trained it on Mrs Flanagan.

"Now you tell me who you really are."

"Veraena Flanagan." The woman smoothed down her wild grey hair and wound it into a bun before releasing it again with a sigh. "I must look a mess!"

"You do," agreed Ailyss. "Paean told me of her favourite teacher. Enough that I can decide for myself whether you are for real."

"Fair," said the hostage. "I can see that you're spooked. I don't know who you are, but I deduce you're one of Paean's friends."

"I am. I'd like to ask you a few questions."

"Go ahead," said the elderly woman. "Mind if I sit down? I'm a bit winded from all that…"

Ailyss nodded. The Mrs Flanagan look-alike sat down on the desert sand. The sun slanted in at an angle.

"What precisely did you teach Paean?"

Mrs Flanagan smiled. "You're from the Solar Wind, aren't you?"

"I am." Ailyss smiled too. This creature was playing her role perfectly. And she did look completely human; which the one Paean

419

had rescued, didn't. Then again Captain hadn't even been able to tell human from Unicate before he had been made aware of the differences. They were extremely subtle.

"I'll tell you straight, then," said Mrs Flanagan. "Not everything I taught was legal. In school I taught English, Math and Social Background. Afternoons they hung around my place and I force-fed them my awful baking and subversive culture and history." She smiled. "Paean never sat still. Little red ant! Both her brothers were better listeners. She was always on some or other mission."

"Such as?" pushed Ailyss.

"You know Paean. Always looking for someone she could help. Lots of times she was out in the richer areas, doing chores and babysitting for a bit of small change, and then buying bread or milk or washing soap and handing it out in Molly Street. Or brewing some or other herbal potion to give to someone who was sick."

It certainly sounded just like Paean. Ailyss was inclined to give this particular Mrs Flanagan the benefit of the doubt. But still…

"What did they do to you inside that mound?" she pushed. "What happened that night?"

"You know," said Mrs Flanagan, "there are two people I'd like to see. The one is your Captain Lascek, and the other is Paean's – er – husband…" she frowned, "Federi. You can keep me at gunpoint if you must, but what I have to tell them is very important and it may help."

Ailyss nodded. Whether or not this version was the original Mrs Flanagan, wasn't yet decided. But the request was fair, and she'd want Captain and Federi to interview her in any case.

"Tell me about Terence," she challenged.

Mrs Flanagan went a bit pale. "That one," she said. "He's dangerous. Any time as dangerous as one of their females."

"Why?"

420

"Because he's so darned friendly," spat Mrs Flanagan. "Polite, sweet-natured, takes your arm like a gentleman and escorts you straight to hell and delivers you to Old Nick personally. With a smile."

"He seemed to be on our side," said Ailyss. "He helped Paean rescue you."

Mrs Flanagan frowned. "What …?"

"You see," said Ailyss, "the point is, you're already aboard! So we don't need two of you, so now we must decide which one of you we shoot."

Mrs Flanagan stared at her with wild eyes, her hand covering her mouth.

"Holy Mary," she muttered. "Hope Paean and Shawn are still safe!"

"You're not worried about Ronan?"

"He's inconspicuous," said Mrs Flanagan. "He doesn't have Annie's Gift. I don't think the Unicate is really after him."

"Annie's Gift," pushed Ailyss.

"Yes," said Mrs Flanagan sadly. "The Unicate didn't execute Annie only for being politically active or discovering sensitive information. She had a gift."

"Kindly elaborate," warned Ailyss, lifting the machinegun a bit.

"She had mind powers," said Mrs Flanagan. "I don't know all the details. From what I understand they run truest in Shawn. Paean has a fair share too. Ronan doesn't. Maybe it's not after all such a bad idea that there's someone looking after Paean. Is anyone looking after Shawn?"

"We all are," said Ailyss. "Answer me one question. You've spent the past two weeks in the Unicate mound being traumatized. How do you manage to be so calm?"

"Girl," said Mrs Flanagan, "there is only so much hysteria in me.

Make no mistake, I had my breakdown. But once I stopped screaming I found that I couldn't go on panicking. So I faced my reality, no matter how gruesome, and worked on coming to terms with it. I learnt a lot more than I ever wanted to find out. This is why I must speak to your Captain."

Ailyss shook her head. This one seemed so authentic! But the other one… She smiled. There was of course one test this one would pass or fail depending on whether she was real.

"I'll organize it," she said. "Just the second Federi returns."

"Is he still in the Mound?" asked Mrs Flanagan.

"Seems so."

The elderly woman shook her head sadly. "He's not going to get out then! You shouldn't have come for me."

"We didn't," said Ailyss. "We came for Patrick from the IRP, and Terence."

"Leave Terence where he is," warned Mrs Flanagan. "He's dangerous. Patrick? Is Patrick human?"

Ailyss nodded.

"Forget it then. He's dead. Do you know what they do with humans?" asked Mrs Flanagan.

"I have a fair idea," said Ailyss. "My question is, how did you survive that?"

"I'm not human," smiled Mrs Flanagan.

Very nearly that gun went off by itself. Mrs Flanagan lifted her hand.

"Not in that sense," she said. "I'm of the Sisterhood. We're immortals looking after people like Annie Donegal."

Ailyss shook her head, unwilling to accept this. "Immortal, how?" she growled.

"We live, we grow old, we die, we get reborn and we remember everything," said Mrs Flanagan. "Humans don't remember between

422

lives. Many humans only get one life anyway. But the Sisterhood does remember."

Ailyss frowned. Sisterhood? She had learnt a lot in the Secret Service; even more in the places she had visited before that, her *first* employers. She had been made to *remember*. And no – a 'Sisterhood' had featured nowhere. But maybe there was a new twist here?

"So that's why they let you live?" she prompted.

"They're trying to duplicate the formula for the Sisterhood," said Mrs Flanagan. "They dug around in my innards trying to find clues. But this is years upon years back. It's part of what I want to tell your Captain. Don't make me go there twice."

"So then, what do you remember of the Fifties?" snapped Ailyss.

"Too much," sighed Mrs Flanagan. "The Fifties were horrible. And the Sixties were worse. Earth was nearly wiped out completely. Falco Demonos did the world a favour. You don't see it that way now, because the Unicate is so awful, but back then – it was live or die, girl. Say thank you that you're living in today's times."

"Then you may know Sherman Dougherty," said Ailyss noncommittally.

"Sherman Dougherty?" Mrs Flanagan smiled. "What a sweetheart he is!"

"That's great," said Ailyss, getting up. "He's waiting for you. And so is Marge, and Richard. They've all been waiting to talk to you again."

"Ah, Richard," agreed Mrs Flanagan.

"That one has a few loose bolts rattling around in his head," commented Ailyss with a grin. "I have no idea how you tolerate him! What a loudmouth!"

"He's a nice person," said Mrs Flanagan defensively. "Just, perhaps, a little simple."

423

Ailyss smiled grimly. Now she had the old hag! The genuine Mrs Flanagan had never yet spoken to Marge, nor Richard. And there was absolutely nothing wrong with the engineer's mind.

*

Space tunnels flew by. Paean leaned against the neck of the Morrigan, relaxing. This could carry on for ages; she felt drowsy.

Suddenly something blue sparked before her eyes and materialized into Furrl.

"You!" she exclaimed, surprised, catching him. "Last I thought Shawn had you!"

"Shawn sends me," said Furrl. "On pain of death if I don't deliver his message. Why is everyone constantly making me death threats?"

"Maybe because you are not trustworthy?" guessed Paean. "What's the message?"

"The Archangel Uryel wants Jitanali to be the new Keeper, but it looks like Anthrim wants the Keepership for himself."

"What? How would Shawn know that?"

"Anthrim told Uryel, at the post-trial drinking fest," said Furrl.

"But Shawn wasn't there," objected Paean. "Or…?"

Furrl capitulated. "I overheard it."

"You happened to overhear it?" Her fist tightened around the little dragon.

"I was eavesdropping!" squeaked Furrl in terror. "It's what we Blue Furries do! We always do that!"

"And Anthrim sends you?"

"Anthrim didn't see me," said Furrl.

"And why weren't you in Shawn's pocket?"

"I escaped from *your* pocket when you lost consciousness in the

Comet," explained Furrl.

"And you homed in on Anthrim and told him everything?"

A guilty silence.

"And now you're telling us so we can fall into his trap?"

"No, no," denied Furrl. "I escaped him! I pretended to obey his orders…"

Paean dug in her moonbag until she found some tape, and wrapped it around Furrl's wings.

"Anthrim knows you're our prisoner," she said. "What do Blue Furries eat?"

"Cosmic motes," said Furrl. "They're everywhere. More in atmospheric environments."

"Good." She stuck the small creature into her moonbag and closed the zip.

"We excrete dense matter though," came the muffled supply. "In liquid and solid form."

A hamster cage for this one, she decided. *Basta*.

The two Morrigan and Paean landed lightly on a mountain plateau. Vlad threw back his dragon head and hooted like a foghorn. Paean gazed at the scenery surrounding the mountain plateau. Lush, green valleys, lakes, some snowy peaks…

There was a flurry of green, and then a dragon landed in front of them, studying both Virian and Vlad in surprise. It was a good size, if Paean had to measure it from nose to tail-tip it would probably come to half the length of the Solar Wind, and its wings, unfolded, compared favourably with those of the ship… but against Anthrim the Red, this little green dragon was a real midget.

The size of dragon a girl could befriend.

"Shrn?" it asked. "Virian? You know each other?"

"You know the Morrigan who fathered me?" asked Virian in

surprise. "Careful of him, Jitanali! I came to warn you! They have some or other vile scheme from the Council…"

"Shrn's a good friend of mine," said Jitanali. "We visit each other every beat or two. But…" she looked critically at Paean, "he seems to have picked up a parasite? How odd!"

Vlad laughed.

"Jitanali, this is Paean Donegal. She is a Founder."

There was that interstellar silence again. Except this time, on a planet with an atmosphere, it came across a lot more convincingly.

"A Founder," said Jitanali after an appropriate pause of awe. "Shrn, I had no idea there were any left in the universes!"

Vlad nodded his dragon head sagely. "She is from Planet Earth. You know, the sister planet to my home."

"The Sanctuary," supplied Jitanali. "Yes, I know Earth."

"Jitanali, don't trust him," Virian warned. "He has some vile scheme –"

"That's enough now," said Paean angrily. "Virian, go home. You're not part of this conversation. It has nothing to do with you."

The manta ray stared at her.

"I can see that Morrigan are raised without a mother to teach them good manners," added Paean heatedly. "Leave Vlad alone, Virian. He's never harmed you. He's Jitanali's friend, she trusts him. In any case you can't make decisions on behalf of your friends! Gosh, are you bossy! You remind me of…" she petered off, then grinned. "Me, I guess," she completed. "When I was younger. So grow up!"

All three great space creatures stared at her in amazement.

"Paean," said Vlad, "I think *you* should tell Jitanali the deal. I'm glad you came along!"

"Gladly," said Paean, slipped off the Morrigan's back and fell, her injured leg collapsing out under her. Vlad's tentacle lashed out

426

and caught her before she hit the ground. He picked her up and positioned her on his back again.

"Paean!" he warned. "Remember your injury!"

"Okay, Vlad, thanks. Now listen, Jitanali. The Intergalactic Council has decided to take the Keepership of Shrn away from Vlad and give it to you instead."

Jitanali gasped.

"But that's not how Keepership works!" she exclaimed. "Shrn, what are your thoughts on that?"

Vlad looked disgusted.

"They can do what they want," he spat. "They have totalitarian power."

"That's not the end of it," said Paean. "At least, some of the Council want you to be the new Keeper, but Anthrim the Red seems want it for himself."

The three large aliens gaped at her in shock.

"That must never happen!" exclaimed Vlad. "He will hunt out my werefolk!"

"And next, all of Earth," completed Paean. "He's huge."

"You don't mind me hunting your werefolk?" asked Jitanali.

"I do mind!" growled Vlad. "But you will need to eat. You're not a Morrigan to scavenge on whatever carbon-based organic substances come along…"

"Weetie-O's," smiled Paean. "And humans from the planet next door, you louse!" And she grew serious. "Jitanali, honestly now. You know how a Keeper is chosen."

"A Keeper is not chosen," said Jitanali. "When someone cares enough to do the job, they become the Keeper. It's a heart-assignment."

"Exactly," said Paean. "Like Federi and Earth. Vlad cared enough to become the Keeper of Shrn. How can the Council take that away from him?"

"They cannot," said Jitanali. "It's not taken or given."

"So it follows that they can't give you the job either," concluded Paean.

"I wouldn't want to take it from Shrn," said the young dragon.

Virian, who'd been quiet for a long while, finally spoke up.

"Shrn," she said, "I misjudged you. I didn't realize you're a Keeper. Morrigan don't make likely Keepers. They are too predatory."

"Morrigan apparently have self-image issues," muttered Paean under her breath.

"The problem we are facing," said Virian, "is not of Jitanali being forced into Keepership of a planet she knows nothing about. It's of deceiving the Council that we are complying, while keeping things the way they are."

"It's really of preventing Anthrim from grabbing the planet," Paean put in. "I doubt he intends to *keep* anything!" And she blinked. "My! Welcome aboard, Virian! You finally got the message!"

"Pardon my reserve, young Founder," replied the younger Morrigan. "I don't know Shrn from any other devious space-warping jelly."

"So what do we do?" asked Paean.

"We get there first," said Vlad.

"In that case I need Wolf, and my Comet," specified Paean.

29 – Anthrim

Federi didn't have any more shipwreck rum. He had smashed his bottle in the middle of that central breeding hall, setting all the chemical explosives off. They only needed a minuscule droplet of alcohol… that, or heat, such as an open flame or a nearby explosion. But without either heat or ethanol, the reaction could not be triggered.

What explosive he had left over, would have to be detonated, either by fire or a trigger. He had no trigger; and fire wouldn't go far in this humid place. He wondered if the damp was a function of Limerick or of the mound.

In his mind he was still playing Falco's violin, raising Falco's mists. The Mound had been mesmerized into listening to the music. He had played himself invisible; the Mound had lost sight of him. The Unicate others stared straight through him where he passed them. This was the best confirmation for his theory.

But he had to keep up the music, or the magic would fail. He slunk invisibly from doorway to doorway, playing up the mists with all that was in him. He had hypnotised the Mound into a daze. All the occupants were standing or sitting around in stupor.

He was at the exit now. He checked his teleporter – Ailyss registered up at the Space Base. So she was alright. He made sure that the signature he saw was her biogenetic field and not only her wrist-com. Yes, all was in order there. He glanced back at the dark entrance he had just vacated. He so dearly wanted to blast the whole place to pieces as a farewell. He knew now that there was no hope for what human prisoners there were in those cells; he had no way of rescuing them.

But he had nothing with which he could make the crater he intended. He peered back in through the doorway once more as he left the mound; then he teleported back up to Space Base.

It was almost unfairly easy for him to move away from that Mound, once he was outside.

"Tzigan!"

"Captain! I'll take you up on that shipwreck rum now."

*

Doc Judith gave Paean a severe dressing down before allowing her to use the cast that had originally been bought in Atuona for Wolf's knee. It wasn't a very good fit. Doc Judith muttered and rumbled, and then moulded an old-fashioned plaster cast around Paean's leg instead, giving her exoskeletal support from hip to knee.

"You're not supposed to be jumping around," she scolded. "And I shouldn't have to do this! I'll have to open it again tonight and see how your wound is healing, because I don't trust it under that cast. It can easily go bad."

"Sorry, Doc."

"You have three hours, then you're back here on New Dome," ordered Doc Judith. "And then you stay in bed, understood?"

Paean nodded meekly, teleported to her Comet and followed the two Morrigan and one dragon to Planet Shrn, through the Galactic Interchange, towards Earth and through a portal.

Once they were hovering above Shrn, Paean tagged her Comet into position and teleported onto Vlad's back. The Morrigan led the two female space creatures to the exact place where the portal from Dracula's Castle connected Earth with Shrn. They circled above the place for a moment.

430

"Pretty," commented Virian.

"I can see why you don't want to give up this place," said Jitanali.

A huge clap of thunder sounded behind them. Paean ducked instinctively and glanced at the threat.

Anthrim was hovering above them, with the two Morrigan from the Council.

"Damn!" exclaimed Vlad and plummeted to ground like a rock, Paean on his back. She couldn't make out a word of what he was bellowing. There was shouting and roaring; one of the Morrigan wrapped itself around Jitanali, restraining her wings so that she crashed straight down. The other collided with Virian.

Paean didn't have time to look much; but what turned into a fight between two Morrigan looked terrible to her. Each seemed to try to engulf the other. Liquid droplets sprayed from them. She stifled a scream.

And then Anthrim's talons tore into Vlad. The Morrigan melted instinctively, forgetting that he had a passenger. Paean grabbed onto a dragon claw, ripped out her dagger and sank it between the dragon's toes.

Not clever. She was kicked away and sailed through the atmosphere of Planet Shrn.

For a moment she was paralysed bloodless. The parachute jump came back to her; but there was no parachute now! She felt her pockets for her teleporter, and her wrist for her wrist-porter. She was still high up; she had a few seconds. But it was gone. Someone had been overcautious again! It would cost her life this time. You couldn't take an assassin's essential tools away and hope they would survive it. Rigid with fear she watched the blue sky with its single fluffy clouds, refusing to look at the ground that was rushing closer.

Furrl! He was in her moonbag! Frenetically she scrabbled to

open the zip and untie the little fellow's wings. And then talons locked around her, too. She couldn't even scream. There was a teleporter leap, and she found herself on the ground. She battled to get air into her lungs; and there was a scream. It came out of her. She wasn't asking it to! It was something completely outside of her control.

A firm hand clapped over her mouth. She struggled and bit and stared at those dark eyes with the countless laugh lines…

With a hiccup she relaxed into his grip and clung to him, sobbing hysterically. He tried to quieten her down, then his patience was suddenly at an end.

"Stop crying, Paean!"

She pulled away a bit and gazed at him. "Not crying!" Though from laughing so hard, tears were indeed running down her cheeks.

Federi laughed too. "Vixen!"

"How did you know I was in trouble?"

"How could I not know? The only question was where you'd come out. It was a setup, little luv!"

"How?" Ah. She knew. Furrl! This time she'd really kill the little rat.

"Not Furrl," Federi corrected her thoughts. "One of the Morrigan from the Council was hidden aboard Perdita's jet. It followed us to New Dome, and listened to all our conversations."

She shook her head and gazed at her gypsy, and saw shadows in his eyes. Dark shadows. Unicate death shadows.

"Where have you been?" she asked quietly. "Not back in the Mound?"

"Rescued your Mrs Flanagan a second time," he said evenly. "Wasn't her, yet again."

She clung to her Assassin. "Aw, Federi! And you went without me?"

432

"You're injured," he replied accusingly. "You really want to lose that leg?"

"No. Really not. Federi – we've got to help Vlad!"

Federi glanced up into the sky. Paean followed his gaze. The battle that went on there was terrible. It looked as though Virian, though she was smaller, was holding up bravely against the large Morrigan. Jitanali was nowhere. She had crash-landed; Paean had seen it happen, a moment before she'd been catapulted into free-fall herself. But the fact that the other Morrigan wasn't up in the air meant one of two things. Either the second Council-Morrigan had died in that fall too; or Jitanali was still keeping it busy.

Vlad was writhing in the grip of the dragon and being systematically pushed into that great beast's throat. Writhing? He was a liquid! She still didn't understand.

"Mind power," observed Federi. "Anthrim's a better mind-mage than Vlad. He's forcing him to keep a solid shape. Vlad is fighting on two levels at the same time."

"Got my tiny bit of Anthrim," said Paean and held up her dagger. "Come!"

Federi teleported into the Comet with her.

"We need Wolf," stated Paean. "Sticky Carbon!"

Shawn glanced up and clapped his sister in a bear hug. "Thought you were gone, lil' sister!"

"Tougher than that, Shawney! Good you're here!"

"I'll get Wolf," he volunteered.

"Just go carefully," begged Paean. "Get Ailyss too." And she loaded the blood of Anthrim the Great into the Comet's Genitron while Federi escorted Shawn to the portal.

It would take too long. Paean keyed the sequences into the Genitron in such a hurry that she had to delete everything and start again. Messing it up would be lethal now.

Hang in there, Vlad, she begged in her mind. *Just hang tight, we're coming!*

*

Federi saw Shawn through the portal and turned back to look at the battle going on up there. Vlad was putting up a heroic fight, but he was already halfway down that great beast's gullet. Federi trained his teleporter on him and readied his submachine gun.

The eye. He'd aim for the eye. He teleported to coordinates just a few metres up from the Morrigan. It launched him successfully to the spot. The older teleporters had a safety feature that wouldn't let one land in the middle of a solid; but there was nothing to prevent one from teleporting to a place in mid-air. A feature he'd have to ask Wolf to keep! As he completed the leap he aimed at the dragon's left eye in passing, and shot a salvo of exploding rounds from his submachine special. Anthrim swiped at him and missed. The gypsy reversed his teleporter leap and landed safely back at the portal.

Those bullets couldn't be more than an irritation, but they were enough for Anthrim to start retching the Morrigan out again. Vlad had grown a whole lot of spikes; from the lacerated and swollen state of the dragon's jaws and tongue Federi deduced that they were loaded with poison. The Morrigan got slippery and vacated that tight spot.

He'd try that again! Federi repeated the same leap, already shooting as he arrived. This time Anthrim was ready for him and caught him in his talon.

"Ah! Prince Falco! Forever the swindler! No wonder your own kind calls you the Traitor! Your own offspring shall condemn you..." He paused and spat, trying to dislodge the poison from his tongue. And then Federi found himself at the loaded end of a deep,

434

penetrating dragon stare. A Truth Gaze.

"You are not Falco the Traitor at all," said Anthrim softly. "You are his descendent! My word, and you had the whole Council fooled!"

"Federi Demonos," said Federi with a smile. "Whether I'm him or not is not quite clear. But I can guarantee you, you'd rather have him for an enemy than me. Anthrim the Great Criminal!"

"You dare," hissed Anthrim and daintily picked the Assassin up in his maw, tossing him in the air like a peanut and catching him in his teeth.

But along with Federi he got another mouthful of Morrigan. Vlad had formed into a ball of spikes again and stuck himself into the dragon's gullet.

"Get out of here, Assassin!" he hissed.

"Vlad! You're defeating the purpose! You'll get yourself eaten!"

"Buzz off, Demon!" snapped the Morrigan of Shrn. "This is not your fight!"

Federi laughed softly.

"You're under the protection of Earth, Morrigan," he pointed out. The dragon's digestive juices were seriously hampered by his allergic reaction to Vlad. He was trying to swallow the Morrigan, and with his claws he tried to pick Federi back out of his mouth. But unclasping those jaws seemed to be a difficult thing for him.

"I'm disabling his jaw muscles," grinned Vlad.

"Two seconds, old buddy," replied Federi. "I know what even Gargantuans are sensitive to! But you've got to be ready to evacuate! Are you?"

"Sure," said Vlad and watched with a smug grin on his amoebial hide how Federi planted explosives in the dragon's teeth, dodging the talons.

Anthrim roared in frustration.

"On your marks, get set, teleport," shouted Federi. Vlad wrapped a tentacle around him and teleported out of the dragon's maws. The explosion ripped the dragon's lower jaw off. Federi stared in horror. The beast was still very much alive. How tough exactly was such a dragon?

Not tough enough, it turned out. From the trees he watched how Anthrim came crashing down out of the sky where he had been performing all these manoeuvres so effortlessly. The old dragon landed on the ground, his bones clearly smashed; yet he lifted his long neck with the destroyed face at the end of it and looked around for Federi and Vlad. He located them and blew an immense flame at them. And then he collapsed.

On his hide sat Paean Demonos with one leg in a plaster cast, collecting her dart.

"Poor dragon," she said softly and patted the chitinous red hide. "Not his fault that he was who he was. Rest in peace."

Federi glanced at her, then at Vlad. The Morrigan was hanging off a branch, dripping liquids.

"Vlad?"

"Go help Virian," begged the shifter. "And Jitanali if she's still alive."

"Are you alright?"

"No, you clown. I'm dying."

"How?"

"That dragon had enzymes in his mouth. Started digesting me. Can't stop the process. Go!"

Federi teleported away. Paean tried to call Shawney on her com – and rediscovered that the blasted com wasn't on her. But a second later both her brother and Wolf teleported in next to her.

"Alright," said Wolf, "now for the clean-up. When something caustic spills in a laboratory, one washes the place down. Let's get this miserable piece of shifter into the bath."

*

In Jitanali's heart, dragon fires of anger burned brighter than the sun. She hadn't asked for this. The one moment she was lounging in the sun, dreaming; the next, drawn into these lethal politics. Led into a trap by the very Morrigan of Shrn whom she'd trusted. Why? Couldn't he have foreseen this?

Her wings were destroyed; she felt as though there were only broken bones in her sleek body, especially in her left hind leg and her right front leg; but she was alive and, so far, unvanquished. The smaller Council Morrigan, Narrenshee, had tried to get away. But Jitanali had grabbed her in the last moment and showed her why Morrigan feared dragons. What was left of Narrenshee, was pulsing its last in a semi-liquid blob on the ground.

The bad thing was that the native creatures of Shrn were beginning to gather around her. Hunters, scavengers. They were crawling closer, some of them holding long sharpened sticks in their prehensile front paws. She couldn't move. It wouldn't be an easy death. She couldn't believe that these were the creatures Shrn felt so protective of that he was unwilling to relinquish the Keepership.

She had seen the battle between Anthrim and Shrn. Her friend had spent too much time in the jaws of the dragon to escape death. He was going to dissolve from the digestive enzymes; a slow, painful death. Her heart bled for him, and no less for her younger friend Virian who had so surprisingly turned out to be Shrn's daughter. Dragons cared for their offspring. So Jitanali could understand the sentiments that had made the Morrigan come and look for his child after all these ages.

Virian had crashed down, not as steeply as she herself had, only

437

minutes back. Jitanali hoped her younger friend would survive. She had seen the digestive tube that Belarius had managed to inject into Virian. She had also witnessed, from her green hiding place, the spectacular explosion that had ripped Belarius apart. Somehow those little Earth animals seemed to have amazing powers.

The Shrn creatures crept closer, their pointy sticks, bared fangs and ragged claws ready. Jitanali turned a sad green Dragon's Eye on them and watched them. She wasn't even going to try to explain. These here were too primitive to understand.

And then the small black-maned Earth male was there, with his missile shooter held casually in his hand. He ignored the Shrn folk and came right up to her head.

"Are you alive, young one?"

Jitanali sighed. Yes, she was – but she wouldn't be for long, not disabled as she was.

"The Council did you in," muttered the male, touching the ridge above her eye. "Poor Jitanali! You know who I am. I'm Falco Demonos – er, Federi. The Traitor – or as close as it gets. I'm the Keeper of Earth."

It sounded to her as though he wasn't really sure who he was. But then he released her eye and turned his back to her and faced down the Shrn predators, who were significantly larger than him.

"You know who I am, don't you!"

The effect was astounding. They started whimpering and backing away with great caution.

"I'm not going to hunt you down individually, although you mangy lot deserve it," said the Keeper of Earth. "You stay well back! If your Keeper goes and fetches help to keep you scurvy dogs under control, you don't threaten the helper!"

They grovelled in the dirt, whining like puppies. Federi shooed them with a sudden explosive gesture.

"Back off! Scoot! Scatter!" They bolted in all directions.

Another Earth male approached, trampling loudly through the undergrowth. The Keeper turned and nodded at him.

"Hey, Wolf. She's damaged. Got to get her out of here too. The Were Folk can eat Anthrim and the two other Council traitors."

The male called Wolf inspected her from all angles.

"Should get her to Calypso. Won't scare any people there."

"Good," agreed the Keeper. "Should ge

t them all to Calypso, actually."

"How?"

"Hm! Good question."

"We can teleport," said Jitanali with a smile. "What it's going to help I don't know, because we'll die anyway."

"It will help," said Wolf. "And you won't die. We've got Doc Judith!"

Paean sat next to Vlad on the damp leaves of the forest floor, her hand on his hide. The Morrigan didn't have enough energy left to shape into anything discernible. He lay in a puddle of clear liquid, with more liquid seeping out of him smelling faintly of sea water. There were no more colours in his skin; now and then a bit of electricity fizzled across it. Virian had found them and was lying next to Paean in a similar state of collapse.

"Hang in there, you two," the Irish girl begged. "Not long now! Going to fix this!"

It was hard to recall that only two months back they had been hell-bent on eliminating the Morrigan. Back then they had considered him a dangerous enemy.

Shawn teleported in, the Genitron clamped under his arm.

"There'ya go!"

Paean accepted the machine, dug in her moonbag and extracted two syringes.

What was eating Vlad, was dragon digestive juices. Virian on the other hand was being liquidized by Morrigan enzymes. Of the two, Vlad was in the worse state. He had been chewed too, and was losing fluids. Virian was more mentally traumatized; Paean didn't know how to fix that.

She loaded a sample of the shifter into the Genitron and ran a check. Leila crawled out of her moonbag and sat there, waving her feelers, waiting for instructions.

It took five minutes to get the dragon protein analysed, and another ten of frantically searching the database for something that could disable that enzyme. All the while Vlad's life was slipping away and he was seeping away into the ground.

Wolf and Federi joined them a little while later. By now the Genitron was synthesizing an antidote for Vlad.

"We shipped Jitanali over to the Oasis on Calypso," Wolf updated the sibs. "Ailyss and Perdita are looking after her. And Michelle too. Let's get these two Morrigan over there as well!"

"You take Virian," said Paean. "I don't think this one is currently portable."

"Bring the Solar Wind," suggested Shawn.

Federi glanced at the smaller Morrigan. "We'll need a bucket to transport her too," he commented. He removed his wrist-com and put it on Vlad's back. "Help yourself, old pal. Talk to the Solar Wind."

Vlad did an impression of a smiley line-drawing and absorbed the wrist-com. Federi rolled his eyes.

"I'll have to organize you a new one," commented Wolf with an equable shrug. New wrist-coms for Federi were standard issue. "Come, let's scoop up this one here."

"Hold on a minute." Paean drew up a sample of Virian into a

syringe. She really needed another Genitron. She couldn't start this process until the other one was complete.

"Hang tight, little luv," said Federi and teleported out. Less than a minute later he was back with a second Genitron.

"We know now that the Council is evil," said Wolf when they were all gathered on Calypso, nursing various space creatures back to health.

"Not necessarily," replied Radomir Lascek, studying the havoc. "We know that there was a sub-group within the Council that was bad. Three in total: Anthrim, the Morrigan called Belarius and that other female Council Morrigan."

Paean glanced up from where she sat tending to Virian. She'd been teleported with the two Morrigan; Doc tolerated her being out of bed merely because she was working the Genitron for creating new medications for the creatures. Doc Judith was trying to set the bones in Jitanali's broken limbs. They were beyond broken; they were shattered into fragments.

"Of course there should be twelve Council Mages," said Lascek. "I'm wondering who will be recruited to complete the Council now."

"That's a scary thought, Captain," said Wolf.

Federi stood to one side watching the scene, saying nothing. He studied the way his wife helped tirelessly, despite her own injury. She was holding up extremely bravely. But if she took it too far now...

There was one more thing he had to do. He teleported in next to the fake Mrs Flanagan and teleported with her. To a deserted, impoverished street with all the curtains on all the houses drawn. And toys strewn around gardens.

"Go home," he told her.

Mrs Flanagan ghosted around Molly Street, disoriented. Then she headed resolutely for the bus station. Federi watched her. Home. Indeed. Back to the darned mound in Limerick!

That very much settled it! He teleported into the Solar Wind's boardroom and went on a round, looking for the first Mrs Flanagan look-alike. Outside the portholes, the beautiful white beach of Oasis Bay, Calypso, lay dreaming in the sunlight. He and Captain had moved the Solar Wind to the Calypso Base, after which the Captain had left the ship in Jon Marsden's hands and had returned to where the Intergalactic Council was still wallowing in the mud crater near Miami. The crater looked worse for it. There would be a small lake, in the near future. Federi's mind ran ahead plotting what he'd do now with that piece of land he had, after all, legally purchased. It may be under water now, but...

He found Mrs Flanagan pottering around the bathrooms, disoriented. He spoke to her. She looked at him with uncomprehending eyes. He wrapped the teleporter field around her and took her to Molly Street.

"Go home," he told her.

The Mrs Flanagan copy did an exact duplication of what the first one had done. She moved about the street disconnectedly, passing her own front door several times without recognizing it, and eventually ended up at the bus station. Waiting for something to take her to Limerick. He wrapped his teleporter field around her once again and took her across the street from the Mound.

"Go home," he instructed. She went straight into the Mound.

Ha. Thought so. Federi shook his head. Poor little luv! Her teacher was in all probability dead. But just in order to make completely sure, he had to brave that terrible place one more time...

The little red ant teleported in next to him, nearly giving him hiccups.

"Thought you're patching Morrigans," he scolded.

"Thought you were conferring with Captain," she replied. "You're not going into that Mound again, alone!"

"Well, you're not coming along with that leg of yours!"

"Wait," she told him and teleported away.

Damn! She shouldn't teleport so jolly much! He'd have to negotiate a Brurite bullet from Dana again soon. Poor Dana, with her girls decimated like that...

Paean returned, straddled on the motorbike she had stashed at Marge. "Ready?" she asked him. "Hop on?"

Ha! That should sort the Mound! He took the pillion seat, and she navigated the bike towards the mound.

A second later she found herself on the Dublin docks, with the moon shining over the harbour.

"Hey!"

"Got to brief you first, sweetheart," said Federi gravely. "'s not what you think."

It had been supposed to be their honeymoon. He took her to a coffee place, ordered her a meal – she dug in hungrily, when last had the girl had something to eat? He watched her wistfully over a glass of champagne – yuk, the stuff was too sweet for his taste – her cream-coloured skin under the myriads of freckles, her soft curls...

And he unpacked. About the sentient Mound, the creatures that were the Unicate queens, the workers, the child-like larvae; the way he'd hypnotized Mound Rhyn with a mental rendition of Falco's violin; the uncanny choreographed workers... and what had happened to Patrick. What had happened to the children of the Toll, and the elite school class of Johnsson – why Johnsson had preferred dying defending a base against the Unicate... what Captain had told him about his and Rhine Gold's gruesome find at the Antarctic Unicate base...

443

"Little luv…"

"Then she's dead," said Paean, crestfallen. "I was afraid of that. One more friend, gone." The tears of fatigue, overload and grief trickled over her cheeks; but they were silent. She sniffed and wiped across her face. "Federi, from all this nightmarish business the one good thing I got is you. Please don't go back in there!"

He sighed. "There is no safe place for us to raise our children."

"We can settle on New Dome, or Calypso," she said. "Even Shrn. I made a pact with Grww."

"The battle over Shrn is far from decided," Federi pointed out. "What are you talking about, my treasure? We're not settling for some alien planet! Earth is ours! She's my planet! Not on your foot will I allow the Unicate to finish her off!"

"I forget," she said with a heart-broken smile. "You're the Keeper of Earth."

"That's just what the blasted aliens call it," said Federi. "Here on Earth we call it giving a damn."

"But I'm going with you, Federi! 's my planet, too!"

He took her face into his hands and kissed her. Until everything else disappeared around them. Until they were in the Assassin's Cabin on the comparatively deserted Solar Wind. On Calypso. This didn't matter, at this particular moment.

And when she was asleep, he gazed at her exquisite features some more, her face at peace, her hair feathered across the pillows. Once again, she'd never seen his piratical betrayal coming.

It had been necessary. If Doc Judith had no control over her where she was supposed to look after her on New Dome… Anyway he didn't think the valeriensis would hinder her wound from recovering.

"I love you," he whispered as he planted another light kiss on her brow, and teleported out.

444

He sat on the quay at the Dublin Docks for a while, getting his mind back into the frame for attacking the Unicate. She was not going back into the Mound. If it cost him every trick in the book. He brought her motorbike aboard the Solar Wind and locked it into the little storeroom at the very stern of the lower crew deck; a storeroom where items were kept that had nothing to do with the curious new crew. She wouldn't think to look there.

And then he teleported back to Limerick, wishing that it weren't necessary. And knowing that it was.

30 – Mound Rhyn

S.I. Lucy peered out of Federi's shirt pocket.

"Master? The Solar Wind thinks you're taking an unreasonable risk."

"Lucy? Disconnect from what the Solar Wind thinks," commanded Federi. "Tell her if she dares to wake up Paean, she'll be in such deep trouble she won't know how to fathom it. Not with her most sophisticated sensors."

S.I. Lucy ducked back into his pocket. It was good to have the little spy with him, he thought. There was a possibility that Unicate was insensitive to roaches.

Alright. He needed to find the vibe again. That, or a way to remain invisible to the Mound. He picked his way into the Mound.

The Council had returned to discuss the Shrn Breach. Lascek plied them with much rum, as before. This carried on for a number of hours; the angels discussing amongst themselves whether Anthrim had had a right to attack Shrn and Jitanali. They came to no conclusive result, only the general agreement that it was a rather disagreeable situation.

They didn't know that Shrn, Virian and Jitanali were in fact still alive; and Lascek did nothing to enlighten them.

The last of the huge aliens had finally vacated the mud hole at Miami and fluttered unsteadily back to their interstellar homes. Radomir Lascek breathed a sigh of relief and gazed at the devastation strewed with rum bottles. His daughter, tall, proud and

446

very pregnant, stood by his side gazing across the wasteland.

"That's a landfill," she commented eventually. "If I'm not mistaken."

"They buried the Everglades under it," growled Radomir Lascek. "Back in the Sixties. Just before the Unicate descended. It was one of the many things they did. Ask Sherman."

"I know," said Rushka. "He talked about it. Trouble with Sherman is, you never know when he's telling a story and when he's talking about history!"

"This isn't history," said her father with a sigh. "This is here and now, as you see. To think that our Tzigan paid money for this piece of garbage-laden ground…"

"At least they're gone, Papa."

He put his arm around his daughter's shoulders. His brave little Rushka. His wrist com bipped once. He glanced at it.

"What?" The Solar Wind's message didn't make sense. He had to read it twice. "What in hell does he want back in there?"

"He's gone back into that mound?" Rushka shook her head. "Captain, someone ought to back him up!"

"Someone?" Radomir Lascek smiled grimly. "My girl, to the Wingnut! You've got to get on the Solar Wind and stand in for me!"

The Wingnut, the Captain's Perdita Jet, stood at the edge of the mud crater. The Captain and his daughter boarded it and closed the hatch, and then it described a flaming arc towards Calypso on the other side of the sun.

*

What was it about Falco's violin? Federi tried to find the thread of thought again as he wended his way through the Mound, playing Romanian gypsy songs to her on his mind violin. She seemed to be

447

happy this way, lulled into a dreamy state. There were grey workers moving about, but they ignored him. He wondered. He had injured the Mound grievously, he had killed her Queen, twice now. Did she not mind? Was the sound of that violin so seductive, so soporific? It had to be, he thought. He couldn't imagine how else Falco had ever negotiated with this entity.

Were all the mounds connected, or were they different minds? He'd dug a girl out of high security of one of these mounds before. Right after which she had turned him in at the police. He wondered if she had possibly been a copy, too. And what had happened to the original... the Toll, he acknowledged with a heavy heart as he made his way deeper and deeper into the damp underground.

Alright. He knew now where the nursery was. That was one thing. And the dungeons. But if Mrs Flanagan was in neither – there had to be yet another place the Mound kept prisoners. He opened doorways and peered into empty chambers. The Mound had a lot of those. Federi wondered if that was where the workers slept – if they ever slept. Or if it were something else that had been deserted. He wondered if other mounds had anything in those chambers, or if it was simply part of the internal structure of the alien, like those little sacs in a lung. In some of the chambers there were food supplies. The workers seemed to live mainly on the same kind of diet as humans – bread, grains, potatoes, apples and so on. There was no meat of any sort stored anywhere, but that stood to reason. They'd want to refrigerate that somehow. Either that, or they ate it fresh, or perhaps the workers were vegetarian. Ha! How likely was that?

His plan had three corner posts. He was going to bring Paean a small piece of worker, and an egg, and Mrs Flanagan. For the egg he'd have to get back into that breeding hollow. The small piece of worker he could pick up on his way out, with S.I. Lucy's help. But to find Mrs Flanagan – that was the real challenge. Because whatever he found this time – it was his last chance for finding the genuine article. He had brought enough explosive to blow up the whole mound, and was planting it conscientiously all along the way.

He had expected there to be other stuff in the mound too – laboratories perhaps, or office equipment beyond the upper regions where there were some computer-like devices in the office cubicles, but at the least, munitions stores. Guns. Bombs. Explosive. He was rather baffled at the simplicity of the Mound's insides.

This was no good. The structure was huge! He could spend days ghosting around in here! He'd have to risk it and dig into the Mound's mind once more. He prodded her gently.

Are you enjoying the music?

The response was a sleepy, contented feeling that was nearly a purr. Federi smiled. The alien was intelligent, and had a musicality that was nearly human. He complimented her, then sent a stray, absent-minded little thought of Mrs Flanagan into the ether.

There! He'd glimpsed it, fleetingly, before the Mound covered her own thoughts from him. She hadn't meant to reveal the whereabouts of the old lady. She was throwing thoughts at him of Mrs Flanagan in the dungeons, locked up with the other prisoners – another copy, Federi knew. He shrugged mentally. It was of no concern to him. Playing '*Fa Lescek*' to this alien beauty was a lot more important than anything on Planet Earth.

Had Falco actually called the Unicate with his violin? Federi couldn't imagine it. But then… rats and blast, next mission: He had to find that violin again! He'd left it when he had fled from the massacre, as a boy, and the violin hadn't been his top concern. His sister had. Still breathing, begging him to run and save himself. And hours later, after watching over her and his parent's cooling bodies, he'd had to flee again, never to return…

A soft keening surrounded him. He realized that he'd been

449

transmitting his pain in his music, and the Unicate was affected by it. She could feel the emotions, although she couldn't associate with them. He had to get his mind on a happier track. He thought of the sea and the Solar Wind and endless blue hours with wind and sun and white bulging sails and the wonderful rush of the prow wave. Up in the Crow's Nest, or by the prow, or sitting idling in the storage deck… and a beach in Southern Free, where he had spent some time as a bum when he was a teen. Picking oysters off the rocks and reed rats off the coastal tangle.

He could clearly sense the confusion of the Mound as she tried to assimilate the images and feelings of those unfamiliar places. He smiled. He wasn't too far from the nurseries now, he knew; but she had practically told him how to get to the other place… he mustn't think about it now. Just keep on walking, deeper and deeper under the ground…

The air was cooler down here. Around the nurseries it had been muggy; here it was nearly draughty. How the Mound got that right he had no clue, but he played her a song of Romania in winter. And of his beloved Southern Free, with the breakers on golden beaches and the endless veld in the inland. S.I. Lucy wiggled nervously in his pocket. He patted her to reassure her. It was alright.

Another doorway…

Green light, cold passages. Nearly a refrigerator. And here he found the alien technology he'd so sorely missed elsewhere. There wasn't much – but then it might be that the Unicate didn't need much. There were horizontal tubes of volcaniplex – or it looked like that; arranged like sun beds. They were empty and standing open; green light shone from their bases, and their bottom halves were filled with some sort of jelly-like substance. He continued along the passage. The temperature was enough to make him thankful that he was wearing his wind jacket. He hadn't bothered taking it off after taking Paean back to the Solar Wind, in his arms. Hypnosis wasn't something Federi used a lot on his wife. He saved it for utter emergencies.

The passage made a turn, and ended in a closed door. Federi tickled the lock open, all the while playing violin to the Mound in his mind. Lock? The lock was an illusion, he realized; designed to slow down trespassers and workers. He pushed the door open, which was hardly more than a membrane. How much else in the Mound was illusion?

The air in here was freezing. There were five beds in here, of the same tubular kind as outside. But these were closed. And they were occupied. Federi looked through the glass into the beds, to see emaciated, shrivelled human forms – and one dead bottle-nosed dolphin. These customers were all dead, he derived. Nothing was alive in here. But the one bed in the corner held Mrs Flanagan. Suspended in jelly, and not yet quite skeletal.

Oh hell. He teased the bed open. The jelly parted. He peered at the body. She didn't necessarily look dead, but she didn't look all that alive either. The Assassin, playing 'Abandoned' to the Mound in his head, felt for the old lady's pulse in her throat. When he discovered it, too slow but present, he nearly jarred in fright. One pulse per... what? He waited. Yoy! Twenty seconds! And her body was cold to the touch. Fridge-cold.

Federi picked the stiff form up out of the jelly, placing a firm hypnotic image in her place before closing the bed again. Aargh! Would she bite him if she came to? Would she be sane? Would she even – he shuddered and turned his back on the chamber, carrying the frozen old lady like a statue over his shoulder.

Hells' bells, he could have done with a spare pair of hands now! Or Paean's motorbike. He retraced his steps back to the level where the breeding chambers were. He'd have to put her down somewhere when he went looting an egg! He found an empty cubicle just up the passage from the nursery and hid her in it, casting gypsy luck over her and closing the door. He turned back to the passage, remembering uneasily how he'd walked straight into a Rebellion soldier back in the Pacific when he'd done that round of that Schooner. But nobody confronted him here, though several workers hurried past. He played the '*Malaguena Espagnola*' in his mind. New tunes; he hadn't known them back in Romania. But maybe Falco had; sheet music was freely available back in his day.

"S.I. Lucy," he briefed his tiny accomplice, "your job is to get a teeny tiny piece of worker and come back to my pocket."

"Yes, Master!" S.I. Lucy flew down to the ground and scuttled off.

Federi opened the door to the breeding hall. There were still traces of the devastation he'd sown earlier. Workers were clearing away the burnt bits of their fellows that hadn't been consumed by the explosion. Pieces of tattered cocoons hung from the ceiling. How to find anything that lived, in here?

Veraena Flanagan opened her eyes. The icy cold had stopped. She was in a small brown room underground. She had no idea what she was doing here, or where she was, or why she wasn't in her bed at home. She'd had a nightmare of which she couldn't remember a thing except the hysterical fear. And an echo of a childhood nightmare... But all that was gone somehow, replaced by – nothing. She felt numb, drained. As though life were basically a small brown hollow in the ground, and that was all. A completeness. She couldn't think clearly. She sat up, shaking her head and rubbing some jelly-like substance out of her eyes. She didn't know how it had got in there, or what it was. And she felt centuries old, like the old Stone Giant from the folk tale.

Federi looked into the niches where he'd seen them stash the eggs and found that further back in the hall, some of those were undamaged. He slunk over there, between the workers who didn't even glance up. He picked up one egg, very gently, glanced at it – suppressed a reaction of ghastly shock and hid the thing under his wind jacket. He played '*Dance with the Devil*' for the Mound as he sauntered out of the room. He was still moving in the protective hypnotic mist; she didn't really know where he was, but she was loving the music and not wanting it to stop.

He left the nursery and entered the passage – and was face-to-face with Radomir Lascek and his Kosaka cannon.

"*Madre de Diablo*, Captain!"

Radomir Lascek laughed softly. "Good to see you too, Tzigan. What's with all these Unicate slaves? They seem dazed!"

Federi blinked. Not so darned dazed anymore, anna bottle! He concentrated hard on playing another Sarasate piece, but the Mound was coming to. He could sense it. S.I. Lucy teleported back into his pocket.

"Mission accomplished, Master!"

"Great!" Federi grabbed the Captain's sleeve and pointed down the passage. "That door!"

A hole opened in the wall of her cave. Mrs Flanagan gaped at the huge bearded man who was suddenly there, picking her up off the floor. She hadn't even tried standing up yet; she was still too drained from the cold.

"Who are you?"

"Radomir Lascek."

She stared at him, shocked. "Radomir Lascek," she repeated in awe. And then she spotted Federi. "Falco! You're alive!"

"Only Federi," said the gypsy apologetically. "Come!"

The workers were beginning to converge on them. Federi swore softly, trying to get the music to work again. Panic wasn't a good frame for working hypnosis! Between him and Captain they didn't have enough hands. Radomir Lascek needed both his hands to carry the woman, even though she didn't weigh much. His Kosaka gun hung on its strap, unusable. Federi had his gun in his left hand; in his right arm he clutched the egg under his wind jacket.

"One second," said Radomir Lascek and put Mrs Flanagan down. She wobbled, and her legs collapsed out under her. Lascek activated his com. "Now," he called into it.

Federi helped the elderly woman up and put a firm arm around her waist. Radomir Lascek raised his gun and shot a path into the Unicate workers.

"Captain, the *valeriensis*," suggested Federi. "'s many of them!"

"Do you have any on you?"

"Sure!" Federi let go of Mrs Flanagan, who wobbled but didn't fall to the ground this time. He dug in his pockets and extracted the tiny breakable vaporizer balls that carried the virus in condensed format. On breakage of the glass ball, the virus would be dispersed into the air. A special construct, once again by Wolf. Only he hadn't had any on him, earlier today. There weren't many yet, because they were handcrafted. He had managed to get hold of ten.

He flung one into the Unicate crowd and proceeded straight through them with the Captain, who was carrying Mrs Flanagan over his shoulder by now. She had passed out from the virus.

"Are you sure it's her, this time?" asked the Captain sharply.

"From where I found her – definitely," said Federi.

The Mound sounded alarm. It started as a low keening, and

escalated to a high-pitched whistling. Workers converged on Federi and the Captain from all sides, blocking off passages. They folded from the virus capsules Federi flung at the floor and passage walls as he went along. He didn't want to use them all, so in bursts he and Captain shot a path into the throng.

Where did so many come from? It bothered Federi. The Mound had to have many more areas he'd not yet explored.

And then they were in the upper passages, where the air felt fresher. Machinegun fire greeted them. Federi ducked into a side chamber, pulling the Captain with him.

"Captain, I'm nearly out of capsules. We can throw one last one, but then we'll have to make a mad dash for it–"

"Federi, hold your wild birds. Those are our guys!"

"What?"

"Watch," said Radomir Lascek. He left the cubicle, Mrs Flanagan still over his shoulder, and held up his hand. "Hold the fire!"

The machinegun fire stopped. Unicate others littered the floor. Federi shook his head as he stepped over them, on his way to the entrance. Unicate forces lined the walls, saluting at the Captain.

"You know," said Radomir Lascek when they stood outside, "for what am I Planetary Leader if I can't abuse it to rescue my associates?"

Federi grinned. "How did you find me?"

"You left a trail of plastic explosive for me to follow," grinned the Captain.

"There's that," said Federi, waited for the Unicate soldiers to clear the Mound, and detonated it.

31 – Lim

Paean opened her eyes. She was in the Cabin of Dreams – and it jingled. Waves rocked the Solar Wind. This was amazing.

Federi was there, sitting cross-legged on the bunk next to her. In his hands was something small. But he wasn't fiddling with it; he was gazing at her, watching her slowly wake up.

Half-real images of a white hospital room with green light came back to her. She'd been under semi-sedation for a while. Always drowsy, mostly asleep. How long? More than two days, she was suddenly quite sure.

"Federi?"

"Hey, little luv!"

"Why am I being kept under sedation?"

"Chains didn't work that well," replied Federi, and laughed brightly. "Only kidding, little luv. Because your leg needed that gap to heal. It's better now. Doc said you can get up today."

"How long was I out like this?"

"Three weeks, about," said Federi. "Not out, only subdued. You don't remember? Our long, deep conversations? You and me, talking about the future? Mrs Flanagan coming in?"

"Mrs Flanagan?" Paean sat up abruptly. And her smile dropped away. "Right. She's a fake."

"Not this last one," said Federi. "She spent a good part of her first few days in screaming fits. Then she thought I'm Falco. Well, that's fair," he added. "Sometimes I still wonder myself if I'm Falco. But this Mrs Flanagan is real. Ailyss has quizzed her, Sherman has chatted to her, there is nothing to indicate she's another copy – most of all, Paean, I picked her right out of the cloning chambers of the Unicate mound."

"The Mound in Limerick?" asked Paean. "You went back in?"

"Mound Rhyn," said Federi. "She's destroyed. Blown to bits."

"You did go back in," said Paean accusingly.

"Guess who came to pull me out?" smiled Federi. "Captain himself."

"Ah!" Paean grinned broadly.

"Brought you a present from the Mound," added the gypsy. "Coming?"

She got up, wobbling a bit and establishing her balance on the newly healed leg. It would take getting used to, and strengthening.

Paean followed Federi to the lower crew deck, into the laboratory. He opened one of the refrigerators. She peered in – and gave a yelp of surprise.

Through the translucent membrane, the inhabitant of the Unicate egg was staring darkly at her.

"It's a baby!" she exclaimed. "What is it doing in the fridge?"

"It's not a baby," countered Federi. "It's a Unicate *Other*. Wolf wanted to shoot him into the sun. I brought him for you so you can study what the Unicate is made of; but I wanted to put him on ice, so to speak, for you to study him. Seems to me he survives ice quite well." He lifted the egg out of the fridge and placed it on the bench top.

"He looks as though he knows everything," said Paean, shivering lightly.

"He knows a lot more than we do," agreed Federi. "Sentient for the last billion years, probably. Captain's called him Lim, after the Mound in Limerick."

"'e's not going back into the fridge!" determined Paean. "Poor

457

little mite must be cold!"

"How you can feel sorry for him…"

"'e freaks me, alright," admitted Paean. "But… Now, Federi, how am I supposed to study the little chap?"

"Genetically," he said. "Check what genetic differences there are between Unicate *Others* and humans."

"So, you're saying I must stick a needle into the little guy?"

Federi rolled his eyes and located a clean syringe and needle, and drew some liquid out of the egg through the membrane. He handed it to Paean, and she loaded it into a Genitron.

Five minutes passed, during which Federi made himself comfortable on the bench top, taking his bit of woodcarving out of his pocket and sanding it. It was nearly finished.

"This doesn't make sense," said Paean.

"What?"

"Federi, could you draw again – and this time try to get hold of a tiny bit of the baby itself? A bit of skin or some blood – anything."

Federi stuck the needle into the egg again, and had quite a dance with the unhatched Unicate *Other* before he could present Paean with a tiny bit of the creature's skin – and Lim was glaring at him through the translucent membrane.

Paean ran the test again, with the same results.

"Federi, I've got bad news."

He glanced up.

"Terence was right," said Paean.

"Terence?"

"The Unicate *Other* is genetically one hundred percent human."

"But that can't be! At least the embryonic genes must be different! It's inside an egg!"

"That's not an egg," said Paean. "That's a foetal membrane."

"And that means?" asked Federi, though he knew the answer.

"No virus, no prioid, nothing of that sort is going to work," said Paean. "Maybe if we could get a sample of one of the queens, as you observed – they're a lot more alien than the workers…"

"I'd have to tap a fresh mound for that," said Federi and shuddered. Nemiscau. And the Hub. Going into the Hub struck him as a death wish.

"Lim," said Paean and peered at the odd baby inside the membrane. And she started humming a sweet Celtic lullaby.

Federi peered at his young wife, amazed how singing to a baby – even a Unicate *Other* baby – changed her face; from a sharp young assassin and a bossy know-it-all she transmuted into a soft, sweet child-minder with dreamy eyes.

Apparently Lim thought so too, because he relaxed and closed his accusing eyes and went to sleep, not any creepier than any other newborn baby encased in a membrane.

"If he's genetically hundred percent human," said Paean softly, "maybe all he needs is a decent upbringing? Shall we try?"

Federi shied away. He wasn't raising any Unicate spawn!

She watched his reaction with raised eyebrows.

"Paean," he said, "try to understand. This thing is not a normal baby. It's not even human."

"We'll smuggle it between our own lot of Solar Wind babies," she suggested. "Look: We've got a full nursery already, what with Ronan's Donal and Séamus, Dana's Arawn, Rhine Gold's … aw, I have no clue what they're calling their bairn. I think Lim will be in good company; the lot of babies will be raised together in any case. Kids have to run in packs. You know that!"

"I thought you meant that we ought to raise Lim," said Federi with clear relief. "You and I. There's no way. But maybe, mixed into the lot that's already due… but I'd put Ailyss in charge of him."

"I wouldn't put Ailyss in charge of any baby," countered Paean.

"'s not fair to her."

"Not as a childminder. As a custodian. Someone else gives him the bottle. She checks that he doesn't eat the other babies."

It was eventually Lyr who volunteered to look after Lim, once the baby had received a tobusky basket as a crib and was wrapped in soft fleece rugs – around its membranes. Lyr pointed out with a good-natured shrug that he'd raised worse. He studiously ignored Federi's subliminal comment that he didn't think so, and took the Unicate baby into his cabin.

"Is that safe?" fretted Paean. "Lyr is an alien too!"

"He's not, only an Atlantean," replied Federi. "I think he can be trusted." He shuddered lightly.

Paean went on a Solar Wind round, checking where everyone was. The ship itself was still anchored at Oasis Bay. Shawn was in the Crow's Nest, taking a break from planting – there was non-stop planting to be done at the Oasis, and some proper stone-buildings were going up too, so there was no real end to the manual labour. Captain was in the mess hall on the base, a low stone building with long tables and benches in it to accommodate everyone who was helping. Among the helpers were all the gypsies from the Space Base. Wolf was working on a portal-like, fixed structure that used teleporters to transport people from the Space Base to Calypso and back. He called it a Televator. Paean thought that for all his inventiveness, the names he gave his inventions rather lacked sparkle.

Everywhere she went, she was greeted and welcomed like a homecoming princess.

"I don't get it," she told Federi. "I wasn't gone, only under sedation."

"Aha," laughed the gypsy. "But you were under sedation on

New Dome!"

And then Paean found Jitanali.

The young space dragon with the endless fractures was healing; she was so bandaged up and in traction that Paean felt terribly sorry for her. Doc Judith was tending to her, with the help of two wildlife vets who had been commissioned from Earth. Paean chatted to both and came away feeling that perhaps vet wasn't a bad profession either.

Jitanali now had more metal in her bones than an average dragon had in his hoard. She did seem cheerful though, especially seeing that Doc's prognosis for her was very positive.

"She'll forget that she was ever injured," said Doc Judith.

And Vlad?

The Morrigan poured himself into existence next to Paean, causing her to jump in surprise.

"Milady," he said with a suave bow. "How's the injury your humble servant made such a mess of?"

"Healed," said Paean with a grin. "And you?"

"Both Virian and myself would have died," said Vlad dramatically, "but for the biofield restorer Wolf designed."

"You'd have died but for my antidote, and Dana's Brurite capsules," said Paean.

"Of course, of course! But this is an invention you need to see to appreciate!" Vlad wrapped a tentacle around her and teleported with her into the infirmary, where he showed her something that looked a bit like a black box with an indicator light, a switch, a dial and some cables coming out of it.

"What does it do?" she asked.

"It generates a biostatic field to align with our bioelectric fields," said Vlad proudly. "Wolf has also attached one to Mindy's back, to

461

direct the regrowth of her spinal nerves."

"Great! And what happens with Shrn now?" asked Paean.

"The Intergalactic Council has decided to let the matter rest," said Vlad. "Jitanali is given time to recover from her broken limbs. In the interim, I'm still the Keeper. They will decide after she recovers, whether I'm replaced."

"Well, that gives us some time," said Paean.

Virian the Morrigan slunk into the machineroom. She had decided to emulate her father's example and take on a human shape to blend in better with the crew of the Solar Wind. It would be interesting to move among this oddball species for a while and have a look at how they did things.

Wolf glanced up. "Hi, Paean."

"I'm not Paean," said the young Morrigan, "I'm Virian."

Wolf's eyes stretched. For some strange reason the engineer was displaying a stress reaction. This was interesting.

"Virian," he said, "there are rules aboard this ship. You're not allowed to pretend to be someone else!"

"But I'm not pretending to be anyone," objected Virian. "I'm merely taking a human shape."

"Then it must be a human shape that is different from the people aboard," explained Wolf. "Those are Federi's orders, or else it results in chaos. You can ask your father about it at some point."

"Change, how?" she asked, growing a second pair of eyes on her forehead and losing them again.

"Nothing serious," replied Wolf. "The basic shape is good. Subtle changes, like skin tone, hair colour, eye colour… the shape of your eyes… you know."

"Hm." Virian scowled, and reflowed.

Her hair turned from red to turquoise; her eyes, lilac and quite a lot larger. Her skin tone rippled towards a bluish tinge.

"Better?" she asked. "Will these subtle changes do?"

Wolf laughed. Virian now looked like a blue cartoon version – still of Paean though.

"That's fine," he said. "Nobody will be able to confuse the two of you now."

That evening Paean sat on the jetty that led to where the Solar Wind lay anchored; watching the sun set over the Calypsean sea.

Federi sat down next to her. She glanced at him. She had not heard him approach…

"So everyone's happy?" she asked.

He smiled and pressed something small into her hand. She looked at it in the reflected glow of the waves. And she emitted a tiny squeal of delight.

"A wooden ocarina! You got it right! This is the thing you've been carving since we were on Anya Miller's ship, there in Miami!"

He smiled. "Try it!"

She played on it. It had a soft, muted sound; different from a clay whistle though the principle was the same.

"Sweet!" She gave him a stormy hug. Federi was a little slow to release her.

The next few minutes, she tried all sorts of tunes on the ocarina. It came with a leather string attached, which she used to hang it around her neck. The sun finished setting to her music, and the early stars came out. They were the Solar System's stars; only the opposite season as on Earth. Before Paean had become a seafarer she wouldn't even have noticed; but now it struck her as strange.

Federi had his arm around her and was gazing up into the twilit skies.

"Somewhere out there is Pirate Haven," said Paean, pausing in her play.

"What? I thought that's right here!"

"Och…" Calypso was lovely, and she wanted to be part of it; and of course Earth needed her, as always. But she felt that out there were still worlds to be discovered. And one of them…

"And what's wrong with Calypso?"

"Same as Island Base," she said with a sigh. "Federi, a respite is a good thing, and I love the occasional rest, but – I'm not old, and a place like this makes me feel retired. I'm a pirate! I want to go explore, meet more species, discover more worlds…"

"Clone more prioid," laughed Federi. "Yes, you're a pirate, alright. Little luv, your old Tzigan was just waiting for you to finish healing from your leg injury. Our honeymoon isn't over yet, and neither is our mission."

"So what's next?" she asked.

"Federi wants to check on the mansions on Tortuga, for the pregnant fairies. Then I plan to build something – a resort on water or something – on my patch of ground west of Miami. Want to steal us a yacht so that we can sail around the world a little. No big deal. Want to go back to Romania, find the remaining gypsy groups, and – little luv – Falco's violin! Want to check what's going on in Nemiscau, and in the Hub…" He fell silent.

Paean reached across with her left hand to clasp his right that was on her right shoulder, and they sat like that for a long, silent while. From the shore, sounds of music drifted over. Captain had ordered a Ceilidh.

"The Intergalactic Council asked me to take a position," said Federi softly.

"What?"

"To join their ranks," he explained. And he stared up at the stars with his eyes narrowed to slits.

"That's an honour," said Paean, impressed.

"Not an honour, yodiho," he countered quietly. "Not a blasted honour. They asked it so they can keep a closer eye on Federi! Won't do them that favour, not on my left foot!"

"You turned them down?"

"The Intergalactic Council," said Federi, "tricked Falco into Keepership of Earth; tricked him into signing a contract with the Unicate, and then withdrew when the Unicate became the problem that she is. Federi is wilier than Falco. My grandfather was never trained as an assassin from childhood. I'm out of their league. They don't know what to do with me."

Paean smiled.

"So they are keeping their enemies close," he said. "Ha! But Captain was quite eager to accept their offer, once they knew that I wasn't taking the bait."

"Captain?" asked Paean, worried. "That's bad!"

"Ah no, that's brilliant," replied Federi with a sparkling smile at her. "Captain has them all in hand. It's good that he can monitor them that closely."

Paean chuckled softly.

"Should keep him out of trouble, too," observed Federi. "Stop him from thinking up constant work for me and my Tzigane."

Shawn came walking along the jetty.

"There they come, calling us to the Ceilidh," sighed Federi.

*

465

Solar Wind Log, 13 January 2117.

We are currently anchored in Oasis Bay, Calypso. Patching up two Morrigan, one dragon, and an old woman's psyche.

Got a Unicate egg aboard. Wolf wanted to tie the thing to a rocket and launch it into deep space. Paean wanted to deliver it to the doorstep of a mound, like a foundling. Federi wanted to put it out of its misery, one bullet, minimal pain... but why pass up on such a prime opportunity to study the Unicate? The baby is an orphan. Its mound has been destroyed. How is it going to respond? Would it fit easily into another mound? If so, it can be used as an agent. Does it still have a mind and thoughts of its own? Is it going to create its own mound? Will it bend to the will of another mound? Will it bend to my will? Can it be taught loyalty?

All these, highly interesting questions. It comes from Limerick. I believe Lim is an apt name for it. Vlad is terrified of it; but Vlad, as has been established, is an old coward. I'm pleased we managed to protect him from justice. Very proud of my crew the way they came up for that Morrigan. Saved me from having to explain why I didn't exactly want to have him executed...

Mrs Flanagan, this time hopefully the genuine article, is petrified of the Unicate egg too. She's scared of Vlad as well, and of Dana, and the croaches... The poor old bird is a bundle of nerves. Will have to order Paean D to clone something!

Got Federi back aboard, thank the Pope and several of his heathen saints! Now we can have a change from the endless sushi! I used to think fish and chips is boring... I suspect, all the man needed was that honeymoon, that bit of rest, that public acknowledgement that he and Paean are, indeed, married. They can say it was a shotgun wedding, it happened on a death mission...

It would be nice to have Rushka around a bit more, but she's spending a lot of time up at the Space Base. I suspect she and Ronan want to move in there when the progeny arrives.

Anyway, it's been a good run, signing off for now
R Lascek, Pirate Captain.

The Solar Wind series:

A mostly teenage crew of motley pirates sails the Earth's oceans on a freedom ship, the Solar Wind. Their Captain Radomir Lascek is not only a wily old sea-devil, but also a politician with a big picture on who should take over the Earth... and then the solar system... and what hey, how about the neighbouring world... and overthrow the intergalactic forces that be... The Earth is infested with an uncanny military world government, the Unicate, costing countless human lives. They don't seem entirely human; their decisions and actions run contrary to anything one would consider normal. Radomir Lascek doesn't have a solution for the Unicate. The best he can do is rescue precious people and keep them safe. But aboard, he has someone who holds the answers: The mysterious gypsy, Federi. Except that Federi has a split personality...

Follow-on series:

1. The Shooting Star.

After understanding the true nature of the Mounds, Federi is uncertain how to tackle the Unicate further. Instead, he commandeers a beautiful ship and transforms it into a magical present for his Paean.

But the Intergalactic Council has not forgotten about him, and neither has the Unicate...

www.ingramcontent.com/pod-product-compliance
Lightning Source LLC
Chambersburg PA
CBHW050913030726
47503CB00007BB/2279